# NEW
# BEGINNINGS

# NEW BEGINNINGS

## LEGEND OF THE SPEAR SAINT
## BOOK ONE

A. T. Valentine

Podium

# NEW BEGINNINGS

# CHAPTER ONE

# Expecting Turbulence

The funny thing about being utterly terrified is that the mind eventually decides enough is enough and shuts itself down.

So when Rowan found himself hurtling through miles of air, he was all about the hurtling part of the equation for the first few minutes. After his mind shut off? Well, it was one really stunning view.

*Really put things into perspective. I guess instead of a last meal, I'm getting a last sight.*

"Aaaaaaaahhhh!" Blake's scream ruined the moment.

"Would you please stop screaming!" Kayla was a notch more cranky than anyone else, but it was profoundly funny that she'd take issue with Blake's screaming when there were . . . more pressing issues.

Blake quieted down as a huge smile stretched across his face. His scream didn't contain an ounce of panic or fear. It was an expression of unadulterated exuberance, and his arms were outstretched like he was trying to hug the world itself.

"And you, Rowan. Why did you think it was a good idea to flip off a goddess!" Kayla yelled.

Rowan managed to shrug his shoulders and hoped Kayla got the message. "I thought it was a dream! And she was being rude! How was I supposed to know that they were real?"

"The idea that maybe, just maybe, we were talking to a whole pantheon of gods and it'd be good to play things safe?" Kayla shouted back. "Now we're all going to die."

"The view," Blake shouted. "It's worth it."

He was right. The planet underneath was absolutely massive. There was no hint of the spherical shape. Just tons and tons of landmass and water, like a painting with an assortment of blue and green colors.

*Definitely not Earth. That's for sure.*

They weren't going to die. At least Rowan didn't think so. If the gods took offense to his little display of disobedience, they could have just thrown them into a vat of lava instead of going through all the trouble of dropping them out of the air.

*Unless the goddess got super pissed and tampered with something. So instead of being sent to a new world, we're going to be splats on that new world.*

The ground was starting to get close. Rowan could see that they were aimed at the absolute center of what looked like a city, into the largest and most notable structure around.

*Well, it was a good run, if a bit short.*

Moments before his violent reunion with the ground, Rowan turned to the sky and flipped off the gods one last time.

It might have been a bit premature. His bones weren't turned to mush, and he was very much not a kebab as the group somehow slipped past the structure's pointy spires. Their descent slowed to a near stop. The inertia of all that force should have ended them. Instead, Rowan felt oddly airy and light as his feet drifted the last few inches and touched down on the ground.

Actual solid ground.

"Hmm . . . Three? Fortuitous. Welcome, heroes!"

The words snapped Rowan back into the moment. He had been staring blankly ahead, still trying to process the fact that he was still alive.

Rowan raised his eyes from the floor to take in the speaker. The man was wearing pristine white robes. The top of his head was graced by a few clinging gray hairs, but that didn't detract from his stature. Next to him were a dozen spear-toting guards as well as two metal-armored knights.

Where Rowan wasn't sure what to do and Kayla seemed content with glaring at anyone and everyone, Blake took everything in stride.

"Thank you, dear sir! By the grace of the gods, I am here!" Blake said as he stretched his hand out for a handshake.

Rowan, to put it lightly, cringed. The speaker, too. His smile cramped at the edges before he found the right response.

"And we are glad, heroes. You have come to our kingdom in a time of great need. The demons are gathering. Heroes, the kingdom needs your support."

"Happy to help. Just let me know what to do," Blake proclaimed.

"And we thank you for that," the speaker replied.

"Who are you?" Kayla demanded.

"A priest," the speaker said.

"What does that mean?" Kayla asked.

"I practice magic as a follower of the goddess Sarina. May her holy light shine upon us all."

While Kayla tortured the priest with her questions, Rowan glanced around the room. The floor they stood on was marked by a glowing magic circle. Golden statues that looked suspiciously similar to the gods they had recently met were lined up around the edges of the room.

"I understand that you have many questions," the priest said, likely already tired of Kayla's inquisition. "However, before all else, I must ask that you follow me. You have an important audience to attend, and I hope you will show poise when you do."

"What if we don't want to?" Kayla thrust her chin out defiantly.

One of the knights unsheathed his sword. A pretty good answer to her question.

The priest turned and went toward one of the room's doorways. Blake fell behind the priest, and after a few soft grumbles, Kayla and Rowan followed suit.

Beyond the arched doors was a series of sweeping fields. In the distance, walls tall enough for giants met the sky. As Rowan glanced back, he realized where they had landed.

*A palace. A real damn palace in a real castle.*

As the group made their way forward, they were greeted by row after row of soldiers practicing maneuvers with spears in their hands. Whatever was happening here was serious business. Rowan wondered if there was some kind of war going on.

One thing was certain, the soldiers would falter in their drills and glance at the passing convoy of priest, knights, and three very out-of-place Earthlings. Some of the braver ones would even give whoops of joy before their instructors cut such celebrations short.

After what felt like a very long walk, the priest made a sharp turn and led them to a new set of fields where there were more training dummies than people. Unlike the packed soldier fields, these fields had servants holding towels and trays lining the fences.

The men and women using these fields—and Rowan noticed near equal numbers of both—were much more impressive. They were built like world-class athletes, and each move they made produced audible gusts of wind. Their swords and axes screeched through the air, impacting the training dummies with staggering amounts of force.

As they walked, some of the people paused their training and openly stared at them. Rowan stared back. At some point, the priest took another turn and headed back toward the palace.

*They want us to see something. The troops? Or is it the other way around—they wanted to parade us in front of everyone?*

The priest picked up his pace on the way back, and they soon found themselves in a new hallway. But for a palace, the halls were oddly stark.

The only decorations were giant paintings drawn in painstaking detail. Everywhere Rowan looked, the paintings depicted men locked in combat with monstrous beasts of every conceivable size and shape. The most disturbing of them was a painting of an army marching against a solid wall of darkness. There was a vividness to the image that chilled Rowan's blood.

*So the gods still sent us to die. Just in a more roundabout way.*

The priest ushered the group into a massive space fit for an audience with a king. Which was exactly what happened.

"Step forward, heroes, and let me have a look at you, the souls who will stem the tide of demons threatening our lands." The voice that boomed out as soon as the doors were open was magnetic and powerful. The space itself was half-full of lushly clothed men and women, with pockets of knights behind each of them. But the highlight of the room was the man who was evidently the king.

The throne the king sat on was not glamorous. It was there to highlight the man who sat on it, not the other way around. The king himself was powerfully built with wide shoulders. There was a sword on his hip, and the pommel was inlaid with gemstones of every shape, size, and color. But what caught Rowan's attention was the king's gaze. Flickering up and down, the man's pale-green eyes weighed the trio's worth.

The show of soldiers in the field and the spartan halls with bloody paintings all suddenly made a lot more sense.

*Here's a man ready to do whatever needs to be done for his kingdom's future.*

That's when something a smidgen distracting happened. A blue box, floating in midair, appeared in front of Rowan's face.

**Wisdom: +1**

Rowan flinched. He looked around at the others, but none of them seemed to see the blue screen. Or if they did, they were giving Oscar-worthy performances of nonreaction.

**System Initialization.**
**Please stand by . . .**

*System, like, a game system? A status?* The words suddenly floating in front of Rowan were entirely disinterested in his inner turmoil and trudged on relentlessly.

**Soul Scan . . . Complete.**
**Physical Scan . . . Complete.**
**Mental Scan . . . Complete.**
**User Initialization Complete.**

The hallucinations, because that's what they *obviously* were, disappeared a second later. Just in time for the king's next set of speeches.

"Heroes, the fate of our kingdom rests on your shoulders. The demons are marching and a demon king has been sighted. The gods have sent you, along with others, to fight against the demons and save humanity. We, the kingdom of Rhys, stand behind you."

"Thank you, King . . ." Blake's voice trailed off.

"Harold. Harold Rhys the First," the king stated. "Heroes, it is now time for you to become full citizens of our world and receive a blessing from the gods."

The king nodded at the priest, who flicked his hand and showered a warm mist over the three of them. For a few seconds, nothing happened, leading Rowan to think that this was a case where the symbolism was more important than the actual substance. But those thoughts scattered immediately when a full band of triumphant trumpets blared in his ear. In front of him, a new box forced its way into Rowan's view. This one, however, didn't have the standard blue background and was instead golden with intricate filigree adorning its edges.

**Congratulations. The gods have deemed you worthy of a blessing!**

**Blessing of the Stalwart Hero**
**From Aristaeus, the God of Soldiers and Rural Craft**
**Grade: Unique**
**Description: You are the determined champion of the people.**
**Effects:**
**1. When fighting with allies nearby, the whole group receives more experience and loot depending on your contribution.**
**2. When fighting with allies nearby, your damage resistance is enhanced.**
**3. When fighting alone, you'll be more likely to encounter streaks of bad luck.**
**4. Believers of Aristaeus will aid you in your journey.**

As Rowan finished reading the screen, he glanced at Kayla and Blake. This time, they seemed to have gotten their own messages and were staring into the blank space in front of them. So whatever was happening was personalized to each individual.

Rowan read through the blessing again. With mentions of experience and loot, it felt like he was in some kind of game. Something that shouldn't be possible. But after his experience with the gods and subsequent plunge through the sky, he hesitated in making a firm judgment. At least for now, everything seemed real enough, if only a bit strange.

Luckily, it seemed like Rowan had a choice in everything.

**Do you wish to accept this blessing?**
**WARNING: Declining a blessing will severely limit**
**your advancement.**
**Yes / No**

Rowan's first instinct was to hit the "no" button.

As if the priest could read his mind, he spoke up again. "The gods are shining down upon you, heroes. Accept your divine blessings; they will aid in your journey against the demons. May Goddess Sarina protect you all."

Rowan scanned through his blessing again. There was no way that the priest was pronouncing Aristaeus as Sarina. *A different god blessed me. That kind of makes sense, especially given that I did offend one of the goddesses. A god of soldiers and rural crafts doesn't sound too bad.*

He mentally hit the "yes" button.

**Status Screen Activated.**

**Rowan Clairfont**
**Level 0 Unclassed (+)**
**EXP: N/A**
**STR: 5**
**VIT: 5**
**DEX: 5**
**PER: 5**
**INT: 5**
**WIS: 6**

**Deck (0/4):**
**[Heart] Empty**
**Blessings:**
**Blessing of the Stalwart Hero (Aristaeus)**

"Let me reassure you, heroes. What you witnessed before you was no trick or illusion. All citizens of our world, Zeimal, are given a blessing by the gods and obtain a status screen that details our attributes," the king thundered. "The gods have another gift to bestow upon you: your Heart Card. It is now time to see what path you are meant to tread. Priest, draw the inspection circle."

The priest sank to his knees, and his lips moved in prayer. Rowan traded a glance with his two companions and saw equal confusion in their eyes.

A moment later, spools of light began to unravel from the priest, drifting down to the ground where they resolved into various symbols that eventually made up a glowing circle. When the spectacle was done and the circle was softly glowing, the priest stood back up and motioned for the heroes to stand at the center.

"Announce yourself one at a time and step into the circle so that all may witness the gift you have been granted," the king declared.

Blake didn't need extra encouragement. He practically leaped into the glowing magic circle. "My name is Blake Trevlin. I am one of the chosen heroes!"

Even before his introduction was done, a solid pillar of purple light erupted around Blake. For all his excitement, Blake flinched at the change. In contrast, the nobles leaned forward as they focused their attention on the image of a card resolving itself above Blake's head.

The card showed a figure holding a sword of solid light against a squirming background of darkness. Accompanying the card was a floating blue screen, one that seemed visible to all, judging by the reactions in the room.

**Advanced Runic Configuration (Inspect) has found:**
**Light Scion**
**Grade: Epic**
**Blessed by: Goddess Sarina**

Seconds later, the hovering card plunged into Blake's chest, and the newly minted hero slumped to the ground. Everything happened so quickly that Rowan didn't even have a chance to react.

"Help Hero Blake stand!" the king commanded. The priest gingerly walked into the magic circle and helped Blake to his feet.

Before Blake was back upright, the nobles exploded in shouts.

"Hero Blake, in my house, you will find the most staunch supporter! Our skill with the sword—"

"Your skill? My house has produced a sword master every generation!"

"Hero, our family's skill with light spells—"

"Enough!" The king's soft words overpowered the nobles' bickering. "Hero Blake, that's an excellent card. Light Scion. Anyone in possession of it would be considered most fortunate. You are meant to follow the path of the paladins, and we will speak more on the subject later. I believe it's the lady's turn."

The priest nodded for Blake to exit the circle on the side, which he did after flashing a quick grin at the nobles.

"What if we'd rather keep our blessing private?" Kayla asked. Her voice was flinty, like she was gearing up for a fight.

"It'd be in your best interest to share your blessing with us. We cannot support you properly otherwise." When the king's voice fell, the knight that had brought them to the throne room took a step forward.

Kayla got the message.

"Kayla Evans." Kayla announced her name like it was a defiant challenge as she stepped into the circle.

The light show repeated itself, though the card that emerged was decorated with an intricate figure turned to the left. Overlapping the figure was a ghostly figure facing to the right.

**Advanced Runic Configuration (Inspect) has found:**
**Echoing Whisper**
**Grade: Epic**
**Blessed by: God Ziraela**

Kayla left the circle as soon as she was able, and as she did so, Rowan noticed the way the runes dimmed. Concentration creased the priest's face, and he slumped a little as the circle regained its glow. Clearly, there was a cost associated with the entire process.

**Perception: +1**

Rowan ignored the message as he glanced toward the nobles. Unlike their shouts of support before, they now mumbled among themselves as they looked in the king's direction.

*It's not the card, can't be. It doesn't look too different from what Blake had. The only other variable here is her blessing. Ziraela.*

Rowan made a note of the god's name.

"I believe that Hero Kayla will have a bright future with the Mages' Tower," the king said. And Rowan could almost hear the nobles releasing their collective breath. "It is quite fortuitous indeed that we are blessed by talented heroes. Of course, that leaves our third hero. I am quite curious to see where his talents lie, since both might and skill are now covered. Three heroes instead of two—it must be Sarina's blessing."

The change in topic was not exactly subtle, but it still worked.

Rowan used the silence that followed to ask a question. "Excuse me, Your Majesty, but when you say 'instead of two,' what does that mean?"

"Young hero, that's a good question. In the past, two heroes have been summoned to our kingdom when a demon wave is coming. The first hero has enormous physical might, and the second soul has great magical talent. To see three of you among us today is a sign of how much Sarina favors our kingdom."

The king had a self-satisfied air about him, and his words provoked murmurs of agreement from the nobles.

A shadow of doubt began to cross Rowan's mind. It was evident that Goddess Sarina held a lot of sway in the kingdom, and he had insulted one of the goddesses earlier. *No way, it can't be.*

Stepping into the runic circle, Rowan waited as the lights appeared around him. Soon, a purple card with a golden halo sprouted out of thin air above him. The card gracefully descended, stopping in front of his face.

As Rowan's eyes focused, he saw a picture of an indistinct figure gripping a spear, the tip pointed at some unseen foe. Darkness swirled around the figure, but the person's eyes shone with a determined golden light. The edge of the card was engraved with an intricate border, and at the top, in the most beautiful font Rowan had ever seen, were the words *Keen Spear*.

**Advanced Runic Configuration (Inspect) has found:**
**Keen Spear**
**Grade: Epic**
**Restriction: This card locks the cardholder out of wielding**
**other weapons.**
**Blessed by: God Aristaeus**

The card jabbed into Rowan. It felt exactly like how it sounded. It was like someone was performing surgery, rummaging and rearranging things inside his body like it was a furniture showroom.

When the pain passed and Rowan straightened himself out, he found the room deathly quiet. The massive space echoed with silence.

The first person who broke the quiet was a red-faced, sputtering noble. He pointed a crooked finger at Rowan as if a great injustice had been done.

"This is ridiculous! What kind of hero relies on a spear?"

The words broke the silence in the hall, and a moment later, the other nobles joined in the outcry.

"Aristaeus? What will the ordinary soldiers think?"

"We must make sure that news of this doesn't leave the room. Rhys is a kingdom blessed by Goddess Sarina, a greater god. If news that a hero with such a blessing got out . . ."

"I demand a trial by blood!"

Rowan could see violence in the eyes of the nobles. Keeping hope, he turned to the throne. There was only one person whose opinion really mattered in this room. Unfortunately, Rowan found the king glaring at him with cold eyes.

*Well, shit.*

The only piece of good news came from Blake and Kayla. The two of them, despite the much warmer reception from the kingdom, stepped into the magic circle again to stand beside Rowan. And the dozen guards who had been part of their original welcoming convoy also rushed forward to protect them, their spears gripped in white-knuckled fear.

There was something very wrong with the situation, that much was obvious. But there was something tugging at the far ends of Rowan's consciousness that screamed danger.

As one of the nobles pushed a guard's spear away, Rowan realized what was wrong.

The guards were holding *spears.* They were dressed in cotton and boiled leather tunics, simple clothing. But the knights behind the nobles were clad in full metal armor. More importantly, the knights had an array of different weapons from swords to axes to even morning stars.

*But no spears.*

So when a metal-clad knight buried their sword into a spear-holding guard, Rowan was pretty sure he was going to die.

# CHAPTER TWO

# A Rough Preview

Time screeched to a halt.

Rowan had seen death before, usually in some movie or TV show where he was sure that the actor would stand back up once the cameras stopped rolling. This was different. For one, there was a horrible, squelching sound when the sword entered the guard's body. And the guard himself made a gurgling noise, trying to say something and instead spraying blood into the air.

But Rowan could only focus on the fact that the guard twisted his neck and stared right into Rowan's eyes. A flurry of emotions whizzed across the man's face. Fear, anxiety, and hope. And then the guard slid off the sword and slumped down to the ground.

Time sped back up again.

"Enough." The king's voice halted everyone in the hall. "I allowed a few moments of distress to steel our heroes to the realities of our world. But you've gone ahead and made a massacre in my halls."

The large knight fell to his knees. "Your Majesty, I never—"

Rowan never heard the end of that sentence. Replacing it was the sound of a sword slipping out of its sheath and a fine red mist spraying into the air. The knight wasn't just dead, he was gone.

"What the hell is going on?" Kayla screamed.

"The demons threaten the existence of this kingdom and everyone in it," the king said, his voice cutting through everything in the hall. "Some of the nobles here today are too young to remember. But when Sarina blessed our kingdom, she also left behind a prophecy. One day, an unworthy hero would be summoned, one who would ally with the demons and ultimately destroy our great kingdom."

"And you think that it's us?" Blake asked. "We were plucked out of our lives by your gods and sent here to help you."

"Perhaps, perhaps not. But the sign of three heroes is one that we cannot ignore," the king said. Around the room, the nobles murmured their agreement.

Blake and Kayla edged closer to Rowan. On the one hand, Rowan was glad that his friends were going to be with him in the chaos. On the other hand, a small part of Rowan wished that they were somewhere else, safe from the wave of metal knights about to charge forward. His card had apparently violated some custom, and now, all three of them were going to meet this world's equivalent of aristocratic mob justice.

"Why are you so sure it's one of us?" Rowan said.

The king paused. "Sarina said that when the time came, it would be obvious. That's why we have the trial by blood."

Rowan didn't like the sound of that.

"The gods bless those who are victorious in combat," the king continued. "We fight for our lives every day. Against monsters and demons. Only those worthy live on. You will fight to the death. Citizens of Rhys, clear a space."

His command was obeyed by nobles and guards alike. Two of them carried the now-dead guard to the side of the room. But unlike the nobles and knights, a couple of the guards glanced back at Rowan and dropped their spears to the ground.

"So, what, you want us to fight for our lives?" Kayla demanded.

"Yes, I do," the king answered. "The fate of our kingdom is no small matter. We have to be sure that you are heroes sent to save our kingdom, not the apostles of an apocalypse."

"If this is about my card, I'll accept whatever punishment that you deem appropriate." Rowan stepped forward and stood at the edge of the disappearing magic circle. "Let Blake and Kayla go; they have nothing to do with this."

"I apologize, Hero Rowan, but this is no callous matter. Your card puts you at a disadvantage. That is true. But I will not recklessly endanger my kingdom. All three of you must undergo the trial by blood. I promise that it will be a fair process. May the goddess shine upon you. Begin."

Before Rowan could protest further, one of the knights with a mace stepped forward. He made a slight bow before charging at the three of them. As Rowan braced for impact, Blake screamed and rushed forward.

The enemy knight hesitated slightly before raising the mace he was holding. Blake, on the other hand, responded by pulling his arm back and winding up a punch. It looked like a classic Blake thing, trying to punch a knight who was wearing a sheet of metal. Rowan abandoned his stance and ran forward, intending to knock his friend away from the impending mace strike.

Blake never threw his punch. His hand position was off, like he was trying to pull something out of thin air.

And somehow, he actually did. A bar of solid light in the rough shape of a broadsword coalesced in Blake's hand and he wasted no time in slashing it at the knight.

*Light can't cut through metal.* Rowan was still trying to get over the shock that his friend was gripping something that looked like pure light. It was bending every law of physics known to mankind.

The knight paused when he saw Blake's weapon. After a split second, he tried to twist away from the fully formed sword. He was too slow, and the surprise-induced hesitation meant that Blake landed his strike onto the knight's shoulder and the light sword effortlessly slid past both metal armor and bone.

Halfway through his strike, Blake twisted his sword and slashed into the knight's breastplate. Once again, the light sword met zero resistance as it passed through the armor. The knight looked down at his wound, then back up to Blake.

"True Hero Blake. I'd be honored if you could take my card," the knight said as he crumpled to the ground.

Blake released his sword and backed up. The bar of light faded away moments later. In its place was the outline of a card, which floated up from the knight's body and sped toward Blake a moment later.

"Hero Blake, you have passed the trial by blood. You may leave the circle," the king said.

"Not without my friends," Blake said. Another classic Blake move. He was rough around the edges, but his heart was made of gold. His face looked pale, like he was trying to fully process the implications of actually killing someone. "Either you let us all go, or none—"

Before Blake could finish his sentence, a knight from next to the king's throne blinked forward, grabbed Blake, and then returned to the throne. As Blake struggled in the knight's grasp, the king signaled toward the nobles.

Kayla seemed loath to waste time on shock. She dashed forward and grabbed the fallen knight's mace before another challenger stepped forward.

"Do something!" she hissed at Rowan and kicked one of the spears in his direction.

Moving on a weird sort of autopilot, Rowan did. He dropped into a crouch, and his fingers fumbled around for a few seconds before they wrapped around the smooth wood.

**Keen Spear prerequisites met.**
**Your mind is keener with a spear in your hands.**

The panic, the doubt, the fear. They didn't exactly disappear. They were, however, put on mute. Rowan's thoughts felt smoother, like someone had reordered the mess in his head.

In fact, as Rowan moved forward to support Kayla, he could feel his muscles working in concert to maintain his balance. His feet rocked just slightly forward so that he could get a tiny bit more leverage if needed, and his elbows made a slightly sharper angle to better control the spear. More than anything else, he felt confident. He knew where the tip of his spear was, where it could go and, most importantly, how it could do maximum damage.

It was perfect timing. A knight was charging at Kayla's back, sword poised for a strike. And Rowan intercepted the charge by stumbling forward and pushing the spear in the knight's direction.

Rowan knew that his actions probably looked clumsy. He felt as if he had lost control of the weapon. But some instinct within him was telling him that this was the only way to angle the spear so that the tip would slip under the knight's raised arm and into a vulnerability. Not a lethal one, thankfully. Rowan wasn't ready to think about killing another person.

The knight realized the same thing. He paused in his charge, stumbling slightly under the momentum, and blocked the spear with his arm guard. At an angle, Kayla spun around and began swinging her mace.

"Die! Die!" Evidently, Kayla had no qualms about taking a man's life.

But despite her attitude and the scary weapon, she wasn't a match for the knight. After being caught off guard by Rowan's attack, the man warily stepped to the side and slipped away from her swings. His next slash caught both Rowan and Kayla by surprise, drawing a long gash in Kayla's arm.

"Shit." Rowan cursed as he leaped forward, placing a smart strike that pushed the knight back. With a few seconds of respite, Rowan scanned his surroundings and saw that there was now a half circle of knights around them. Escape didn't seem like an option.

*One problem at a time.*

The knight came forward again, and the two of them beat the enemy back. With the numbers advantage, Rowan and Kayla could cover each other. As the knight came forward again and again, Rowan realized that the man was, in fact, trying to hurt Kayla first.

*They're not aiming for me?* In the back of Rowan's mind, he pieced together the facts. The violence had originated from his card reveal, but it was Blake and Kayla who were the primary targets. *Why would they want Blake and Kayla dead?*

When the knight charged again, Rowan feinted a thrust at the man's unprotected face. After drawing the correct reaction, he aimed the spear down and smashed the tip against the knight's forward leather boot. Kayla didn't even miss a beat. When the knight lost his balance, she was already swinging her mace, and a moment later, a card rose from the knight and plunged itself into Kayla.

"That's it, right?" Rowan turned to the king, the spear still in his hand. "You can't possibly expect us to take on a knight by ourselves, with no training and against seasoned warriors."

"Hero Kayla dealt the final blow. She's our hero," one of the nobles cried.

"Silence," the king boomed. He looked at the two of them with heavy eyes. "Hero Kayla and Hero Rowan. Perhaps the prophecy is meant for another time. The two of you have passed."

Rowan waited a few more seconds before relaxing slightly. Bad idea. The spear he had held in a white-knuckled grip slipped between his numb fingers and clattered to the ground, taking the odd clarity and surety of his thoughts with it. All of a sudden, it felt like the adrenaline had rushed out of his body and the room rocked under his feet. It took all of Rowan's effort to stay standing.

"Priest, see to the wounds our heroes have sustained," the king declared, motioning to the same priest who had cast the identification ritual earlier.

The priest moved forward, his disposition entirely unchanged by the events that had gone down.

"Stay away from me!" Kayla's words were accompanied by a swing of her mace. But where it had at least garnered respect from the knights, the priest simply brushed it aside and caught her wounded forearm.

Light glowed from the priest's hand, and the wounds on Kayla's arm began to heal at a pace visible to the naked eye. In mere seconds, the only reminder of it was the blood that still stained her skin.

"It is . . . unfortunate that this day has been marred by such events, yet we must move on," the king said, his words ringing against the walls. "Heroes, servants will see you to your rooms, so you might be tended to and given a short respite. Gather yourselves, make yourselves presentable, and then join us for your welcoming feast. There is much still that we need to discuss, and I promise that our nobles are looking forward to sponsoring heroes as promising as yourselves."

The king's eyes lingered momentarily on Rowan as he wound down his speech.

When the servants stepped forward to guide them, Rowan followed. There really didn't seem like a better option. He was in a new world, surrounded by a crowd of murderous royalty and nobility. He'd have to get used to that.


"So you're saying that you can send us back?" Kayla, wearing a forest-green dress that matched her light-green eyes, leaned across the table. "You're saying that we can just choose to leave?"

The king shook his head. "You have been ordained with a divine quest, and only its completion will release you from your duty. What I said was that you will be granted a choice when victory has been achieved against the demons. A choice where you can either stay in the world you have saved or return to your homes and back to your original lives."

"So we have to do as you say. Otherwise, we never get to go back." Kayla slumped down in her chair. She, like Rowan and Blake, had been dressed in the garments of this new world. Gone were the T-shirts and jeans. Replacing them were layers and layers of thick fabrics. "I'm not a fan of this."

"Perhaps, but maybe once you see what this world has to offer, you'll change your mind," the king said as he snapped his fingers. Servants pulled away from the walls and brought forward a variety of meats, vegetables, and drinks. The king pointed at one of the glass flasks that contained a deep red liquid. "Tower Master, would you like the honors?"

An older lady sitting next to Kayla laughed. She stood up and muttered something that Rowan couldn't quite catch. Instead, he saw something much better.

The red liquid took on a life of its own, swirling out of the flask and making its way through the air before finally sloshing into Kayla's cup.

"Hero Kayla, meet Filipa, tower master of our kingdom's Mage Tower," the king said. "Are you not going to pour me a cup as well?"

The old woman smiled as a second stream flew out of the flask and into the king's cup. "Echoing Whisper—it's been a long time since a hero with that card graced our kingdom," the tower master said. "Hero Kayla, I promise you that you'll soon become a great mage. Perhaps, King Harold, you might be inclined to gift our newest student something? I've found that a little deal sweetener goes a long way."

"You're right," the king said, not at all offended by the tower master's casual remarks. "Hero Kayla, could you describe the effects of your Heart Card for us?"

"It's called Echoing Whisper," Kayla said as she looked at the older woman, who encouraged her on with a gentle nod. "The description is, *Your voice is joined by another, allowing you to incant two spells at once. The wielder of this card unlocks dual casting.*"

"Ah, a dual caster. It seems we're in luck." The king's eyes took on a blank look as he began looking at something in front of him that Rowan couldn't see. Moments later, a blue card materialized out of thin air and hovered in front of Kayla. "How about this? Ball Lightning, Rare Attack card. But you'll only get this if you agree to join the Mage Tower, to be personally instructed by the tower master herself. It's the best place in the kingdom for a mage."

Kayla's gaze darted between Rowan and Blake, neither of whom could offer any support to her. "I . . . sure. I'll do that."

"A good choice," the king said as the blue card fluttered down to the table. Kayla immediately grabbed it. "For the second matter, Hero Blake. Your card, Light Scion, destines you to walk the path of paladins. The best paladins in the kingdom are here in my royal guard. Would you like to train here? In the palace?"

Blake brushed his raven-colored hair back and nodded. It wasn't like he could say no to such an offer.

"Good," the king boomed. "Let it be known that Hero Blake has joined the royal guard."

The nobles at the feast gave a hearty cheer. Some of the more ambitious ones leaped out of their seats to congratulate Blake and offer minor gifts in the form of jewelry, promises of wealth, or even their daughter's hand.

At first, Blake blinked furiously at the onslaught of gifts. And then he smiled with teeth so white they hurt to look at. Rowan could tell that his friend was starting to have a good time. There were two things in life that mattered to Blake: helping people and finding new thrills.

There was no correlation between the two. Blake was the kind of person who'd jump in the middle of a street to save a kitten. And if he got to risk his life in the process, that was just an extra bonus.

Rowan was different. He wasn't the type to be a hero. Sure, he had harbored fantasies of saving the world, but when rubber met the road, he was out of his depth here. He picked up his glass of unidentifiable juice and chugged it down. The feast had gotten underway, and somehow both Blake and Kayla could pretend that the earlier attempts on their lives hadn't happened. But try as he might, Rowan couldn't shake the thought that every noble drinking and eating at the table had watched as they were almost killed by knights just a few hours earlier.

"Not one for feasts, Hero Rowan?" A middle-aged noble slipped into the seat next to Rowan.

"The food's good," Rowan offered as he sized up the noble. The people of this new world had an odd quality about them. It was like they had more vigor than any modern person. Even the wrinkled-looking priest who guided them into the audience room had moved with a grace that stood in stark contrast to his apparent years.

"I'd hope so. If the king's table offered you no joy, then I'd shudder to think how you'd feel about the rest of our food," the noble said with a smile. The man looked about the same age as the king, just with a few more strands of gray hair.

"Right, and you are?" Rowan asked.

"Kayden. Baron Kayden Sutton, at your service." The baron gave a shallow nod.

"Baron Kayden, I don't want to be rude, but are you sure that you want to be here talking with me?" Rowan gestured around himself, especially the seats that were now empty since their occupants had gone to greet Blake and Kayla. He had chosen one of the corner tables, where he felt just a bit safer than being in the middle of the massive room. And no one had bothered to ask him to move to a more prominent position.

"You're a hero, right? This feast is in your honor. But no one's here to congratulate you," Kayden said. Rowan knew that these were plain facts, but somehow they still stung. "In some way, you and I are in the same boat. Do you see that fop by the king's side?" Kayden angled himself to subtly gesture at one of his fellow nobles.

Rowan looked in that direction and found a young noble with a drink in hand. The noble's cheeks were suspiciously ruddy, which somehow complemented his animal fur clothing.

"Yes?"

"That's the newly minted Duke Treagon. He now holds vast tracts of land south of the capital. In fact, one could say that he owns the entire southern portion of the kingdom, all but one small barony at the very edge of the kingdom. My barony. And his lands? They once belonged to the House of Sutton."

It took a moment for Rowan to put two and two together. Treagon had taken land from the House of Sutton, and the baron's last name was Sutton. "I'm, uh, sorry to hear about that."

"Don't be. My plight was self-inflicted. A man must have his principles, and they're only called principles if you're willing to lose something to uphold them." Kayden straightened in his chair. "In that vein, I'll be honest with my intentions. I hope to sponsor you."

"Sponsor me?" Rowan asked.

Kayden blinked before a look of understanding dawned on his face. "Excuse me, perhaps I jumped the gun. I thought that you already knew, given how Hero Kayla and Hero Blake have both been sponsored."

"I really don't know what you're talking about," Rowan said, a slight edge creeping into his voice.

"Right. Sponsorship is an ancient tradition in the Rhys kingdom. When the first heroes arrived, the great houses made a pact with them. In return for support from the houses, the heroes agreed to give them a certain percentage of what they earned fighting the demons. Today, there are hundreds, if not thousands, of things that a noble house takes care of for their sponsored hero. Your training, party members, meals, laundry, and a lot more. Most important is your deck. The nobles can find the right cards to pair with your Heart Card. Without a properly balanced deck, even an Epic Heart Card loses its power."

"Okay, so you're looking to help me, and in return, you get a percentage of whatever I earn?" Rowan asked.

"Exactly. To be honest, House Sutton no longer has the wealth it once did, and I've lost much of my family's treasured card collection. But there is one thing that you'll find in me that you won't get from any of the other nobles in this room: I lost my lands and my wealth because of my belief. This belief."

Kayden tapped the air in front of him a few times, and a blue box popped up in front of Rowan.

**Kayden Sutton**
**Follower of Aristaeus**

Before Rowan could register what the screen meant, he was hit with a second notification.

**Blessing of the Stalwart Hero upgraded**
**Believers of God Aristaeus are more likely to provide aid and help in any way they can, provided it doesn't interfere with their personal goals.**

# CHAPTER THREE

# Noble Alignment

Rowan hesitated. It all sounded a bit too good to be true. Was the baron hoping to get his support and eventually reclaim the former Sutton lands? Or was this just a genuine offer to someone blessed by the god that the baron believed in?

"You're not sure. This is a lot to take in all at once," Kayden said, as if he could read Rowan's mind.

Rowan nodded.

The baron took a breath in as he looked around the room. His gaze paused on Kayla, who was engaged in a lively conversation with the old woman next to her.

"There, tell me, what did you make of everyone's reaction to Hero Kayla back in the audience room?"

"It was different than Blake's reception," Rowan said. Even now, not a lot of nobles were approaching Kayla. Most opted instead to squeeze in among the crowd in front of Blake. "But it's not her Heart Card. The tower master seemed happy to take her, and the king complimented the card. If it isn't that, then it had to be her blessing."

"Correct. The goddess who sponsored your friend is . . . rather infamous. She's one of the greater gods like Sarina, powerful and respected. But people hesitate to even utter her name. Goddess Ziraela is the goddess of secrets and schemes. There's a myth where those who say her name will find their secrets exposed soon after. So when Hero Kayla was blessed by the goddess, it made the nobles think twice before associating with her, not to mention that the fact that Goddess Ziraela isn't the patron god of Rhys."

Rowan noted the fact that the baron had used the goddess's full name in the conversation. Either he didn't believe that his secrets would come to light or he didn't have secrets at all.

"I don't think anyone has to worry about Kayla scheming or anything. The worst they can expect from her is a broken nose, and that happens right away."

The baron simply offered up a smile. "The greatest followers of Goddess Ziraela often bear the most disarming of masks. Your friend seems to be doing quite well for herself despite everything. Having the support of the Mage Tower will offer her a lot of leeway, and her card is a powerful one."

"You mentioned something about a patron god for the kingdom. Who is that? Just so that we're clear," Rowan asked.

"Goddess Sarina is the new patron god of the Rhys kingdom," Kayden responded. He paused for a fraction of a second before continuing, "The Rhys kingdom previously believed in a different god. Aristaeus. Unfortunately, he was a lesser god. And so when the kingdom had the opportunity to be blessed by a greater god, we leaped at the chance. Sarina has been our patron for a little more than two decades now."

"But you still follow Aristaeus," Rowan said.

"I do. As does the House of Sutton. We're devout followers of Aristaeus, which hasn't made us many friends at court." Kayden motioned at the other nobles, who kept sneaking glances at the two of them.

"So it was my blessing? The chaos in the audience room?" Rowan asked. He was starting to get comfortable talking with what seemed like the only normal noble in the whole place.

"It wasn't *just* your blessing. Your card, too. Aristaeus is the god of soldiers and rural crafts. He's often seen as someone more practical," Kayden said.

"And by practical, you mean common."

The baron sighed. "Spears are a commoner's weapon. They lack the promise of other weapons. A bow offers more range and safety, and better mobility to boot. Swords offer more damage, and the cards you can build around them are exceptional. Even daggers and axes have their place. Spear wielders are stuck in the middle. Not enough mobility to dance around your foes, not enough defense to bull through hits, and not enough damage to bury enemies quickly."

"And there's nothing I can do about it?"

"Usually, a spear pairs reasonably well with a shield, and many knight classes use the two in conjunction to cover both offense and defense. Your card, however . . ."

"It has a restriction that locks me out of wielding weapons," Rowan finished the thought.

"Shields are off-hand weapons in the eyes of the system, but weapons, nonetheless. This locks you out of options that would have made up for your shortcomings," Baron Kayden said.

"And I can't change my Heart Card into a new one?" Rowan asked.

"Gods, no. It's called your Heart Card because it can never be removed. It can grow stronger, sure. And in rare cases, it can be altered. But it cannot be changed," Kayden said.

"What about spears? There's never been a successful spear user? Ever?" Rowan asked.

"The best only ever climb to the Rare tier. There was one such case where a man found a spear that was a powerful artifact, uncovered from the ruins of an old mage tower at the very edges of the frontier. That led him to advance until the upper edge of a Rare class, level 58 or 59, I forget which. He was lost fighting against the demons. As a hero, you're expected to rise above the Epic tier, to reach at least level 60. But no one has ever seen an Epic-classed spear user."

"Okay, fine. But that just means I have a bad card. Life sucks. Boo-hoo," Rowan said, venting his frustrations slightly. "The reaction was more than that."

Instead of answering, the baron poured himself a drink, downed it, and then repeated the process for the second drink.

"Your blessing. Aristaeus isn't welcome around here. Not anymore. Devout followers of Sarina will see you as a threat to the stability of the kingdom," Kayden said. "They'd rather scrap your card, like they did all the other spear cards."

"I'm not talking about that. The knights were—" Rowan paused as a thought occurred to him. Two thoughts, actually. The first was that this was probably not the right place to ask why the knights wanted to kill Blake and Kayla. The second thought was around the new piece of information from Kayden. "What happens when someone dies? Their Heart Card. What happens to it?"

"When something dies, a card in their deck drops at random. That applies to both demons as well as people like us. If you only have one card in your deck, then that card will drop," Kayden said. He raised his head and looked into Rowan's eyes. "I know there is much you still don't understand about the system of our world, and I would be happy to fill you in on the details. But perhaps it'd be better to confirm our relationship before I get myself in trouble for saying too much."

Rowan took a deep breath and shoved his list of questions down. "So what's your offer of sponsorship?"

The baron's smile was soft. "The House of Sutton offers Hero Rowan all the aid our house can give. Including, but not limited to, house cards, adventurers and soldiers under the Sutton banner, and Baron Kayden Sutton himself. In exchange, we ask that Hero Rowan give us twenty-five percent of his loot."

Rowan drummed his fingers on the table. "Okay, so one more question. What are my other options?"

"I don't know if another house would be willing to offer terms like mine," Kayden said. Rowan silently agreed, especially given that the baron was the only person willing to sit next to him. "The king held a private session with the nobles earlier. He plans to send you out of the capital, one way or another. The alternative to my house sponsorship is to venture out on your own, with whatever title of nobility and a small plot of land our king sees fit to grace you with. Heroes in the past have done that, but to varying degrees of success. I do not wish to force your hand, but that is the truth."

Rowan swallowed and looked away from the man, scanning the crowds of nobles clustered around his friends.

Kayden seemed earnest. The baron didn't need to admit that he'd fallen out of favor. He could have promised a lot more than he could actually offer. Instead, he'd been genuine, and Rowan appreciated that.

Rowan briefly considered haggling, but there wasn't much more he could think to ask for. Kayden had already promised the full support of his house. As for loot percentages? None of that would matter if he was eaten by some demon. A higher percentage meant more incentive for the baron to train and help him.

"I, Rowan Clairfont, accept."


Over the next few days, Rowan mostly stayed in his room. To say that the kingdom was mistreating him would have been a lie. His meals were delivered, the room itself was large and comfortable, and there was even a bathroom with running water. But when he tried to leave the room, the knights at his door escorted him to the garden and back. Any attempt to go explore the palace or even just find his friends was denied.

So when Rowan heard news that he was going to be sent to the Sutton barony, he was excited. From stray conversations here and there, he learned more about his destination. For one, it was at the edge of the kingdom, about as far away from the palace as possible. It was also located next to the frontier, the first in line to get hit if demons crossed over.

With the message was also an update about Kayla and Blake, both of whom Rowan hadn't seen since the feast. Apparently, both heroes would continue living inside the palace, under the direct attention and in the company of the king. Blake was already training with an Epic-classed paladin while Kayla made the trek to the Mage Tower for tutoring.

As soon as the message was delivered, Rowan found himself escorted with only the clothes on his back to a humble-looking carriage.

The bright spot in all this was the baron. A smile lit up the man's rugged features when he caught sight of Rowan.

"Ah, there you are," Kayden said. "I thought I would be kept waiting much longer."

That brought Rowan up short. "They only just told me you're here for me."

"Is that so?" Kayden's eyes narrowed dangerously, but Rowan thought the baron looked more resigned than angry. "Well then, may I receive the official notice of the hero's dispatch to my lands?"

The knight that the baron was addressing cleared his throat and stepped forward. "By leave of the king, the hero Rowan Clairfont is hereby to accompany

Baron Kayden Sutton to his holdings, where the hero is to receive training and support in preparation for the demon wave."

"I accept." Kayden lowered his head. "And I confirm that Hero Rowan Clairfont is now in my charge. I vow on my life to protect him and help him grow in whatever way I can."

As the two of them got into the carriage, Rowan expected a cramped, uncomfortable affair. The carriage's exterior certainly inspired no confidence with its boxy look. But there was more than enough space for the two of them inside, and when he sat down, the seats were comfortably plush.

Some surprise must have shown on Rowan's face. "I may no longer be a duke, but there are some discomforts and indignities I refuse to suffer." Kayden laughed. "I would rather ride on horseback all the way back to my barony than be forced to endure an uncomfortable carriage."

"How long is the trip?" Rowan asked. "You mentioned that your home is all the way south?"

"If no unpleasantness happens to befall us, then it should take just over a week for us to reach our destination. Do not worry. I promise you won't be bored," Kayden said.

If Rowan was a more suspicious man, he would have found that comment alarming. But he got an early glimpse into his future after the baron rapped on the wood and the carriage surged forward. As Rowan sank into his seat, the baron began a rather innocuous introduction on noble titles.

Barons were at the bottom of the nobility ladder. Above them were viscounts, earls, marquesses, and dukes. Only four dukes existed at any one time, all related to the king directly, and eight marquesses served under them. From there, the web of nobility only expanded, and that was before they ever got into individual noble houses and their connections.

As the sights whipped by outside the carriage, the baron doggedly explained the nobility in the kingdom, their importance, and how many nobles could lay claim to each station. It was all a land-based system. The kingdom only had so much land, which meant that it could only support so many nobles.

Baron Sutton was one of the few nobles outside of the normal chain of command. Due to his past as a duke, he reported to the king instead of a viscount. And his barony was therefore only subject to the king's tax.

Kayden would occasionally pause in his explanation and begin quizzing Rowan on what he had said a couple of hours ago. The man was relentless. The only moments of peace Rowan got were when he went to sleep. And even then, the carriage never stopped moving. Somehow, the coachmen at the front never needed a break.

Rowan's head was practically splitting in half when, halfway through the third day, they took a break and the baron urged him to join him outside.

"This isn't a trap, right? You're not going to start teaching me about some noble house's flower while we're eating?" Though the forced cramming was unpleasant, Rowan had to admit that he was feeling a lot more comfortable around the baron.

Kayden laughed, shaking his head as he stretched. "No. No more of that. We're finally far enough away from the capital to do something more interesting."

Rowan had learned his lesson. He immediately backed up, trying to go back into the carriage. "Nope. No. Can't make me. The last time you said something like that, you made me run alongside the carriage for an hour while shouting about nobility ranks."

Unfortunately, Rowan's attempts to flee were stopped by a firm grip on the back of his shirt. "And now we know that you desperately need to work on your stamina, lad. This is like that, so stop whining."

"Wait, I have a serious question," Rowan said. It was alarming how easily Kayden could pick him up. He seemed to have more strength in a single pinkie than Rowan did in his entire body. "The knights, they should have torn through us. There's no reason why we should be alive right now. Why didn't they?"

Before answering that question, the baron looked around. They were in the middle of miles and miles of grassy plains, with only two coachmen and a group of riders that were accompanying the carriage.

"Well, there are two reasons why," Kayden said as he satisfied himself that no one else was around. "The first is that the king never meant for any of the heroes to get hurt. It was meant to scare you and nothing more."

"Scare us by killing his own guards?"

"Something like that," Kayden said softly. "The lives of commoners aren't valued in the kingdom. A single Uncommon class is rival to dozens or even hundreds of Common classes. The second reason is that the palace is placed under a giant formation. One that disables the use of cards and forcibly reduces a person's stats, so that the stronger you are, the weaker you become. The only exception to that rule is the king and those that he designates."

"So our lives were never in danger? Even in the trial of blood?" Rowan asked.

"No, that was true danger. If you had failed the trial, you would have died." Kayden looked into Rowan's eyes for a second before breaking contact and glancing at the riders. He called one of them over.

"I think we've done enough on the mind side of things today. Two points in intelligence in just as many days is a pretty good accomplishment," Kayden said, steering the conversation to a new topic. "Now, it's time we start working on your body more. That single point in vitality you got is not good enough."

"I'd be happy to help Hero Rowan with that." The rider dismounted from his horse and joined the conversation. The man had a wide grin on his face, and even though he looked nothing like the baron, Rowan got the sense that they were cut from the same cloth. "With your permission, of course, Baron."

"This here is Jacob," Kayden explained. "He's one of the best swordsmen in my barony. The sword and spear might be different weapons, the basic footwork between the two is the same. If you mess that up, you'll find yourself on the ground, lad. And you don't want to be on the ground."

"Hero Rowan, pleased to meet you," Jacob said.

Rowan looked at Jacob. Technically, heroes were automatically considered lesser nobility. And technically, Jacob didn't need to grin so menacingly.

"So how are we going to—"

Like the baron, Jacob wasted no time with pleasantries. A wooden stick materialized in his hand as the lesson began immediately. Rowan was prodded, poked, and pushed into position over and over again. His instructor was exacting in the way Rowan was to bend his knees, how he was to brace himself, the exact shuffle-step he had to make to maintain a sense of balance regardless of whether he was advancing or retreating.

The lesson went on for *days*. Or at least it felt that way. Kayden later assured him that he'd only trained for a total of two hours, but Rowan refused to believe such obvious lies.

It was two days after that, on the fifth day of their journey, that another change took place.

For the second time during their trip, they set up camp. Apparently, even the seemingly indefatigable coachmen needed sleep. And Rowan was starting to get used to his new life. He didn't need any help to set up his own tent, and he'd even argue that it didn't look crooked . . . if he tilted his head slightly.

As soon as that was done, Rowan shuffled his way over to the back of the carriage, where he knew Jacob was waiting for that day's footwork lessons. He didn't expect to spot the baron there, too. Kayden normally watched from a distance by the fire, chuckling quietly with his men and occasionally motioning in the hero's direction.

"You're going to train me today? Kayden?" Rowan knew that he should be grateful to the baron. After talking with some of the men, he realized that Kayden was putting his whole house on the line. Nobility was hereditary. The king could downgrade Kayden to a baron, but he couldn't kick him out of the ranks of nobility without proper justification. But if anything happened to Rowan, Kayden could forever lose the Sutton name. Even so, the training of the past few days, both physical and mental, strained any goodwill that Rowan might have felt.

"If only I were so fortunate. No. We have a good baseline for what you are capable of. The speed at which you can learn. How quickly your body adapts to training," Kayden said. That was true. Rowan had earned a couple points in all his stats, from strength to dexterity to even wisdom. His body didn't ache quite as much, and he was capable of enduring much more than before. "Now, it's time to see just how useful that card of yours is. Give it to him."

The baron motioned to Jacob, who opened one of the traveling trunks attached to the back of the carriage. He brought out a spear.

Rowan's breath briefly caught in his throat. The last time he'd wielded a weapon, it was a matter of life and death. He almost flinched as the memory of metal parting skin came to his mind.

And yet, the sight of the spear awakened something in him. A part of him wanted to grab the spear. Badly. He wanted to replicate the feeling of confidence he had with a spear in hand. His mind had cleared. His body had obeyed. Neither had become more powerful, but they both worked better. Like a machine that had just been cleaned of rust and cobwebs.

The baron took the spear and shoved the blunt end into Rowan's chest. "Take it, lad."

With shaky hands, Rowan did.

**Keen Spear prerequisites met.**

# CHAPTER FOUR

# Humble Heroing

For a long moment, Rowan did nothing but breathe. His hands were glued to the spear. He relished the ease with which he could feel his body and marveled at the way he could track the movement of each muscle. He was in control. That, of course, was when he got bonked.

"I'm not here to stand around and watch you breathe, lad," Kayden said as he pulled a wooden stick back. "Get your head on straight. Now, there will be no swinging that spear at Jacob here. What I want you to do is go through the footwork exercises with him again. See how they feel."

It felt amazing. Better than amazing. Even when Jacob added new motions to the routines, Rowan only slipped up a handful of times. His legs seemed to have a mind of their own, moving to the right spot before Rowan consciously gave the command. His body also began to remember the motions. If it took ten repetitions to get a motion right in the past, it now only took two or three.

By the end of the session, Rowan was heaving lungfuls of air. In spite of that, his grin threatened to split his face.

"Stop that right now." Kayden's voice was harsh, cold enough that it snapped Rowan right out of his good mood. "I've seen that look before. Young men get their first card, and they feel invincible. What you're practicing are the bare-bones basics. Children learn how to do that."

Anger bubbled up in Rowan's chest and he lashed out. "Then why bother teaching me how to do it?"

"Just because they're taught to children doesn't make them unimportant. The footwork lessons that Jacob taught you will be the foundation that everything else is built upon," Kayden said as he waved Jacob away. "But I won't let you get a big head. You'll get popped by the first monster that comes along. Now, come here. Bring the spear along."

Rowan regretted snapping at Kayden. Still, he let out a heavy puff of air before he followed. They settled down in front of the baron's tent, and he motioned his men to disperse.

"Is that smart?" At a questioning look from the baron, Rowan clarified. "I mean . . . I have a spear. You don't have a weapon at all." And it was true, the man had set his sword inside the tent and hadn't bothered to wear it after they made camp.

Rowan expected several different possible answers. What he didn't expect was for the baron to break out into laughter.

"Lad, I could stand in front of you in my undergarments and you wouldn't be able to scratch me. You've felt what those stats you've been getting are doing to you. Now, imagine the stats a former duke has. Imagine what a combat Heart Card might be able to do. Or my full deck, for that matter."

"I get it," Rowan mumbled.

Kayden raised a hand. "No, you really do not. And that is normal. You asked why the knights seemed so weak. Here's another answer. They weren't used to being so weak, to lose their system stats and cards. You haven't felt the benefits of the system, not really, and so you don't know what that feels like. Everyone who enters the palace feels as naked as a newborn baby."

"All the more reason to leave," Rowan said.

"More than that, there are no records of a hero ever coming to us from a world operating under a system," Kayden said. He motioned to the broader world. "It's strange, to think that people could live in a world without a system."

That bothered Rowan. A lot. Not simply because he was apparently leagues weaker than the baron, but also because he didn't understand a thing about the system.

"What is it? The system?" Rowan asked.

"No one really knows. It has been there for as long as things have existed. I can tell you this. From the lowliest monster to the greatest of the gods, we all use the same system," Kayden said.

At that, Rowan blinked in disbelief. "Wait, you're saying . . ."

The baron grinned. "Yes, just like you and me, the gods, too, are system users. Now, they're as far beyond me as I am beyond you. But if you know which texts to reference, you'll find that quite a few of our gods were not as divine once upon a time."

"But, if anyone can become a god, then why do you worship them?" Rowan asked.

"When did I say anyone can do it, lad?" Kayden said. "Do you really think that all you need is a Heart Card, a weapon in hand, and enough experience to fill your levels? It's much harder than that. If you want to upgrade your class-rarity tier, you need the right catalyst. Or the right Heart Card."

That caught Rowan's attention. "A Heart Card is helpful for that? And what's a class? Or a catalyst, for that matter?"

"The tier of your Heart Card determines how far you can climb without obstruction. Class rarity is divided every twenty levels. A Common Heart Card means that you'll find trouble reaching level twenty, which is the domain of Uncommon classes," Kayden said.

"But my Epic Heart Card means that I can reach level eighty without trouble," Rowan said.

"Level seventy-nine," Kayden corrected. "Each class comes with a class card. An Uncommon class gives you an Uncommon card for your deck. And a catalyst is . . . a trophy. One that you can get by slaying an enemy of the appropriate level, rarity, and strength. It's what you must do to move past the limitations of your Heart Card," Kayden answered.

"I know people were excited about our cards. Well, Kayla and Blake's cards," Rowan said. "But . . . how rare are Epic cards, really?"

"The Heart Cards of heroes are always Epic," Kayden said. "Commoners can, at best, hope for an Uncommon for their Heart Card. Most will get Common cards."

Rowan wasn't sure he liked the implications. "What about nobles, then?"

"There is a component of inheritance when awakening a Heart Card. The higher your parents have climbed, the better your card will be. Most nobles will awaken to an Uncommon card. Royal offspring most often get Epics. Both have the potential to awaken a tier higher. Of course, inheriting a Heart Card directly before it is awakened is an option, too."

"Directly?" Rowan asked. He had half a mind to pull up his system screen and read everything over again. "When I got my card, the system prompt said that it was bound to me."

"Slaying a cardholder gives you the chance to claim one of their cards. For most nobles, if they know that death is coming, they will . . . expedite things, and ensure that some part of their deck is passed onto their descendants," Kayden said.

"So, nobles just keep getting stronger, then?" Rowan asked.

"Correct. This is why the age of a kingdom is an important thing to keep in mind. No one knows how many high-tier cards old kingdoms might have hidden away. Or what they might do with them, if pushed too far."

For a long few moments, the two of them sat in silence. Rowan was certain he disliked what he'd heard. Card hoarding reeked of classism. He decided to ask another question to distract himself. "Why do all heroes get Epic cards, then?"

"I'll be honest with you, lad, no one knows for certain," Kayden said.

"But, there's been how many heroes before?" Rowan asked. "You made me listen to the various noble lineages and how many of them claim to be related to heroes, too! How can no one know?"

"You saw the message when you got your card. The system evaluates everything about you. Some people argue that there's something about summoned heroes' worlds that nurtures the conditions the system values better. Others argue that the ritual simply reaches out and catches only the souls deemed 'worthy,' and that other souls in your world would follow the average of ours just as consistently." Kayden paused as his face twitched. "It is not spoken of very often. But, once in a blue moon, a commoner might be able to awaken to an Epic card."

"So, we're just the lucky ones?" Rowan asked.

Kayden shrugged. "There are those who claim that the summoning itself is what gives you the advantage. After all, it is a fact that all heroes . . . well . . ." The baron's voice trailed off as he looked away. "Never mind. The important thing is that every hero gets an exceptional card. Yes, even you. The inherent value of an Epic card, especially a hero's card, is much greater than you can imagine."

The two of them stared at a nearby campfire for a few minutes before they retreated to their own tents. Before the night ended, Kayden promised Rowan that his training would be kicked up a notch. And that he'd actually learn how to use the weapon he was stuck with.

It was an unusual turn of events, to say the least.

Over the next few days, Kayden took over the training for Rowan, citing that none of his men were spear wielders but that his expertise would let him make do.

At first, Rowan thought of this as an upgrade over the hellish training that Jacob had put him through. He was wrong. The baron taught only a single move: set, thrust, and shuffle to repeat the motion with a different dominant hand. Supposedly, the hand swapping was crucial in battle because it changed the angle of attack.

Finally, when Rowan got bored by repeating the same motion thousands of different times, he made the mistake of trying out a grand sweep, imagining the swing shattering the defense of his enemies and cutting them in half.

Before he knew it, he was lying on his back.

"If you're looking to get yourself killed, there are easier ways of doing it than trying to use your spear like a club. The spear is powerful, but if you do big moves like that, a monster is going to find your gaps and tear open your throat," Kayden said. "Like I did."

As Rowan got back to his feet, he wondered if all the children in this new world were trained like this.

"The power of the spear is that it's a versatile weapon. You can use it as a makeshift staff in an emergency," Kayden continued. "But once again, you need to build your foundation. The point of a spear is to stab its pointy bit into your enemy, not use it like some other weapon. Right now, you don't have the stats or the skills to try anything other than the simple thrust."

After that, Rowan stuck religiously to what he was taught.

Surprisingly, he could feel himself making progress long after the motions had become ingrained into his mind, body, and soul. The thrusts were becoming a hair quicker, and there were somehow still a couple of extra movements that he could cut down on. In the words of the baron himself, Rowan wasn't flailing the spear mindlessly now. Instead, he was flailing it with some idea of how to stab someone other than himself.

Rowan would have been content to continue this way until they arrived at their destination. But exactly a week into their journey, a bit past the point when he'd been informed that they had already entered the baron's holdings, they came across a group of harried field workers rushing down the road.

To Rowan's untrained eyes, it looked like the workers were running to get lunch. But Kayden stretched his head out of his carriage and signaled for Jacob to ride ahead and catch up with the farmers.

When Jacob came back, Kayden dipped his head to hear the report. A couple moments later, he pulled his body back into the carriage with a contemplative look on his face.

It was bad news. Rowan had become fluent in the baron's facial expressions, especially this one, since it so often led to some kind of escalation in his training, or a particularly unreasonable request. The baron had worn the same expression before he'd suggested Rowan try some innovative stretching, also known as obscure torture methods, that led to his seventh point in dexterity.

"It seems we're fortunate, lad," Kayden said. His grin was positively radiant, but it only chilled Rowan's bones. "These fine folk here have a demon problem in their fields, and you are going to sort it out for them."

Rowan wasn't exactly forcibly marched down the road to his impending fate, but he wasn't given much of a chance to wiggle out of what was coming, either. He'd barely managed a squeaky "what" before the baron pushed him out of the carriage.

"What exactly am I fighting?" It was only thanks to the spear in his hand that Rowan had enough presence of mind to open his mouth again. Still, he hated the way that his voice warbled and he couldn't help but remember being swarmed by a group of knights bent on killing him.

"Just a couple of corrupted animals," Kayden said in an offhand manner. "A trio of boars. They slipped past the frontier border, and now they're threatening people's livelihoods. Can't exactly leave such things alone, can you, hero?"

"Boars," Rowan repeated. He dearly hoped the animals were the same as the ones he was familiar with. There were stories and videos online about how deadly these animals could be, but for a first opponent, they sounded much less threatening than dragons or wyverns. "Three of them."

"You'll do fine. Remember what I taught you in the last few days. The only reason these boars are here is because they didn't warrant being hunted down."

"Why not?" Rowan asked. Anything was better than focusing directly on what was to come.

"The frontier stops any powerful monsters, demons, or corrupted beasts. If any strong ones do manage to cross somehow, a hunting party is dispatched," Kayden said as he twirled his finger in the air. "This is well in line with what local militia can handle. And you're a hero. It's going to be a walk in the park."

*A new hero. Brand-new, level zero!* Rowan knew better than to contradict Kayden. For starters, he now trusted the baron. Despite all the torturous mental and physical training, Rowan now knew the man as someone fairly even-keeled. If he thought something was doable, it was usually possible, even if the process left Rowan sore for the next two days. And compared to before, Rowan now had a bit more training with the spear. *That has to count for something.*

On impulse, Rowan brought up his status screen.

**Rowan Clairfont**
**Level 0 Unclassed (+)**
**EXP: N/A**
**STR: 7**
**VIT: 9**
**DEX: 7**
**PER: 7**
**INT: 8**
**WIS: 8**

**Deck (1/4):**
**[Heart] Keen Spear (Epic, Passive)**
**Blessings:**
**Blessing of the Stalwart Hero**

The training, both physical and mental, had worked. His stats showed improvements across the board. The only part of his screen that bothered him was the insistent blinking of the plus sign next to his unclassed status. But the baron had assured him that it was something to worry about only once he hit ten in all stats.

Rowan began making his way forward with his spear. He was so taken by his thoughts that he almost missed the fact that no footsteps accompanied his own. But that was *fine.* He was a hero, and he would fight like one.

The closer Rowan got to the affected fields, the more apparent the problem got. The noises the boars made were high-pitched and angry. He'd be lucky if the noises didn't give him nightmares in the future.

Finally, Rowan found them. The three boars were not perfectly clumped together. Of the group, two were a decent distance away while the last one was rooting through a vegetable patch of some kind, less than fifty paces away.

Up close, Rowan could see that the corrupted boar was an ugly thing. Its body was a twisted mass of angry muscles, accented by the occasional clumps of fur that clung on. The worst part was its tusk, rough and blunted. This wasn't a creature that relied on precise strikes but rather brute strength. It probably hadn't met an opponent it couldn't overpower yet.

And Rowan was about to fight it.

Tightening his grip, Rowan sneaked forward, hoping to score a hit without going face-to-face with the monster. The gods didn't smile on him. About ten steps away, Rowan's luck ran out. The boar suddenly grunted and whipped its face in Rowan's direction.

The two stared mutely at each other for what felt like an eternity. The boar was the first to ruin things. It opened its jaws and screeched.

*What kind of monster has teeth like that and still eats vegetables?*

The boar's mouth reminded Rowan of a shark's rather than a boar's. Rows upon rows of razor-sharp teeth lined both the top and bottom. The perfect meat grinder. Rowan didn't want to find out how it'd feel to get bitten.

The monster tensed up when it realized that Rowan wasn't going to flee. It ended its screech and kicked back its legs. After a moment to gain traction in the soft dirt, it began rocketing forward.

Rowan planted his feet in the stable ground of the road and braced his spear. If he was right, then the beast didn't have much maneuverability. Its speed was working against it.

As the boar came into reach, Rowan thrust his spear forward, sidestepping as he did. The attack worked as intended, leveraging the beast's momentum to rake across its side in a long, jagged line. But the boar showed surprising agility, twisting its head at the last second and catching Rowan's shirt with its tusk. The momentum carried Rowan in the direction of the beast's charge. Thankfully, he managed to regain his balance before the boar's next charge.

Behind Rowan, more screeching sounded, and he risked a glance to find the other two boars speeding his direction.

*Not good.*

Rowan bit into his lower lip, hard, and tasted copper. He couldn't afford to be hemmed in from both sides.

When the original boar drew closer, Rowan decided to change tacks. Instead of thrusting downward, he held his spear low, practically planting the back end of his spear in the ground and angling it upward. The boar kept charging.

*Five steps. Four. Three. Two.*

Rowan stood his ground. His heart began beating so loudly that he could barely hear anything else. *One.*

He could see the blood in the boar's eyes as he jumped to the left. The delay was expensive. A tusk grazed Rowan's side, and he felt a force lift him into the air before being dumped on the ground.

It took several painful seconds for Rowan to hoist himself upright. Even breathing was a chore. He strongly suspected his ribs were cracked, but he forced himself to stumble toward the now-stationary boar.

The end of the spear had dug a shallow path in the road, driven into the dirt by the momentum of the boar's charge. Luckily, the weapon had done its job. The boar was squealing and twitching on its side. Its hooves were kicking up dirt, but it wasn't a threat anymore. Especially since the tip of Rowan's spear was lodged deep in its chest.

*One down. Two more.*

Rowan had no clue how long he had until the other boars were on him. Pushing his broken body, he fumbled at the spear's shaft, struggling to pull it out of the beast's chest.

"Careful!" Kayden's voice came just in time for Rowan to dive to the side and narrowly avoid a pair of nasty tusks that were about to skewer him. Even better, his spear had come free in the struggle.

"I got it," Rowan yelled back as he felt his training kick in. Set, thrust, shuffle. The third boar shrieked in surprise when Rowan aimed a well-placed thrust to its side, drawing blood but not much else.

As Rowan moved, he positioned the fallen boar behind himself. It limited the attack angles from the other two. When the second boar came rushing in, he repeated the same sequence and sent it squealing back with a new wound.

From there, the battle became grueling. The boars would dance forward and Rowan would have to send them back with a thrust, each contraction of his chest muscles sending a fresh wave of agony through him.

Slowly, Rowan began to understand his opponents. One of the boars was clearly more interested in self-preservation, but the other was in a rage, charging again and again only to be stymied by Rowan's spear or get tripped up by the carcass.

It was in that moment that Rowan realized the value of Keen Spear. Despite the pain, risk of death, and truly ugly monsters, Rowan kept his calm. He exploited the anger of the boar, landing precise strikes that seemed to hit an artery each time. When the beast finally fell after what felt like hundreds of different wounds, Rowan even had the energy to give a small smile.

The final boar glanced at its two dead companions and whimpered. It ran away.

Rowan had no strength left for a chase. He tried to loudly taunt the monster, only to see it run away even faster.

*Shit, if it gets away, then it might . . .*

Before Rowan could finish that thought, he saw the baron strolling through the farm. And for the first time, Rowan realized why Kayden insisted on repetition and perfection.

When the king had acted to strike down the knight, Rowan had failed to see any movement. For all he knew, it was some kind of royal power that had turned an entire person to mist. Now, when the baron closed the gap between himself and the fleeing boar, Rowan could appreciate the strength difference. The man looked like he was just walking, but every step was performed without any extra motions and brought him a bit closer to the sprinting monster boar.

His strike was also a lazy thing. Kayden simply brought his sword down, and the boar's head parted from the rest of its body. Its momentum held true for a couple more seconds before it collapsed onto the ground.

"Not horrible," Kayden said, appearing next to Rowan in seconds. He had the same contemplative look on his face as before. "I was hoping you could strike down all three. At least you showed bravery. Oh, what you did was stupid, lad, but certainly brave."

Rowan's response was to collapse on his back.

*I want to pass out. Please let me pass out.*

"None of that now. On your feet." When Rowan didn't react quickly enough, an iron grip caught the front of his shirt, pulling him up effortlessly.

"Fine, fine!" Rowan hissed out, stumbling upright.

The baron watched Rowan with wry amusement before offering a vial of red liquid. "Drink that, lad. It'll make you feel better."

Grumbling a word of thanks, Rowan took the vial and chugged it down. The liquid was a bit heavy, with a hint of sweetness. But when the liquid passed his throat, it transformed into genuine magma. An unbearable heat coiled in Rowan's chest, then shot down to where his ribs ached. The pain flared, and Rowan was convinced he would pass out. But after a few moments, the heat and pain began to fade, leaving behind a warm, numbing sensation.

"Wh-what was that?" Rowan wheezed.

"You know, you should ask questions like that before accepting a potion from someone. Especially once you meet my daughter," Kayden said, slapping Rowan on the back. Oddly, he experienced no pain. "That was a healing potion. You'll feel numb while it works, but you'll be right as rain in a couple of hours. Better-quality draughts work much quicker, but this doesn't warrant those."

As the healing potion did its magic, Rowan forced himself to hobble the distance to their carriage and collapsed on its doorstep.

While he panted, half-numb and mostly alive, the baron made his way to the field workers who had alerted them to the whole mess. He calmed those who seemed upset and shook the hands of those who had grim lines on their faces. The carcasses of the boars were left to them and quickly butchered on the spot.

The baron also ordered the soldiers out into the fields. Rowan saw why pretty quickly. They came back with bits and pieces of previously alive workers.

Eventually, the carriage began moving again.

As he looked out the window, Rowan began to realize that he had seen more death in the past few days than his entire previous life combined. In a normal world, he'd need an extensive amount of therapy to make sure there wasn't some lingering mental trauma. Instead, the baron hopped back in the carriage and began the next set of lessons on the strengths of the noble houses.

*I am going to survive it all.* The determination ignited in Rowan's chest. *I don't care whether my card sucks, or what it takes. But I'm going to survive whatever this world throws at me.*

As the carriage drew closer to its final destination, Rowan almost managed to convince himself that he'd survive. Almost.

# CHAPTER FIVE

# Setting a Foundation

As the carriage rolled deeper into the baron's estate, Rowan began getting a slight pressure in the back of his mind. It was like a small weight had settled on his head. When he tried to get rid of it, a status screen popped up.

**Battle Results:**
**EXP:**
**[Corrupted Boar] +5**
**[Corrupted Boar] +10**
**Loot:**
**2x cards**
**Claim?**
**Y/N**

*Wait, loot?* The prospect of getting actual useful drops was more than a little exciting. So, before the rest of his mind caught up with suggestions to ask Kayden for his advice, Rowan hit yes.

**Experience assignment failed, no class found.**
**TIP: System experiences require a class to be assigned.**

The first screen that showed up was a disappointment. By not having a class, Rowan had lost out on the experience portion of his loot.

But before he could mourn the lost experience, two white flashes of light sparked beyond the blue screen. When Rowan dismissed the experience screen, he found two cards that each rotated once before becoming corporeal enough to flutter to the ground. Kayden smiled at the sudden appearance of the cards.

Slightly embarrassed by what he had done, Rowan scooped up the cards as swiftly as he thought was proper.

His excitement wasn't meant to last.

**Reckless Rush (Common, Active)**
**Rush toward your enemy, increasing your movement speed and**
**dealing increased impact damage.**
**Bind card to your deck?**
**Y/N**

Rowan was pretty sure that he didn't want a card like that. As powerful as the boar's charge had been, Rowan couldn't see himself sprinting forward and attacking like that. In the small amount of combat time he had, he was much more of a strategic fighter, poking for weaknesses instead of trying to overwhelm enemies with absolute might.

The second card was somehow worse. He couldn't even use it.

**Coarse Fur (Common, Passive)**
**Your fur becomes tougher and bristly, more easily turning blows.**
**ERROR!**
**You are incapable of adding this card to your deck at this time.**

That was it. Two cards, both Common. Rowan knew that the odds of him getting some kind of amazing loot on his first monster kills was low, but somewhere deep inside of him, he had hoped that his very near brush with death would mean something good. The only consolation prize appeared when he checked on his status screen. His vitality had ticked over to ten.

*Wait, does the body of the boar count as loot?*

Rowan turned his gray eyes on his companion. After glancing at the cards, Kayden had turned his attention back to the scenery slipping by outside the window. In their agreement, they had agreed that twenty-five percent of his loot would go to the baron. Rowan wasn't sure how he could split a card into fourths.

"If you have something to say, lad, spill it out," Kayden said.

"The cards, how do I—"

"Don't worry about them." Kayden waved Rowan off. "I know they're Common cards; the light was white. They're probably not good for your deck. Just hold on to them for now."

Rowan nodded. "There's something else. And I don't want to sound ungrateful. But wasn't I supposed to get seventy-five percent of all my loot? Wouldn't that include the boar corpses? If they have value?"

"That's true," Kayden said. He paused and turned to face Rowan with a sly smile on his face. "That's very true. The two boars, they were probably level three or four. Beyond the experience and cards they drop, there's also the meat, which is edible, the hides, which are somewhat useful, and the bones, which can be crafted into a variety of items due to their toughness."

Rowan waited. He knew Kayden well enough to know that there was going to be a "but" sometime soon.

"So the total value of the materials should be around twenty gold all considered. And most of that comes down to the value of the bones. So you should be getting fifteen gold." Now, Kayden's smile turned into a grin. "But the potion you drank is worth twenty-five gold. So technically, you're running a ten-gold deficit."

"But you gave it to me!" Rowan protested.

The baron broke into laughter. "Yes, and that's the kind of trick nobles happily use to get people to owe them. I do admit I should have asked, but you were in shock. I knew you would want to help those people. There's also the small matter of those cards being arguably more valuable than the carcasses."

Rowan huffed and rolled his eyes, but let most of his anger pass. "You can have the cards! They're both not my type. I can't even use one of them."

"Thank you, but you should keep those. They might come in handy in the future, or you might be able to trade them away," Kayden said. "Our agreement comes into play later when you're earning more. A truckload more."

That brought Rowan to a new topic. It was pretty amazing that this new world would just happen to use English. "You just described something that I'm pretty sure doesn't exist in this world. How are we even talking right now?"

"You don't know? Is this not part of the basic knowledge you were taught on arrival?"

"Basic knowledge?"

Kayden settled back into his seat with a sigh. "I should have known. The reason we can talk is by the grace of the gods. When you were summoned here, it came with certain benefits. You'll be able to converse with every language-capable creature. If records are to be believed, you will hear every language as though it were your own."

That made some sense, Rowan thought. The gods wouldn't want their chosen heroes to flounder and struggle to communicate after they were summoned. Still, hearing anything be referred to as the "grace" of the gods was off-putting, especially since Rowan had seen these gods once before.

The silence for the remaining carriage ride didn't feel particularly awkward, especially since they soon caught sight of their destination.

A part of Rowan expected the baron's home to be something like a large village or small town. After all, the man had been more or less demoted to the lowest rank of nobility. It was also at the far edge of the empire, right about at the frontier.

So when tall, thick walls began appearing in the distance, Rowan wondered if they had somehow overshot their destination and reached the frontier. After some squinting, he could make out crenellations. The walls weren't just for show—they were built to handle trouble.

But Rowan saw the baron relax, the same way someone might when they caught sight of their home. Except in this case, that home was about the size of a city.

*The baron has a castle?*

As it turned out, Kayden did. A small castle, to be fair. The castle was built around what looked to be a small hill, with a sprawling settlement emanating beyond the walls.

The settlement itself looked like it was flourishing. The streets were actually paved with checkered stones. The houses looked to be in good repair, predominantly built out of stone as well.

*Does the baron have a quarry?*

Most telling was the welcome the baron got. When people realized it was his carriage rolling into town, they waved and smiled, and a couple of them even cheered.

In that moment, it struck Rowan that for all of Kayden Sutton's ramblings on nobility, he'd never revealed the details of his own house.

"Do you have a family, Kayden?" Rowan asked.

"Uh . . ." For the first time since Rowan had known the man, the baron was caught off guard. Kayden winced as he composed his response. "You'll meet some of them soon."

Rowan could sense that it was futile to push more on the topic. And like Kayden had said, he would meet them soon, one way or another. The wince was odd, but Rowan couldn't think of any reason the man would be reluctant to speak on the subject.

As they rolled through the gates separating the castle from the wider town, Rowan expected some procession of maids and butlers to greet them. Something to match the splendor that he had seen so far.

Instead, they were greeted by a harried-looking boy in a livery coat, who immediately started to work on the horses, and an older gentleman in a dark suit.

"Welcome home, Lord Kayden. Your daughter and Lady Sutton are waiting for you inside." With that bit of formality out of the way, what was almost a fatherly smile slid onto the older gentleman's face. "How did the summoning go? Did our good King Harold get what he wished for?"

"Ah . . . On that subject, Garrett, meet Rowan Clairfont, a young hero we have the honor of hosting. And Rowan, meet Garrett, our butler. He's indispensable."

Several emotions flashed across Garrett's face. Shock, worry, a hint of . . . hope? His expression slipped back into a polite mask as he turned to face Rowan. "Lord Clairfont, I apologize for my late greetings. It is truly an honor to host a hero."

"It is an honor to be here." After debating what the right response was, Rowan chose a line that he had heard uttered in movies and speeches. "You can call me Rowan."

"Of course, Hero Rowan," Garrett responded.

Before Rowan could try to get the butler to try a more informal name, Kayden stepped between the two of them. "Come, lad. We need to introduce you to my family. Garrett, could you help the coachmen get situated? They did well."

"My pleasure, Lord Sutton." Garrett bowed.

The castle was oddly cozy. The stone was clearly old, worn until it was glossy by the passage of time. Still, someone had made it all a bit more hospitable. Warm-colored rugs, a couple of nice, cheerful paintings, and an occasional vase with flowers did a lot to soften the cold stone.

It didn't help Rowan relax. All of a sudden, he realized that he was about to meet the lady of the house, a previously-married-to-a-duke noble lady, while wearing the baron's spare clothes.

The baron noticed Rowan's fidgeting and grinned like a shark. The baron was a large man, but Rowan's clunky build made it so that the clothes were still uncomfortably tight. It hadn't mattered during the training sessions, but now, everything felt wrong.

Pushing open massive oak doors, the baron led Rowan into a large dining room that was more or less lifted out of a *Harry Potter* movie. The room was big and lined with massive wood tables. At the end of one such table, looking tiny, were a few plates of food.

A tall, willowy woman stood as they entered, and there was something about her that subtly threw Rowan off. "Finally, Kayden! We expected you days ago. If you were going to be late, the least you could have done is—"

Her protests were cut off when the baron rushed up to her and lifted her in a hug.

"Put me down, you brute! You *smell*!" Lady Sutton exclaimed.

"I'm happy to see you, too," Kayden said. The two soon devolved into quiet muttering.

With the two side by side, Rowan realized that the proportions of Lady Sutton's body were odd. Her arms and legs were just a little too long, and her fingers reminded him of the videos of pianists he'd seen in the past. It wasn't anything that made her look ugly—the opposite, actually. She seemed to have a natural grace thanks to those characteristics.

"Mother, Father . . . you are embarrassing yourselves. And in front of an audience," a new voice protested. Rowan searched around and found a girl around his own age. She remained seated, warily looking between him and her parents.

"Ah yes, our audience, as you put it. Camilla, Olivia, allow me to introduce our guest and charge, Rowan Clairfont, one of the summoned heroes our kingdom was blessed with," Kayden said. "And Rowan, Camilla Sutton is my wife. Olivia, my daughter."

This produced two diametrically opposed reactions in the ladies. The lady of the house looked stricken before her eyes accusingly snapped onto her husband. Her daughter, however, straightened and looked at Rowan with undisguised glee. Several seconds later, she slumped down in her seat again and let strands of forest-green hair obscure her face. A small part of Rowan's mind was stuck wondering whether the color was natural.

"I welcome you to our home, Hero Rowan. It is not every day that we get to house one such as you," Camilla finally said. Something had passed between her and her husband while Rowan was distracted by their daughter.

"Thank you for your welcome, Lady Sutton." Rowan tried for a smile. He knew it looked strained.

"We were not expecting a guest, but that's easily rectified." Camilla had a death grip on her husband's hand as she dragged him down next to her, at the head of the table. "Now please, do regale us with your tale of how we got the honor of hosting a hero."

While they picked at their food, Kayden was forced to go into exacting detail of what had happened.

Camilla contributed nothing of substance throughout, her face unreadable. The baron's daughter had nothing to say, either. She was stuck staring at her plate, a contemplative expression passing over her face occasionally.

Rowan had no clue what to make of it all. Kayden had clearly not consulted his wife or daughter when he decided to take a hero home. Even if they were too polite to object to him outright, the idea that the barony was going to be anything but welcoming was like a cold stone in Rowan's stomach. As much as he hated to admit it, Rowan had taken a liking to Kayden despite the baron's torturous training. He doubted that anyone else in the kingdom cared about him as much as the baron.

At least the food was good. Rowan had grown sick of the road rations less than a day into their journey. There was only so much one could do with dried meat and hard bread, even if they were turned into a makeshift soup. So, the warm, delightfully seasoned meat and vegetable dishes were doing a wonder for his palate.

When the conversation wound down and the food was mostly gone, Camilla took charge of the conversation for the first time. "Well, I know you two must have had a trying journey. Rowan, if you would follow Garrett, he will get you settled and direct you to a bathroom."

Rowan knew a dismissal when he heard one, so he politely excused himself with a few words of thanks and followed the butler.

"You shouldn't worry, you know," Garrett whispered. The words snapped Rowan out of his melancholy. The old butler was briskly leading him to their destination, but the tone of his voice was kind. "You will be welcome here. We'll do our best to assist you. Please don't hold her attitude against Lady Sutton. She just doesn't like to be surprised."

Rowan didn't know how to respond to that, so he simply said nothing and waited as, over the course of the next few days, the butler's words came true.

"Faster! Come on, faster! My one-month-old kitten could run faster than you," Kayden shouted.

"Does your kitten have a system?" Rowan shouted back, surprised he could find the breath for it after running for hours.

"Of course," Kayden responded. He grabbed a spear from a nearby rack and chucked it, nonpointed end first, at Rowan.

Rowan slowed down and caught the spear, feeling the same rush of relief wash over him. He was starting to get used to the power of his Keen Spear card.

"Hold position," Kayden barked.

Rowan brought his right leg back and stood almost parallel to the spear. He slid his right hand to the back of the spear while his left gripped the middle portion.

"You know, this is much worse than the training we did on the road," Rowan said. Even though his body was on the verge of collapse, he felt oddly disconnected. Like it was someone else who was going through all that pain and he was merely an observer.

"It's meant to be," Kayden said. "Thrust position."

Rowan pushed the spear forward and appraised the motion. He could have been a bit faster, but the spear didn't wobble after the strike. He was getting better. "I appreciate all this training. But why are we doing this again? I thought the whole point of a system was so that we didn't have to train like this."

"Ha," Kayden scoffed. "Anyone can kill monsters, gain experience, and level up. That's easy. What's not so easy is making sure that a person gets the most out of every level. The limit for an unclassed person is ten in all stats. Normally, that'd require training from birth to even have a shot of reaching. But you're a hero. The gods gave you a chance to catch up. But there's always a give and a take. Can you guess what the take is? Shuffle."

Rowan pulled the spear back, swapped hands, and shuffled to a new position in a single motion. It was smooth enough that he felt proud of the technique. "I have to work harder than other people?"

"Exactly. Even a single stat point at this stage makes a world of difference," Kayden said as he watched Rowan's stance. "Good stance."

"So why can't I train after I get a class and level up a bit?" Rowan asked. His body wasn't as sore as before. Somehow, whenever he held a spear, fatigue would start to melt away.

"Because the system is also a give-and-take," Kayden answered. "It offers amazing benefits when you level up. It uses mana, in some way that we can't understand, to bolster a person's physical and mental faculties. But each point that you get from leveling up drives you farther away from what you could achieve on your own."

"Which is a bad thing?" Rowan asked.

"In some ways, yes. Once you start leveling up, it becomes incredibly hard to increase stats through training. It might take you years of strength training to get even a single point of strength. Usually, the system would rather give you experience instead of raw stats." Kayden motioned for Rowan to go through the stances at his own pace. "So right now is your best chance of getting stats while only paying the low, low cost of being exhausted."

Rowan thrust the spear out as he lobbed his next question. "So how do stats work with leveling up?"

"Every level you gain, you get two points to spend," Kayden said. "Now you get why we're doing this? You're gaining at least two stat points every day right now."

"Just an excuse to torture me," Rowan mumbled.

Kayden caught that comment. "Oh, you haven't seen torture yet. Do a thousand spear thrusts. Now, it's probably time to talk about proper noble etiquette. I'm guessing you'll need it if you want to stay on Camilla's good side."

For better or worse, both the butler and baron were right. When Rowan gave the proper greeting to Lady Sutton later that day, she became markedly friendlier.

The baron's family seemed to take all their meals together. And Rowan was naturally invited. Over time, he got more accustomed to the place, making friends with Garrett and learning more about the past glories of House Sutton. Apparently, they had been very close to one of the past heroes and found their standing through holding steady in their support of the hero.

While the rest of the house was warming up to Rowan, the baron's daughter was the opposite. It wasn't that she was hostile—she just never spoke up. And Rowan could have sworn that he saw her staring at him on a couple of different occasions.

Not that there was much time to dwell on such things. Kayden soon added two more parts to Rowan's training. The first was fun. Instead of stuffy nobility bloodline lessons, Kayden began teaching the strengths and weaknesses of different classes. There were the classic fantasy classes like [Knight] and [Mage], and then there were just as many specialized classes like [Cultist] or [Baker].

But it was always a bit of a downer when Kayden ended each lesson by emphasizing that Rowan's class had been set in stone thanks to his card. He had to take [Spearman] as his class. The only reason he was learning about the other classes was to know how to counter them if the time came.

The second new addition was less fun. So far, Rowan had found an equilibrium with the baron's training. The exercises were tiring. The knowledge was interesting. The endless spear grilling was actually enjoyable. So when Kayden mentioned sparring, Rowan was excited to see what would happen.

His hopes were dashed when Kayden summoned a maid from the castle to be his sparring partner—a dainty, smiling woman in her early thirties who arrived still wearing an apron.

And then Rowan had made the mistake of looking at the grinning baron and raising an eyebrow in question about his opponent. A second later, his world was flipped upside down, and he landed roughly on his back, all air driven from his lungs.

When Rowan got back to his knees, he found the maid smiling with her hands behind her back. "What are you? A [Brawler]?"

The maid giggled. "Hero Rowan, you're hilarious. My base class was [Maid]."

"[Maid]?" Rowan echoed. That threw him for a loop. In all their discussions about class, Kayden had mostly focused on battle professions. And Rowan was pretty sure that [Maid] wasn't a battle class, unless there was some major translation issue going on. "What kind of [Maid] class does that?"

"A [Battle Maid] of the Sutton house," the maid answered. "Ready to continue, Lord Rowan?"

It was a trick question. Before Rowan answered, he was tossed in the air again.

With the maid's help, it only took a week to max out Rowan's physical stats. In that time, he never once touched the hem of her apron. The woman moved like the wind. No matter what Rowan did, she'd find the right angle to dodge, parry, and counter.

During that time, the baron's entire staff found it hilarious that Rowan would flinch away from every maid that passed him in the castle's hallways. Rowan himself was less amused and more proud. For the first two days after the [Battle Maid] was introduced, he had been squaring up at every maid on instinct. Flinching was much better than trying to fight the people doing his laundry.

Perhaps because of all the suffering and trauma, Rowan grew at a speed that shocked even himself. As he sat in Kayden's study, the baron asked him to open his system window. It was glorious.

**Rowan Clairfont**
**Level 0 Unclassed (+)**
**STR: 10**
**VIT: 10**
**DEX: 10**
**PER: 10**
**INT: 10**
**WIS: 10**

No one threw him a party or showered him with gifts when Rowan reached ten on every stat. But the baron had emphasized how much those stats would help him and how much they'd do for his survival. Seeing them for himself, Rowan couldn't help but feel a sense of accomplishment. It felt like he was finally getting the hang of this new world.

And so, it was with glee that Rowan finally focused his intent on that blinking plus mark.

It was time for him to pick a class.

CHAPTER SIX

# Class Considerations

**Class prerequisites met.**
**Classes available for selection:**
**Scribe, Scholar, Orator, Mathematician, Cleaner . . .**

Rowan had expected a lot of things for his class selection. What he hadn't expected was how many supposedly mundane classes he'd be given access to. From what Kayden had said, most people were generally pigeonholed into a couple of classes by the system. It seemed that heroes weren't like that.

"I can check out what a class does without picking it, right?" Rowan asked as he glanced at Kayden. The baron chuckled and nodded.

Rowan clicked on Scribe first.

**[Scribe]**
**Scribes are a crucial part of bureaucracy everywhere, and a**
**skilled scribe is worth their weight in gold.**
**Over the course of your life, you have proven your skill at taking**
**notes, copying text, and facilitating correspondence. Now, you**
**can improve upon these skills further.**
**By picking the [Scribe] class, you become more skilled at quickly**
**and efficiently filling out documents, copying them, or drafting**
**them. Your handwriting will also improve.**
**Attached Card: Nimble Hands (Common, Passive)**

*I mean, this is just the result of the public education system. Who knew it would be good for something?*

Rowan quickly closed out of the window. He had absolutely no intentions of becoming a low- or high-ranking bureaucrat, even if it wouldn't get him killed.

Rowan clicked onto the [Orator] class next. *How do I even have this one, though? I suck at public speeches.*

**[Orator]**
**Orators sway opinions and direct people's efforts using their words alone.**
**An orator's value shines when they're allowed to work with large crowds.**
**Over the course of your life, you have delivered speeches in front**
**of a large audience that evoked strong reactions several times.**
**Now, you can hone your voice further.**
**By picking the [Orator] class, your voice will hold greater sway**
**over all those you address. People will also feel more inclined to**
**listen to you and your opinions.**
**Attached Card: Earnest Speech (Common, Passive)**

*Strong reactions?* Rowan wanted to scoff. He'd been in a few school plays, mostly in a villainous role, and gotten to deliver a few monologues. Wouldn't that qualify him for the [Actor] class instead? He took a second to check. *Oh, yep, [Actor] is in the list. Guess I unlocked [Orator] through presentations, or maybe in addition to [Actor], then.*

There were a few more interesting classes, like [Beast Tamer], but he elected to skip over those and went straight to the one that really mattered.

**[Spearman]**
**Spearmen find their place at the front line of battles, standing**
**their ground so that others may be protected. In numbers,**
**spearmen become an impenetrable wall.**
**Over the course of your life, you have fought valiantly in defense of**
**others with a spear in hand several times. Now, you have the opportu-**
**nity to master the use of this weapon and strike down your foes.**
**By picking the [Spearman] class, you improve the power of your**
**attacks with weapons that resemble a spear. Learning spear**
**techniques also becomes easier.**
**Attached Card: Empowered Thrust (Common, Active)**

A sad little smile sneaked onto Rowan's face before he could help it. Even the system acknowledged that spearmen were best fielded in *large* numbers. Still, it was the best bet he had, and he'd make do with it.

Without further ado, he hit yes.

Small white sparks flashed in front of Rowan's eyes. It wasn't like what he'd experienced during his Heart Card bestowal, or even when he got his blessing. After an unimpressive light show, he had a class.

The most visible part of that change was reflected on his status screen.

**Rowan Clairfont**
**Level 1 Spearman**
**EXP: 0/25**
**Mana: 50/50**
**STR: 10**
**VIT: 10**
**DEX: 10**
**PER: 10**
**INT: 10**
**WIS: 10**
**Deck (2/4):**
**[Heart] Keen Spear (Epic, Passive)**
**[Class] Empowered Thrust (Common, Active)**
**Blessings:**
**Blessing of the Stalwart Hero**

Rowan clicked on the Empowered Thrust card.

It was a plain white card that showed the tip of a spear, wreathed in blue flames. The illustration was nowhere near the complexity of his Keen Spear card, but it still somehow looked better than the other two Common cards that Rowan now had.

**Empowered Thrust (Common, Active)**
**Empower the thrust of your spear using mana, increasing its destructive potential.**

The description of the card left much to be desired. In spite of that, Rowan was excited. This was his first step to getting stronger.

"I see that everything's gone smoothly," Kayden said, serving himself a drink and offering one to Rowan.

"Yep." Rowan forgot his etiquette lessons for a second and slipped back into casual speech. He waved the drink off and practically bounced in his seat. "I'm ready. What's next?"

"Oh? You understand your new class and card? Their power and limitations?" Kayden teased.

"About that—it says that the card uses mana." Rowan pushed the Empowered Thrust window to the baron, a trick he had learned while in the carriage and playing around with system windows. "But it doesn't tell me how much mana. Shouldn't it have a mana cost listed?"

"Heroes," Kayden sighed. The word was equal parts annoyed and amused. "The history books are littered with heroes asking that question. So many of you have preconceptions about the system, in spite of growing up without one. There is no mana cost listed because your cards aren't blunt tools that you can just call upon."

"So how do I use it?"

"For some, it helps to actually say the card's name aloud at first." Kayden paused. "Obviously, that's not something you want to do in battle, especially against opponents who can understand speech. Most transition to mentally calling the card's name. Once you have mastered it sufficiently, however, you will be able to instinctively use it with no casting delay."

"But how does mana play into this?"

"Think of the card as a skill," Kayden said. "Every person has a certain amount of mana within them. Most of the time, it sits dormant. But in times of great need, you can tap into that mana pool and accomplish great feats. The card simply gives you a way to use that mana in a productive way."

"Can I remove the card? Switch it out for something else?" Rowan asked.

"You can." Kayden nodded slowly. "It's not encouraged until you learn the card, and even then, class cards are different from the rest of your deck. They're the centerpiece."

"Right," Rowan said, happy with that answer. But it felt like everything that the baron said just led to more questions. "What does it mean to learn a card?"

"Cards are tools at the end of the day. They guide your mana in a way that you can't do on your own right now. Or, at least, can't easily do right now. But some people can produce the effects of their cards after they've had them for long enough, without having the card in their deck. It takes years of effort to reach that point."

Rowan appreciated that the baron would always answer Rowan's questions, no matter how many or how small.

"And I'm guessing that the more familiar you are with using a card, the better you can do it and the stronger it gets?" Rowan said.

Kayden shrugged. "Yes and no. Empowered Thrust is a Common card. You will always be limited in how much you can do with it. There are one or two exceptions, but the higher the tier of the card, the more nuanced its use gets."

"But I'm still going to train using it until I'm about to pass out?" Rowan guessed.

The same contemplative smile hung on Kayden's face again. "Exactly. Train, train, and then train some more. Before that, I am your sponsor. House Sutton might not be the grand place it once was, but we still have more than enough honor to uphold our end of the bargain."

Kayden gestured at three items laid out on his huge desk, and Rowan leaned closer to take a look.

"May I?" Rowan asked when he found two cards and an odd item that reminded him of a metal cigarette case.

"Of course. They're for you."

The moment Rowan picked up the first card, a system window popped out in front of him.

**Stable Footing (Common, Passive)**
**With this card, it is much harder for foes to disrupt your balance.**
**Traversing difficult terrain also becomes easier.**

"I thought you said you didn't have any cards for a [Spearman]," Rowan said, enamored by what the card promised. Footwork was the bane of his existence. He couldn't count the number of times he'd been tripped, pushed, or otherwise tricked into landing on his glutes over the course of his footwork training.

"It's true. I don't have any [Spearman] cards. Luckily for you, Stable Footing is one of the special cards that can strengthen any combat class. A [Swordsman] or even an [Archer] could use it," Kayden said.

Rowan clicked yes, and the card flashed white before disappearing from his hand, safely added to his deck.

"I can't wait to try this out."

The baron couldn't just let him feel happy. "That card should help you. However, I do have a request. It would be best if you unequipped it while we train. I know you're tired from getting pushed around, but the experience you are getting now will be invaluable for you later."

"Yeah, I know. I won't always have that card," Rowan said, and then noticed Kayden's expression. "Will I?"

Kayden motioned to the next card. "Before I answer that, look at the next card. It's a support card."

**Inspect (Uncommon, Active)**
**The user can expend mana to try to inspect any item or person.**
**The quality and amount of information gleaned differ based on**
**the tier difference. This card can only be used to inspect items or**
**people of Rare or lower tiers.**

"This is amazing!" Rowan exclaimed. He had gone into the boar fight blind. If he had known a bit more about the boars, it would have made a huge difference in his fighting tactics.

"Yes, which is why that particular card and others like it are so valuable. The only reason I have it at all is because it's one of the few I've kept from my family's collection," Kayden said.

"Thank you. I really appreciate it," Rowan said. He meant it.

Rowan bound the card, and this time the flash of light was green instead of white. Impulsively, he tried to use Inspect on the baron.

What was followed was distinctly unpleasant.

For starters, the sensation of using mana was downright strange. Some kind of dormant strength stirred awake within him and flooded out in the form of a wave. Except the wave crashed right into some sort of barrier around the baron and rebounded. If Rowan had been standing, he might have collapsed on the spot. Instead, he just felt a strong vertigo sweep through his body, and he tried not to puke.

"Ha. So much like my son," Kayden laughed. But even in his daze, Rowan could hear the hint of some deeper emotion within the baron. "When I first gave him one of those cards, he tried to inspect me, too. You're lucky you have a tougher stomach than him, lad, or I would have forced you to scrub my study clean."

"Everything hurts." Rowan had his head in his hands, trying to wish the rapidly building headache away.

"In some ways, you're lucky that you used it on me. It's considered extremely rude to inspect someone. If you're thinking it's a perfect tool to use from stealth, don't. The person you use it on *will* feel it, and it's not a pleasant thing at all. Here, feel it," Kayden said as he brought out a cigarette-like case that looked similar to the one on the table.

Before Rowan could protest, the baron's own Inspect landed. It felt like a hand had plunged into Rowan's chest, rooted around in there, and then stolen a piece of him. It made him feel naked.

"Okay, I get it. But why do I feel like this?" Rowan groaned, setting the Inspect card aside for the moment. His headache was definitely not going away.

"Check your mana, lad," Kayden said.

With more than a little effort, Rowan did.

**Rowan Clairfont**
**Level 1 Spearman**
**Mana: 30/50**

"That took twenty mana? But how? I didn't even—"

"You tried to use an Uncommon card when you were at the Common tier. And you tried to use it against someone much stronger than you. And it was your *first* time wielding a card." Kayden's voice wasn't accusatory, but it wasn't kind, either. "Let me repeat myself. You're lucky that's all you're feeling. Now, I prepared this for you. Inspect it." Kayden pushed forward the metal case engraved with a shield emblem.

Rowan looked at Kayden and confirmed that it wasn't a trick. He took a deep breath and used the card again. The metal case's status window made him do a double take, and then he went over it once more for good measure.

**Soul-Bound Cardholder (Unbound)**
**This rare and powerful artifact draws on the knowledge and skills of an enchanter with an extreme understanding of the system to provide its user with the ability to store and manage a limited deck of cards. Normally, a person would need to spend a couple of seconds when changing a card due to a built-in system delay. The cardholder bypasses that. A user can equip and remove cards between the decks and cardholder with no delay at all.**
**The user cannot store cards they are incapable of binding to their deck.**
**Current Capacity: 0/5**

"Holy card god," Rowan whispered. There were a couple of significant things that Rowan had learned over the past few weeks. But the most serious one was how important cards were in his new world. The nobles had almost lynched Rowan because of a bad card. But the cardholder changed the game itself. It meant that a person could effectively double their deck size.

"As I said before, I'm your sponsor," Kayden said. "There aren't a lot of cardholders, but any self-respecting noble house will have enough of those to equip the most important of their members. In fact . . ."

Rowan picked up on the baron's pause. "Yeah?"

"In fact, I suspect that your fellow heroes will have higher-quality cardholders. There are some that can hold up to fifteen cards. Rumors have it that royal family members have cardholders with even higher capacity. But it's not an overwhelming advantage."

"It's not? Sure sounds like it is."

"A cardholder allows you to switch cards from the deck to the holder and back. But you can't switch cards in the middle of combat." Kayden's smile became a little feral. "In fact, it's often been an issue for nobles who like to use support cards outside of combat. If they get ambushed, they're cut off from their more powerful battle cards. That's why it's common practice to have no more than one or two support cards in your deck at a time, depending on your tier."

"Huh, that makes sense," Rowan said.

"All right, enough talking. Up, lad. We're not going to waste the entire day like this."

Kayden didn't literally drag Rowan to the training courtyard, but it was a close thing. There was a silver lining. The moment Rowan gripped a spear, he suddenly felt much better. The cobwebs that had stuck to all his thoughts cleared, and even his headache eased a smidgen.

"So your Heart Card helps with mana fatigue. Good to know," Kayden said.

"Is it? Or are you just going to go rougher on me?" Rowan groused, even if a part of him was glad his card had once again proven useful.

"Of course we'll go harder. I want you to strike that training dummy using only your own strength. Then, do it while using your default class card," Kayden commanded.

Rowan obliged. He squared up against one of the wooden dummies and punched the tip of his spear into the wood. It was a solid strike, with the tip an entire inch into the dummy.

Pulling the spear out, Rowan gave himself a moment to breathe and focus.

"Empowered Thrust!" Rowan screamed.

The differences between using his default class card and Inspect were immediately apparent. Whereas the latter had violently ripped Rowan's mana from him, Empowered Thrust let his mana flow outward.

The mana swirled out from the center of his being, through his arms and into the spear. The spearhead glinted under the sunlight, and this time, it slipped into the dummy like a knife through butter. The tip of the spear was a vicious, six-inch-long spike. The entirety of it had sunk into the wood.

Before Rowan pulled the spear out, he quickly checked his mana.

**Rowan Clairfont**
**Level 1 Spearman**
**Mana: 9/50**

Rowan had no clue how quickly his mana pool refilled. However, even if the card had used more than the single point of mana, it was more than worth it. He pulled the spear out and grinned like a loon before attacking again and again, the tip of his spear blazing. The feeling was intoxicating. Weeks of training, more effort than he'd ever put into *anything*, finally seemed worth it. He kept using **Empowered Thrust**, feeding every bit of mana into it.

And then he was on his face, someone was shaking him awake, and his head hurt far more than before.

"Wuhwezzat?" Rowan mumbled, spitting when he got a mouth full of sand and gravel.

"I said, lad, that I *really* wish you were less like my son. What is with young idiots doing the *exact* thing they shouldn't every time?" Kayden's words were soft, and Rowan had to strain to hear them.

"Wuh's happening to me?"

"I assume you're wondering what's wrong? Your mana pool is what's wrong," Kayden said. It sounded like he was an entire world away. "When you use too much mana too quickly, it hurts. When you reduce yourself to less than a tenth of your total, you'll feel sluggish and exhausted. When someone manages to bottom out to zero? They get to eat dirt. I should have left you out here on your own."

"Am fine," Rowan said.

"Of course you are. A good sunburn and a full body ache from sleeping on the ground would have been a good lesson. You're lucky I'm a gracious host. And that my wife would have killed me." That last part was said in a quiet grumble.

"How long was I like this?" Rowan's tongue was numb and not cooperating, and he had to speak at a snail's pace to make sure his words came out fine.

"Long enough. When you're feeling better, go back to your rooms. You'll be useless for the rest of the day," Kayden said as he turned away. "But you did good today, lad."

Rowan felt a surge of emotions. It would have been too much effort to express it all. Instead, he managed to roll onto his back, watching the clouds drift by.

*I'm a part of this world now. A real part.*

Rowan wasn't sure if he was referring to the powers he had gained from the cards or the way the baron had been treating him the past few days. It was all tangled up in one big ball of emotions that sat on his chest.

When he managed to drag himself upright, Rowan stumbled his way to the nearest wall and narrowly avoided face-planting into it or the ground. From there, progress back to his room was slow and plodding. He was going to flop into his bed and forget about everything else. If nothing else, his headache demanded it.

"Pssst! Over here!" A voice sounded to his right.

"What?" Rowan wasn't amused. He looked around blearily and jolted awake when he saw the baron's daughter sticking her head around the corner.

"Over here!" Olivia hissed at Rowan. It occurred to him that she thought she was being stealthy. "Come on."

She motioned for him to follow and then disappeared. She was back a few moments later to glare at him when she realized he hadn't, in fact, followed.

"You've got to be kidding me," Rowan muttered, watching the girl beckon with ever-increasing urgency.

Finally, Rowan sighed, shrugged, and decided to give it a shot. *Might as well see what my sponsor's daughter wants . . .*

# CHAPTER SEVEN

# Party Prospects

Rowan would have been a lot more impressed if Olivia Sutton did a better impression of sneaking around. She had somehow led the two of them into three maids in the short walk from his room to wherever her destination was.

*I'm the one who's on the verge of collapse, so how am I the one who's making sense?*

Finally, the girl turned down a smaller hallway, found a slightly crooked door, and dashed inside. She poked her head out a moment later when Rowan didn't follow.

"Okay, fine. I'm coming," Rowan muttered as he hobbled after her.

Once he was inside, Olivia shut the door and bolted it. Rowan would have been more alarmed if he wasn't so damn tired. He doubted that the baron's daughter would really hurt him, but as he surveyed the room, he wasn't so sure anymore.

The room was a toxic explosion waiting to happen. One large table sat in the middle of the room, and on it were half-full, entirely exposed jars with colorful liquid still in them. That would have been fine if not for the fact that there were also random clumps of powder next to these jars and whenever fumes from the jars touched the powder, they'd make tiny sparks of light. And to add one final wonderful touch to the room, a haze hung over the floor, the combination of different fumes all spooling down.

Despite all that, Olivia seemed right at home.

"So, what do you think?" Olivia asked. "And how come you're so bad at being sneaky?" Before Rowan could respond, she went down a different line of questioning. "Wait, you look off. What's wrong with you?"

"I just finished—" Rowan had just begun his answer when Olivia jumped to his left and stared intently into his face. The sudden movement threw him off guard.

"Mana exhaustion? Weird. You're *sure* you're a hero? Well, fine." Olivia turned to rummage through the mess on the closest table.

"Pretty sure I'm a hero," Rowan grumbled.

Moments later, the girl gave a small whoop and pushed a vial of green liquid in Rowan's face. "Here, drink this!"

"Uh, what exactly is this?" Rowan asked. "My parents taught me to not take candy from strangers. I'm pretty sure suspicious potions fall under that same category."

"Are you saying that you don't trust my potions?" Olivia demanded. She pushed her lips out in mock hurt.

"I trust your father," Rowan said slowly. "But we haven't talked yet, and today, you dragged me into a strange room and handed me a strange potion. How do I know it's safe?"

"It only happened one time!" Olivia exclaimed.

"What? What one time? Are we even having the same conversation?"

"I promise, it won't happen again. The potion reacted violently when it was shaken. But no one even got hurt because it happened before they tried to drink it. I don't get why we can't get over that."

"One of your potions *exploded*?" Rowan's voice went squeaky.

"Oh, you didn't know . . . Then you have nothing to worry about! It was a long time ago. And it was a small explosion. Now, do you want this or not? I promise it'll fix you right up." Olivia swirled the potion vial, and whatever was in it responded by glowing softly. Rowan thought about taking cover before thinking that he'd probably be safest next to the mad alchemist.

After a very long hesitation, Rowan took the potion and downed it.

Thankfully, nothing exploded. And the potion both tasted and felt better than the healing potion. A sort of cool feeling sank throughout Rowan's body, numbing the pain that had taken root there. In a matter of seconds, he felt almost as good as he had before using the **Inspect** card.

"Wow. You weren't kidding," Rowan said. "It actually worked."

"See? I knew you'd get it. My potions might not be *registered*—" Olivia spat the word out like an insult. "But I guarantee their effectiveness! It's been forever since one of their effects got away from me. At least a month, if not more!"

"A month?" If Rowan had known this piece of information, he might have made different life choices.

"I know! I'm impressed, too!" Olivia exclaimed.

Rowan took a moment to look at the girl. *Really* look at her. She was more animated and excited than he'd ever seen her.

"So, you're a scientist? Potion brewer?" Rowan asked. "I have no clue what the right class name would be."

"I'm nowhere close to those two-bit potion makers. I'm an [Experimental Alchemist]!" Olivia said.

"At least normal potions don't explode," Rowan muttered.

"It's an Uncommon class!" Olivia half shouted. "I'm level 23."

Rowan blinked. At least on the surface, that sounded impressive. "And I'm level 1. You got me beat."

The girl almost seemed taken aback by Rowan's admission. She pulled back.

Trying to make conversation, Rowan tried a different beat. "I'm surprised that you took a support class. I thought that most nobles were supposed to take combat classes."

"The world doesn't revolve around combat classes, you know? I bet you that I could take you on in a fight."

"You could," Rowan said. "I'm level 1, remember?"

"Right, sorry," Olivia said. Rowan's words took the wind out of her ire. "I promise that my class matches up to the combat classes out there. It's like I have a mage class, except in the form of potions. I'll be able to do things that they can't even imagine. I just need time and an opportunity . . ."

Here, Olivia looked at Rowan meaningfully. The only trouble was, he had no idea what she was trying to imply.

"What kind of opportunity?"

Olivia glanced back at the table, where one of the jars was beginning to shake while being heated.

"As a hero, you need other people around you to help," Olivia said. "No one hero is an island. I wanted to ask—"

Before she could finish her thought, the liquid in the jar started whistling loudly. She snapped to the heat source, one that somehow resembled a portable stove with its controls, and turned the heat down.

"If it's not a good time, we can do this later," Rowan said as he took a step back. This really didn't seem like the right place to talk about anything.

And then the world turned into pure chaos.

The room didn't exactly explode, but it was close enough for all intents and purposes. The first thing that happened was the door disappearing. One moment, it was a heavy maple barrier that blocked access to the rest of the castle. The next moment, it was gone.

"Olivia!" Kayden bellowed. "I heard that. What did I tell you about your secret experiments! I can't rebuild half our home every time you set it on fire! Would it kill you to do your experiments with someone else looking on?"

Then the baron noticed Rowan, which brought a second round of questions before the first could be answered.

"What are you doing here? What are you doing with my daughter?"

Rowan had always known that Kayden was stronger than he looked. Now, he realized just how strong. Every instinct within Rowan was shouting for him to curl up in a ball and hide from the baron's wrath.

"I was just about to leave." Rowan paused, trying to figure out how to explain what had just happened. "Your daughter noticed that I was suffering from mana exhaustion and she offered me a potion to help with that. That was all."

Kayden tried to control his emotions, failed, and then whirled on Olivia. "You asked to join his party, didn't you? How many times do I have to tell you that the frontier is nowhere for an alchemist to be? I don't care what you say, it's a no."

Olivia froze, her eyes going wide as she tried to figure out an answer.

"Wait, hold on," Rowan said. "Join my party? What are you talking about?"

Kayden turned toward Rowan in slow motion. Like he needed every second to figure out what to do next.

"She—my daughter, Olivia—what exactly did she say to you?" the baron asked.

"We talked about potions and her class," Rowan said. "What's all this about a party? I don't have a party. Do you want to join my party?"

"No!"

"Yes!"

Kayden and Olivia both yelled at once and the father-daughter duo turned to glare at each other with near-identical expressions. Rowan *almost* found it funny. Almost. Unfortunately, it was now apparent that he'd found himself in the middle of a family spat.

"Olivia, you're an alchemist. You aren't meant to traipse around the wilderness or fight your way through dungeons! You are supposed to stay at home and do all your experiments. It's why I've turned a blind eye to all this," Kayden said, the momentum of his initial fury fading slightly.

Olivia pounced on that weakness. "And you know that I need to adventure. I'm already slowing down on my leveling. And even if I somehow get enough experience to get to 40 before I die of old age, how am I supposed to get a Rare class with just crafting experience?"

"We'll cross that bridge when we get there. Crafters hire people to help them level all the time. There's nothing shameful about it," Kayden said.

"I'm not going to be some pampered lordling crafter!" Olivia shouted, successfully reviving the previously waning argument.

"Stop that shouting immediately!" Kayden yelled back. "You should know better by now!"

Things quickly devolved from there. Rowan was more than a little scared when Olivia decided to grab a potion and chuck it at the baron. Kayden swatted the potion away with a mini fireball. All of a sudden, the knowledge that Olivia had previously made exploding potions was at the front of Rowan's mind.

And despite all that, the two of them never once stopped their argument.

Rowan slipped his way to the now-missing door and was about to escape when he found his path of exit blocked by an equally imposing member of the Sutton household.

"What is going on here?" Although Olivia and Kayden were still engaged in a full-force shouting match, Lady Sutton's whisper somehow cut through both of their arguments.

Both nobles stopped in their tracks and looked at Camilla. She looked like a force of nature. Her hair was floating and tiny bolts of electricity were zipping from different strands. Rowan took a step back and tried to find the most inconspicuous corner to fade into.

The father and his daughter broke into a flurry of excuses but they were fighting a lost cause.

"No. Enough," Lady Sutton said. "The two of you are behaving like children. You"—she pointed at her daughter—"go to your room. And you"—she pointed at her husband—"explain to me what happened, though I have a decent clue already."

Olivia slipped by her mother without argument, disappearing beyond the door while Rowan found himself suddenly envious of her.

"Hero Rowan is here as well," Kayden said.

Lady Sutton turned her gaze. "Knowing my husband and daughter, I doubt any of this was your fault, Hero Rowan. I apologize for anything that they may have done." She stepped out of the way and Rowan quickly found his way back to his room.

The moment Rowan saw his bed, the day's events suddenly caught up to him. Whatever Olivia's potion had done for his mana exhaustion, apparently it came with a side effect. Rowan was asleep before his head even hit his pillow.

For the next few days, the house was a battleground. Neither the baron nor his daughter were willing to back down, and they carried out their arguments in secret, away from Lady Sutton's wrath.

Rowan's training didn't really suffer from the ongoing drama. Not exactly. Rowan himself was the one who suffered. Kayden became even more of a taskmaster, pushing him ever onward. Rowan was forced to work through his drills, use up all his mana, and then exercise again when his eyes could barely stay open.

On the bright side, the ordeal provided Rowan with a very comprehensive look into how his mana regeneration worked. Each point in wisdom represented three points of mana regeneration over the course of an hour. So, at ten wisdom, he stood at a respectable regeneration of thirty mana per hour, or one mana point every two minutes. That wasn't too bad. Rowan didn't have to sleep or rest to regenerate his mana.

On the other hand, the regeneration was also a curse. Each point in intelligence meant three extra points in Rowan's total mana pool. At a fifty mana capacity, he would regenerate his entire pool in less than two hours. Which also meant that the mana and card training cycle would start back up every two hours.

Eventually, the temporary war between father and daughter came to an end. Lady Sutton summoned the two of them, along with Rowan, to the baron's study.

"This childish spat of yours needs to end," Lady Sutton said.

"Camilla, I think you know my position," Kayden said. The baron looked around the room and found that his other chairs had been removed from the study. The only two left were occupied by either Lady Sutton or Rowan. "Could we do this sitting down?"

"No," Camilla said. She gestured at Rowan, who was in the process of giving up his seat. "Stay. They deserve to stay standing for how immature they've been. Did you two really think that I wouldn't hear your arguments?"

It was Olivia's turn to try to convince her mother. "I'm not the problem here. Father's clearly—"

"You are. You've burned down more sets of equipment than I can be bothered to count, you're impulsive, and you don't care about your own safety as long as you get to satisfy your curiosity. If you're like this at home, I can't imagine what you'd do if you went off to adventure," Camilla said.

"See? Olivia should stay home," Kayden added. "Here, we can protect you and—"

"Don't think you're blameless in this, either." This time, the pale-green eyes of Lady Sutton pinned down her husband. "How long are you planning to baby her, Kayden? We both know the reason she's like this is because you refuse to let her learn her lesson. How many times are you planning to replace everything she destroys?"

When both Olivia and Kayden seemed sufficiently shamed, Camilla turned her attention to Rowan. "I'm sorry to bring you into our family drama, Rowan. But the two of them have been so caught up in their own arguments that they forgot to ask your opinion. I'd like to ask you this: Do you want my daughter in your party?"

Rowan had a new appreciation for the phrase *caught between a rock and a hard place*. With all three pairs of eyes stuck on him, he wanted nothing more than to just disappear. He could see that Kayden's eyes were glinting dangerously and Olivia's fingers were twitching toward her belt, where a string of different vials hung. *So either being trained to death or getting pelted with exploding potions. Lovely choices.*

Taking a deep breath, Rowan did the only responsible thing he could think of. "Olivia. Question. Why should I accept you as a member of my party?"

While Lady Sutton looked amused and Kayden appeared stuck between offended and hopeful, Olivia was more than ready to take things in stride.

"Easy," Olivia said. "You simply can't find a better or more dedicated alchemist in the entire kingdom. I might not make the best potions or the most potions, but I can make potions, tonics, and salves for all types of different situations."

"But why would I want that?"

Olivia paused, as if she'd never considered such a question before. A second later, her expression cleared up as a system window popped up in front of Rowan. "Take a look at this."

**Pursuit of Brilliance**
**Grade: Epic**
**Description: The effectiveness of every unique alchemical item
you produce will be doubled, and the effectiveness of items
crafted from your original recipes is boosted by fifty percent.**

"I'm an [Experimental Alchemist]," Olivia said while Rowan read the description on the card. "The class pairs perfectly with my Heart Card. It allows me to craft anywhere and improves the odds of discovering new recipes."

"Wait, hold on. Olivia, what recipes do you know?" Kayden asked before Rowan could think of his next question.

"Several different healing potions, one type of mana potion, and an assortment of different potions," Olivia said proudly.

"Could you walk us through what the other potions are?" Kayden asked with the same contemplative smile that Rowan had learned to dread.

Olivia realized the trap she had walked into. Her eyes darted between her father and Rowan before she hung her head in defeat. "I might have created certain explosive compounds that can be used in combat."

"And these explosive compounds, how did you find them?" Kayden asked.

"Father!" Olivia yelled before glancing at her mother and toning down her voice a notch. "My class is great for discovering new recipes. But it assigns a permanent percentage chance for all my potions to mutate. Most of the time, it's a positive mutation, like higher potency or longer lasting. But sometimes the mutations destabilize the potion, and then . . ." She motioned with her hands to indicate a boom.

"So it means that you have a solid chance of blowing up everyone around you, even when making a well-established potion and following the most stable formula," Kayden said.

"And what about your Stable Creations card?" Camilla asked.

Olivia's face froze before she broke into a giant grin. "Right, exploding potions aren't a problem anymore unless I want to make them. The Stable Creations card stops the mutations. The only downside is that I never get to make anything new, and that's what gives me the most experience."

"Would you prefer to have nonexploding potions, Rowan?" Camilla asked.

Rowan nodded his head furiously. He couldn't imagine what he'd do if he was drinking a potion one day and then it exploded in his face.

"Then that settles it," Camilla said. "You'll be getting the experience from the monsters anyways."

Throughout the whole exchange, Rowan kept an eye on Kayden, noting that the baron's expression went from angry to proud to quiet resignation.

"Olivia, is this really what you want?" Kayden asked.

"Yes." The admission was quiet but firm.

"Very well," Kayden said and took a deep breath. Rowan saw that the baron was remarkably well composed. "I suppose, Rowan, this isn't such a bad thing. Olivia will cover your healing needs. She might not be a dedicated healing class, but you wouldn't have been able to get one of those anyways."

"Wait, why?" Rowan asked.

"All priests and healers of the divine inclination serve the goddess of light, Sarina," Kayden said. "I don't need to tell you that they won't welcome you among them, let alone serve as your party members."

"She has a hand in all [Healer] classes? Sarina?" Rowan asked as he looked at the other two in the room for confirmation.

"Not all," Kayden said. "But [Healer] classes without affiliation to Sarina are extremely rare, almost unheard-of in humans, regardless of which kingdom you're in."

"Healing-adjacent classes are common among elves," Camilla said. "You won't find many unless you travel all the way north."

"So my potions are more effective than normal. I have some elven blood in me," Olivia said proudly before realizing the look her father and mother were giving her.

Rowan, on the other hand, ignored all the social cues and bulldozed ahead. "Quick question, do elves have green hair?"

"Not all elves have green hair. They have more hair colors than can be counted. I inherited my ancestors' hair color," Olivia answered.

Rowan glanced at both Kayden and Camilla.

"There was elven blood in my ancestors," Camilla answered Rowan's unspoken question. "It happened a long time ago, when the relationship between races was better."

"Okay," Rowan said, ready to get out of the tangent he had brought on. "It sounds like an alchemist is my best option. Is everyone okay with it?"

Olivia furiously nodded her head. Camilla poked her husband, who grumbled but also gave his blessing to the new party member.

"All right, then, Olivia, welcome to the party," Rowan said. As his voice fell, he realized that there was some new piece of world trivia he had missed. He almost jumped when a new system window appeared before his eyes.

**Olivia Sutton is suggesting the following contract:**
**Rowan Clairfont and Olivia Sutton will enter a party together. As part of a party, Olivia Sutton will become your ally. This doesn't stop Olivia from dealing damage to you, accidental or intentional, but for skills or blessings that work better with allies, Olivia will count as one.**
**Accept?**

"Do you see the system contract?" Olivia asked.

Rowan nodded. "Yes, but what's a system contract?"

"Huh? You didn't sign one before?" Olivia sounded genuinely surprised, but she didn't wait for Rowan's answer before launching into her explanation. "It's when you ask the system itself to enforce the terms you agreed on. The consequences of breaking a system contract are quite severe."

Rowan hit yes.

**A contract between Rowan Clairfont and Olivia Sutton**
**has been established.**
**The contract can be modified or dissolved if all parties involved agree to the changes.**

It was surprisingly easy to form a party, Rowan found, and quite useful, too. As soon as he'd sent them an invite using the system and Olivia accepted, an odd feeling bloomed in his chest. If Rowan was forced to look for Olivia in a pinch, he had a vague feeling what direction he should head in.

**You have formed a party!**
**Current party members:**
**Rowan Clairfont (Leader)**
**Olivia Sutton**

All of a sudden, Rowan was assaulted by Olivia in the best and worst way possible. She tackled him with a hug, and before he could react, the two of them toppled over the poor chair Rowan had been sitting in. For a moment, all Rowan could think of was how Olivia smelled like all kinds of different alchemical ingredients. It wasn't a bad smell.

"You won't regret it," Olivia whispered in a voice so soft that even Rowan could barely hear her. "I'm gunning for the [Combat Alchemist] class when I upgrade to Rare."

Rowan had no clue what to make of that. But there was one thing for sure: As Rowan disentangled himself from the mess, he glanced up to see Kayden staring at him. There was no smile or grin on the man's face. Instead, Rowan could see the baron's anger rising.

"Rowan, I just realized that we're late for your training session," Kayden said. Rowan was almost entirely sure that the training session had been made up on the spot. "I think we should get going."

*Is it too late to change my mind and apologize?* As the baron's hand slammed down on his shoulder, Rowan came to the conclusion that it was.

"Take Olivia, dear. She's now a part of the party. Some combat training would be good," Camilla said.

It was a good thing that Olivia had come with Rowan.

As soon as Rowan stepped foot on the training field, Kayden tossed him a spear.

"Let's do some live sparring today," Kayden said with his signature smile. Right before Rowan's eyes, the baron transformed himself into a wrathful god. He exuded a pressure that made it hard to breathe. And the pressure only intensified when Kayden pulled out a wooden sword. "We've been a bit too lax on the training recently. I think it's time we—"

A purple sphere flew at the baron and he sidestepped out of the way while also countering with his sword. As the sword met the offending object, the sphere exploded in a deep-violet cloud.

"Olivia, this is sparring, not a playground for you to test explosive, poisonous, or acidic concoctions," Kayden warned.

"We're a party now. Me and Rowan," Olivia retorted. "If you wanted to do live sparring, then we should fight together as a party. That's the only way we learn."

For the first time since Rowan had met Kayden, the baron didn't have a response. Instead, he grunted and charged toward Rowan.

*Set, thrust, shuffle.*

Rowan could almost picture his movements in his mind as Kayden drew closer. He pushed his spear forward right between the gap of a stride during Kayden's charge and shuffled to a new position when the baron had to slow down his momentum.

Olivia followed that up with a flurry of different offensive potions. Rowan watched as different glass vials and flasks flew through the air and burst into different colors when Kayden parried each of them. Quite frankly, if his new world had anything at all like a Geneva Convention, Rowan was absolutely sure that he wouldn't want to be anywhere near Olivia.

"I'm out," Olivia suddenly said. The vials stopped flying.

"What?" Rowan asked.

"I don't have any more potions. Watch out!"

The last part of Olivia's warning was in response to the baron's sudden charge. He closed the gap between him and Rowan in the matter of a few steps, and before Rowan could respond, a sword swing knocked the spear out of his hands.

As Kayden pulled his sword back to take his victory, Rowan's salvation came in the form of the trusty Sutton butler.

"Lord Sutton, I beg your pardon. Lady Sutton has news. It's about the frontier," Garrett called out. Kayden might have still finished the swing if not for the urgency in the butler's voice.

"Show me," Kayden grunted as he threw his sword to the weapons rack. "You two, follow along."

Rowan followed as the baron passed through the castle, arriving at a room he'd never seen before. The space itself was large, filled with dozens of different tables with maps strewn across them. People were bustling through, looking harried as they carried messages from Lady Sutton, who stood in the middle and gave out commands.

"What's going on?" Kayden called out.

"It seems like the demons are unusually active today," Camilla said, pausing in her commands. "Now that you're here, dear, it's time for you to take control."

Rowan fell back to the side of the room and whispered to Olivia, "What does this mean?"

"It means that the frontier forces failed to do their job," Olivia responded. She pointed at a map near them showing the southern part of the kingdom. The demon territory was marked in black, stretching like an inkblot across a large swath of land and bordered by a variety of kingdoms, big and small. "There's probably been a breach. They usually send messengers ahead of the horde to warn us. But there's only a few days before the demons hit our towns."

"What's our plan?" Rowan wasn't going to turn tail and run. Kayden, for all his flaws, was a good man. Rowan was going to stay and help in any way he could.

"Dad's going to meet the main demon force," Olivia said. "But the problem with a breach is that the demons scatter. There'll be small groups of them, and they might attack any of the villages or towns."

"So what do we do?" Rowan asked.

Olivia responded with action. She pointed at one of the villages at the eastern end of the baron's lands. "Dad, Rowan and I are going to protect Felton's Mill."

"Absolutely not, you and—" Kayden stopped what he was doing and trained his gaze on Olivia.

"Dear, Olivia already made her decision to adventure," Camilla said. She gently laid a hand on the side of Kayden's arm. "Felton's Mill is far from the frontier. Whatever trouble gets there is going to be fairly minor. It's a good first adventure."

Rowan was sure that "good first adventure" was a euphemism for *safe and out of danger*.

"Sure fine," Kayden said. "You two, take twenty soldiers with you."

The baron turned back to the people in the room and started shouting commands. It was inspiring. The man would listen to a problem, digest it for a second, and then send out a command that seemed to be the perfect solution. Rowan watched as different people came into the room with panic written over their faces and left the room with a look of confidence. It was remarkable.

He could have watched the baron work for hours, but Olivia pulled him out of the room.

"I'll pick the soldiers," Olivia said. "Go get dressed in riding clothes and light boiled leathers. Meet me at the front gate."

As he went to get dressed, Rowan found that a part of him was genuinely excited.

The hero was marching to war.

# CHAPTER EIGHT

# Combative Advancements

R owan didn't expect the war to come to him first.

On the way to Felton's Mill, one of the soldiers spotted a couple of loose beasts. And so Rowan decided to kill two birds with one stone. He'd get a feel for his new strength and stop the animals from rampaging through the countryside.

But when he watched almost twenty corrupted beasts sprint toward him, the plan suddenly seemed a lot more rickety. It wasn't just a couple of beasts. There were a couple of foxes, a sickly-looking deer, a menacing wolf, and a group of approximately ten boars. It was like the world's worst zoo, with animals that seemed to come out of nightmares.

And then one of the boars suddenly sped up, overtaking the rest of the corrupted animals.

"Shit, shit," Rowan cursed. *It's probably the **Reckless Rush** card.*

As the corrupted boar came into range, Rowan sidestepped the charge. He wouldn't call the motion smooth, but it was much better than clumsy. For the most part, he kept his footing and had a fairly large margin of safety.

The boar sailed past Rowan, tusks flying but not latching onto anything. It squealed in anger when it realized that it had missed its target.

"Nope, you don't get to be angry," Rowan said as he stabbed his spear into the boar's flank. He silently activated his **Empowered Thrust** card and felt the mana flow through him. It swirled around his chest before rushing into the tip of the spear.

The boar was still in the middle of its turn when the spear reached its target. The glowing tip sank deep into the monster's muscle before Rowan pulled it back out. He must have hit something vital, because the boar suddenly lost its momentum. By the time Rowan was ready to place his second strike, the corrupted animal was on the ground. Before it could get back up, Rowan took aim and finished his enemy.

Behind him, a small explosion went off. A quick glance confirmed that Olivia was in her element, chucking vial after vial of explosive liquids at the larger cluster of animals. For once, Rowan was thankful for his foresight in staying far enough away from his mad alchemist ally.

"Olivia, let a couple through," Rowan called as he squared up to greet the next attacker.

Two of the foxes emerged from the giant dust cloud and sprinted right for Rowan.

The foxes were slower than the boars, but they came with their own challenges. As they got closer, one of the foxes veered to the side, splitting Rowan's attention in two different directions. Luckily, Kayden had trained Rowan on how to fight multiple enemies.

Rowan took a quick step forward and lunged. His spear shot out so quick that it was just a blur. It slammed into one of the foxes, instantly taking it out of the equation. Rowan pulled the spear back and twisted in place to face the second fox.

As his foot squelched in the wet mud, Rowan's stance was almost ruined by the sudden loss of balance. But that's where his new deck came into play. **Stable Footing** guided his foot through the uneven mud to a more solid spot and saved him from a nasty tumble.

Even as he adjusted his stance, however, Rowan landed a precise strike directly on the second fox's head. He stared at how easy things were.

Less than two weeks ago, he had nearly been killed by a corrupted boar. Now, he felt like he could mow down as many of these monsters as he wanted. In a strict sense, he was still limited by his mana, especially since **Empowered Thrust** usually took one to two points of mana each time. But those were mere details.

"Rowan? Ready for the rest of them?" Olivia asked as she chucked a few more vials at the horde of monsters, pushing them back once again.

"I'm ready," Rowan yelled back. She almost didn't need to ask him. When Rowan had formed a party with the baron's daughter, he'd begun to get a faint sense of where she was and the rough strokes of what she was thinking. The sensation had sharpened when they'd initiated the battle, too. Right before she'd spoken up, he had felt a rush of intent from her, like a premature warning.

"On my mark," Olivia yelled. "Now!"

Olivia slung a new vial at the monsters. Before it slammed against the ground, she began running back, putting as much distance between her and the battlefield as possible. The vial released a low purple haze, which the monsters charged through without a single worry.

For a second, Rowan was worried that their plan had backfired. The corrupted animals seemed immune to the purple gas. And then one of the boars stumbled and found itself rolling head over stomach. Soon, almost all the monsters were missing their steps.

*PETA would have a field day with me in court.*

Rowan stepped forward, and in the span of a dozen **Empowered Thrusts**, the animals all met their ends. The most stressful part of the whole thing was when the wind shifted and he was forced to retreat in a hurry lest he inhale some of Olivia's concoction himself.

"Why didn't we do that earlier?" Rowan asked.

"Because you needed a test. That's what Father made you fight on your way to our keep, right?" Olivia asked as she pointed at the original boar that Rowan had defeated.

"Yeah, fighting it is a breeze now," Rowan answered.

"Good." Olivia hopped back on her horse. Next to her, the soldiers hadn't even bothered to dismount. "It'd be a bad thing if you couldn't take them on. These are all Common monsters, not even demons."

As Rowan found his own seat, the system apparently decided that the fight was over and began distributing the loot.

**Battle Results:**
**EXP:**
**[Corrupted Boar] +5 x 12**
**[Corrupted Deer] +10**
**[Corrupted Fox] +12 x 4**
**[Corrupted Wolf] +16**
**Loot:**
**18x cards in Party Loot Inventory**

"You know, I almost didn't believe Father when he said that you needed to be rescued from fighting corrupted boars," Olivia said. Her tone wasn't mean, but she was definitely poking fun at his expense.

"You try being shoved into a new world, given weird new powers that you barely understand, and then being told to fight stuff that looks like it came right out of a nightmare," Rowan countered. "Actually, if the boars are so weak, then why did they wreak so much havoc? I almost beat one without a class." The image of dead farmers floated into Rowan's mind.

Olivia twisted in her saddle to look at Rowan. "You mean why do most people run away from them?"

"Yeah."

"The system," Olivia answered. "The difference between having just a single useful fighting card and a deck of random cards is huge. Monsters and demons naturally get cards that are suited for them. Most of us don't get that advantage. But no matter how powerful the system is, it can't teach you how to fight or give you the courage to stand your ground. Anyways, you handled the last group of monsters better than I thought you would. Let's try just explosive potions next time."

"Don't you want to use the explosive potions less?" Rowan asked. Potions exploding next to him did not sound like a good time.

"More, actually—the explosive potions are literally the cheapest potions I can make. They're not even real potions, if you want to get technical about it," Olivia said as she somehow found the focus to flip her hair. "Part of [Experimental Alchemist]'s class card is the ability to take a bunch of different materials and stabilize them before sealing them in a vial. If I pick ones that react badly to each other and undo the effect, it produces a nice boom. It's cheap, it's easy, and you can *always* find conflicting materials."

"So, let me get this straight," Rowan said. His voice went dead as he realized the implications of what Olivia had just said. "You're saying that you're always walking around with a bunch of bombs that could potentially go off?"

"In a way," Olivia said before changing the topic. "Did you level up? You probably did with all the experience that you earned."

Rowan glared at her for a few moments longer before refocusing his attention to the system screen.

**Congratulations, you have leveled up!**

**Rowan Clairfont**
**Level 4 Spearman**
**EXP: 15/100**
**Mana: 30/50**
**STR: 10**
**VIT: 10**
**DEX: 10**
**PER: 10**
**INT: 10**
**WIS: 10**
**Available stats: 6**

**Deck (4/4):**
**[Heart] Keen Spear (Epic, Passive)**
**[Class] Empowered Thrust (Common, Active)**
**Stable Footing (Common, Passive)**
**Inspect (Uncommon, Active)**
**Blessings:**
**Blessing of the Stalwart Hero**

"Holy crap. I just jumped three levels," Rowan said. He repeated the phrase again in disbelief.

"Yeah, that's expected." Olivia's words snapped him out of his daze, and he gave her a confused look. "Come on, most of those monsters were level 3 or 4, so obviously they'd give you full experience. That means each boar should give you at least three to four points of experience after my split."

"Four?" Rowan asked.

"Yeah, did I get that wrong?"

"Uh, no," Rowan said. For some reason, he wanted to keep the specifics of his blessing to himself. It had changed once before when Kayden showed that he was an Aristaeus follower. "Did you get experience, too?" Rowan asked.

"Kind of. The system splits the experience of enemies defeated evenly between party members," Olivia responded.

"So, this is a normal leveling pace?" Rowan asked.

"More or less. Things get tricky from Uncommon and onward. But your class actually becomes useful then, so it balances out. I actually got no experience out of that. Those were Common enemies, so they don't count for my progression anymore. It's to discourage people from gaming the system by fighting enemies too strong or too weak," Olivia said. "You should also see that we have eighteen cards to claim. Don't mess with those yet—we don't have anywhere to keep them if we claim them right now."

"All right, not touching the cards," Rowan said even though his hand itched to accept the cards. With his cardholder, he could store the Inspect card away and maybe equip another attack card.

"Also, pick out where you want those stats to go if you haven't already, and be smart about it. Don't hoard them," Olivia said as she urged her horse forward.

*What do I know about my class so far?* Rowan thought, thinking back on his training and the two battles he'd been in. *I need to be able to dodge, and I need to strike quickly and hard.*

When put like that, his initial investments seemed obvious. He focused on the unassigned points and invested them in the corresponding stats.

**Rowan Clairfont**
**Level 4 Spearman**
STR: 12
VIT: 10
DEX: 14
PER: 10
INT: 10
WIS: 10

A jolt tore through Rowan's body, and the horse almost bucked him off in his moment of weakness. Once the sensation passed, power coursed through him.

His fingers tightened on the saddle more powerfully, and balancing himself suddenly became easier.

"A rush, isn't it?" Olivia teased, giving Rowan a considering look. "Enjoy it, because leveling up really slows down after a while."

Rowan did enjoy it. Assigning the stats also filled him with a buzzing energy that he was dying to burn off. When they came across another group of corrupted animals, he was downright eager to face them.

What Rowan didn't realize was how much the extra stats changed things. As he charged at a group of foxes and squirrels, his legs seemed to have rockets strapped to them. The difference that four points in dexterity made was absolutely massive.

The best part was that Rowan felt completely in control of the extra speed. Where he'd still been a bit slow when dodging away from the monsters before, he now felt like he could dance right through them. And for the first few, he did. One of the foxes lunged for his thigh, and he twisted to the side while driving the end of his spear into its flank in a single motion. Then, in an instinctive movement, he ducked when a squirrel launched itself at his head like a mini missile.

Of course, that's when the rest of the animals ganged up on him, and he was reduced to a half-panicked mess of wide blows and desperate dodges. It was incredibly difficult to fight the critters when they were practically on top of him, and he was clubbing the animals more than he was stabbing at them.

But the stat gulf was something that the monsters couldn't just overcome. The extra dexterity did wonders for his reaction speed. A couple of minutes later, Rowan emerged from the fight harried but victorious.

"That's why you don't fight close range when you have a spear," Olivia called out. "You need a potion, mighty hero?"

"Hey, I won, didn't I?" Rowan yelled back. Despite his tough words, his face was bright red. He deserved the ribbing for the rookie mistake of charging in like that.

"Should have let me help you. Heroes have parties for a reason," Olivia said. "Ideally, we'd have another two party members to shore up our weaknesses, but I can do a lot of crowd control and terrain management, like I did with my poison-cloud potion."

"The purple potion?" Rowan grumbled. "Doesn't that color just scream poison?"

"It does. And that's intentional. Because, spear hero, if I just started chucking poison onto the field, I'd do more harm than good. Do you want to be on a battlefield when the next breath you inhale could be full of poison gas? The purple makes it easier to track, and frontliners know exactly what areas to stay away from."

Rowan had no witty response to that. Instead, he preoccupied himself with the system screen.

**Battle Results:**
**EXP:**
**[Corrupted Fox] +10 x 3**
**[Corrupted Squirrel] +5 x 4**
**Loot:**
**25x cards in Party Loot Inventory**

Felton's Mill wasn't exactly far off. But as they got farther from the baron's castle, their pace kept getting slowed down.

By the fifth group of corrupted beasts, the soldiers started joining in on the fights. Individually, Rowan could see that they were slightly stronger than him. But together in a group, they became a slaughter wall. No corrupted beast, boar or wolf, could get past the flurry of spears.

After the eighth attack, the officer attached to the group called everyone together.

"What's wrong?" Rowan asked.

"There are too many beasts," Olivia explained, her face grave. "This isn't normal. We're in a relatively protected part of the barony. There shouldn't be this many beasts."

"Could we have just been unlucky?" Rowan asked.

"Luck is something that farmers count on," the officer said. "We assume the worst. Always."

"I agree," Olivia said. "Either the demon horde is much larger than we expected or the battle's been shifted."

"Neither case bodes well for Felton's Mill," the officer concluded. "We'll do double speed and ignore the monsters on the way. I'll feel a lot better once we see what's going on at the village."

Olivia nodded her agreement, and Rowan, seeing no better option, did so, too.

Over the next couple of hours, the group avoided different groups of corrupted beasts. The frequency of these encounters rose as daylight soon started shedding away. After a few close calls, the group finally saw the village.

Rowan had heard both Olivia and the others refer to Felton's Mill as a village. In his mind, that equated to a cluster of straw houses that opened onto the surrounding fields, with perhaps a mill at the center. What he saw was a sturdy-looking wooden palisade, large enough to be a small castle. And thanks to the lanterns hung on the walls, Rowan could see that the officer's words had come true.

The village was under siege. Hundreds of people were guarding the walls and using pretty much every medieval tactic that Rowan could think of. The more professional-looking militiamen used bows and spears, while the villagers threw rocks and poured boiling water down onto the beasts.

It wasn't looking good.

The monsters seemed to be of a different breed than the ones Rowan had previously faced. Arrows bounced off the creatures' hides more often than they pierced, and the stones and water were at best slowing them down. As the animals jostled against the walls, Rowan could occasionally hear screams. Human ones.

"Off your horses, men," the officer ordered, and his soldiers obeyed instantly. "Flat formation!"

Rowan followed the first half of his order, copying the soldiers and hurriedly tying his horse to a nearby tree that looked sturdy enough. When it came to falling into formation, however, he was woefully unprepared. The two neat rows of soldiers offered no spot to squeeze himself in.

"Not you, Hero Rowan," the officer said. "Let us clear the way for you first."

"Are you sure about this?" Rowan said. The twenty soldiers that had tagged along were almost nothing compared to the horde of monsters.

"Of course," the officer said with a smile. "Formation, ready."

The men began to unsheathe their weapons. The first row wielded spears identical to Rowan's own, while the second row took out lightly curved short swords along with heavy shields. The officer himself gripped a large double-headed axe in one hand and a shield in the other.

"Time to earn our mead," the officer roared. "Formation, **Fearless Charge!**"

As one, the soldiers broke into a run, gaining momentum far faster than should have been possible. When they met the beasts, Rowan realized that he had severely underestimated his traveling companions.

*They shouldn't be called spearmen. They're harbingers of death.*

The wall of soldiers crashed into the beasts with glowing weapons, easily mowing down the opposition. Where a single spear might have faltered, the momentum of the soldiers together was enough to push hundreds of corrupted beasts back.

Rowan watched the soldiers literally step on the bodies of their enemies to continue their charge. It was both gruesome and a raw display of power.

The rush finally faltered when the soldiers crashed into the main body of the horde, but by then it was too late. The officer shouted something unintelligible from their position, and the spears retreated to let the second row of soldiers forward. In moments, the corrupted beasts at the front of the horde met a whirlwind of steel from the curved swords.

As soon as the village defenders became aware of the reinforcements, a cheer rose from the wall, and their efforts redoubled. Arrows flew unsparingly into the thickest pockets of the horde.

A black miasma that somehow stood out against the night sky flowed down from the wall, rapidly spreading over the horde and making the beasts visibly falter. To follow up that display, a figure launched itself off the wall and down into the press of animal bodies, killing more than a few on impact. Rowan couldn't make out much, but he could tell that the fighter was wielding a truly ridiculously large shield. It looked bigger than the person themselves, and they used it proficiently to literally pulp the surrounding corrupted beasts.

What had once looked like an insurmountable obstacle was being rapidly demolished right in front of Rowan's eyes.

"Impressive, aren't they?" Olivia's voice was solemn. "My father was only allowed to bring a tiny portion of his men to the barony. Most of his standing troops were ordered to stay behind and serve the new duke. They had to. The king would have seen their insistence to follow my father as rebellion."

Rowan wasn't sure what to say to that, opting to instead watch silently as the soldiers tore through the horde. In a matter of minutes, the battle was done. The corrupted monsters lost their will when the worst injuries they could inflict on the soldiers were mere surface wounds. It didn't take long before they fled.

"Looks like it's our turn." Olivia grinned as she went to untie her horse.

"Our turn?" Rowan asked as he copied her motion.

"Remember what I said about the system? It's only a part of a person's strength. The same thing applies to a group of people. If they know that their lord's daughter is among them, it'll do wonders for their morale. And a hero? It'll be like a buff that doubles their stats," Olivia said. "And looking at how big that horde was, we'll need every bit of help we can get."

Rowan moved toward Felton's Mill. It was time to see if he could play a convincing hero.

# CHAPTER NINE

# Bracing for Impact

Rowan sometimes wondered what it would be like to have people cheering him on, especially since a near-death experience had interrupted his initial arrival in the new world. He got his answer as he walked into the village, the massive wooden gates pulled open by the militia who had been manning the walls.

He didn't like it.

And there wasn't anything that he could do. The villagers all showed relieved expressions, and a couple even gave shouts of joy. But he couldn't help but feel that this relief was misplaced. The soldiers had been the people who cleared the monsters. In fact, Rowan had slowed down the arrival of reinforcements by fighting the stranded clumps of corrupted beasts for easy experience. It was false glory.

*I should have done more, somehow.*

The feeling only grew as he got his first good look at the villagers. They weren't destitute or malnourished, but they were clearly common working folk. Even the militia wore armor that didn't conform to their bodies properly, making them look like people playing at being soldiers rather than competent combatants.

These were people worried about the next harvest and the local gossip, not a group ready for combat.

"Welcome, welcome to our humble home." The man who spoke wasn't old, but he was definitely middle-aged. Time hadn't managed to grind down his mobility, however. He strode through the crowd easily. "I'm the chief of this fine village, name's Desimir."

The officer in charge of the arrivals met the chief halfway, accepting a firm handshake. "I'm Sir Bron, sent by Baron Sutton to reinforce Felton's Mill. This is Hero Rowan, and the baron's own daughter, Olivia Sutton, a member of his hero party."

The officer—Bron, now that Rowan finally knew his name—motioned dramatically in their direction. There was a moment of tense silence where Rowan watched the gathered crowd and they stared back at him, but then they broke into even louder cheers.

He heard snippets of what they were saying, and they all seemed certain that with his arrival, they were safe.

That only made an odd feeling curl through his chest, putting him on edge.

Even the village chief looked suitably impressed, rushing in their direction and grabbing Rowan's hand before he could even think to protest. "Thank you for coming here. We can't thank you enough for protecting a small village like ours. You, too, Lady Sutton. We all know how much the baron cares about these lands, but having you here is a true relief."

Olivia looked almost as uncomfortable as Rowan felt, but she still managed to carry herself with poise. "Of course, Chief Desimir. We're happy to have the chance to assist you, right, Rowan?"

"Of course." Rowan rushed to chip in, forcing his smile to look more genuine. "We'll do our best to keep everyone safe."

"Having a hero to protect us is a true inspiration," Desimir said, and Rowan couldn't tell whether the chief was being sarcastic or genuine. "We don't have—"

"Desimir," Rowan cut in. "I hope you forgive me for diving straight into things. Is there somewhere we can speak in private?"

"Yes, I'm sorry. I got carried away there," Desimir said. "Please, follow me."

The chief took a second to bid everyone return to their homes before leading them to the far end of the village toward one of the larger houses.

Rowan took that chance to look around. The village wasn't as old as he'd assumed, or it had been rebuilt recently. Some of the houses had a fresh look about them, and even the more weathered buildings hadn't started to show true signs of age.

The buildings themselves were also more numerous than he'd expected. Just by the number of homes alone, there were probably several hundred families living in the village.

As soon as they were in private, Bron was all business again, even before their host could introduce them to the woman and child that were already in the house.

"How long has that beast horde been troubling you? Did they hit just before we arrived, or have they been an ongoing issue?" Bron asked.

The chief blinked, then motioned toward seats arrayed around a massive table right in the living room. "They arrived a couple of hours before you, but one of our [Hunters] spotted them and warned us a couple of days ago. They took their time ripping through the forest. I'm afraid it'll be a tough winter without meat to supplement things."

There was clearly some worry on the chief's face at what the future held. But Bron was worried about something more immediate.

"You can take whatever can be salvaged from the carcasses outside," Bron said. "But I don't think food's going to be one of your problems. Not this winter."

"This isn't just a simple roaming horde?" Desimir's voice trembled, but he was keeping it together remarkably well.

"I'm afraid not, Chief Desimir," Olivia said, delivering the bad news. "There was a breach on the frontier, and now we need to handle the cleanup."

"Shit," Desimir cursed softly.

Bron sighed, running a hand through his short brown hair. "With a horde that big, there has to be a demon nearby commanding the group. I might be wrong—I hope I'm wrong—but we have to prepare for the worst. I hate to ask this, but what are your numbers here? How many will be able to help us fight?"

The chief hesitated, his eyes fixed on the desk for long moments before he spoke again. "Three hundred eighteen, last we counted. Out of that number, however, only around fifty are combat or combat-adjacent classes. Another ten or fifteen could manage fighting, but they don't have classes that help. The rest can help man the walls, but I wouldn't rely on them for much more than that."

"You people won't have to venture outside the walls. That's our job," Bron said as he rapped his knuckles against a table. "I also noticed some pretty powerful magic assisting us and a formidable shield bearer. Are they from here, too?"

The village chief shook his head, a wistful smile on his face. "I wish that they were, but they're just passing through. Mercenaries. We sent out a quest when we thought the beasts were just an isolated group that got past the frontier."

"I'll talk to them," Bron said. "The baron pays well, especially in emergencies. And it's safer here than trying to adventure through the plains right now. What about defense? What do you have?"

Olivia chose that moment to insert herself into the conversation, pulling out a couple of potion vials from her seemingly bottomless pack. "I have something that might help. These potions can be used to harden wood, making it as strong as steel."

Rowan watched with amusement as Olivia began a one-woman potion show. She had evidently held something back in what she told the baron. Her repertoire went far beyond a couple of healing and explosive potions.

"Miss Sutton, if I could ask, how many potions do you have?" Bron said.

"I brought my entire backlog," Olivia said. "About a hundred potions, maybe a couple fewer because I spent a lot on the fights earlier."

"But that won't be enough for an entire wall," Bron said, bringing the baron's daughter up short.

"I can make more. As long as I have the ingredients, I can pump out as many potions as we need," Olivia said.

"But we're out of the baron's keep," Bron said. "The only places we can find worthwhile herbs or materials are deep into the surrounding forest. But with a potential demon around, we can't have you going out alone. I could send some of my men with you, but their effort is better spent here, especially when we don't know if the materials you need can even be found locally."

"What about explosive potions?" Rowan offered. "Those are cheaper and probably easier."

"I can do that," Olivia said, grateful for the lifeline. "Those are cheap—all I need is some help finding the right ingredients, but they should already be in the village."

"Sounds good. Olivia, your potions *will* be helpful. We just need to figure out where to use them," Bron said. "We can use what you brought to reinforce the gates. They're the most vulnerable point in our defenses at the moment. Chief Desimir, could you coordinate with Olivia later about the explosive potions? But before that, we'll need to repair any damage to the wall and maybe dig a shallow moat to make things harder for the demons."

"I can get people working on that immediately, Sir Bron," the chief said. "I doubt many will be eager to rest immediately after the scare we just had."

After a brief hesitation, Bron shook his head. "Not tonight. It's too risky to do it in the dark. We'll start tomorrow morning. I'll oversee the digging, and my men will accompany any lumberjacks you send out in case more beasts show up while they work. For now, I'd just ask everyone to get some rest."

"Of course," Desimir said. His face sagged slightly as he came to the next topic. "We're a pretty small village. I don't know if there's going to be enough housing for the soldiers. I'm sorry. I know we should—"

Bron raised a hand to stop the village chief. "Do you think you could find two rooms?"

"Definitely. I can give you the two spare rooms we have in our home." Desimir gestured to the back of his home, where a wooden stairway led to a second floor.

"Not me. They'll be for Miss Sutton and Hero Rowan. They've both had a long day, fighting to clear our path here. I'll join my men, and we can set up tents in the village square. If that's no bother to you."

"No trouble at all. I'll have it cleared of the tables and benches immediately."

Bron nodded in approval, and the two men stood. The chief paused only to fetch a girl that Rowan assumed was his daughter, judging by their respective ages, and directed her to assist Rowan and Olivia before he left for the village square.

The room itself was pretty cozy, and Rowan relaxed for the first time in the day. He would have liked nothing more than a few moments to himself to unpack both his belongings and his feelings.

It wasn't meant to be. Olivia barged into his room mere moments later.

*Did she even unpack?*

"Ready to see what we actually got out of all that fighting?" Olivia grinned, all worries temporarily forgotten as she collapsed on the bed. It creaked ominously under her, making her flinch, and Rowan worried about his back in the coming days.

"What are you talking about?" Rowan sighed, collapsing in a small chair in the corner of the room.

"You're seriously telling me you forgot already? All the cards we looted?" Olivia stared at Rowan until a red flush appeared on his face.

**Party Loot Inventory: 72x cards**

*That's a lot. And we just fought, what, five groups of beasts? That's more cards than beasts. Maybe it's the blessing?*

The extra hunting had also done wonders for Rowan's levels. His leveling had slowed, but he'd still gained enough experience for two new levels and four extra stat points. He quickly assigned two points to strength and dexterity each.

"Seventy-two cards," Olivia said. "Common, of course, but we can't really complain about that. Who knows, we might even get something relatively useful? Ready when you are, party leader." Olivia seemed happy with what they'd achieved. That was a good sign.

Rowan hit the "yes" button, and an array of card screens unfurled in front of him, almost blinding him for a second. Olivia jerked a little, too, so he could only assume she was going through the exact same thing.

It was an absolute mess, and Rowan strongly suspected that you really weren't supposed to go so many battles without checking your loot.

**Reckless Rush (Common, Active) x 15**
**Rush toward your enemy, increasing your movement speed and**
**dealing increased impact damage.**

**Coarse Fur (Common, Passive) x 12**
**Your fur becomes tougher and bristly, more easily**
**turning blows.**

**Goring Tusk (Common, Passive) x 7**
**Your tusks deal increased damage to enemies, and the inflicted**
**wounds heal slower.**

*I now have everything I need to role-play as a boar.*

"Why does the system give us these fur and tusk cards? Does it expect us to grow tusks and use them?" Rowan asked.

"Gods, no," Olivia laughed. "We'll scrap them. The system allows a person to scrap their unused cards into fragments that can then be fused back together for another card. Each scrapped card leaves behind one fragment, and it takes four fragments to create a new card."

"What about the **Reckless Rush** cards? Scrap as well?" Rowan said. "I can't see it being very useful for my build, but maybe some of the other people could use it."

"I'm not sure if they'd want it, either," Olivia said. "**Reckless Rush** is one of the most common cards for frontier villages—everyone here probably already had a chance to get a copy. What we can do here is something better. Since we have more than ten **Reckless Rush** cards, we can merge them together and raise the card to Uncommon, where it becomes **Relentless Advance**."

"Huh, neat," Rowan said absentmindedly. He had already gone to the cards that came from the foxes, and those were a whole lot more interesting.

**Vicious Bite (Common, Active) x 13**
**Inflict a devastating bite on your foes, drawing more**
**blood than expected.**


**Light Step (Common, Passive) x 4**
**Your every step is muffled and harder to discern.**


**Nimble Body (Common, Passive) x 2**
**You can contort your body in unexpected ways, both to evade**
**blows and pass through spaces you normally couldn't.**

*We can actually use some Nimble Body and Light Step. Well, I guess we can use Vicious Bite, too, but I'm not sure if I want to be biting some monster.*

With how many cards they got, Rowan began to wonder if it was possible to farm cards like this. If it took ten Common cards to get an Uncommon card, he could have a full deck of Uncommon cards in no time at all. Acquiring cards was far easier than he had imagined, which brought up the question of why the baron seemed to think that nobles had a stranglehold on cards.

Rowan pushed those thoughts out of his mind. It was hard not to. The cards they got from the squirrels downright amused him.

**Skilled Climber (Common, Passive) x 5**
**You can scale any tree and balance on every branch with**
**increased ease.**


**Savage Claws (Common, Active) x 2**
**Rend and tear with your claws until the job is done.**

**Friendship Is Power (Common, Passive) x 3**
**All your stats are boosted by one point for every member of your**
**race with this card within five yards of you.**

It was easy to see the pattern now: Almost all the corrupted beasts had some combination of three different Common cards, two of which were passive, while the last one was active.

With three counterexamples, it was easy to see that the sets from the wolves and deer were actually not complete. In either case, they didn't seem too much like cards that Rowan wanted to use.

**Innocent Gaze (Common, Active) x 3**
**Your appearance is your weapon, and you wield it to mitigate**
**people's aggression and fighting spirit.**

**Hasty Retreat (Common, Passive) x 2**
**You can temporarily increase your speed and agility**
**when fleeing enemies.**

**Eerie Stare (Common, Passive) x 3**
**Unnerve your foes and crush their spirits with your stare.**

The wolf card, in particular, surprised Rowan, since he was pretty sure they'd handled a decent number of wolves. "Hey, Olivia?"

"Hmm?"

"Is it possible for an enemy not to drop a card when they die?"

"No. Are your numbers not adding up? What's wrong?"

"The wolves—I can only find one card that looks like it came from them. **Eerie Stare.**"

"Oh, that." Olivia chuckled. "You know, sometimes, animals have the same cards. Wolves have **Coarse Fur** and **Vicious Bite** to round out their deck."

Rowan blinked, not having expected that. However, there was one final card that was bothering him, all the way down at the bottom of their loot list, and for some reason, even just looking at it filled him with dread.

"What do you know about this one?" Rowan focused and sent her a status window.

**[Heart] Demonic Encroachment (Common)**
**You have accumulated enough demonic mana in your body that**
**you've been permanently altered by it, granting you new and**

**unusual abilities. Accumulate more of it to grow further. This Heart Card supersedes whatever Heart Card you used to own and takes its place.**

Only one **Demonic Encroachment** card had dropped, and Rowan knew it was bad news when he saw the look that crossed Olivia's face. It was somewhere between utter fear and complete disgust.

"Rowan, listen to me carefully," Olivia said, her voice void of any excitement. "Do you see the dice at the bottom of that screen?" She was referring to a tiny icon at the bottom of the screen standing above the words *Roll for Card?*

"Yeah I do," Rowan said.

"I want you to pass on rolling for this card, okay?" Olivia said. "Just press the dice and then hit the decline-roll button."

Rowan did as she instructed, then watched as she immediately materialized the card and let it drop to the floor. She pulled out a handkerchief and picked it up gingerly, careful not to let her skin touch it, before bundling the card up.

"I'll be right back. Wait for me here," Olivia mumbled and was out of the room before he could even ask about what was going on.

The entire thing had shaken him, and not just because of her reaction. When she'd finally summoned that card out of whatever space the system was keeping it in, his senses had screamed danger. There was something instinctively repulsive about the card.

To calm himself, Rowan materialized the other cards and organized them in neat little piles to distract himself.

"So that's taken care of," Olivia muttered, not even bothering to walk all the way to the bed. She flopped down on the floor with her back against the wall. "Please don't scare me like that again. It's not good for me."

"What was that thing? I mean, beyond the obvious, of course," Rowan said.

"A corrupted Heart Card. They're extremely rare. As in, they're not really supposed to be a viable drop at all." Olivia paused as she let out a breath. "Corrupted Heart Cards are among the most dangerous cards out there. If you're careless with one, you'll be reduced to a [Corrupted] class."

"What does it mean to be a [Corrupted] class?" Rowan asked.

"You go insane," Olivia stated. "Corruption drives a person insane, but it also makes them stronger, faster, and even increases their regeneration. There are people who seek out corrupted Heart Cards on purpose, thinking that they can perform rituals to use the cards safely."

"Sounds like it could be useful," Rowan said, thinking of the danger that he had seen so far. "I mean, I'm not going to use it. But I get why people would want it. This is a dangerous world, and if they have a choice between life and death, they'd probably choose life."

Olivia hesitated, obviously uncomfortable. "You're not . . ."

"Of course not. Why would I want to go insane when I already have an Epic Heart Card?" Rowan said.

"Good," Olivia said as she exhaled. Both of them briefly fell silent before Olivia forced cheer back into her voice. "Hey, how about we check out those cards properly and try our luck with some merges and fusions, yeah?"

Rowan gave her a wan smile, but complied. It didn't take them a lot of time at all to separate the cards into "keep" and "scrap" piles. Cards like **Nimble Body** and **Light Step** could be useful, so it would be a waste to throw them away for a chance at something better.

The moment Rowan picked up ten **Reckless Rushes**, a new system window popped up in front of him.

**10 x Reckless Rush (Common, Active) detected.**
**Would you like to merge all ten cards into Relentless Advance**
**(Uncommon, Active)?**
**Note: This process cannot be reversed.**

Rowan pushed the "yes" button and felt a surge of energy as the cards merged, and a warm glow spread through his veins. A stream of white light emerged from the stack of cards, weaving together until a spark of green began to pulse at its center. The color grew, taking over the white light and illuminating everything in a light shade of green.

**Relentless Advance (Uncommon, Active)**
**Rush toward your enemy, building up movement speed and**
**damage as you go. Your impact damage grows in proportion to**
**the ground covered during your advance.**

"Huh, that's pretty neat," Rowan said.

"It is. Do you have space in your deck? It'd be good to equip this, just in case you need it at some point," Olivia said.

Rowan did. He removed the **Inspect** card, placing it in his cardholder, and equipped **Relentless Advance**.

"All right, so should I upgrade the other cards?" Rowan asked. It didn't seem like an Uncommon **Coarse Fur** would be very useful, but he was open to have his mind changed.

"No, those go straight into the scrap pile. You don't need Uncommon fragments right now," Olivia said. "Just pick one of them up with the intent to destroy it. The system will do the rest."

**Coarse Fur (Common, Passive)**
**Your fur becomes tougher and bristly, more easily turning blows.**
**Scrap the card?**

The effects of scrapping a card were equally impressive. Two lines of white-colored light ripped through the card he was holding, neatly separating it into four different pieces. A moment later, the light intensified, and three of the fragments evaporated. A final corner was left to drift slowly to the floor, now completely featureless.

"I never get tired of seeing that." Olivia muttered with a grin, grabbing a card of her own and scrapping it, too. "Let's get through them quickly, and then the fun can begin."

The two of them reduced everything into fragments, saving just the **Eerie Stares**, **Friendship Is Power**, **Nimble Bodies**, and **Light Steps**. In the end, they were left with an even forty card fragments.

"Want to go first? You've never done it before." Olivia offered Rowan four scrap pieces. Somehow, she looked like a seasoned gambler in that moment.

**Four Common scrap pieces detected. Would you like to fuse**
**them into a Common rank card?**

Rowan took a deep breath, then gave the system his answer. The four featureless card pieces slipped out of his fingers, briefly turning incorporeal. He watched, awe coloring his face, as they slotted perfectly together, that same white light flaring up again. Except, this time, the light melted the edges of the scrap pieces together until a new card was revealed in a flash of light.

**Enhanced Harvest (Common, Passive)**
**The yield of your fields will always be slightly better**
**than the work put into them and the weather conditions**
**should allow.**

Rowan's eye twitched. Olivia started shaking, covered her mouth, and then lost it as she broke into raucous laughter.

"It's not funny," Rowan growled, refusing to acknowledge the flush that was threatening to spread to the entirety of his body.

"How? How do you immediately get a [Farmer] card? What's your luck?" Olivia was barely getting her words out through her laughter.

"You try then, if you think you'll be luckier!" Rowan scoffed, pushing the pile of scraps toward her.

It took her a few more moments to get her laughter back under control, but Olivia complied. When the whole show was over again, they could do nothing but stare.

### Skillful Juggling (Common, Passive)
### Your juggling will be the talk of the town, so why not challenge yourself with something beyond balls and pins?

"Is it because you're a clown?" Rowan tried to duck, but the baron's daughter still managed to nail him right in the forehead when she chucked the card at him. "Oh, come on, don't be mad! I'm sure you'll get something useful next!"

"I swear, I've never seen a fuse this bad," Olivia said as she picked the juggling card back up and scrapped it. "No one's going to want this card anyways."

Rowan resolved to have Olivia fuse the rest of the fragments herself. That way, he could avoid the ribbing and instead laugh at Olivia's expense.

Unfortunately, that's when they were rudely interrupted. "Excuse me, Miss Sutton, Lord Rowan. Lieutenant Bron is looking for you."

CHAPTER TEN

# Woodland Friends

Fifteen minutes later, Rowan and Olivia were getting instructions from Bron.

"Good, you're here. We're a little short on manpower." Bron got right down to business as soon as he saw them. "We're going to shore up the defenses at the village as much as we can over the next few days. That means wood. We're sending some lumberjacks to the eastern forest. My men will protect them, but someone needs to scout around for threats. I don't want them caught out when the attack comes."

"You need us to scout? What should we be looking for?" Rowan asked.

"It should be obvious when it comes. More than obvious. If an attack comes, it'll be slow and heavy. As long as you keep moving, it shouldn't catch up to you." Bron paused. "There'll probably be some loose packs of corrupted beasts roaming around. I'm sorry to put the two of you in danger—I wouldn't be asking if this wasn't absolutely crucial."

Rowan nodded. "No, I'm happy to help."

"Just the woods? What about the plains to the north?" Olivia asked.

"Just the woods, and only daylight scouting while we're working on the defenses," Bron responded. His gaze focused on something beyond Rowan as he rushed off. "Chief, we need to talk about your men."

Finding himself dismissed, Rowan traded glances with Olivia.

"Bron couldn't have just told that soldier to relay that to us?" Olivia quietly grumbled.

"He probably wanted to do it himself," Rowan said. "Just in case anything got lost along the way."

"What's there to lose? It's just, 'go scout in the woods to the east.' Anyone can deliver that message," Olivia said.

"I'm sure Sir Bron had his reason," Rowan said, walking back to his room. "What should we do about the fragments?"

"Store them somewhere safe," Olivia said. "I'm too tired to deal with them tonight."

Rowan agreed. "Good night, then."

"Good night."

Rowan realized that he was not a fan of the woods.

In his mind, they were these wonderful pockets of tranquility, unspoiled nature away from all the concrete jungles he'd grown up in. And on Earth, that might have been true.

In this new world? They were a sort of hell.

Bron had said that there would be small groups of corrupted beasts. What he hadn't mentioned was the fact that the beasts were ambush predators. Until now, Rowan had been fighting the monsters on flat plains where he knew exactly when and where they were coming from.

So when a corrupted fox sprang at his face, Rowan's manliness vanished. He shrieked two octaves higher than what his voice should have been able to do and used every single point of his stats to twist and skewer the thing with his spear. It was easy fighting these corrupted beasts now, even if they were a jump scare.

"What would people think if I told them that their hero was screaming like a little girl at a corrupted fox?" Olivia laughed. "You should have seen yourself. I don't think even I can scream that high."

Rowan toughed out the ribbing.

"Do you think we'll see more beasts like this?" Rowan asked as he pointed his spear at the fox.

"Maybe. It's possible that some of them are circling back in hopes of a good meal. The blood from the fight at the village is bound to attract stragglers," Olivia said. "If that means I get to see more of a hero screaming, I'm not complaining."

Rowan paused and checked his cardholder.

**Rowan's Soul-Bound Cardholder (4/5):**
**Inspect (Uncommon, Active)**
**Nimble Body (Common, Passive)**
**Eerie Stare (Common, Passive)**
**Light Step (Common, Passive)**
**Note: The cardholder can't be used in combat.**

In theory, a cardholder was the same as carrying a stack of cards in a pocket. Olivia had explained that the difference was the speed at which a swap could happen. Without a cardholder, someone would need to stop, unequip a card, fetch the card, find the right card, and equip it. The cardholder made that instantaneous. And the fact that cards in a cardholder couldn't be lost or stolen was an extra bonus.

Rowan removed the **Stable Footing** card from his deck and replaced it with a **Nimble Body** card. Since the fighting was going to be in such close quarters, it was probably a good idea to focus more on flexibility than solid footwork.

Soon, Olivia's wishes were granted. They came across a small group of corrupted beasts, and Rowan fell upon them in an attempt to wash away his dishonor.

**Nimble Body** was exactly the right choice for the confines of a forest. Typically, a spear would have been rather limiting, especially since the deeper they went, the more clustered together the trees got. But with the card, he could perform moves that would have previously left him writhing on the ground with a bad back.

The beasts were soon dispatched, and the duo began to sweep through the forest.

The only close call Rowan had was when Olivia ran in front of him to chase down a couple of squirrels and in his haste to back her up, he let two foxes ambush him. In a moment of card-enhanced genius, he pivoted on the spot, stabbed one of the ambushers, and contorted into a low crouch. The second fox sailed over his head in its attack, and he swept the spear upward against the beast.

Rowan knew the baron would have disapproved of how reckless and "pointlessly flashy" the sequence of attacks was. But the moves were good. His spear threw the fox off balance for long enough for him to use **Empowered Thrust** and dispatch the second attacker with ease.

As Rowan took a deep breath to calm himself, he was beginning to appreciate the power of **Keen Spear**. But when he saw Olivia trudging back, even **Keen Spear** wasn't enough to keep his anger in check.

"Squirrels got away?" Rowan asked.

"The flighty little bastards," Olivia cursed. "I hate them. I'm going to have a feast one day and the only meat allowed on the table is roasted squirrel."

"I mean, did you really have to chase those squirrels? That put both of us in danger," Rowan hissed.

"Hey, I wasn't the one who asked for this assignment," Olivia retorted.

Rowan took a deep breath, pushing down his emotions. "Are you okay? Hurt anywhere?"

"No."

"Then what's wrong?" Rowan asked.

"It's just, I can't exactly fight here properly, can I?" Olivia said.

It made sense. The alchemist had always hung back and chucked various explosive potions at their foes. The potions were powerful, but with trees all around, she'd be lucky if they didn't bounce back.

"You have the sword right there?" Rowan asked.

Olivia scowled at the sword in her hand. She had always kept a short sword at her waist and drew it as soon as they entered the forest. He supposed that should have been his first clue that not everything was going to plan.

"Yes, and I *am* trained to use it. Neither my class nor my Heart Card lock me out of holding a weapon, but they do stop me from using combat cards. So the only card I have that's somewhat fighting oriented also drains my mana like crazy," Olivia said as she sent a screen of the card in question.

### Honed Mana Edge (Rare, Active)
**Coat the edge of a blade with a dense layer of mana that makes it possible to cut through most Common, Uncommon, and Rare materials.**

It was the very first Rare-ranked card Rowan had laid eyes on, and its power was apparent from its description alone.

"The card, it's impressive," Rowan said. **Empowered Thrust** was great, but it wasn't an unstoppable attack.

"There's only one problem—it's me." The admission seemed to cost Olivia her pride as she bunched up her shoulders. "My first class was [Alchemist] and I'm now an [Experimental Alchemist]. The last time I put points into strength, dexterity, or even vitality was when I was level 5. Sure, I can use a sword just fine, but I don't have the stats to back it up. It's meant to be a last-resort kind of thing, not my main method of combat."

"What about the other potions?" Rowan asked. "Maybe you could use that poison cloud?"

"Well, I can't very well waste all my *expensive* potions on some random animals."

Olivia was getting agitated again, but Rowan's temper was flaring right along with hers. He hadn't forced her to come with him. She'd signed up for it, combat and all.

"So what do we do? Stick together, keep scouting, and if we start hitting danger, you use the big potions?"

"Are you saying that I'm useless, is that it?" Olivia demanded.

"No, I'm . . ." Rowan fell silent. There was something else going on here, and he was just the punching bag for Olivia's emotions. Once again, **Keen Spear** came into play, keeping Rowan from escalating the argument.

"I just, I wanted to get away from my family. To fight for myself. To contribute." Olivia's voice was almost a whisper, and it hitched for a moment as the fight went out of her. "All Father wants is for me to become a glorified healing-potion dispenser. But what I want is to become a [Combat Alchemist] when I hit level 40.

I want to adventure. It's just, the fighting parts of my path don't appear until I get a Rare class."

Rowan was about to apologize when a series of grunts sounded to his right. He turned to see a handful of corrupted boars and foxes in the distance, huffing as they began their charge. Before Rowan could do anything, Olivia ran forward. The blade of her sword suddenly erupted in a blue glow, and Rowan could hear it humming with power every time she swung it. It went straight through whatever happened to be in its path, whether it was wood, skin, or bone.

The boars were no match for an enraged Olivia. She took out all her anger on them and didn't even blink when they tried to rush her. In some very overtaxed swings, she sliced through them.

Rowan's contribution to the fight was minimal, merely acting as her backup so she wouldn't get ambushed and taken down by a cheap shot.

*That's weird, there's not a single squirrel among them. Did Olivia scare them off earlier?*

By the time the last corrupted animal fell, Rowan realized he had a bigger problem. Olivia began stumbling and then almost face-planted to the ground. He caught her.

"Whoa, hey, Olivia. Easy there. Are you hurt?"

"Uuuurgh, mana. Out of. Need potion," Olivia muttered.

Rowan managed to awkwardly reach around her and grab the pouch. That's when the real problem presented itself. All the vials looked different and they all looked dangerous. The last thing he wanted was to feed Olivia an exploding or poison potion.

"Um, what does that look like, exactly?"

"Blue. Glows. Silver specks," Olivia said softly.

Her pouch was also a maze. There were the outside pockets, each of which contained at least two to three vials. Rowan went through all of them and found potions of every color minus blue. Moving on to the center storage, he threw the main flap back and froze.

The pouch was so much bigger on the inside.

It was like he was looking at a suitcase. One of those extra-large ones that was borderline legal. Compartment after compartment was filled with what he assumed were materials, several odd-looking tools, and so many potions. Thankfully, the blue ones were in a section all their own, so it didn't take him long to locate one.

"Good," Olivia said, the effusive expression of gratitude for Rowan's hard work. She snatched the vial and threw it back like one would a shot of alcohol.

The effect was immediately apparent. Color crept back into her skin, and her expression, previously scrunched up in pain, eased. She gave a happy little sigh and finally opened her eyes. It was only then that she seemed to realize that she was still in his arms, and her face erupted in crimson.

"Oh. I'm so sorry." Olivia sprang away, almost tripping in her haste to put distance between them.

"Don't worry about it." Rowan liked to think his voice was steady as a rock, but he really didn't trust himself when his face was also heating up.

Olivia looked at Rowan, then at the slain monsters, then back at Rowan. A smile crept onto her face, which then burst into a round of giggles. The laughter was infectious, and Rowan found himself grinning as well.

"I guess that's the end of Olivia the swordsman," Olivia said. "I'll figure out a formula for some kind of cheap, mass-production poison and we'll never talk about this again?"

"What's with you and trying to make destructive potions?" Rowan said as he got back up and headed along their scout path. "Aren't alchemists supposed to be making all kinds of support potions?"

"Sure. I can do those, too. But those are far more dangerous than a simple poison potion," Olivia said. "What do you think those potions draw on? They produce the bursts of strength, endurance, speed, or whatever by draining your body. But in the moment, you feel invincible, which makes them addictive. If you drink one too many, you'll outright die due to exhaustion or malnutrition, depending on the potion. It's the same reason you can't just keep chugging healing potions to become an unstoppable juggernaut. Your body would literally eat itself alive."

"So, no enhancement potions?" Rowan said.

"*Some* enhancement potions. *Occasionally.* I never said I don't have them. I'm just saying we don't need them for everyday stuff," Olivia said. "If the beast waves get worse or a dem—Never mind. I'll bring them out when we need them."

"Sounds good." Rowan nodded.

The rest of their day shaped up to be more productive. Neither lingered on their spat and instead spent their extra attention picking useful plants, herbs, and fungi.

"How did you even find that?" Rowan asked when Olivia once again beat him to a plant, one that had been tucked underneath a large stone.

"You can do it, too. **Inspect.** It's useful for more than artifact and enemy appraisal. The key to using cards is understanding where their limitations are. A master can use a Common card to beat someone with a Rare card."

"Wait, hold on." Rowan rubbed his temple. "We came out here to scout and you're using one of your deck slots for **Inspect?**"

"It's useful. I might not have a physical enhancement card in its place or whatever, but I can spot all these plants, and I can tell you that not a single beast we've come across so far today was over level 4."

Rowan frowned and brought up his status screen. She was probably right, since the monsters were only giving him around four or five experience each, and that was *with* the hero blessing experience bonus.

*I know that experience is technically getting split between us, but that's still low. It's going to take me forever to get to twenty and upgrade my class.*

"Why does everything have to give less experience once it's below your level?" Rowan complained, glaring at the surrounding trees like they were personally to blame.

"I mean, it makes sense. Experience is the system's reward for overcoming challenging situations. If you could get experience no matter the difficulty, things would be absolute chaos," Olivia said.

"Just because people could level up faster?"

"Not only that. If *every* enemy slain gave you some experience, people who wanted to hit max level would have every incentive to go out there and hunt down everything they can get their hands on. When you do that, you're no different than the [Corrupted]."

"I guess it makes sense," Rowan said. On second thought, he could easily see several very negative effects of such a thing. "They'd completely exterminate all the weaker monsters. The lower classes would be completely incapable of advancing."

At that, Olivia paused and gave him a look before her eyes suddenly widened. "Weaker monsters?"

"Yeah? Did I say something wrong?" Rowan asked, pausing in his step.

"Monsters aren't the only ones who give experience. Part of why we hunt down the [Corrupted] is because they'll slay entire towns for experience," Olivia said.

The image brought a chill in Rowan's mind. He thought back to the painting he had seen in the palace—a whole group of soldiers walking into the darkness.

The day only improved from there, and they fell into a nice rhythm. Olivia used her sword, helping to cover Rowan's blind spots now that she wasn't trying to hide how uncomfortable fighting without her potions made her.

Rowan was also really benefiting from getting to practice actual combat. All the theory and being shoved around by the baron or his maid was beneficial, sure, but in an environment that could turn hostile at any moment, he could *feel* himself improving.

Part of that was due to his experience bar ticking up and some extra stats. By the time they took a break for lunch and Olivia broke out a traveling alchemy kit to brew up some potions, Rowan had managed to hit level 7. He immediately threw the two points into strength, bringing him up to eighteen in both strength and dexterity.

Frankly, it was ridiculous how much stronger and faster he already felt. If he was gauging things right, ten had put him firmly above average and roughly at an Olympian level of fitness. With sixteen in a stat? He was superhuman in both strength and dexterity.

Olivia was much happier after the break, too. Her brewing had been successful, and she was now a proud owner of a whole new array of deadly potions.

So when they ran into a small pack of wolves, nine of them in total, it was an almost-easy fight. Their attacks were sharper, their movements more nimble, and their coordination was night and day compared to what they had started with.

It felt like nothing in the forest could threaten them.

Of course, that's when it all went wrong.


"Why do you hate the squirrels so much?" Rowan asked as he twirled his spear.

"It's not that I hate them," Olivia said. "I just don't like it when they look back when they're running away, like they're taunting me."

"Personally, I'm a bit more worried about the fact that they can half fly through the air," Rowan said as he swerved the spear to avoid hitting one of the trees.

"Wait." Olivia froze.

Rowan immediately fell into a combat stance, eyes scanning for the threat. He found it sitting in a tree a moment later. "A squirrel? I guess we're taking our revenge, then."

Olivia held still.

When he didn't get a response, Rowan pulled back his smile. "Wait, what level is it?"

A motion to Rowan's left made him jerk in that direction, and the same thing happened to his right. There were at least a dozen squirrels around them.

All of them holding perfectly still.

All of them watching the duo.

That's when Rowan saw them. His eyes spotted squirrels hiding behind roots, or in the bushes, or in the crowns of the trees. There was a whole army of the tiny critters. They might have looked cute, had they not been corrupted. Instead, they looked like irate squirrels on steroids.

"Friendship *is* power," Rowan whispered. If all the squirrels had that card, and beasts tended to get the same sets, and if they all got a single point of stats for every friend that shared their card . . .

*Oh boy, are we in trouble.*

The infernal squirrels waited just long enough for Rowan to realize what was happening before they struck.

Juiced by their dexterity stats, the squirrels didn't just leap forward. They flew. Before Rowan knew what was going on, he already had a couple of critters on his armor. And they weren't shy about using their claws.

The only saving grace was that despite ridiculously boosted stats, the squirrels hadn't suddenly turned into apex predators. Their claws, even with high strength, were still tiny. And as they scratched away at Rowan, their paws got caught in his armor.

To his credit, Rowan didn't hesitate, either. His whirling, slashing, and stabbing spear still carved through the little furry monsters.

It didn't matter. Every fallen squirrel was immediately replaced, and if a single strike of their claws couldn't make it through his defenses, a hundred would. What filled Rowan with dread was that most of the squirrels shook off his attacks. The extra vitality points meant Rowan's attacks just weren't strong enough.

Olivia had become a storm of steel. Her card was doing miracles, slicing through the buffed-up squirrels like they were made of butter. She was putting a serious dent in the monster numbers.

But it was a losing battle. The squirrels soon realized that they didn't need to leap at the humans and could instead scale them like trees. Rowan punted as many of the monsters away as he could, but the hissing and spitting critters kept coming dangerously close to his neck.

It was the same story for Olivia. One of them slipped past Olivia's blade and started to clamber up her robe. She flung it away with her free hand and then immediately followed up with an explosive potion, consequences be damned.

The resulting explosion bought them a few moments as the squirrels staggered, seemingly impacted by the noise much more than they were.

*I guess high perception stats aren't entirely a good thing.*

"Run?" Rowan yelled.

"No," Olivia yelled back.

Rowan tried to think of why. His mind worked faster than it had ever done before.

*The main flaw of the squirrels is their diminutive size and weak bodies. That's why they can't take advantage of their increased strength. But dexterity—they were already fast. Now, they're probably supersonic.*

And then, in a moment of clarity, Rowan realized that he had been wasting brain cycles on the wrong thing. He could have used the time to think about how to get out of this situation.

*I'll do that next time. If I'm not mobbed to death by squirrels.*

Olivia was thinking for the two of them. She barreled into Rowan, knocking him over as her left hand shoved something into his mouth when he tried to protest.

On the ground, Rowan saw the tide of squirrels flow toward them and closed his eyes in resignation. They could have delayed their fate by a couple of minutes if they could fight standing up. On the ground and with Olivia on top of him? There was nothing he could do.

"Hold your breath," Olivia whispered into Rowan's ear. Instinctively, he took a deep breath and watched as a purple fog obscured his vision.

*Poison. She's using poison to cover us.*

The squirrels didn't have the benefit of Olivia whispering in their ear. They charged right into the fog, and most of them began to stagger as soon as they took their first breaths. A few persisted long enough to reach them and attempt an attack or two.

Rowan rolled himself over, trying to shield Olivia from these determined critters. Their attacks were like tiny needles, enough that he could feel the damage but not enough for him to take them too seriously.

But the squirrels were the least of Rowan's issues. The two of them had traded a swarm of corrupted squirrels for being stuck in one of Olivia's poison clouds. Rowan's earlier exertions caught up to him as his lungs screamed in ever-increasing agony. He needed to breathe and soon.

That's when he noticed the lump in his mouth, the thing that Olivia had given him earlier. He nudged it with his tongue.

*Some kind of candy?* It was definitely melting in his mouth, if extremely slowly.

Rowan managed to endure another few more torturous moments before instinct finally overpowered reason and he gasped for air. Predictably, the miasma surrounding them rushed into his lungs, producing an unpleasant tingling sensation.

*We're going to die because of squirrels. The mighty hero, killed by breathing an ally's poison after being surrounded by squirrels. That's going to be a tale told for generations.*

"Rowan?"

Something was calling his name. He assumed that it was the grim reaper.

"Rowan?"

The voice sounded like Olivia, which shouldn't have been possible. Rowan ignored it as he took another breath. It was better to die a quick death than a slow one.

"Rowan!"

Rowan flinched, opening his eyes as he realized that it was actually Olivia calling out his name. He could barely make out her face, since the cloud of poison was frustratingly persistent.

"Thanks for, uh, trying to protect me. Good to know that chivalry isn't dead. But can you let me up?" Olivia said.

"Okay," Rowan said, still unsure of how he was having this conversation. He collapsed to the side of her. "So, did we die? I'm going to be honest, this isn't what I expected at all."

"You know you're fine, right?" Olivia muttered. "I gave you the antidote. It just needed a bit of time to work, which is why I told you to hold your breath."

"Oh, that's neat," Rowan said. His mind began processing what had happened, and he sat back up. The poison was heavier than air, pooling across the ground and rapidly losing altitude. Sitting up brought his head above the cloud, giving him a rough view of what had happened.

It was a slaughter. Dead squirrels were littered on the ground around them.

Next to him, Olivia stood back up and stomped at the nearest squirrel. When Rowan looked in her direction, she had a mischievous grin on her face. "You remember how I was talking about a feast of squirrels? The poison I used fades quickly, and the residue left inside the body isn't harmful. So guess what's on the menu tonight?"

For a few long, tense seconds, Rowan just stared at her. "Olivia, you really are your father's daughter."

"Hey, what does that mean?" Olivia asked. Rowan ignored her and began collecting some of the squirrels. "Hey!"

As they stumbled back into the village later that day, ridiculously weighed down by all the squirrels, Rowan still wasn't sure whether he'd meant that as a compliment or not.

# CHAPTER ELEVEN

# New Waves

People liked those who fed them.

That was true both on Earth and in the new world Rowan found himself in. In spite of Bron's insistence that food wouldn't be an issue, the villagers weren't quite convinced. So when the two of them came back with the lumberjacks with a giant sack of squirrels, they were greeted with enthusiastic cheers.

But more than the new food, Rowan suspected that there were two more reasons why the people seemed in such a good mood. A part of his newfound popularity was owed to his status as a hero, but a much larger portion was likely due to the fact that the last few days had been tense for the village. It wasn't an easy thing to watch increasing numbers of corrupted beasts roaming around your home, wondering when someone would get hurt. And so, the importance of Rowan bringing back a sack full of the infernal critters was blown way out of proportion.

The feast that Olivia had in mind was quickly made into a reality. The whole village, minus those manning the walls, attended. As Rowan watched the affair, a new thought floated across his mind.

*Hope is more important than reality. These dead squirrels changed nothing, but to the village, it meant everything.*

For the first time since he chose his class, an unbidden system screen popped in front of him.

**You've gleaned a fundamental truth of your race.**
**Wisdom: +1**

Rowan swiped the screen away when Olivia shoved a roasted squirrel in his direction.

"Are you sure this is edible?" Rowan asked. Corrupted beasts looked exactly as the name implied, like they had been tainted by some evil magic. Although he knew that people in this world ate the meat, he'd successfully dodged the same fate up until now.

"It's amazing," Olivia said with a full mouth. "Extra sweet to be eating something that tried to eat us not so long ago."

Rowan really couldn't see the appeal. But against his better judgment, he accepted the squirrel. Olivia gestured for him to get on with it. Taking the smallest of nibbles, he tried the center meat.

In his mind, the corrupted beasts were barely edible sources of food, only to be eaten in extreme hunger or hate. He expected a gamey taste, or something that was both stringy and dry. Somehow, the squirrel meat was neither. It was shockingly tender and complex in flavors. Rowan took a larger bite.

"Why is this so good?" Rowan grumbled to Olivia, only to find out she could offer up an actual answer.

"It's the mana," Olivia said between large bites of her own serving. "Regular meat isn't as delicious because normal animals don't have mana infused into their flesh."

"Wait. Mana?" Rowan leaned closer to his companion. "Demonic mana?"

It might have been Rowan's imagination, but Olivia's face turned a slight shade more pink. "Mana's not poison. As long as you cook the meat thoroughly, there's no danger. If you wanted to make a rare steak, you'd need to treat the meat with potions and cleansing spells. The higher the tier of the monster, the better its taste. Generally."

"Oh? So there's some stuff you definitely don't want to eat no matter what?" Rowan teased, taking another bite now that he knew it wouldn't poison him.

Olivia rolled her eyes. "Plenty. Undead are obviously out. There are also plenty of poisonous monsters—a single bite of them would reduce you to a literal puddle of melted mess. Then there are dragons." She shuddered, scrunching up her face. "No one in their right mind wants to eat a dragon. Although they're as high-tier as it gets."

Well, that was concerning. Not the eating bit, since Rowan wasn't particularly in the market for dragon meat. What did matter was the mention of an apex predator that had pretty much been in every fantasy story that ever existed.

"What's so bad about dragons?"

"Besides the fact that they're the closest thing to natural-born divine creatures?" Olivia asked rhetorically. "Probably the fact that some of them have, in fact, ascended to divine status."

"So they're tough and mean. And if we eat one of them, the rest of the dragons won't look too kindly at that?" Rowan asked.

"They actually don't care about that. But let me know if you ever hunt a dragon that's ascended to divinity." Olivia paused. "Dragon blood and flesh carry a special type of energy. The first thing you have to contend with after eating dragon meat is that energy. There are legends of people eating dragon meat and obtaining special achievements and titles. But there are also legends of people mutating into a draconic race. However, the most common outcome is . . ."

"Death?" Rowan finished his skewer and chucked it at the large bonfire in the center of the village.

"Death." Olivia nodded as she offered Rowan another skewer. He took it.

"So how common is it to run across a dragon?" Rowan asked with genuine curiosity. He wasn't planning on a dragon expedition anytime soon, but that didn't stop him from asking questions.

"Thankfully, they're very rare. Most live in isolated areas, or all the way up on the Lost Continent to the north. The only time dragons willingly venture out and meet mortal races is when something horrible or notable happens. Say, if all the heroes die trying to kill the demon king, and the demon king manages to fully manifest in our world with all his power and the power he stole from the heroes. That qualifies."

*I guess it's good to know that if we mess up, some dragons will wake up and pick up the slack.*

The celebration, much needed or not, didn't continue for very long. There was plenty to do still, and people were tired from a day of hard work. After a couple more skewers, both Rowan and Olivia went back to their rooms.

Rowan couldn't exactly put his finger on it, but he was sure that his relationship with Olivia had somehow changed that night.

In the morning, Bron knocked on their doors, politely asking where the squirrel meat had come from. He'd missed the previous night's festival due to work on the moat, and when Rowan rubbed his eyes open, he first thought was that the officer was angry at not being invited to the party. Reality was a bit different.

"I sent the two of you on a scouting mission. And you come back having hunted an entire chitter of squirrels," Bron groaned, massaging his forehead. "How'd you miss the fact that there were hundreds of squirrels trapping you?"

"It wasn't obvious," Olivia protested. "We came across some squirrels at the start, but they weren't a tough fight and ran away."

"And that didn't clue you into trouble? How many times did you see corrupted animals run from you?" Bron asked.

"Twice, technically," Rowan said, coming to Olivia's defense. "Once when a boar tried to get away after I killed its friends, and then yesterday when the horde broke from your charge."

"Hero Rowan," Bron said, visibly keeping his emotions in check to accommodate someone who knew nothing of their world. "The first isn't unexpected. Boars are shockingly smart animals. And hordes always break when they meet overwhelming strength. These animals might be corrupted, but they aren't dumb enough to be slaughtered, not unless there's something else forcing them to fight."

"So . . . squirrels running means they're smart?"

"No, squirrels running means they're a part of a chitter," Bron said. "Those little nuisances are about as smart as a rock, *on their own*. Once you put enough of them together, things get complicated. If there are only Common-tier squirrels around, they just run around and attack things. But if they were smart enough to scout, retreat, and pull off an ambush, there was probably an Uncommon-tier squirrel in charge. You're lucky to have come out alive."

"And above that?" Rowan was curious now, wondering what the squirrels could potentially achieve. "What if the leader is Rare or even Epic tier?"

"Then we run away. Rare is beyond anything that we can hope to deal with ourselves. Once the leader hits Rare, the intelligence of the entire chitter goes up. It acts like a little general, directing its troops with surprising intelligence. And Epic? There's a rumor that one of them is running around the Galeden continent with a woodland empire."

"Isn't it a good thing we took down the chitter, then?" Rowan ventured.

"You mean that I took down the chitter?" Olivia butted in with a smug grin.

"Yes, yes, good work," Bron admitted. "It *could* have been bad if they decided to attack the village."

"So, we're off the hook?" Rowan asked.

"No. I'm not letting you out of my sight again. The two of you will be helping with the moat." Bron seemed to take a ton of pleasure from delivering the news to Olivia, and his grin only grew when she groaned and protested. "It's time to love digging."

Even if he was determined to bring the wrath of an upset superior down on their heads, Bron was at least kind enough to give them a chance to sort through their loot first.

And that was a very good thing, indeed.

While Rowan had been content to ignore the loot when there were better things to do, he could swear that his loot notification had grown into a physical weight pressing down on his chest. Apparently, even if the individual experience of the squirrels eventually became negligible in the face of their low levels, that didn't impact their drop as much, at least for now.

So, Rowan stared at the big, bold number in muted astonishment.

**Cards in Party Loot Inventory: 468**

Some of those cards were obviously from other beasts. However, by far, the bulk of the number was made up of the squirrelly friends.

"Is this really a normal number of loot drops?" Rowan asked in a daze, earning himself a smirk.

"Aren't you glad you have me in your party? Just imagine if you didn't have a talented, wonderful alchemist such as myself there to support you," Olivia teased, though her self-glorified speech lacked its normal punch, seeing as she was currently seated on the floor next to his bed.

Rowan opened his mouth to tease her about her apprehensions in the forest, but be it his recently improved wisdom stat or just common sense, he decided against that.

"Yes, yes, whatever would I do without the wonderful alchemist who decided to take pity on me and wander the world with my poor self," Rowan groused playfully instead.

He didn't expect her to suddenly look away from him, or for the tips of her ears to betray the fact that she was blushing.

"Let's just go over our loot, shall we?" Olivia mumbled, probably delving into her loot screen, since Rowan was hit by a system request to join her a second later. He accepted, then had to resist the urge to gape at the absolute wall of cards that popped up.

**Vicious Bite (Common, Active) x 7**
**Coarse Fur (Common, Passive) x 13**
**Goring Tusk (Common, Active) x 4**
**Reckless Rush (Common, Active) x 8**
**Skilled Climber (Common, Passive) x 127**
**Savage Claws (Common, Active) x 242**
**Friendship Is Power (Common, Passive) x 67**

Rowan's attention went to **Friendship Is Power** first. After all, it had left a strong impression after their last encounter. So, to see so few of those popping up in comparison to other cards was more than a little disappointing.

Then again, he also noticed that **Eerie Stare** was completely missing from the wolf loot drops, and they'd killed quite a few of those.

"Hey, do you have any idea why we got so few copies of **Friendship Is Power**?" Rowan asked, choosing to consult the expert in the room.

"What, did you expect that you'll keep getting a ton of Rare cards just like that?" Olivia sounded amused, shaking her head a little. "Honestly, getting this many? That's extremely nice. I'd chalk it up to your hero luck, if anything."

"See, when you keep talking like this, the difference between a Rare-tier card and a Rare card really gets confusing," Rowan returned.

Olivia scoffed. "Honestly, I bet this is a problem with all the heroes. You really don't have a good benchmark on how tough it is to get some cards to drop, even if you kill the right enemies. Me? I'm extremely happy with these results."

"I was kind of looking forward to what a higher-tier **Friendship Is Power** could do, to be honest." Rowan admitted, plopping down on his bed. "It would be nice to have something like that in our back pocket, just in case."

"Well, we can still get a couple of copies. Want to try?" Olivia asked.

Rowan hesitated for just a second, but his curiosity and a tiny bit of greed eventually won out. The result made him snort.

### One for All (Uncommon, Passive)
**All your stats are boosted by two points for every member of your race with this card, or by one point for every member of your race with its lower-tier equivalent, within five yards of you.**

"If we could arm the entirety of our forces with these . . ." Rowan trailed off, shrugging and handing off the card to Olivia.

"Yeah. But it doesn't work like that. With a group of people bunched up in a small space, you're practically asking for an area-of-effect attack. It works for the squirrels because their numbers are so large. If twenty percent of a human army is wiped out? Their morale breaks," Olivia said with a wistful sigh, then shook her head. "Any of the others worth keeping, you think?"

"Maybe we should hang on to the squirrel cards, just in case we want to upgrade them all the way up to Rare?"

Olivia worried at her lower lip for a few moments, but eventually shrugged. "It's as good a choice as any. It's not like we're going to fuse all the fragments. But we really need to stop wasting time. If we don't go find him soon, Bron *will* send someone to drag us all the way to the moat. Literally."

"What if we lock the doors?" Rowan asked.

"Go ahead. Try it. Might be funny to watch." Judging by the malicious grin Olivia gave him, he really didn't want to do that.

"Fine. Fine. I'm getting up." Rowan sighed and climbed out of the bed, stretching as he went.

Olivia fell into step with him, and together, they went to face their fate.

Back when he was a kid on Earth, Rowan was pretty sure that he had tried to dig a really big hole once. The prospect of uncovering whatever lay underneath the ground seemed like a lot of fun, enough that he'd spent the entire afternoon in the sun. That night, as he experienced what it was like to have an old man's back, he'd vowed to never dig again.

Things were the same in his new world.

After a couple days of digging, a piercing pain had taken root in the small of Rowan's back. It permeated into everything he did, be it walking, talking, or, gods forbid, leaning forward. His hands also suffered. Rowan had thought that the spear training had done plenty, but that was evidently nothing compared to shovel work. Blisters turned into open sores, which then became rock-hard calluses.

He gritted his teeth through it all.

On the other hand, despite being built like a noble princess, Olivia was in much better shape. Her hands were just as dirty as his at the end of each day. But after a quick wash, hers came out dainty and fine, while his looked like a dog had chewed them. Whether it was because she had higher stats or because she had built up a tolerance for digging, Rowan couldn't say.

But the moment Olivia realized Rowan was suffering, she came to his aid. She helped him clean his hands and poured a potion over them. The effects were immediate—almost all the calluses disappeared and further digging didn't aggravate his hands in the same way. She also gave him a potion to drink, and it did wonders for his messed-up back.

And then, driven by the power of stats and sheer grit, the work was finished.

The moat was three meters deep and lined with wicked-looking stakes that promised pain and suffering. The wall itself was repaired from the damage it had taken during the skirmish and reinforced in weak spots. It was even sporting some improvements. Previously, defenders were standing more or less out in the open, with the top of the wall coming barely up to their shins. Now, they had a barrier about shoulder height with slits for when they needed to attack.

As far as Rowan could tell, they were as prepared for trouble as they could be without tearing the whole thing down and rebuilding it in stone. And that was a very good thing. Just hours after they'd finished their work and were winding down for the day, a messenger rode into the village. Or up to the village, rather, since the gates were shut and a guard posted already.

When she saw the messenger, Olivia's face lit up. Unfortunately, the news that came wasn't the type she was looking for, especially judging by how she shoved the letter intended for Rowan into his chest.

*Rowan,*

*I am sorry that our time together was interrupted so suddenly. There is much I wanted to teach you still, and we never had the time to sort out the question of your remaining party members. I have sent word to the settlements in my barony, and if they can be reached, people will soon make their way to you at Felton's Mill. I will also try to encourage more mercenaries to assist your position, so you will be better prepared for trouble ahead.*

*Unfortunately, that is not the only news I have for you. The matter of the frontier's failure is a greater threat than I expected. We will not falter, but be warned that you and Olivia might be pushed harder than I would have liked. Keep my daughter safe, and know that you can rely on her when danger strikes.*

*—Aristaeus's own,*

*Kayden Sutton*

Rowan took a deep breath. It was the baron, no doubt about that. In the back of his mind, Rowan had expected something like this. The small details added up. The groups of corrupted beasts roaming around the countryside. The fact that Bron was still out trying to shore up defenses. And how the baron had sent a messenger instead of coming himself.

But Rowan still took the letter like a punch to the gut. He had hoped, even convinced himself, that there would be months of training before he actually had to fight real enemies. Now, it seemed that he'd have to start fighting before he was even level 10. Before he upgraded his class to Uncommon. And before he was truly comfortable with the spear.

After giving Rowan his letter, Olivia clutched her own letter and fled back inside. After thanking the messenger, Rowan did the same.

Up in his room, he carefully burned the letter, destroying any mention of Aristaeus. Maybe it was paranoia, but he didn't feel comfortable just leaving information like that lying around.

*It's not like my blessing is a secret*, Rowan snarkily said to himself in the safety of his own mind. *The giant display that the king put on made sure of that. Everyone who's anyone knows that I've been blessed by Aristaeus.*

But Kayden was true to his word. His encouragement meant more and more people arrived at the village.

Some were farmers, individuals or small families. These were mostly people who lived on their own. They tended their fields and under normal circumstances enjoyed the safety that the baron afforded them. Now that there was an active demon problem, they looked to the nearby villages and towns for protection.

A lot of them looked worse for wear. Olivia had explained in the past that most people in the world sported Common classes with levels around 5 to 8, which meant that even a level-4 corrupted boar was deadly if they didn't have the right cards in place.

The second major group of arrivals were mercenaries. They mostly showed up in groups of four. And unlike the farmers who had been molested by the dangers plaguing the land, the mercenaries were healthy enough to laugh, joke, and even show off the kills they'd accrued on the road.

The third group of arrivals were four scouts. Even when others pointed out the scouts to Rowan, he had a hard time finding them from the top of the wall. They moved through the terrain like shadows, slipping into the grass or mud in the blink of an eye.

And the scouts didn't bring good news.

"Saw a couple of fourteens, and a sixteen, even. Can't say how many are on their way. We couldn't get close enough to the main horde," one of the scouts relayed.

"Why?" Bron asked.

"We were attacked," the first scout said with shame on his face. "Somehow, the monsters realized we were there and they caught us by surprise. A group of weasels snuck up to us. Almost tore my throat out when they attacked."

"Weasels?" Bron asked in disbelief.

"Yes sir," another of the scouts jumped in. "I think they were still Common monsters. But we were caught off guard. We expected the usual—boars, wolves, and the like. Instead, we saw squirrels, deer, and the weasels. Exotic species."

Bron grunted. "So we have burrowing weasels. Anything else?"

"We have about six or seven hours before they get here. Maybe nine, if we're lucky and they come across something to distract them," the scout replied. Unsaid, of course, was that whatever, or rather whoever, ended up attracting the horde's attention was likely doomed.

"Good." Bron looked around and found the eye of Desimir. "We're raising the alarm now. Get everyone inside and ready. I don't want any surprises."

A couple hours later, the adrenaline had begun to wear off. Rowan was standing with Olivia at the top of the wall, straining his eyes to see something new on the horizon. For the first time, he was starting to doubt the intelligence of the scouts.

To cut down on the boredom, he flicked open his stat screen. At one point or another during their squirrel scuffle, his experience had ticked over into level 8. This was a minor blessing, since he'd chosen to put the stat points he got into vitality.

**Rowan Clairfont**
**Level 8 Spearman**
**EXP: 52/300**
**Mana: 50/50**
**STR: 16**
**VIT: 12**
**DEX: 18**

**PER: 10**
**INT: 10**
**WIS: 11**


**Deck (4/4):**
**[Heart] Keen Spear (Epic)**
**[Class] Empowered Thrust (Common, Active)**
**Nimble Body (Common, Passive)**
**Relentless Advance (Uncommon, Active)**
**Blessings:**
**Blessing of the Stalwart Hero**

"You never get used to the waiting." Bron's voice cut through the silence, and the two of them turned back in surprise to find the officer standing behind them. "It's one thing to fight. It's a whole different issue to just sit there and wait for violence to come to you."

All along the wall, people were silent.

"Any advice?" Rowan asked, for nothing else than to fill the uncomfortable silence that followed the officer's words.

"People often say that war is a game of strength. Or that fighting is a matter of who has the sharpest sword," Bron said, his voice carrying across the entire wall. "There's some truth in that. But these monsters only know bloodshed. They don't know that you have your entire families behind this wall and that you'll fight to the last drop of blood to keep them safe. The greatest factor in war is conviction. We will win. We must win. Because we're fighting a war that we can't lose."

The words did their job. Rowan still felt tension, but next to him, Olivia smiled as she stopped fiddling with her potions. Logically, he knew that the best thing to do was rest, but his heart kept beating faster and faster.

*What's that?* Rowan squinted. The forest outside the village had been pushed back. Huge fields of ugly dirt and tree stumps littered the ground, culminating in a massive moat. In the forest, something had twitched. It might have been a trick of the light.

It wasn't. Howls, yips, and all sorts of unholy noises rose up in a clamor from the forest, making everyone flinch.

"Everyone to your positions, now! Remember your instructions!" Bron bellowed, his voice carrying over the entire village.

Rowan pulled his spear close and felt his breathing slow. Like Bron said, this was a war that he couldn't lose. He was going to win. He had to.

# CHAPTER TWELVE

# Threat Assessment

Rowan had expected things to immediately and horribly go wrong. They didn't, which was a surprise, but a welcome one.

The beginning of the siege went exactly the way that Bron had planned. The corrupted beasts behaved no differently than rabid animals intent on slaughtering everything in front of them. They crashed into the moat, needlessly impaling themselves while the defenders on the wall kept raining down lethal projectiles.

To that end, the role Rowan played was exceedingly minor. He couldn't exactly jump down from the walls and start spearing the monsters. That was suicide. Instead, he and all the other short-range fighters were relegated to support roles. They transported arrows, relayed orders, and generally tried to smooth things along without getting underfoot.

It sounded easy in theory, but lugging heavy containers up and down the stairs to the wall was pure torture. Like digging, the stats made Rowan superhuman, which meant that he was also doing much more work than before. He estimated that he had probably carried the equivalent of a small car's worth of stuff up the wall each hour.

But the defenses held.

Briefly, Rowan swapped out his **Nimble Body** for **Inspect** and confirmed what the scouts had said earlier. Most of the beasts in the wave were above level 10, some of them even at 16 or 17.

The mindless attacks from the high-level corrupted beasts were scary, but they were just that. There was very little danger.

Several times, a beast stronger than the rest would charge the wall, building momentum and nearly jumping high enough to reach the top of the wall. It was an impressive show of raw strength, but the defenders showed their appreciation with arrows and more esoteric attacks like fireballs and giant rocks.

No one in Felton's Mill was celebrating.

The beast horde seemed endless. No matter how many arrows were shot or how many stones were thrown, the beasts kept coming.

"How are there this many beasts?" Rowan asked Olivia in one of their rotation breaks.

"I don't know," Olivia replied. She watched as every villager and mercenary who knew how to draw a bow, even improperly, was drafted by Bron for shooting duty.

"What's that?" Rowan was pointing to one of the mercenaries. The man was stepping on top of the protective front of the wall and swinging his sword down at the horde. The sword was glowing, and with every swing of the blade, projectiles of energy would rain down on the corrupted beasts. Wherever the crackling, bladelike projectiles passed, mangled flesh was the only thing that remained.

"Sword beams," Olivia answered. "It's one of the main reasons why swords are in fashion these days. Someone can be both melee and ranged with a sword. Granted, they can't deal as much damage as a dedicated [Archer] or wreak as much havoc as a [Berserker]. But it's a good generalist weapon."

Before Rowan could ask his next question, Olivia was called away from her break. She ran forward and pulled out a string of potions from her pouch. As she went through the wall, she'd take a look at the defender, determine where they were flagging, and give most of them a blend of herbs. Every so often, she handed over one of the potions.

Rowan decided to end his break early. As he got to his feet, the ground seemed to shift underneath him.

*This is ridiculous. I'm going to have to switch out one of my cards for Stable Footing at this rate.* Rowan stomped his foot down, hoping to get the numbness out of his legs. When he still had trouble finding his balance, he looked down to find the ground shaking. *Wait. This isn't me. Are we having an earthquake in the middle of all this?*

He spent a few moments wondering if the earthquake would mess up their wall, before shouting snapped him out of his reverie.

"Look out! Under us! Something's—" One of the villagers tried to warn everyone, but her scream was cut short when a spray of dirt shot up from the ground and consumed her.

A chitinous claw emerged from the ground, and new screams echoed around the village. By the time the owner of the claw emerged from the ground, a group of mercenaries was already in position against the threat.

As Rowan got a good look at the monster, he drew in a sharp breath. Where the corrupted boars and squirrels looked like normal animals that had been injected with growth hormones, the new monster looked like it had been created in a lab run by a mad scientist. It was an unholy cross between a spider and a scorpion. Six legs, two tails, and two pincers. If that wasn't enough, the fact that it was the size of a small car was enough to spell bad news.

"Demonic Stalker!" Bron's yell floated over them. "Watch out for its tails! It can—"

One of the mercenaries threw himself to the side as a spray of dark liquid left the monster's barbed tails.

"Spray acid, got it," the mercenary yelled back as he blurred ahead with a short sword and small buckler in hand. His weapon took on a faint yellow glow as he swung at one of the tails. "Let's see how well it does with only one tail."

Somehow, the sword cut away a chunk of the stalker's tail. But it was like the monster couldn't feel pain. It trained its eyes on the mercenary and lashed out with one of its feet. The man barely got the buckler in place before being thrown back by the weight of the blow.

The others began to swarm the monster, raining down blows on the spindly limbs of the abomination in an attempt to cripple it.

Rowan was about to help the fight when the entire village began trembling. Dozens of different stalkers emerged from the ground, some larger than others, but none as big as the first one.

Without giving himself a chance to overthink things, Rowan gripped his spear tight and charged into the fray. He targeted the closest available stalkers, triggering **Relentless Advance**.

In hindsight, that was a risky decision. Ever since equipping the card, Rowan had never once used it. He had no clue what to expect, besides whatever the description had been. In spite of that, the experience felt easy. Natural. It was like the world itself *wanted* to close the distance between him and his foe.

Rowan aimed right where the smaller stalker's singular tail met the rest of its body, calling on **Empowered Thrust** and feeding it several points of his mana for extra oomph.

It worked. The spear pierced into and *through* the tail, leaving a dangling tail on the monster. It went into a frenzy, and Rowan's **Nimble Body** was the only thing that saved his life, letting him lean away from the blows in ways Rowan thought should have snapped his spine.

Rowan furiously backpedaled as he dodged, using his spear to mostly block the nearly random attacks from the monster. Then, spotting an opportunity, he leaned inward and aimed at the inner side of a joint, figuring that it would be much easier to escape from a stalker without all six of its legs.

Bolstered by **Empowered Thrust**, Rowan succeeded. The spear sliced into the soft shell and the monster lost its balance. Almost by instinct, Rowan pushed forward, took a moment to channel more mana, and drove his spear through one of its eyes.

The monster gave one last struggle before falling limp to the ground. Rowan threw another thrust at the monster for good measure before looking up and taking in the situation. All around him, the mercenaries were wrapping up their own battles. Most of them had been held back from the wall due to their short-range combat styles, which meant that they were in the perfect position to intercept the stalker attack. Around thirty stalkers had emerged from the ground, and all of them were now lying dead.

It wasn't a one-sided victory. Rowan could see at least three mercenaries lying in growing puddles of blood while another half dozen were injured. Some were clutching at severed limbs, which somehow seemed light compared to one of the female mercenaries, who had taken a blast of acid to the face and was screaming as the acid bit deeper into her head.

Before Rowan could do anything, one of the more grizzled-looking mercenaries stepped forward, bringing his sword down. The downed woman stilled, and no one said a thing.

Rowan felt a hint of bile rising at the back of his throat. All he could think of was that people weren't supposed to die like that. This should have been a fantasy world, where all the bloodshed and suffering was somewhere in the background. Instead, it was all around Rowan.

Things moved faster than he could process them. A hair-raising howl sounded right above him. He brought his spear up, only to find Bron bisecting a massive wolf. The blood splattered down and Rowan felt drops splash against his face.

*This is real.*

Rowan pulled his spear closer and felt himself calm down slightly. Without new vibrations in the ground, he felt safe enough to run up the stairs, taking as many steps as he could at a time. Once up there, the picture wasn't pretty. More and more of the beasts were successfully making leaps, landing on the wall outright.

He had no idea where Olivia was. Before panic could claw its way down his throat, Rowan remembered the party benefits and relied on the vague pull to find her. Forgetting his fear, he began fighting through the monsters that had made the leap. He used every bit of training from the baron in his attacks. Stab, thrust, shuffle, twist. The movements became a blur. His body was acting before his mind even realized what was going on.

And then he saw her.

Olivia was on her own, facing not one but two beasts, a wolf and a vaguely reptilian monster. Without a single moment of hesitation, Rowan engaged his **Relentless Advance** again and thundered right into the side of the nearest beast. Even though it was only the second time Rowan was using the card, he was beginning to get the hang of things. He activated **Empowered Thrust** while also using **Nimble Body** to aim for the wolf's rib cage.

The attack was true. The spear bit into the wolf's chest and plunged deep. That was when Rowan realized he had made a mistake. Anything that Olivia had trouble fighting was probably above the Common rank, which meant that it was at least ten levels higher than Rowan, with all the extra stats that those ten levels brought.

His worst fears came true when the wolf stumbled sideways from the attack but somehow remained standing. It cranked its head toward Rowan and then swiftly snapped out, its jaws closing around the hero's right arm.

"Shit," Rowan cursed, twisting around the spear with his left hand. The motion probably wreaked havoc on the wolf's organs, but it also tightened the wolf's bite. A couple moments later, the stalemate was finally broken as the wolf lost its strength. Unfortunately, its jaw was still clamped around Rowan's arm when it crumpled to the ground, bringing Rowan down, too.

Rowan cursed again, letting go of his spear to unhinge the animal's jaws. That was a mistake. The moment Rowan's hand left the spear, a spell of exhaustion washed over him. His vision went black as his breathing became shallow. Fumbling around, Rowan gripped the spear again and brought things under control.

On the other side, Olivia was much more at ease against a single opponent. She danced around the reptile's claws and tail, her sword lighting up for the briefest of moments when she chose to retaliate. She was being a lot smarter about her mana usage, though even the smallest of strikes left impressive wounds on the animal.

Her opponent was obviously getting hurt. But it also seemed of a tougher variety than the enemies Rowan normally fought. Long after it should have fallen, it was still in the fight.

With gritted teeth, Olivia's hand dipped into her potion pouch, producing a very small vial. The next time the beast tried to bite her, she chucked the potion into its mouth with expert precision.

It must have been some kind of poison, because the next thing Rowan knew, the monster shuddered and fell over. It was almost anticlimactic how the fight ended.

"You okay? Let me see that." Olivia was on Rowan a second later, helping him free his arm.

Rowan didn't protest as she fussed over his wound, pouring an odd, fizzy potion on it and then following it up with a healing solution. It gave him plenty of time to finally get his spear back from the thieving carcass.

He did keep his eye on the rest of the wall, but the situation almost seemed to be calming down. The massive beast that Bron had personally slain was obviously a cut above the rest, and its lesser brethren had taken advantage of all the chaos to jump in. Now, they were getting beaten back down the wall.

Before anyone could celebrate, one of the defenders pointed at the sky. "In the sky. Monsters!"

Rowan looked and found a whole flock of things that looked like prehistoric dinosaurs heading their way. To call them birds would have been a disservice to the avian kind. These monsters were essentially skeletons with a thin layer of skin on their wings. But the largest feature by far was their legs. At least two-thirds of their body was dedicated to the disturbingly handlike appendages with long sickle claws.

"Bombers!" Bron bellowed. For the first time since Rowan knew him, the officer seemed genuinely worried. "Bombers! Mercs, get up here. I want every archer protected. Archers, shoot those damn things down. Focus on them!"

Rowan turned back to the baron's daughter, still with her head bent and treating his wounds. "Hey, uh, are we okay? What are bombers?"

"It's a shorthand," Olivia said as she pulled out bandages from her magical pouch that seemed to have everything in it. "No one calls them by their proper name. They're nasty little buggers that demons breed and keep around as disposable minions. The stalkers burrow underground; the bombers attack from the air. They'll snatch you right up with their massive legs, take you as high as they can, and then drop you on your allies. If you're not dead at the apex of the flight, you will be when you land. And you'll probably take someone else out, too."

"Uh, sounds nasty." Rowan wasn't sure what else he could say. "So don't get grabbed?"

"Yeah, don't get grabbed," Olivia chuckled. She finished the bandaging of Rowan's arm and tied it up, eliciting a hiss from Rowan. "Come on, it's not that bad. I even used numbing bandages for you."

"You try getting your arm bitten by a monster wolf," Rowan retorted halfheartedly. His gaze was still in the sky.

Olivia noticed his gaze and turned to look at the flock flying closer. "Make sure you're not in the way of that big guy at the head of the flock. That's an Uncommon. The others, you should be able to handle."

"Should?" Rowan asked. "How? Throw my spear up in the air?"

"They dive to get you. Make sure to stab at their wings and damage them as much as you can. Their skin tears as easy as paper. But their brain and chest organs are behind a solid layer of bone, and those bones are tougher than steel," Olivia said. "But don't worry, this isn't our fight. The bombers will focus on the archers first because only the archers pose a threat to them. All we have to do is make sure the wall doesn't fall."

That sounded simple. In theory. Rowan tested his arm, and it moved just fine. He made a note to thank Olivia after the battle. *The wonders of having a healer.*

Soon, the bombers were upon them, and like Olivia predicted, they aimed for the archers and left most of the melee fighters alone. Almost every archer had a soldier, mercenary, or villager as a bodyguard, but accidents still happened and Rowan could soon hear bloodcurdling screams as unfortunate souls were dropped from the air.

He would have paid more attention to the bombers if it wasn't for the fact that the rest of the horde was almost upon them. The earlier slaughter had killed hundreds if not thousands of monsters. But at the same time, it produced a pile of corpses tall enough to both plug up the moat and make it easier for new enemies to launch themselves up the wall.

The first thing Rowan skewered was a godforsaken squirrel. The little guy came charging up with a mindless screech, and he managed to put it down with a basic thrust. The second thing he killed was a badger and, knowing the stories about those from his old world, he enhanced the strike with mana.

Soon, he lost count of his kills. It was set, thrust, shuffle, and the whole process over again. Beads of sweat rolled down his forehead and collected beneath his chin. Gradually, his vision narrowed to the threats in front of him and nothing else. He clobbered, skewered, and shoved. No monster got past him.

Until he came face-to-face with a bear. A corrupted bear.

The thing was huge. Rowan watched as it pulled itself up, the entire wall groaning under its weight. Its head alone was almost as large as Rowan's entire body. It was built like a juggernaut and not something that Rowan ever wanted to mess with.

Still, he had to try.

With a sputtering mana pool, Rowan used **Relentless Advance**, comboing the card with his other two cards for an enhanced stab at the monster's eye. The beast tilted its head at the last second, and the blow landed on its cheek. The spear clashed with whatever natural defenses the beast had and didn't leave so much as a scratch.

*Shit. Uncommon.* The size of the beast was clue enough that it was something an entire tier higher than what Rowan could handle at the moment. The good news was that he had his own Uncommon helper.

"Get out of the way!" Olivia yelled as she chucked a potion right as its face. The resulting explosion sent Rowan staggering back but only blackened the bear's fur.

It moved with speed that should not have been physically possible for something that was the size of a small house. But in the blink of an eye, Rowan was staring at one of its bear paws rumbling down at his head.

Before he could even close his eyes, the paw landed on a bloody shield face carved in the shape of a snarling wolf head. The displaced air produced a boom so loud that Rowan thought he was going to go deaf. But he was alive. And the rebound of the blow sent the bear staggering, its hateful eyes widening as it fought to regain its balance.

Then, two things happened in very short succession. First, a dark cloud of miasma descended on the bear and seemed to have a life of its own as tendrils of smoke wiggled into the bear. And second, the shield that had intercepted the bear's attack started to glow. The blink of an eye later, it rocketed out.

Rowan watched all this in a daze. He desperately wanted to help, but none of his muscles responded.

Luckily, he wasn't needed. Whereas Rowan's full-power thrust had been ineffective, the shield bash was not. There was a loud, echoing crunch, and the bear was *shot* back into the horde, crushing more than a few of the monsters with its bulk.

It didn't move again.

"Good job out here! Do be careful not to overdraw your mana reserves," the shield bearer quipped, turning around to give a brief smirk.

Rowan just blinked, staring blankly. The man who had saved his life had animal ears. They were pristine white, extremely fluffy, and twitching as the man tilted his head. Behind the man, a tail lazily waved from side to side, and Rowan dared think it was even more luxuriously fluffy than the man's ears.

"Th . . . thanks," Rowan finally managed, pulling himself together. He realized how stupid it had been to assume that there were only humans in this world, especially when he had seen Kayden's wife, Lady Sutton. And with that realization, he knew that losing his mind on a life-or-death battlefield was a very bad idea.

"Don't mention it. Happy to help." The response didn't come from the shield bearer. Rowan blinked as he tried to find the speaker. When he finally did, he wondered if perhaps he had hit his head.

Next to the shield bearer was a humanoid dog. Or that's how Rowan's mind chose to interpret things. Where the shield bearer still looked human, the new miasma producer was fully canine. Its head looked exactly like a wolf's, covered in fur and ending in a short muzzle. More than that, this was a tall wolf-person who was some kind of magic user. Their paw, not a hand, held on to something between a staff and a walking stick, but much more unpleasant-looking. The body of the staff was crafted out of some black, gnarled wood, but it was inlaid with strips of white that formed odd symbols and glyphs. Rowan strongly suspected it was bone, especially because the head of the staff was a grinning, horned skull.

For a second, Rowan wondered if these were the demons that were plaguing the lands. Then, he remembered the fight he saw when first arriving at Felton's Mill. The shield bearer had launched himself from the wall to support Bron's men. And the black miasma was part of how the monster horde had been beaten back.

And then they were gone. The shield bearer had short, stumpy legs that pumped with incredible strength as he bounced to the battle. The wolf-mage gave Rowan a smile, or maybe a snarl, and then calmly walked to join its companion.

Once they were a safe distance away, Rowan turned to Olivia. "Those were humans?"

"Humans?" Olivia choked. "What part of that was human to you? Those are beast folk. They're our allies. I didn't think we'd see them so close to the frontier."

Rowan grabbed his spear and got into a fighting stance. Beast folk or not, the two of them were responsible for that part of the wall. And the monsters were still coming. The only good news was that flying bombers had disappeared from the sky, and the ranks of the monsters seemed to be thinning.

Rowan glanced at his mana, a pitiful four out of fifty. *Shit. That's not good.*

Olivia must have noticed, because she tossed him a mana potion that he immediately downed. It helped, but as he began using his cards again, it felt like someone was squeezing his head in a vise. His vision became so blurry he was occasionally uncertain whether he was looking at one enemy or two, or even how many limbs he had.

He kept fighting. Spearing wolves, foxes, and even squirrels. Each time a monster poked its head over the wall, Rowan was there with his spear.

And then it was over.

"Victory!" Bron's voice boomed over the village. Even though the volume was there, Rowan noticed that there were undertones of exhaustion in the words. "They're retreating. We won!"

Cheers went up all along the wall, followed by a louder echo from lower in the village.

"It's over? Really?" Rowan staggered back and bumped into Olivia. Somehow, she looked worse than he felt. Her armor was covered in soot and blood, mixing into a nasty combination.

"It's done," Olivia said as she slipped her hand in his and began tugging him down the stairs.

The trip down the stairs and off the wall was tricky, and they almost pitched over the side of the stairs. Rowan had no clue what happened next. All he remembered was seeing a bed and dreaming of a single thought that brought a smile to his face.

They were still alive.

# CHAPTER THIRTEEN

# A Flash of Fangs

When Rowan finally woke up the next morning, the sun was already high up in the sky. He found himself only halfway on the bed and every part of his body ached, a sort of seminumb feeling that promised pins and needles of pain later.

So he stayed in bed a bit longer and distracted himself by bringing up his battle log.

**Battle Results:**
**EXP:**
**[Corrupted Wolf] +75**
**[Demonic Stalker] +125**
**[Corrupted Fox] +60**

. . .

**Loot:**
**128x cards in Party Loot Inventory**

Rowan scrolled through all the kills he had made. He could only remember a tiny portion of them; most of the fighting was now a blur even though it had just happened yesterday. One thing did stand out to him: The monsters all seemed to give far more experience than he expected. Where the level-3 and -4 boars only gave a handful of experience points, the monsters from yesterday all left him with double-digit experience.

That almost made him sit up. All that experience combined together would mean . . .

**Rowan Clairfont**
**Level 12 Spearman**

**EXP: 322/650**
**STR: 16**
**VIT: 12**
**DEX: 18**
**PER: 10**
**INT: 10**
**WIS: 11**
**Available stats: 8**

Level 12. Eight whole stats. Rowan smiled so hard it hurt. In theory, there was plenty wrong with the stat screen as well. It was concerning how quickly the experience requirements were ramping up. And the fact that his current experience was listed as 322. He liked fives and tens, and it kept things nice and neat. *It was the bloody squirrels, wasn't it?*

Thankfully, it was hard to be cranky when there were eight whole stats to distribute. If there was anything that soured his mood, it was that he didn't know what to spend the stats on.

Rowan's first impulse was to bump both his strength and dexterity up to twenty-one. Those were big, significant numbers. He hadn't taken the time to confirm his suspicions, but based on how ten had been so important to reach before he took a class, maybe twenty came with some extra benefits?

On the other hand, there were some more pressing issues. Namely, his perception. Several times yesterday, he had almost lost track of a foe because of how fast and nimble they were. He had enough speed and good enough reflexes to respond, but that mattered less when he could barely spot death coming at him.

With great reluctance, Rowan spent four points on perception, then two each on strength and dexterity. The system went to work, leaving a deep ache in his muscles and bones. That, he was used to. What he didn't realize was what bumping perception up by four points at once would do to him.

Every inch of his skin suddenly felt like it was dipped into acid. His sense of taste went on the fritz, things dancing across his tongue that he had no name for and that made him want to puke. His hearing, too, was filled with static and overwhelming noise, robbing him of all coherent thought.

The only mercy was the fact that the process didn't last for long. A few moments later, Rowan wondered why he had never done this before.

The world was *alive* around him. He caught sounds and snippets of conversation outside when there was near perfect silence before. There was a pleasant scent in the room, something vaguely floral and medicinal. And his vision . . . it was like someone with horrendous eyesight getting glasses for the first time. The vibrancy of color, the way light played and refracted through the air, and even the dance of dust particles—all of it blew him away.

And yet, he managed to forget all that when he turned his head and his eyes landed on the sleeping form of the baron's daughter.

For what felt like the longest time, he just stared. Olivia was a bit of a mess, her clothes all ruffled and stained by mud and blood. There was a long, shallow cut right above her left eye, clipping her eyebrow. Her hair must have escaped the ponytail she put it into for the fight, because there were clear tracks of blood staining her green locks.

Rowan was struck by how relaxed she looked. Normally, even when she was resting, there was a coiled eagerness to everything she did. An animating force that pushed her to do something. All that was gone now. Ironically, it made her look a little older, more mature.

He might have been stuck there staring at her if there wasn't a potential monster horde outside. He prodded her cheek. "Hey. You alive?"

Olivia groaned and mumbled something, turning her face and burying it into the sheets. "Go away. Tell my father I'm not getting up today."

"I'm not sure about you, but I'd rather be looking through loot than sleeping," Rowan insisted, poking her again.

Olivia froze, and then shifted so one of her green eyes could peek at the world. "Rowan? Why are you in my bed?"

"Actually, I'm pretty sure *you're* in *my* bed," Rowan answered. "To answer the question, though, I have no idea. I blacked out after we won."

"I did, too." Olivia checked to make sure she was decent before pushing herself onto her elbows. "Oh god. We ruined these sheets. The chief's wife is going to be pissed. Wait, he *has* a wife, right?"

"Nope. She passed a couple of years ago. Some kind of sickness. Had a daughter and son-in-law, though, and an adorable grandkid." Olivia hadn't spent as much time getting to know the villagers, but Rowan had more or less forced himself to know as many people in the village as possible. Most of them were very pleasant. The chief's family, in particular, was nothing but kind and friendly. But they seemed scared, and he could hear a rough edge under their voices.

"Okay, fine. We'll talk about how you know that later. Why, exactly, did you ruin a good thing and wake me up again?" Olivia asked.

"Check your system logs." There really wasn't much else to add.

"That's a lot of cards," Olivia muttered. There was a certain dazed quality to her voice, and he couldn't ignore it.

"Something wrong?" Rowan asked as he got comfortable in his spot. "You don't sound too happy."

"No, it's just that we've been getting cards left and right lately." Olivia sat up as well. "Just by defending the village, the barony gained at least a thousand cards. Getting this many cards isn't normal. Normally, you'd need to go looking for corrupted animals or demonic monsters."

"And with the invasion, it's like the demons are delivering the cards to us," Rowan said.

"Father used to say that each demon invasion is a great reshuffling of the noble houses. Cards that used to be sought after are now common," Olivia said. "This is horrible, don't get me wrong. A lot of people could have died. A lot of people *did* die. Still, opportunities like this don't even appear every generation. It's ironic—we only get the opportunity to become powerful when the world itself is threatened."

"Or it's the other way around. There's no need to be powerful if a world-ending threat doesn't exist," Rowan offered.

Olivia was quiet for a second, but she eventually nodded. "Well, no point in thinking too much about it."

**Your party member is viewing the loot report.**
**Open loot inventory?**
**Yes / No**

Rowan hit the "yes" button and let the cards unfurl in his vision. Just like last time, he was briefly overwhelmed. There were so many cards, he didn't know where to look. But then a flash of green caught his attention.

**Flash Freeze (Uncommon, Active)**
**Send your mana out in a wave, covering everything in a thin layer**
**of ice and dealing ice damage to foes within ten feet of you.**
**The severity of the damage is proportional to**
**the amount of mana invested.**

"How'd we get an Uncommon card?" Rowan asked as he sent the screen over to Olivia.

"An Uncommon? We probably defeated an Uncommon monster at some point," Olivia replied, her attention taken elsewhere.

"We did?" Rowan mumbled as he expanded the list of monsters to look at each and every kill. Halfway down the list, he found it. At some point, the two of them had defeated something worth a whopping 250 experience points. A [Corrupted Winter Tapir]. Just the name alone was enough for Rowan to pay more attention to it. "How's the card?"

Olivia refocused her attention, and a smile blossomed. "It's a mana card." When Rowan didn't show the appropriate levels of appreciation, she made a face and continued. "It's a card that gives you a mana skill, something that you can use to channel your mana directly."

"And that's rare?" Rowan guessed. He mentally toggled a pass on the card, the same way he had done with the Corrupted Heart Card.

"You have no idea," Olivia said as she summoned the now-uncontested card. It was a pretty thing, the glacier-blue image glittering under the sun. "Cards like these come from monsters that can innately use mana. They're incredibly hard to find."

"So you're going to use it?" Rowan asked.

Olivia paused in her excitement as her eyes went glassy. Rowan assumed that she was looking at her deck. "Maybe, if I can make enough space for the card. The other cards synergize quite well with my class."

Rowan nodded absentmindedly. His attention was already on something else.

**Nimble Body (Common, Passive) x 17**

He immediately rolled for all of them, and grinned when Olivia immediately passed on them. The cards rained down on his chest, and he gathered ten as quickly as he could.

**Nimble Body** had been one of his impulse picks, and when paired with **Empowered Thrust**, he could attack at angles that would have been impossible before. More than that, it also gave him the flexibility to dodge without losing his balance. To say he was excited about an improved version would be an understatement.

**Contortionist's Physique (Uncommon, Passive)**
**You can control your body in new and unexpected ways and with startling precision, allowing you to move with precision and pass through gaps you normally couldn't.**

"Yes, yes, yes," Rowan chanted, practically forcing the card into his chest while unequipping **Nimble Body.** It settled into his deck with a thrum of power that pulsed through his body, and his aching muscles actually relaxed a fraction.

Testing things out, Rowan focused on the various muscle groups, finding that he could both perceive them and tense them individually. It was like someone had mapped out his body, then transmitted the knowledge right into his brain. *I could probably recreate that scene from* The Exorcist.

"I don't like the way you're grinning. Stop it," Olivia joked, tossing one of the Common cards that were now scattered all over the bed at his face.

Rowan just laughed, unbothered. "You have no idea how amazing this card feels. You've got to get one for yourself."

He illustrated his point by pulling his arm so far back that it cracked three times in a single motion. Demonstration over, Rowan sank back down into the bed with a content sigh.

Olivia scrunched up her nose at him in distaste, and she shook her head in an adamant no. "Nope. You can have your weird physique card, I'll stick to my build. Besides, I can't get as much out of it as you can."

"Wait, why not?"

"You're a dexterity build, dummy. Don't think I haven't noticed how much better your speed and reflexes have gotten. Cards all have stats they work well with. Do you really think someone with ten or less dexterity could use the **Nimble Body** series of cards half as well as you do? The majority of my points are in intelligence and wisdom."

Rowan considered that for a moment, and it made perfect sense. He definitely couldn't get far with the **Flash Freeze**. It would probably drain him in two or three casts max, and then he'd be a sitting duck. Or passed out in the middle of a battleground.

"Do you think my stats make **Relentless Advance** more effective, too? I mean, if it's rushing an opponent, it has to have something to do with strength and dexterity, right?" Rowan asked.

"Probably? But if you think about a boar, they're mostly strength and vitality builds. Not dexterity," Olivia said, her finger on her chin. "If you want to have a good baseline for the way your stats affect the card, you'd need to compare with someone else that has it. Not that a lot of people are likely to agree to such testing."

Rowan was about to be an idiot and ask why not, but it was pretty obvious. Even now, he didn't know what Olivia's full deck was. He knew that she could make potions, some of which were more like bombs than enhancement brews, but he had no clue what her full deck looked like. If people were that cagey about their cards, then they were probably equally unlikely to be using them for testing.

"Does anyone ever do that kind of stuff?" Rowan asked. "Proper testing on cards and such? That feels pretty important."

"Of course. The mage association does it often. However, if you want to browse the results of their research, you need to be either a member with high enough access or you need to pay a whole lot of money. More than we can afford now that my father is a baron, at any rate. The imperial academy also does some testing and research, but only high-ranking nobles and the king's men go there."

Rowan heard a slight edge in Olivia's voice when she mentioned the academy. Instead, he refocused on their loot.

Most of it was not that exciting.

The best of the loot were sixteen copies of **Eerie Stare** and nine copies of **Light Step**. Those, Rowan grabbed with Olivia's blessing.

**Malevolent Gaze (Uncommon, Passive)**
**Cow your enemies into submission and reduce the stats of an**
**enemy you lock eyes with by ten percent if your intelligence and**
**wisdom total is higher than theirs.**

**Malevolent Gaze** was perhaps Rowan's best card outside of the ones he currently had in his deck. Rather than a simple reduction to an enemy's morale, the card had grown into something with a real effect. Its effects fell somewhere between a passive and active card, yet no mana cost was mentioned for its use.

The only problem was his stats. With the dependence on intelligence and wisdom, he wasn't sure how much mileage he'd get out of the thing.

"You sure you don't want this one?" Rowan asked, drawing Olivia's attention away from her **Flash Freeze** and showing her the description of **Malevolent Gaze**.

"Huh, I didn't know about that one. It's from the wolf drop, right? How many duplicates do we have of those?" Olivia asked.

"Nine. We're one short of getting another Uncommon," Rowan said. To be so close to another upgrade definitely bothered him a little.

"Hrm. Well, it can definitely work with my build, and it would give me more options in combat beyond just my potions. **Flash Freeze** is going to help immensely with that, too. I'll hold on to the card for now," Olivia said as she took the card along with all the **Eerie Stares**. "With how many wolves we had to fight, I'm sure someone has a copy they're willing to trade for one of our cards or just for scrap."

Rowan nodded, moving onto the second combination.

**Ethereal Step (Uncommon, Passive)**
**Your steps are nearly silent and deceptively light, bypassing all**
**pressure-based Common-tier traps and all standard or lower-**
**quality Uncommon-tier traps. The effectiveness of higher-tier**
**traps against you depends on your dexterity values.**

Rowan didn't see an immediate value for the card. Still, given that it was an Uncommon card, he stowed it away in his cardholder.

Scanning the rest of the card drops, Rowan zeroed in on another unusual card drop. He knew which beast this particular card came from instantly.

**Acid Spray (Common, Active)**
**Shoot a stream of corrosive acid at your foe, dissolving flesh and**
**weaker materials. Your acid can damage most Common-tier items**
**and sometimes destroy them entirely.**

That was a nasty card. Surprisingly enough, the system didn't hit Rowan with a warning that he couldn't equip it. To double-check, Rowan tracked down the **Coarse Fur** cards, of which they'd gotten twenty-one duplicates, and the warning was right there. *Interesting.*

"Hey, couldn't you also use this for your build? You're all about poisons and explosions. Feels like a natural fit," Rowan teased, forwarding Olivia the card info.

"What in the world dropped this?" Olivia asked, but she did roll on the card, and Rowan chose to pass on it.

"Demonic Stalker. I had to fight one of those when they dug their way into the village." Rowan hated the mere mention of those things. "There was even an Uncommon tier among them."

"I might use it for brewing potions," Olivia said as she summoned the card to look at the art. "We might need to hunt down some more of these cards for it to be useful, though."

"Maybe someone'll want to trade for the cards we have," Rowan said. "Or we can try to scrap our cards. We have a lot of fragments and useless cards piled up."

"Later. There's a trick to fragment fusing. Usually, it's better to have a whole bunch of fragments and fuse them all at once," Olivia said. "For now, I think it's time to clean up and find something to eat. We definitely need a change of clothes."

Rowan had to admit that it was a little funny to watch Olivia cautiously crack the door open and then scout the hallway before scurrying into her room. He wasn't sure what she was worried about, but he left her to it.

A couple hours later, they finally ventured out of the village chief's house and into the chaos of everything happening outside.

Everywhere they looked, someone was hauling in beasts, butchering them, or packing away monster materials. The villagers worked away with smiles on their faces, and even the mercenaries were pitching in with gusto.

Rowan felt a little ill when he saw that the stalkers were being scavenged too, but felt a little better when he realized the villagers were after the exoskeleton, claws, tails, and venom sacs instead of the creature's flesh.

The two of them found Bron at the top of the walls, more or less where they'd left him the previous day. Instead of commanding the troops in battle, the officer was now overseeing another round of repairs for the wall.

"Ah, the hero party joins us humble mortals," Bron drawled, spotting them before they reached him. "I almost thought you would be lost for the day. You did look cute, though, all collapsed on the bed like that."

"We didn't—I mean, nothing happened," Rowan stuttered, blushing even harder. A glance at Olivia revealed that she was suffering just as much as he was, and her blush was even more apparent when contrasted with her green hair.

"I know, lad, I know," Bron laughed, clapping him on the shoulder. "I hope you understand I still have to report everything to the baron, though. No lying to my liege, not if I want to keep my job. Or my head." The man looked to be relishing their discomfort a bit too much.

Rowan groaned, refusing to give in to the urge to bury his face in his hands. If he couldn't beat Bron at his game, he could at least go for a distraction. "How was yesterday? We won, but at what cost?"

Bron sighed, his cheer dropping away in favor of resigned weariness. "It went about as well as it could have, with fliers and burrowers added to the mix. There were losses, you saw that much yourself, but we handled ourselves well. I'm just worried about what this means for Baron Sutton's troops. If things are this bad here, then . . ." Bron trailed off, but there was no real need to finish.

"At least the worst is over for now, right? I doubt we're going to see another attack this quickly after such a large horde," Rowan offered. There were small mountains of monster corpses piled around the village. Rowan had a hard time imagining that there were many more of those corrupted beasts around.

It seemed like that was the exact wrong thing to say. Right as Rowan's voice fell, a howl ripped through the air.

It was a terrible sound, like the cross between a wail of sorrow and a scream of rage. A feeling of dread welled up in Rowan's chest, and Bron snapped his attention to the forest. Rowan followed the officer's gaze and saw nothing for the first few moments. Then, be it because of his heightened perception or because the creatures had drawn near, he saw the threat.

It was a noble out for a stroll with his dogs. Or rather, it was something that resembled a noble and beasts that resembled dogs. The faces of the beasts looked half-melted, and even their skin seemed to be slipping off their bones. Weeping sores were strewn all over them, leaking pus and blood that steamed.

But the noble was far stranger. It wore no clothes, giving Rowan a direct view of its purple-gray, distinctly nonhuman skin. Its torso was massive and wide, wrinkled skin folded all around, and all stuck on top of comically stubby legs. A total of six long, spindly arms jutted out of its body. Two from the shoulders, two on its front, and two on its back. They ended in fingers that could have belonged to a pianist, if they weren't tipped by claws.

It leaned forward, and its two frontmost arms landed on the ground, effortlessly supporting its weight in spite of the fact that the limbs were over six feet long and perhaps as thick as a normal person's wrist throughout. The arms then lifted its entire bulk, swinging the creature out of the cover of the trees, depositing it on the ground almost gently.

"Morsels . . . many . . . yes . . . divine scent . . . near . . ." A voice echoed out of the monster, muffled and lilting, while its lips didn't so much as twitch.

"What the hell is that?" Rowan hissed, drawing his spear and relying on **Keen Spear** to center himself.

Bron replied, "A demon."

# CHAPTER FOURTEEN

# Flower of Malice

*This is real life. This is reality*, Rowan mouthed silently.

A part of him still looked at the new world through the lens of an observer getting to witness something fantastical. It was still a bit hard to believe all the system screens and the stats. In fact, they offered him a comforting sense of distance from everything, where he could keep up the illusion that this was all just a game. A hard game, to be sure, but a game nonetheless.

The demon stripped all of that away, laying bare a startling truth about his new world: Death was watching, lurking, and out to get him.

*This is real life.*

**Keen Spear** flared, keeping Rowan's mind clear and giving him enough wits to manage a joke. "Why is it just standing there?"

It was true. The demon just stood there, making no real move since revealing itself. Even its eerie canine army was perfectly still, looking more like melted wax figures than real creatures.

"It's probably enjoying this." Bron gritted out the words, eyes narrowed. "Demons can feed on the negative emotions their sheer presence produces."

"What happens when it stops enjoying this?" Rowan asked.

"Bad things," Bron breathed. He steadied himself against the protective parts of the wall. "If I were a betting man, I'd say that thing is at least Rare tier. Putting it down will be difficult."

Olivia's face scrunched up as she spat out her thoughts. "Bron, I know you have your own party, but I need you to join ours."

Rowan was a bit surprised at how easily Bron accepted Olivia's request. And at how the two of them were still thinking about fighting the demon. All that was running through Rowan's head right now was how he could survive an encounter with the demon, not how they could defeat it.

**Bron Hollander is requesting to join your party, accept?**
**Yes / No**

Rowan hit the "yes" button and, a second later, their party got their third member. An odd kind of force filled Rowan's body, likely some kind of buff from Bron's class or status.

*Maybe that's why he's an officer while the others are soldiers.*

"Good. Now, I want you to have this," Olivia said. The care she showed when retrieving the potion in question was a bit alarming, given how carelessly she handled her exploding potions. When Rowan had asked her to handle the explosives with care, she dismissed his concern by saying that the bottles and vials were enhanced and wouldn't break unless there was intention behind the motion.

But when Rowan saw the potion in question, he understood why she used such tenderness. It looked like a miniature galaxy caught in a bottle, coruscating and revolving around a center so bright he couldn't look straight at it.

**Potion of Heroic Might (Unique)**
**As one of the three named pieces produced by Olivia Sutton so far, this potion is a unique marvel of tricky alchemical processes. Its creation almost led to tragedy, but its frightening potential has been constrained to suit the purpose of its creator.**
**Effects:**
**All stats +20 for sixty minutes. [Burning Braveheart] status applied for the potion's duration.**
**WARNING:**
**This potion cannot be safely imbibed by anyone with an Uncommon or Common class and will act as a poison if the attempt is made.**
**[Burning Braveheart]**
**Your will and body are bolstered by the power of the Crimson Ember, granting you immunity to negative status effects and bolstering your might.**
**WARNING:**
**If your body cannot contain the power of the effect, it will slowly immolate itself, bolstering the power you've been granted but worsening your condition.**

"That's a lot of warnings," Rowan whispered, awe leaking into his voice. The plus-twenties would almost triple his total stats—it was the equivalent of adding sixty levels at once.

Bron looked at Olivia, who returned his gaze with just a bit of distress in her eyes.

"Is there anything else I should know?" Bron asked softly.

"You'll also benefit from my **Pursuit of Brilliance** card. That means you'll get double the potion's effectiveness." Olivia paused as her voice broke. "Don't use that potion unless you have to."

"I understand," Bron said. He took the potion and tucked it near his chest. "Thank you, Miss Sutton."

Rowan was a bit too distracted to pick up on the social cues at that moment. He looked out at the demon and its hounds before glancing back to Olivia. "Got anything for me?"

Olivia huffed as Bron walked away. But she dug into her supplies again. "Nothing as powerful as that. But at least you can pop this as soon as we're officially in trouble."

**Lesser Potion of Might (Common, Top Quality)**
**Concocted out of powerful reagents collected from creatures who symbolize might, this potion will lend part of their power to the person who consumes it.**
**Effects:**
**All stats +5 for sixty minutes. [Boosted Toughness] status applies for the potion's duration.**
**[Boosted Toughness]**
**Your body is bolstered by the might of creatures whose bodies are well beyond yours, granting you a medium increase to your physical resistance.**

"No warnings for this one?" Rowan asked, gripping the off-brown potion tighter. The potion wasn't as powerful as the earlier one, but Rowan was still plenty happy with it.

"Besides the fact that you'll be half-dead when the effect wears off? Not really," Olivia said. "It's not a Unique, but I'm the one who came up with the potion, so you still get a fifty percent bonus."

Rowan wanted to ask what that meant for odd numbers like five, but then figured he'd find out soon enough. That really only left one thing for him to say. "Thanks."

That earned him a small smile and a nod before Olivia grew serious again.

"I don't know how long it wants to toy with us, but I say we do something about that," Olivia muttered, casting a glance at the demon. "I'm going to try using my **Inspect** on it."

That one caught Rowan's attention right quick. "Are you sure that's smart? I tried using it on your father, and it didn't go well."

"I can do it. My **Inspect** is a rare one, and I'm an Uncommon specializing in mind stats. It won't be pleasant, and it'll definitely provoke a reaction. But at least we'll have some idea of what we're facing."

"That sounds like a plan to me," Bron said as he walked back. Behind him, Rowan could see that the villagers and mercenaries were standing a bit taller than before. Whatever Bron had done had given them a dose of confidence.

"Here goes," Olivia muttered.

And then it was like the world itself sprang into action.

A blue sheen covered Olivia's eyes, and for a second, it looked as if she was peering into the soul of the demon. And then a grunt of pain escaped her lips as she staggered back.

On the other end, the demon jerked like it had been slapped right across its ugly face and screeched in anger. All the canine monsters that had been as still as statues suddenly broke into motion, yipping and howling as their feet ripped up the ground under them.

"BRING ME THEIR BODIES! I WILL DEVOUR THEIR PHYSICAL FORMS AND FEAST ON THEIR SOULS!" the demon howled, its voice ringing out without any lip movements at all.

"Soldiers, to arms! Mercenaries, block the gates! Everyone else, retreat to your homes immediately!" Bron bellowed, moving closer to Olivia and Rowan.

Olivia was in the process of wiping the trail of blood from her nose, but she still sent over the system info she'd managed to get.

## Vastrozot

### L̈ηv3l 51 [RØ†flowēr Caṃlon]

"Shit. Fifty-one, Rare class," Bron cursed. "How'd they let something like this get so deep?"

Before Rowan could answer Bron's rhetorical question, the demon released his chains and the dogs began sprinting forward.

"DESTROY THEM!" the demon yelled after them.

As dozens of different canines made their way through the half-cleaned carnage of yesterday's siege, Rowan turned to Olivia.

"Did you get to inspect those hellhounds? It'd be good—" Rowan shut up as another screen popped up in front of him.

**[Rotsworn Charger]**
**Level 23**

**STR: 28**
**VIT: 9**
**DEX: 34**
**PER: 7**
**INT: 5**
**WIS: 5**

**Deck (5/5):**
**[Heart] Demonic Breeding (Rare)**
**Death's Remembrance (Uncommon, Passive)**
**Pestilent Embrace (Uncommon, Active)**
**Spewing Mucus (Uncommon, Active)**
**Final Promise (Uncommon, Passive)**

It was pretty close to what Rowan expected. The Rotsworn Chargers were like him, high strength and dexterity builds. And where Rowan had no clue what the cards meant, Bron did.

"The dogs. Don't let them touch you. Archers, double-time on them. I *don't care* if you pass out from mana exhaustion—every ranged skill that you have, use it!" Bron roared.

His words had an immediate effect on everyone, and dozens of different attacks in the form of arrows, fireballs, and even rocks flew at the hounds. But because of the distance, most of the attacks bounced off the Rotsworn Chargers at the end of their flight.

While Rowan looked on, Olivia rummaged through her bag and popped a mana potion, getting some color back into her cheeks. This was quickly followed up by a couple secondary potions, and Rowan didn't need a status screen to know she had taken something stat-enhancing. Her face practically glowed.

As the hounds got closer to the wall, there was both good and bad news. The good news was that there weren't nearly as many hounds as there had been monsters in the previous horde. The bad news was that every single one of the dogs was at the Uncommon tier. And when paired with their small size, their dexterity was utterly ridiculous. They'd dodge projectiles with the slightest tilt and then keep charging forward.

Every so often, a clump of incoming projectiles was simply too dense for the hounds to dodge. Most of the damage was too soft to truly take them down, and they'd reemerge behind the smoke with arrows sticking out of their rotting skin. But the defenders sometimes scored a lucky hit, striking at a vital spot or dealing too much damage to be ignored.

When that happened, the hound would whimper for a second before its body bulged, ballooned, and finally exploded in a shower of hissing entrails and disgusting liquids. Everything in the blast radius turned black.

"Shit, are they coming for me?" Rowan asked when he noticed that the hounds were focused on a single point in the wall. Him.

Bron confirmed it a second later with his next set of commands. "They're coming for our hero. Protect him. Make sure none of the monsters get to the hero."

Despite Bron and the defenders' best efforts, the hounds were fast. They zipped their way forward through the barrages and were soon just a couple hundred paces away from the wall. Rowan decided to play things safe. He popped the cork on the potion Olivia had given him, quickly throwing back the brownish liquid while trying not to think about how the potion was made.

If nothing else, the potion was fast-acting. An overwhelming feeling of strength surged through the spot in his chest he'd come to associate with his deck. His body creaked as it spread throughout him, and every part of him changed. His senses surged in power. His muscles coiled and tensed. Even the sensation of his mana pool doubled in intensity.

He checked and found that the increase rounded up, giving him an extra eight in all his stats.

Suddenly, the monsters' breakneck advance was something his eyes could track, and a smirk played across his lips. He took a step forward, trying to get a better look at everything.

Of course, that's when the alchemist cruelly smacked him in the head.

"If you die because of potion madness, I swear I'm going to find a way to resurrect you and then turn you into the royal jester," Olivia hissed. "They're coming for you. Stay in the back."

As the hounds came within a couple dozen steps of the wall, Bron ordered most of the defenders back. The soldiers and defenders who stayed had an air of toughness to them. *These guys are Uncommons. I would bet an arm on it.*

The wall that had given so much trouble to the monster horde yesterday did almost nothing to stop the Rotsworn Chargers. They either leaped straight for the battlements or scrambled up the wall like it was level ground.

In the back of his mind, Rowan knew that his confidence was probably the potion madness that Olivia described. But he felt unstoppable. Putting his strength to the test, he surged forward, relying on his boosted stats to empower his strikes in a way he never could before. A thrust of his spear *nailed* one of the hounds back down to the ground. Another hound tried to bite away the spear, but **Contortionist's Physique** helped him lean backward, out of the hound's range. He used the rebound to swipe the hound away.

Olivia wasn't wasting time, either. As soon as the enemies had drawn near enough, her tried-and-true strategy of hurling potions was employed again. The explosions were notably bigger, which translated into more monsters getting consumed in blasts and spaces where other hounds avoided.

Both of them paled in comparison to Bron. Rowan had never seen the officer fight without his men, but apparently Bron was just as ferocious fighting by himself. He used a long sword that glowed in a light blue. It wasn't exactly like Olivia's **Honed Mana Edge** card, but when Bron sliced through a hound unfortunate enough to get caught by him, the sword emitted a crescent blast of mana that left the other hounds scrambling.

For just a moment, the monsters' assault actually faltered in the face of Bron's might. Then they made him the priority target as they renewed their attack.

As the battle raged, Rowan expected his body to falter. It didn't happen. If anything, he was only starting to find his rhythm. For once, he had to adjust to fighting the hounds, given their tendency to bite at his spear and the desire to not take a corpse explosion to the face. Instead of doing thrusts like the baron had taught, Rowan began batting the monsters away with furious swipes of his spear.

For once, he felt like a hero. For once, he was *in control*.

Off to his left, Rowan heard a wet explosion, a bit too close for comfort. Taking a few steps back, Rowan risked a glance, only for his stomach to turn.

A mercenary had been showered in the monster's pieces, and wherever his skin had been stained, boils and lesions were breaking out. He tried to wipe away the monster's fluids, but it did him no good. In a matter of moments, his entire body was deformed, and he was left gurgling on the ground, somehow still alive.

One of his companions rushed to help him, potion in hand. Before he could even try to apply it, the man stilled.

And then the body exploded in a shower of gore.

Bron cursed. "It's a chain skill. Make distance. Don't try to help them."

But Rowan watched as people who had been splashed were tottering toward their allies, begging for help. The good news was that those hit by the second explosion didn't immediately explode themselves, but in the chaos of battle, no one wanted to take a chance, forming a second line against both monsters and those infected.

"I've got a plan," Olivia yelled, her voice barely audible above the fray. Rowan closed the distance and stood by her. "I need help." She scanned the wall frantically and located the person she was looking for. "You, big shield. Come this way!"

To their right, in an area which was still clear of exploding corpses and puss, stood the beast-folk duo, doing a remarkable job of keeping the wall clear.

But Olivia's words were lost to the wind. Rowan picked up the mantle, yelling as much as his lungs would allow. "Beast folk. Gather to me!"

That got their attention. The two of them exchanged a look and started to fight their way over. Rowan helped, batting as many of the hounds back down the wall as he could. The boost in dexterity gave him an almost superhuman level of control over his body. Each move flowed into the next, and somehow, he kept up with the rushing menaces.

When he met up with the two beast folk, things became much simpler. The shield bearer was an unconquerable bulwark. No matter what the hounds tried, they couldn't get past his defense. And the mage was doing work, too. Waves of miasma rose from around them, and the hounds caught in the fog would either slow down or start stumbling around aimlessly.

When they met back up with Olivia, she laid out her plan. "You have a taunt card? Right?" The shield bearer nodded. "Use it. Full power. I want as many of them focused on us as possible."

Instead of following the order, the shield bearer looked to Rowan. And trusting Olivia, Rowan nodded as if he was entirely sure that Olivia's plan would work. The shield bearer nodded back, planted his feet, and howled.

There was something primal in the sound. Something that woke up a feeling of violence and anger in Rowan's heart.

It took him a couple of moments to throw off the feeling, barely resisting the urge to skewer the man in front of him. For the monsters, their reactions were a thousand times more exaggerated.

Almost every single one of them paused in their fights and turned their eyes toward the shield bearer. And then they came.

A violet-colored miasma rose around them, staggering a couple of the early hounds. But as more and more of them sprinted into the fog, the effects seemed to diminish. Rowan did his best to spear as many of them as possible, but they just kept coming.

"Buy me as much time as you can," Olivia yelled at the center of their formation. Rowan was a mere beginner when it came to mana, barely able to use it with his cards. But even he could feel the storm brewing inside Olivia. It was like she was a tempest, powerful and slow.

Thankfully, the shield bearer could take as much as he could dish. With more than half of the monsters trying to bite and claw their way in, he managed to keep most of them at bay with thunderous charges and heavy swipes. When the hounds tried to circle around him, Rowan was there with his spear, finally thrusting like the baron had taught him.

Even though the teamwork between the beast folk and Rowan was solid, they still found themselves being pushed back. Soon, they were at the back of the wall, surrounded by the hounds on all three sides.

That's when Olivia chose to strike.

All the mana inside her exploded outward. Everywhere it went, ice formed. Rowan shuddered, a gasp ripping its way out of his lungs. The cold gripped him, making his weapon slick, fingers numb, and armor uncomfortably stiff.

But that was nothing compared to what the hounds were going through. As the mana swept over them, cracking sounds rang out. They stiffened as the ice spread upward from their feet. It went to their chests, tails, and eventually heads. By the time Rowan was back in control of his body, the hounds were ice sculptures.

For a tense moment, Rowan still expected the dead creatures to explode. When they didn't, he released a tense breath he didn't realize he was holding, and together with the others, he knocked as many of the now-stiff hounds down the wall as he could. The sound that the iced Rotsworn Chargers made as they shattered at the bottom was like music to his ears.

A couple hounds had survived Olivia's artificial ice age, but Bron made short work of them, blitzing through and slicing them in half while also kicking their remains off the wall before they could explode.

When all that was done, Rowan turned back to see Olivia leaning against the wood. Her face was paler than he had ever seen it but she dug through her pouch and swallowed down more mana potions.

"You okay?" Rowan asked.

Before Olivia could answer, the same dreadful voice sounded again. "That was entertaining, little morsels. Can you repeat that performance?"

Rowan wasn't completely positive, but he thought that the demon's speech was improving. It was like it hadn't spoken for centuries, and now it was relearning how to use its voice. He whipped around and looked at the demon, only to see the forest begin to shake, teeter, and then collapse. Slowly, three gargantuan shapes revealed themselves, breaking past the tree line.

Where Rowan could at least somewhat understand the monsters until now, these new beasts were something else entirely. They were vaguely humanoid, but their massive arms dragged on the ground, while their hands were tipped by sickle-like talons.

They weren't giants, though. Unless giants were supposed to be covered in long black fur that looked more like wires than any sort of hair. Whenever they moved, the fur produced metallic grinding noises, filling the air with uncomfortable screeching.

The worst part about these monsters were their faces, bunched-up things that were dominated by a giant mouth. Almost all their jaws were left hanging open, showing hundreds of pointed teeth.

Even as others faltered, Olivia was on point, immediately taking action again.

**[Diseased Titanic Mauler]**
**Level 37**

STR: 43
VIT: 58
DEX: 18
PER: 5
INT: 2
WIS: 3

Deck (5/5):
[Heart] Demonic Breeding (Rare)
Plague Incubator (Uncommon, Passive)
Titanic Physique (Uncommon, Passive)
Mauling Strike (Uncommon, Active)
Diseased Breath (Uncommon, Active)

# CHAPTER FIFTEEN

# Rotflower Puppets

Rowan felt queasy. The maulers almost came up to the height of the wall, and even if their gait was lumbering, their speed was deceptively fast. They had the same dexterity score as him, and Rowan knew just how much having eighteen points in dexterity meant.

"We need to meet them out there," Bron declared, walking toward the edge of the wall without hesitation. "If they destroy the wall, we're dead, even if we survive this battle."

Then he stepped off. Sounds of combat immediately rang out, and the last few Rotsworn Charger stragglers at the foot of the wall were reduced to bits in record time. The two beast folk didn't hesitate to jump off the wall, either. Most of the soldiers followed their officer's lead while the mercenaries held back.

"I don't suppose I can get a ride down?" Olivia asked Rowan. "All my boosts are applied to mana for better effect."

Briefly, Rowan wondered if everyone around him had just gone crazy. But when the wall jumpers somehow made it to the bottom without breaking their legs, he realized that he might have underestimated the effect that stats had. He shook his head, gave Olivia a smile, and swept her off her feet. The little "eep" she made when they jumped surprised him more than the ease with which he landed.

Olivia handed him a new potion that he downed without hesitation. Strength flowed through him. Specifically, his strength stat went up by five points. Rowan raised his spear. It was featherlight. Riding off that high, Rowan decided that he could finally be the hero that everyone thought he was. He focused on the mauler to his left and charged.

Rowan could hear curses and shouts behind him, but he forgot all that as the wind blew through his hair. There was still quite a bit of distance left between him and the monster he'd chosen. That meant that his **Relentless Advance** had all the time in the world to ramp up.

As the card pulled on his mana, Rowan felt the process like never before. The increased mental stats meant that he could *tell* what the mana was doing, feel it coursing through and out of his body. For the first time, he tried to help it along, to manipulate and urge it to be more effective.

His speed kicked up by another notch as the mauler was drawing closer.

His Heart Card seemed more effective, too. The familiar feeling of forced calm was enhanced, structuring his thoughts in a simple sequence of what he needed to accomplish.

As Rowan looked at the mauler, he could almost read the monster. It was no longer advancing and instead gearing up for a strike with its clawed hand. **Mauling Strike**, if Rowan was forced to guess.

This meant that its armpit was exposed, a stretch of flesh where the monster's fur was thinner, almost nonexistent.

Rowan pushed on **Relentless Advance** even more, accelerating away from the monster's impending blow, and used **Contortionist's Physique** to slide onto his knees and slip perilously close to its arm. Most of his momentum was invested in his spear, the tip of it blazing blue with mana, aiming straight for the target Rowan had picked out a couple moments ago.

At the last possible moment, Rowan came back to his senses and remembered what Olivia had said about potion madness. What he was doing was downright mad. It was too late to pull out of his move now, but there was just enough time for him to hesitate, and instead of thrusting into the monster, Rowan pulled the spear in a slice, cutting through the hard muscle.

A shower of sickly-green blood nearly hit Rowan as the mauler's limb went limp. He dodged only by his continued momentum. His knees paid the price, but they were still strong enough to support his weight when he sprang to his feet.

Behind him, the monster roared out in anger, and Rowan turned just in time to see it grip its own arm and tear it away.

Wielding its arm like a cudgel, the mauler lumbered toward Rowan and swung the amputated limb by the wrist. This made drops of its blood rain everywhere, forcing Rowan to backpedal in fear. If the blood had the hounds' corpse-explosion properties, then it'd be game over before he knew it.

For a brief moment, Rowan caught sight of the other two maulers already in combat and blocking the others from supporting him. Beyond them, there was the village—the walls that had been battered over the last few days and the villagers who stuck their heads out to watch the battle. These were the people he was fighting for.

*This is real life.*

Rowan's confidence returned to him. This time, it wasn't the reckless variety that the potions brought on. Rather, this was the knowledge that if he could survive for long enough, the victory was theirs.

"Come here, you big brute!" Rowan yelled at the mauler. Then he charged again.

This time, he didn't engage his cards, choosing to use his dexterity to carry him forward. The mauler's eyes lit up with glee and it prepared to bludgeon him to death with its own limb. When it tilted backward the slightest amount, Rowan burned all three of his cards.

He used **Relentless Advance** to gain a spurt of speed, **Contortionist's Physique** to tilt his angle, and poured as much mana as possible into his spear tip with **Empowered Thrust**. But instead of stabbing forward, Rowan took aim and threw the spear right at the thing's face.

Throwing a spear wasn't something he had tried before. The baron had warned that such a move should be a desperation attempt, one that would leave him defenseless. More than that, he hadn't used **Empowered Thrust** with a spear that had left his hands. Mana began to pour out of Rowan, keeping his connection with the spear alive for just a moment longer.

And that moment was all he needed. The spear, with the full power of Rowan, who now had almost twenty-five points in strength, sailed forward and met the monster's eye. And it didn't stop. The spear came out the other end of its skull, quivering and burning blue for a fraction of a second longer before petering out.

Rowan slowed down and watched as a blank expression slid over the monster's features. Only when the mauler finally toppled backward and landed on the ground with a thump did Rowan start moving again.

He found his spear, cleaned it of the blood by using a bit more mana, and sprinted back toward the others.

Bron had demolished his mauler even faster than Rowan had, neatly chopping the massive monster into different blocks. And the combined efforts of everyone else had taken down the last monster. Despite their giant size, it seemed that the maulers weren't exactly meant for small-scale engagements.

Rowan took a quick glance at his mana and grimaced.

**Mana: 27/100**

"Have a mana potion to spare?" Rowan asked as he fell in by Olivia's side, and had one practically shoved into his chest.

"Don't do something that reckless again," Olivia said, eyes trained on the demon that was content to keep standing there.

"I'll try." Rowan used his teeth to awkwardly unplug the potion.

"Such amusing morsels. Such reckless morsels. You draw near of your own accord. Yes, come closer. Let me see you," the demon said. Its voice seemed to echo, and the words overlapped on each other.

Rowan glanced around and saw grim faces on everyone around. The soldiers lined up behind Bron while the two beast folk made their way to Olivia.

There weren't any grand speeches or clever quips as the group began moving toward the demon. Everyone knew their job: They had to fight. There was no other choice.

If Rowan had been at the top of the wall, he might have recognized what was happening. It was exactly like the painting he had seen in the palace, a group of souls marching toward the darkness because that was the right thing to do.

As it was, he was right in the middle of the group. The first couple hundred paces were easy, as everyone stayed fairly close together while the demon simply watched. But when they were about a hundred paces away, Rowan began to have trouble breathing and his legs felt heavier than ever before.

Rowan looked around to find that most of the group was slowing down. Only Bron was completely fine.

*There's some kind of aura that higher classes give off,* Rowan concluded. As the only Common-tier combatant in the group, he was finally feeling the limitations of his class. There was only a slight tinge of adrenaline against Uncommons, but he now felt a brew of unease, doubt, and fear as he got closer to his enemy.

Still, Rowan convinced himself that he would be okay. *I'm a hero. I just killed a giant. The green blood on my spear is proof that we'll win.*

"Divine morsel. So kind of you to come. Yes, so very kind," the demon whispered, its lips still refusing to move.

Rowan wondered if forcing it to scream would finally do the trick.

"Be ready for any tricks. Demons do not fight fair," Bron warned.

That made the demon chuckle, and it shifted its entire torso so its face was pointing at Bron. "Such unkind words. I will have such fun devouring your flesh. Well, why have you not struck yet, Blade? Do you wait for your master's leave?"

The demon's whispers were like feathers that tickled Rowan's ear, making him shudder. Bron, however, shrugged off the comment as he pulled out a normal-looking potion, knocked off the cap, and downed it. Before the demon could speak, Bron's sword lit up with mana, and he was suddenly *there*, striking at one of the demon's many limbs.

Metal met flesh in a shower of sparks, and the demon cackled as its limbs suddenly surged toward the swordsman. Seeing them up close, Rowan noticed dozens of different joints on each limb. They bent and twisted every which way, coming at Bron from a variety of unexpected angles.

Somehow, Bron became superhuman. The sword was everywhere, blocking, countering, and parrying the blows from the limbs. As the two of them fought, the rest of the group spread out, trying to find weaknesses in the demon.

Rowan was the first to try something. He pushed down the fear in his heart and kicked off the ground, making full use of **Relentless Advance** to add as much power to his blow as possible.

The others added their own power to the attack. A rush of miasma clung to the tip of his spear, and when the demon tried to bat Rowan away with one of its limbs, the shield bearer was there, tanking the hit.

When Rowan's thrust finally reached its mark, it actually sank into demon flesh, causing the monster to flinch slightly.

The tiny distraction was enough to give Bron his opportunity, and his sword's mana shroud intensified as he began slicing.

Two of the demon's arms tumbled to the ground, the stumps spraying black ichor that everyone struggled to avoid. A couple of drops landed on Rowan's shoulder, and his eye twitched when he saw the leather sizzle in response. Luckily, the liquid wasn't acidic enough to completely burn through his armor before its effects ran out.

*Next time I fight, I'm finding a nice, normal monster that doesn't have diseases and acid for blood.*

Still, the demon's floundering provided Olivia with a stationary target, and she was ready to show off. The potion that impacted the demon's hide didn't burst into flames. Instead, miniature storms of electricity kicked up, ravaging the creature's flesh and leaving charred trails in its gray-purple skin.

The shield bearer surged forward again, protecting against all harm by a halo-like aura, and bashed his shield against the demon.

Shockingly, the thing actually swayed, almost losing balance before its back pair of arms stabilized it against the ground.

The soldiers swarmed forward, and Rowan was secretly glad to be outnumbering the enemy for once. The demon's limbs flailed, pushing back the soldiers. Once again, Bron was the only one who could keep up with the demon.

Half of the soldiers were slow in the retreat. And while the blood of the demon was only slightly acidic, the claws at the end of its limbs were dripping with green poison. It swung one of its limbs at the soldiers, letting loose a couple drops of deadly fluid. Those drops ate a hole through everything that they touched, whether it was metal, wood, or human. At least a quarter of the soldiers collapsed, either dead or injured so seriously that they were out of the fight.

"Damn demon!" Bron roared when he saw his men falling. He redoubled his efforts, only to be repelled by the demon's limbs, which had taken on a black shine. When they clashed with Bron's blade, the black corroded the sword's blue haze.

Bron glanced at his blade and canceled and reapplied the card. The new blue glow didn't have any lingering black spots, but Bron's face stayed grim.

Rowan found himself stuck. The demon's limbs were now whipping all around, leaving no room for him to try an attack. The other soldiers hurled themselves into suicide attacks, only to score shallow cuts that healed back in moments.

Olivia, at least, was doing work. She never seemed to run out of potions, peppering the demon with bottles of lightning, ice, and flame. She never used the same potion twice, and despite the demon's whips, she always found the right angle to sneak her projectile through.

They were in a stalemate. The demon couldn't defeat Bron and get at the weaker humans, and no one could deal a decisive strike to the demon. It seemed like it would be a war of attrition, and with the numbers on their side, Rowan was certain they could wear the thing down.

After a few minutes of fighting, the demon seemed to realize the same thing. It tensed its legs and launched itself at the mage beast folk, who stood in the back.

Rowan could do little more than take potshots at the thing as it sailed over their heads, and Bron took the chance to charge a massive blade slash, severing another one of its limbs.

It was the shield bearer who came to his companion's rescue. His shield gave a blinding flash of green light and the demon was frozen in midair for a second. Then, like being sucked by a magnet, it began to fly toward the shield bearer.

It landed heavily on the shield, almost flattening the beast folk behind. Using the opportunity, the demon swung its limbs out, digging at the shield bearer while still stuck to the shield.

"Help him!" Bron called as he rushed forward first. His sword created a deep gash on the demon's back, and Olivia's flames charred another section of its skin. Even with all that, the monster moved like nothing had happened and hopped to the side, gearing up for another pass at them.

Rowan readied his spear for an attack when a voice wormed its way into his ear. "Wait, not yet. Its attention is being drawn by the others. Stay back."

For a second, Rowan thought that it was the demon trying to divide them. A shroud of black smoke around him quickly dispelled that notion. He looked back and caught the eye of the mage beast folk. Around him, the other soldiers, all holding spears, also held back with their own black clouds.

"I'll create an opening. Use it," the voice said.

Rowan tensed his muscles and readied himself to perform his skill combo.

The opening ended up being in the form of a giant wave of black smoke that congealed into a cackling, twitching skull. It rushed forward and slammed into the demon, freezing it in place.

Rowan pushed as much mana as he could into every single one of his cards. The others also took advantage of the opportunity. The other soldiers stabbed with Rowan, charging forward in unison. Bron launched himself into the air, the blue glow on his sword intensifying before the blade carved right through the demon's head, obliterating everything above its jaw.

When the monster was still twitching after all that, the shield bearer spun his shield, turning it into a giant drill that crushed through its limbs and caused a deluge of slush-like black ichor to spill out of its torso. And Olivia delivered the final blow. She tossed an unusually large vial at the center of the demon. When the potion crashed against the demon, everywhere the liquid touched immediately turned into stone that started cracking and fracturing.

For a few long moments, the only thing Rowan could hear was the thundering of his own heart as he readied a second combo. Finally, the demon teetered side to side, then collapsed in the puddle of its own blood, lying still.

"Is that it? Did we get it?" One of the soldiers finally broke the silence, inching closer to the demon and nudging it with his foot.

"Wait, don't! We didn't get the experience yet!" Bron shouted.

The demon *screamed*.

It was unlike any of the sounds it had made before. The sheer force of its voice lifted the soldier into the air like a rag doll. Rowan was thrown backward right into Olivia's arms, and the two tumbled to the ground in a heap.

Only Bron and the mage beast folk kept their footing, the latter due to distance and Bron due to sheer power and skill.

The demon's flesh rippled, pulsing, and then *wiggled*. All the damage they did sloughed off its body along with chunks of quivering flesh. New limbs burst out of its stumps, thumping into the ground and righting the creature once more.

Even the severed head was bubbling, flesh reaching upward and regrowing once more into the expressionless face.

The only good news of all this was that the demon was diminished. Its healing came at the cost of its bulk, and the thing was slimmer now, smaller. That seemed almost trivial compared to the fact that the monster had just come back from the dead.

"Pathetic fool. You take my kindness for permission to show insolence. You will pay, and I will have my meal, no matter what it takes," the demon spat.

Strips of flesh began peeling away from the demon's body, revealing a grotesque mix of petals lined by thorns. Black sludge spilled down from the monster as its limbs began to take shape as vines around the petals.

"Rotflower," Bron called out as he waved everyone back.

"Ah yes, it's been decades since someone called me by my proper name," the demon replied, finally showing a smile. "For that, you get to watch your friends die first."

As the Rotflower spoke, its body kept transforming. From the chest up, Rowan could still imagine the monster as some kind of person. Below that were four ridges of bone and cartilage, while the torso-turned-petals splayed out like some kind of diseased flower. At the center of it all was a heart. A sick, infested-looking thing that somehow still functioned. Each time it pulsed, black sludge bulged through the many, many blood vessels that led away from it, cycling into the vines and petals.

Honestly, Rowan wanted to just turn away, run, and scrub the thing from his memory.

*This is real life. I can't run when things get hard.*

The Rotflower took a step forward and everyone, including Bron, flinched back a couple of steps. It laughed. "Here's a peek at what you'll become once I'm through with you."

The vines shot out and attached themselves to four of the downed soldiers. A couple moments later, the previously dead men stood back up. Rowan saw that their eyes were unfocused and empty, and their bodies moved more like marionettes than living creatures. They moaned in unison, a tortured, unearthly sound, and when their mouths opened, Rowan wanted to gag.

At the back of their throats, he spotted a flowerlike black growth, its roots spreading down and up into the soldiers' bodies.

"No, no more."

"It hurts."

"Kill me, kill me, kill me."

"It's in my brain, in my chest, in my heart."

The reanimated soldiers began to cry for help, straddling the line between being alive and dead.

For the first time since Rowan had known the man, Bron faltered. His face paled as his feet stumbled backward.

"We can't fight like this," Olivia whispered.

"Give up the struggle," the demon said softly. It watched as panic rippled through the soldiers who saw their dead friends stumbling forward. "Your outcome was already determined when you came to fight me instead of running like morsels should."

Rowan could see the group's morale flagging. If the demon could turn the dead into his allies, then the war of attrition was flipped against them. There was a chance that the reanimation was a onetime thing, but Rowan couldn't count on that.

"Send the men back," Rowan suggested. Bron looked at Rowan like he had lost his mind. "They can't fight against their friends. And anyone who dies to the demon can be turned against us. Send them back."

"Retreat. Pull back," Bron commanded, taking Rowan's advice. To their credit, the remaining soldiers didn't just cut and run. They pulled back in an orderly fashion.

"Don't go too far, my morsels," the demon hissed. The smile was still plastered on its face. "I'll find you all soon enough."

With the four resurrected soldiers, it was five against five. But Rowan found a way through the problem by doing the thing that heroes do best.

"I'll take care of the undead," Rowan said as he moved away from the group. "Focus on the demon."

# CHAPTER SIXTEEN

# Burning Bright

The others didn't protest Rowan's decision. Olivia made unhappy noises, but even she could see that Rowan fighting the undead gave them the best shot of winning. And if they lost, then it didn't matter whether Rowan was safe or not. They'd all be dead.

"Is this a battle tactic?" the demon taunted.

"A strategy to win," Rowan retorted.

"Very well. Very well," the demon said. After a silent command, the undead soldiers stepped to the side. "You against my four. And I'll face your four. Let's see who wins."

Bron charged forward, the shield bearer at his side. Olivia and the mage started peppering the demon with their own attacks. And Rowan was now alone. Or rather, he was facing down four undead soldiers that were still moaning about their pain.

The soldiers had been around the same strength as him while alive, and Rowan was willing to make the risky bet that he was now stronger with the potion on his side. The question now was whether the reanimation process gave them some kind of buff and whether his potion would last long enough that he either won against them or the others could take down the demon.

The soldiers seemed content to stand idle while their master battled for his life. Rowan wasn't about to change that. He risked a quick glance at his system screen to check the leftover potion duration and was shocked to find that he had another twenty-six minutes left. He was expecting to be down to the last few minutes of the potion. The last thirty-four minutes had been the slowest time he'd ever experienced.

The four soldiers were spear wielders, like Rowan and it took them a few seconds to re-arm themselves. But once that was done, the break was over. They began charging forward.

"Here goes nothing," Rowan muttered. He engaged his cards.

Seconds into his charge, he was forced to abort and drop to the ground when a spear whizzed inches above his head. Apparently, the undead soldiers didn't have any qualms about throwing their only weapons.

*Death probably does that to a person.*

A swift roll to the left got Rowan clear of two spears that stabbed into the spot he'd previously occupied, and he swiped the shaft of his spear against the legs of the last soldier.

The crack of bones was loud and unmistakable, and the man wobbled, pitching forward. A normal person would have been distracted by the pain of their leg snapping. But this was an undead soldier. The man stabbed forward while falling to the ground and managed to open a cut on Rowan's side.

"Shit," Rowan cursed as he scrambled back. He knocked into something that felt like a wall but evidently wasn't, judging by the fact that the wall sprouted two arms that locked him in place. Rowan's heart was beating so fast that his chest hurt. He slammed his legs against the ground, generating enough momentum to break free.

A fair distance away from the undead, Rowan saw that it was the fourth soldier that had caught him. Even though they were dead, it seemed that the soldiers retained some part of their teamwork. It was going to be a tough brawl.

As the second round of the fight began, Rowan noticed one of the soldiers was slower than the others. *I broke that guy's legs.*

Rowan used his two movement cards to their fullest extent to dodge away from the three too-healthy soldiers and found an opening. Inspired by what he'd seen before their battle started, Rowan stabbed his spear up, aiming right for the back of the man's throat.

It worked. There was an unpleasant squelching noise, but the soldier collapsed, no longer an undead terror.

Much of Rowan's nervousness calmed down. Somehow, the dead bodies were pushed well beyond death and seemed possessed by endless vitality. But they could be killed. That was the most important part.

The kill seemed to scare the other three soldiers. They turned around to face Rowan but no longer charged forward.

Rowan waited for a second before he realized why.

The demon was struggling. Rowan wasn't sure what he'd expected from the others, but it definitely wasn't for Bron to be on fire. Flames lined his entire body, and his eyes burned particularly bright. In the officer's hand was an empty potion bottle.

*Potion of Heroic Might. Bron drank it,* Rowan realized with a start. If the lesser-might potion had almost overwhelmed his mind, he could imagine what the heroic-might version would do to Bron.

Bron blurred, and then his sword was chopping through vines. The demon wasn't an easy target, and the speed of its vines kicked up a notch, a black glow overtaking its entire form. But it was getting whittled down. Each time Bron swung his sword, the demon had to sacrifice a vine or petal to stay alive. Even with regeneration, it was becoming smaller and smaller.

The three soldiers began running toward the demon. Sensing the opportunity, Rowan used **Relentless Advance** and speared them in their napes. It almost felt like cheating to win the way he did. But there was nothing fair in war.

On the other side, the demon was growing thinner, spindlier, but also faster and more desperate. The threat to its life was real now, and it realized that as its smile changed into a snarling expression. In spite of that, Bron was winning. His sword only picked up in speed and ferocity, and the protective glow of whatever card the demon was using was doing less and less.

Bron was paying his own price. The flames were also consuming him. His body was a crimson red, and bits were starting to disappear. It was only a matter of time before there wasn't enough of him left to keep fighting.

Rowan could almost pin down the exact moment the demon realized that, and its combat style rapidly grew more defensive.

But Bron wasn't fighting alone.

Rowan hefted his spear, taking aim. The weapon was bulky, the distance he was aiming it over much longer than last time, and it was definitely not designed to be thrown. He still chucked it forward. While he didn't hit the skull that he was aiming for, the glowing spear obliterated the lower parts of the demon's jaw.

"Its heart!" Olivia yelled. "It only protects that spot."

The mage chose that moment to release another massive miasma skull. It did far less than before and only slightly slowed the demon. But it was enough for the shield bearer to spin up another drill attack that went through the demon's petals and almost reached its main body. Olivia used the opportunity to chuck one of her most destructive potions to date. Ironically, it didn't explode. Rather, it sprayed a viscous, tar-like substance all over the demon. When Bron attacked again, the demon was suddenly an inferno, too.

The damage was too much. The demon focused on regenerating its essential parts, which left a path free for Bron to take a solid hit at the thing. He rushed forward and swung at its core. The blade severed the demon's upper body from its lower plant body. Its human half thudded onto the ground, reduced to just a smoking skeleton with a corrupted heart pumping black ichor onto the ground.

The spray of blood that followed the kill left everyone but Bron scrambling for cover. He simply stood there as his flames purified the liquid out of existence. Then the man approached the downed demon, lifted his foot, and stomped.

Somewhere, in the back of his mind, Rowan heard his system chime at him.

That didn't matter much when the fight wasn't over just yet. Bron was *still* burning away, the fire now reaching down to his bones. He turned back to the group with his sword still bright.

*Oh god, he has potion madness*, Rowan thought. There was no way they could fight Bron. Outside of the man's new strength, it felt wrong to turn their weapons against a friend.

Olivia seemed to expect this, rushing toward Bron with a potion in hand.

"Here. Take this, quickly."

Bron took the opened flask and drank the potion without question. When nothing happened for a few seconds, his face twisted in a mask of rage. He went to open his mouth, but the moment he did, his eyes bulged.

Bron doubled over, heaving and retching. A river of molten stars ran out of his mouth and pooled on the ground. Rowan could do nothing but stare as far more of the material, whatever it was, came out of the man than should have been physically possible.

The stars were also doing all kinds of odd things to the ground.

Plant life suddenly shot up, growing at an incredibly accelerated rate. Flowers, grass, even a tree came to life. In moments, there was a tiny forest on that one patch of land. The magical discharge also had the complete opposite effect on the demon's remains. It melted them into nothingness, eradicating its taint from the land more thoroughly than they could ever have managed.

Finally, the flames died down around Bron and his heaving stopped. He collapsed to the ground, in a puddle of the molten stars. Luckily, they didn't seem to burn away at him.

"We need to get back to the village," Olivia said as she looked around at the forest. The two beast folk mercenaries agreed with her.

As gently as he could, Rowan slung the man on his shoulder. He really doubted that he could be gentle enough with someone who was half burned to death, but it felt right for him to be the one carrying the officer.

The trek back felt impossible. The moment they'd wrapped up the battle properly, a bone-deep weariness had started to drag at Rowan's body. His strength felt like a dry well, too, sputtering and struggling to sustain him.

About halfway back to the village, Rowan was too tired to be surprised when the ground suddenly rushed up to meet him.

Olivia sighed as she looked at Rowan, facedown on the ground. Judging by how quickly he'd fainted, the potion had likely run its course.

"You two better not pass out and leave me to carry all of you," Olivia grumbled.

The shield bearer had already picked up Bron from Rowan's exhausted shoulder, holding the officer on top of his shield. "You're the boss, boss."

"So that's the hero?" the mage beast folk asked.

"That's him," Olivia said.

"He's brave," the shield bearer said.

"That he is." Olivia smiled. There was no part of Rowan that resembled a hero as he lay in the mud. She shrugged and plopped down next to him. "I'll protect him. Could you ask the others to come out and help?"

"Will do, boss," the mage said.

Soon, it was just Olivia and Rowan in the middle of the field. She sighed and took out a few exploding potions as a precaution. Then, on second thought, she pulled Rowan so that he was lying on his back and glared down at his face, willing him to wake up. When that failed, she brushed some of the hair out of his face, flicking his forehead as she went.

"I thought we said no more recklessness," Olivia hissed. Predictably, she didn't get an answer. "Honestly, what am I supposed to do with you?"

By all accounts, Rowan's contribution to the death of a Rare-tier demon when he was just a Common class was a heroic feat.

Unfortunately, he didn't feel very heroic at all when consciousness finally returned to him and he found himself shifting hesitantly under comfortable covers. Despite how comfortable the bed was, he felt positively wrung out and broken. Olivia hadn't been joking when she described the side effects of messing with potions that boost stats.

The thought of Olivia finally forced him to groan in acceptance of the fact he was awake and tackle the day. With great reluctance, the hero forced his eyes open and sat up in bed.

Only to immediately spot a man standing by the door of his room.

"Ah, hello?" the young man ventured, giving a shy wave.

Rowan blinked and tilted his head a little. He really shouldn't have, but he blurted out the very first thing that came to mind. "Am I supposed to fear for my virtue?"

The blush that took over the young man's face was the deepest crimson he'd ever seen on a person before. He broke out into stutters, then finally managed to compose himself enough to reply. "No, sir. Lady Sutton ordered me to stand guard here."

"Right there? On the inside of the door, rather than in front?" Rowan asked, still not over the weirdness of the moment.

"Yes, sir. She said that if you try to do anything stupid, I'm supposed to literally sit on top of you until she comes around to check on you."

That did sound an awful lot like Olivia. And it wasn't like the poor guy was doing anything wrong.

"How long have I been asleep?" Rowan asked. "What happened after I, well, passed out?"

"Lady Sutton had us move you here. It hasn't been that long, really."

"Lady Sutton? As in Camilla Sutton?" Rowan interrupted, hopeful that the baron had somehow arrived.

"Sorry. We've been addressing Miss Olivia Sutton as Lady Sutton since the lady isn't here," the young man replied in a single breath. "Hero Rowan, you slept throughout the night, and it's afternoon now, but you can still get some hot food brought up, if you'd like."

Rowan's stomach chose that exact moment to gurgle loudly, and hunger gnawed at him with a startling intensity.

"You know what? Food sounds like a great idea," Rowan muttered, starting to wiggle out of bed.

"Sir?" The young man hesitated but still dutifully stepped forward. "I'm sorry, but I'm under orders not to let you out of bed. It was explicitly listed as one of the 'dumb things he might try' from Lady Sutton."

Rowan paused, squinting at the man. On the one hand, he really didn't like being ordered to bed rest. It seemed a lot like when the king had confined him to a single room back in the palace. But on the other hand, he was pretty sure that he was safe and that his guard could singlehandedly wrestle him into submission at the moment.

"And did Olivia say anything about when she'd be showing up to check on me?" Rowan grumbled, collapsing back onto the mattress.

"Sir, she's been doing that every few hours. She's been busy getting everyone organized and seeing to the repair of our defenses. With Lieutenant Bron out of commission, she's the highest-ranked officer that we've currently got."

"Bron's not up yet? How is he?" Rowan asked. Somehow, he couldn't really imagine the forceful officer just passing away in his sleep, but the man had been in bad shape even after downing Olivia's potion.

"He still hasn't woken up." The guard's voice was quiet now, reserved. "We don't have real healers out here. Recovery might take a while, but everyone's hopeful he'll pull through."

That, at least, was good. Rowan wasn't sure how he would ever repay the man for the risk he took so they could kill the demon, but he would figure something out.

"Okay, then. If I can't get out of bed and you can't leave this room, could you please ask someone to bring us some food?" Rowan said.

The young guard nodded, popped his head out the door, and shouted someone's name. Loud footsteps preceded a short conversation, but Rowan mostly tuned all of it out.

The system had been there since he woke up but it was now positively blaring in an attempt to catch his attention. The sensation was like someone constantly poking the back of his head. So, with a flex of his will, Rowan let the system windows unfurl.

**Congratulations!**
**You have contributed to the demise of a significantly stronger foe,**
**boosting your loot and experience gain from the battle.**

**Battle Results**

**EXP:**
**[Rotflower Cambion] +12,640**
**[Rotsworn Charger] +250**
**[Rotsworn Charger] +220**

**. . .**

**[Diseased Titanic Mauler] +450 x 2**
**[Rotflower Puppet] +125 x 4**
**ERROR!**
**Maximum experience for tier reached. Choose an upgrade for**
**your class to continue your ascent.**

**Loot:**
**153x cards in Party Loot Inventory**

**Congratulations!**
**You have completed your Common-tier progression, reaching**
**the maximum level (20) of your current class. View class**
**advancement options?**

Rowan stared. And then stared some more.

Just a day ago, he'd just hit level twelve and was preparing for a slog through the remaining eight levels. Now, the system was already bothering him to pick an Uncommon class already.

He couldn't deny the draw of that thought. He knew what Olivia, the mercenaries, and other Uncommon combatants could do. It would be nice to experience that level of strength himself.

However, Olivia had very explicitly urged him not to be dumb. And diving into class selection while half-starved and still in pain would definitely be stupid.

And then it didn't matter. His food was delivered in record time, and he could scarcely contain himself when he saw it. The fare was nothing special—some roasted meat, a bowl of soup, lumpy-looking bread, and a healing potion to chase it all down, courtesy of Olivia. But the simple food tasted better than anything he'd put into his mouth in recent memory, hunger giving it a wonderful edge even over all the cuisine he'd tried back in the baron's home.

Or was that just his boosted perception stat?

Rowan couldn't deny that his sense of taste was boosted just as much as his other senses were. The tastes that danced over his tongue were rich and vibrant and it was like he could distinguish every single bit of flavor.

Unfortunately, that just meant that the taste of the potion was even more foul than he expected. Holding his nose, Rowan downed the entire bottle and found a message underneath the potion bottle.

*If I find you doing something reckless when I finally see you again, I will slam you into that bed myself.*
*—Your aggrieved party member*

Rowan chuckled, leaning over the side of the bed to look for his pack, then carefully folded the note and stashed it away.

There was no way he wasn't keeping it.

That done, he allowed himself a grin and made himself comfortable in the bed again. There were things that were reckless. And then there were things that were stupid. Rowan had done both, and somehow, he was still alive to tell the tale.

Would the fight have gone differently if he hadn't taken down one of the maulers on his own? Or fought the four undead soldiers so that the other could gang up on the demon? He would never know. But what he did know, the thing that he truly believed, was that they were better because of it.

As the sensation in the back of his head grew worse, Rowan convinced himself that maybe doing something stupid was the right way to go. It hadn't got him in trouble yet.

He hit that plus button and went browsing.

**Class evolution requirements met.**
**Classes available for selection:**
**Spearman Adept, Heavy Spear, Spear Champion, Standard Bearer, Spear Wall, Reckless Spear, Mystic Spear**

# CHAPTER SEVENTEEN

# Price of Recklessness

There were quite a few more class-upgrade options than Rowan had expected. From his experience choosing his first class, he knew these classes had been unlocked based on his past actions. This meant that no two people, unless they were trained and guided through battles in an identical manner, would get the exact same class-upgrade options.

*[Heavy Spear]. That's probably from me mishandling the spear and using it more as a bat than a proper spear. And [Spear Champion] sounds like a class that comes from besting other spear users. I guess the undead soldiers count?*

There was one option that was the basic upgrade path for the [Spearman] class—[Spearman Adept]. The baron had previously mentioned the class as something Rowan should take as a last resort. Usually, these basic classes were taken by those who limped their way up and gained experience through unorthodox methods.

Now that Rowan thought about it, a noble being force-fed experience by more experienced party members probably fell under that category. That not only limited a person's combat ability, but it also meant they usually had to settle for a class that was weaker than the others.

Or at least that's what Kayden had said. Apparently, a sign of noble status was how much information they had on classes. And the Suttons had kept track of optimal progressions for almost every class.

Rowan doubted that he could manage something more impressive than killing a Rare-tier demon. If that didn't land him a good class, nothing would. He first scrolled through [Spearman Adept] to understand what the baseline for the [Spearman] Uncommon advancement should look like.

**[Spearman Adept]**
**You have proven your acumen and skill as a [Spearman], allowing**
**you to take a step farther along the path of growth.**

By picking the [Spearman Adept] class, you will get a medium
boost to the strength of all cards and attacks related to the spear.
You will also master and improve in all spear-based combat
skills much faster.
Additional beneficial effects:
A moderate boost to the effectiveness of your dexterity
and strength stats
Boost to combat maneuvers and synergy with other
spear wielders
Class penalties:
N/A
Attached card: Spear Unity (Uncommon, Passive)

Rowan closed the window. The class was barely an improvement over
[Spearman]. The only thing that surprised him were the beneficial effects and the
penalties tabs. It seemed that at the Uncommon tier, classes were becoming more
specialized, pigeonholing the person in a specific fighting style.

Without any penalties, [Spearman Adept] might have been a good choice if
Rowan wasn't sure which spear path to take. But for the moment, it was at the
bottom of his list.


[Heavy Spear]
You wield the spear with ruthless strength, crushing your foes.
You now have the opportunity to further enhance its power.
By picking the [Heavy Spear] class, you will become capable of
wielding heavy spears with the same adroitness as their lighter
variants. You will also gain a significant boost to the strength of
all cards and attacks relevant to strength-focused fighting style,
and improve faster in all related combat skills.
Additional beneficial effects:
A large boost to the effectiveness of your strength and vitality stats
Increased muscle density and size
A moderate boost to your spatial awareness
Class penalties:
Lighter spears break more easily when you use them
Attached card: Crushing Spear (Uncommon, Active)


[Spear Champion]
You are an icon for your troops to follow. Show your strength and
valor and crush enemy champions so that they might be inspired.

By picking the [Spear Champion] class, you will become a skilled front-line fighter and duelist. You will gain a significant stat boost when fighting one-on-one battles. You will also gain proficiency in mastering spear- and shield-related skills at a much faster rate.
Additional beneficial effects:
A large boost to the effectiveness of your strength and dexterity stats
Improved battle instincts and honed bloodlust aura
A significant boost to your hand-eye coordination
Class penalties:
You will suffer stat penalties after declining an honorable challenge to a duel
Attached card: Champion's Resolve (Uncommon, Passive)


[Standard Bearer]
You are the symbol of hope and determination. Raise the flag of your house and rally all those who fight under it.
By picking the [Standard Bearer] class, you will gain access to powerful buffs that can be imparted to all those who battle under your banner. You will also gain bonuses to mastering and crafting battle tactics and maneuvers.
Additional beneficial effects:
A large boost to the effectiveness of your intelligence and wisdom stats
Improved battlefield control and overview
A boost to the effectiveness of all your buff cards
Class penalties:
Decreased effectiveness of all combat cards
Attached card: Rallying Cry (Uncommon, Active)

[Spear Wall]
You are the wall between the hostile world and those you hold dear. Raise your spear and shield and halt the advance of your enemies.
By picking the [Spear Wall] class, you will receive a boost to the effectiveness of all defensive cards and you will master shield-related skills much faster. Any defensive buffs applied to you will be twice as effective. You will also gain stat bonuses when you stand in defense of another.
Additional beneficial effects:

**A large boost to the effectiveness of your strength
and vitality stats
Improved toughness and damage resistance
A large boost to your mental fortitude
Class penalties:
Lower pain awareness
Attached card: Spear Wall (Uncommon, Active)**

Rowan paused. Of the four classes that he had seen so far, both [Spear Wall] and [Spear Champion] were bad choices. Both classes mentioned using a shield, which was impossible with **Keen Spear.**

That left [Standard Bearer] and [Heavy Spear].

[Standard Bearer] was pretty unusual. As far as Rowan was aware, standards were pretty much just extra-long spears with a flag attached. But they were more figureheads than actual combatants. The class might have been a good choice for a noble with a standing army, but Rowan couldn't see himself sacrificing combat ability so that he could become a general.

[Heavy Spear], for the most part, was actually an okay class for Rowan. He kept it in mind as he read through the descriptions for the last two classes and found that, luckily, those two were more on the money.

**[Reckless Spear]
You desire the death of your foes much more than you value your
own safety. You cast aside all defense and strike down those who
dare stand in your way.
By picking the [Reckless Spear] class, you will gain a significant
boost to the effectiveness of all damage-dealing cards. The mana
cost of all relevant cards will be reduced. You will also master all
combat skills and aggressive fighting styles significantly faster.
Additional beneficial effects:
A large boost to the effectiveness of your strength
and dexterity stats
Improved hunting instinct and heightened bloodlust
A large boost to your mental fortitude
Your strikes will pierce defenses more easily and
cause severe bleeding
Class penalties:
A large penalty to all physical damage resistances
You cannot equip heavy armor
Attached card: Blood Siphon (Uncommon, Passive)**

[Mystic Spear]
**Your skill with mana grows, allowing you to tap into the mystical
reservoir of strength. Allow this power to become a core part of you.
By picking the [Mystic Spear] class, you will gain access to minor
spell-casting powers. Your ability to wield your mana will
improve. You will also learn mystical arts at an improved rate and
grow more capable of incorporating them with your spear work.
Additional beneficial effects:
A large boost to the effectiveness of your intelligence
and wisdom stats
A boost to your intelligence-to-mana ratio
Increased affinity to elemental power
Class penalties:
N/A
Attached card: Mana Spear (Uncommon, Active)**

A part of Rowan wanted to pick the [Mystic Spear] class immediately. It was the spear equivalent of spellswords. And if fantasy books were to be believed, spellswords were about as good as classes came.

That wasn't the only reason. Deep within Rowan, he was also a little jealous of the fact that both Blake and especially Kayla had gotten amazing magical skills. Blake was swinging around a sword made of light while Kayla got to play with fireballs and all kinds of different magic. They were having the standard hero-summoned-to-a-new-world experience, while Rowan was out in a minor barony fighting for his life with a regular old spear.

[Mystic Spear] seemed like the perfect class, except, of course, he didn't really have the right stats for it. He'd already invested pretty heavily in his strength and dexterity, and those had saved his life more than once.

The class was also a dreaded hybrid, which meant that he'd potentially ruin his build. He needed strength and dexterity to keep using his spear well and also needed to assign points into wisdom and intelligence in order to take advantage of the spell-casting abilities. By picking it, he'd be forced to invest in four or, at the very least, three different stats.

All that meant he'd never be quite as powerful as other people at his level, leaving him only the option of bullying those weaker. If all he wanted was to clear mobs and earn some loot safely, that was fine.

But considering that the Sutton barony was being swarmed with demons at the moment? He couldn't afford to be distracted.

It was a hard choice between [Heavy Spear] and [Reckless Spear]. They both promised entirely different build paths. [Heavy Spear] seemed like a class that was more stand-and-fight where he had to endure enemy attacks. On the other hand, [Reckless Spear] was more of a glass-cannon build: He'd do a lot of damage quickly, but he couldn't afford to take any damage himself.

Rowan couldn't make up his mind.

The appeal of [Heavy Spear] was that it massively increased his survivability. And that seemed like a good thing given how dire things were. [Reckless Spear] was good in that it'd reinforce his already high offensive capabilities even more, and it also worked well with his current build path of strength and dexterity.

Before Rowan could sink too far into decision paralysis, he realized that there was a third person in the room. His eyes landed on Olivia, who appeared as a complete mess. The bags under her eyes were darker than he'd ever seen, her hair was wild with plenty of strands escaping her ponytail, and she was still in her battle outfit. Despite all that, Rowan found her beautiful. That thought made his cheeks burn and he turned his gaze elsewhere.

"Well, color me impressed," Olivia said, hands on her hips as she took in his condition. "You're not out of bed, and since you're not chained to it, I guess you didn't try to go against my instruction, either. For once."

"It's very nice to see you, too, Olivia," Rowan sighed. A smile tugged at the corner of his lips when he spotted the guard trying to slip out of the room behind Olivia.

"Don't give me that attitude," Olivia hissed, narrowing her eyes. "You know how bad it is for you to completely drain your mana like that. I *know* my father warned you about it."

"What was I supposed to do, then? Just let those poor undead soldiers attack us while we were fighting the demon?"

"Yes. No. Maybe," Olivia said, all bluster fading from her as she finally turned to shut the door and then stomped over to his bed, collapsing on the edge of it. "I was just worried. I *am* worried."

Rowan waited a couple of seconds before saying anything.

"Olivia? What's wrong?"

"Everything." Olivia let out a deep sigh. "The walls need repairing. Cleanup took forever, because we had to avoid a *plague* breaking out. The entire village is scared after the demon came out. The scouts are gone, probably dead. It's why we didn't get a warning that the demon was coming. And now we have no idea what's out there and coming for us, and Bron . . ." Olivia's voice trailed off.

"Olivia? I'm fine. Bron's alive. We all made it," Rowan said.

"No thanks to me." Olivia's eyes were turning red, and Rowan could see the moisture welling up.

"How do you figure that?" Rowan asked. "Without your potions, we would have been doomed. I know I would've gotten eaten by those hounds right away. I don't really fancy becoming a snack for monsters, no matter how cute they are."

That got a slight smile out of Olivia, but it disappeared a second later. Rowan frowned, and considered just dropping the subject, but that idea didn't sit well with him. She looked far too distraught.

"Olivia? You know, it's not like I'm going to tell your secret to someone else. You're the only one I really know around here."

Olivia didn't immediately respond, leaving a silent void hang between them. With every passing moment, Rowan felt more and more like he should say something. He didn't, and his silence was eventually rewarded.

"That potion I gave Bron. I knew what it was, what it would do. I *made* it." Olivia took a deep breath and finally looked Rowan in the eye. "I knew there was a chance it would kill him. I gave it to him and ordered him to die if it came down to it so the two of us could survive."

Rowan could practically *feel* the self-loathing in her words, and he didn't really know what to say. He could try to say that the potion wouldn't have killed Bron, but it had turned the officer into a human fireball. He could say that they'd needed to do something like that, but she already knew that. Olivia had given them a chance to survive the demon attack, but she had done so at the cost of directly hurting someone else.

So Rowan did the only thing that he could and enveloped her in a hug.

Olivia stiffened, and for a moment, he thought she'd push him away. She relaxed into him a moment later, and then her frame shook with quiet sobs as she soaked his shirt with her tears. Her hands balled into fists, gripping the back of his shirt and pulling on it, forcing him to fight back a choke when his collar dug into his throat.

It was awkward, and uncomfortable, but he didn't know what else to do to make things better.

Eventually, Olivia pulled back as her sobs turned into giggles, producing an odd hiccup sound. "I'm a mess."

"And I'm still on house arrest because a certain someone ordered a guard to 'sit on me' if I tried to get up," Rowan said. "I haven't exactly had the chance to freshen up myself."

"Yep, we could both use a bath. Or ten. At least you're up now. You've eaten, right?"

"Yeah." Rowan motioned to the empty tray he'd left on the floor by the side of his bed. "Even had the time to go over my battle report. I can't believe I'm level twenty already."

Olivia snorted. "I hit level thirty-seven. Eight levels from that one battle— this beats potion making by a mile. Did you take a look at our loot?"

"Wouldn't you get a notification if I did? I figured I'd wait for you to visit so we can do it together," Rowan said.

"That's sweet." Olivia's teasing tone was back. "I'm here now."

Rowan navigated to his loot screens, and the cards unfurled in front of him. It was an entire wall of green. In spite of the number of cards, most of the cards were duplicates, especially since they'd only fought four different types of enemies.

The mauler cards were the easiest to sort through.

**Plague Incubator (Uncommon, Passive)**
**Your body is the breeding ground for deadly diseases, granting**
**you resistance to poison damage and rot damage and immunity**
**to lesser illnesses. Your blood and flesh will also spread the**
**corruption brewing within you, punishing any foes that dare to**
**harm you.**

**Titanic Physique (Uncommon, Passive) x 2**
**Your physical might is staggering, granting your strength and**
**vitality stats added potency. Your physical resistance and defense**
**are also boosted, making it more difficult for foes to damage you.**

**Diseased Breath (Uncommon, Active)**
**Channel your mana into breath attacks that will inflict your foes**
**with a variety of negative status effects**
**and crippling illnesses.**

"**Titanic Physique** seems good, but aren't these other two cards pretty much a health hazard for anyone who uses them, too?" Rowan mumbled. Only a madman would choose to sacrifice their body to breed diseases, and having actual deadly breath seemed more like a debuff rather than a skill.

"Yes and no," Olivia said. "Nothing conjured by your own mana can damage you, but **Plague Incubator** sounds like bad news. It's very likely that it isn't very compatible with a human physique, so I wouldn't recommend trying to use it."

"Yeah, no kidding. Guess they're going in the scrap pile."

Unfortunately, the hound cards weren't any better.

**Death's Remembrance (Uncommon, Passive) x 23**
**You carry a passive aura that will weaken the resistances and**
**defenses of all foes within ten feet of you by a moderate amount.**
**They will also perceive you as a specter of death, lowering their**
**morale and inflicting terror upon broken enemies.**

**Pestilent Embrace (Uncommon, Active) x 42**
**Your touch spreads disease and decay, dealing necrotic damage**
**proportional to the amount of mana invested.**

**Spewing Mucus (Uncommon, Active) x 61**
Release a spray of caustic bile that deals necrotic damage and
sticks to your enemies, eating away at their flesh.

**Final Promise (Uncommon, Passive) x 17**
You will never perish alone. Your death releases a blast of necro-
mantic energies that consumes your entire remaining mana pool,
spreading disease and infection in proportion to consumed
mana. If an enemy perishes due to the effects of this card, the
effects are partially replicated on their body.

**[Heart] Demonic Breeding (Rare) x 3**
Your race has been enhanced by demonic mana and bred for combat
and violence. Your mana is inherently demonic, corrupting and
damaging all it comes in contact with. Your affinity for rot, disease,
death, corruption, chaos, and destruction elements is enhanced.
This card can subsume and replace any currently held Heart Card.

**Demonic Breeding** was particularly vile, and Rowan saw Olivia react to it
much the same way she had to **Demonic Encroachment** before. She dealt with
it the same way she had done with the other demonic card, rolling for it and carefully packing it away. Rowan didn't pay as much attention to what she was doing,
especially because the final three cards shone with a blue light.

**Persistent Regeneration (Rare, Active)**
Force your body to regenerate at the cost of energy reserves
or muscle mass.

**Lavish Feasting (Rare, Passive)**
You can devour food in excess, breaking it down using mana
and storing the energy away to be used at a later date. You are
limited to storing energy equivalent to three times your
body weight.

**Rot Shield (Rare, Active)**
Summon a film of rot mana that will cover your body and protect
you from blows, damaging your enemies and their weapons
in the process.

Rowan's thoughts churned as he read and then reread the descriptions of
**Persistent Regeneration** and **Lavish Feasting**. If he was interpreting things

correctly, this was the combo that had allowed the demon to regenerate again and again.

Making up his mind, Rowan turned to look Olivia in the eye, mentally rolling on the two cards he wanted. "These two cards. Is it okay if I take them?"

Olivia gave Rowan a long, searching look. She could tell he was up to something but wasn't quite certain yet what.

"Okay," she finally conceded, even if she didn't sound happy about it.

With that settled, Rowan finally made his choice.

**All available stats assigned.**
**Congratulations!**
**[Reckless Spear] class selected.**

He had a very strong feeling that Olivia wasn't going to be happy with him once she knew what he had in mind for his future.

# CHAPTER EIGHTEEN

# Social Anxieties

Rowan tore into his lunch with gusto. He wasn't exactly the cleanest or most elegant eater in the world, but there was a different reason the villagers were giving him odd looks.

He was on his fifth plate of monster meat, and probably still had room for another five plates. After adding **Lavish Feasting** to his deck, Rowan had set out to make a dent in the food supply of the village. And since he was one of the five who'd faced down the demon, the villagers were more than happy to keep cooking for him.

As the plates began stacking up beside him, their happiness had transitioned into a quiet weariness. Olivia, meanwhile, was busy glaring at him.

Ever since he told her about the class he'd chosen, she had decided to give him the silent treatment. As Rowan reached for his sixth plate, she apparently decided to break her vow.

"I see now that I've made a mistake," Olivia said, crossing her arms and leaning farther back in her seat. "I should *not* have passed on those two cards."

"You couldn't use them anyway," Rowan said between bites. Monster meat beat normal animal meat hands down. This was some of the most tender, juicy, and satisfying food he had ever eaten. And the best part? With each bite, he could *feel* some new part of himself filling up. It was basically a dream come true. He could eat as much as he wanted and not have to worry about stacking on the pounds.

"True, but considering those cards have enabled your madness, I feel personally responsible," Olivia teased.

"You have to see how this is the ideal class and cards for me, right?" Rowan insisted, refusing to back down. "It's the perfect combination for what I need to do, what I need to *become*."

"A reckless food master?" Olivia motioned around them, indicating the gawking villagers.

"A near-immortal, powerful damage dealer," Rowan corrected, though he was forced to make an admission. "At least if the cards work the way I think they do."

"Well, congratulations! You'll have the chance to test them faster than you might like," Olivia deadpanned.

That one brought him up short. Rowan paused his eating. "Why? What's happening?"

"What's happening? Well, let's see." Olivia lowered her voice, leaning in toward him so she could hiss at him at a barely audible volume. "Bron is stuck in a sickbed and hasn't even woken up yet."

"Yes, and we should go visit him later. I still haven't seen him," Rowan reminded her, earning a glare meant to shush him.

"Then there's the fact that beast attacks are ramping up again, and the blasted things are still in the late teens when it comes to their levels, so we need to be careful when handling them," Olivia hissed.

"We should head out ourselves, that way I get to practice and we take care of the issue. Two birds with one stone," Rowan said confidently.

"Would you please just listen for a second? That's nowhere as bad as our final problem." Olivia paused, closed her eyes, and finally sighed before making the admission like it dearly hurt. "We're blind."

"What?"

"We're blind. We can't do any scouting. We won't have advanced warning. All our scouts were wiped out by the demon."

"And that's bad?"

"Horrible. It'd take me hours to explain all the things that a scout does. Without scouts, we have to prepare for everything, which means that we can't prepare well for anything," Olivia said. She sounded so defeated that Rowan was half tempted to give her a hug again.

"There's no one to replace them?" Rowan asked. "Not even among the mercenaries?"

"Not even close. Mercenaries don't need scouts; they're all small parties. If it's danger that they can't beat, they can run. A solid scout needs the right build, the right cards, and the right *mindset*. It's a role full of danger, and it's not even really a proper combat role. Most people just won't have anything close to it."

Rowan sighed, rubbing his forehead. He had no real idea what he could offer in this situation. "We can do some light scouting when we go out there, right?"

"We?" Olivia asked back. "With Bron out of the picture, we *don't have a commander* anymore. I'm all we've got. If I leave, who's left?"

That was a good point. Rowan almost said that he could just go alone, but he shut that thought down. If he was ambushed by some monster and hurt, he'd just be creating more problems for Olivia. More than that, if he was caught in front of some monster wave that was coming and it became a choice between saving Rowan or putting the village at risk, it'd be a no-win situation.

He couldn't really afford to traipse around on his own.

"But we need someone to look around. If scouting really is that important, we need to at least try something. Maybe we can't get a couple hours' worth of notice, but it'd be better than nothing. And I bet some of the soldiers could take up the command responsibility for a few hours. It'd be good for them to get some leadership time in," Rowan added. "You can't direct everything when we're in battle."

"You are so infuriating sometimes, you know that?" Olivia hissed, but he could tell that she was coming around to his reasoning.

"There's a whole list of reasons why we need to go out, at least today," Rowan concluded for her benefit, ignoring her comment. "After that, we can figure something out for the long term."

"Fine, but I seriously hope you know that I won't tolerate more stupidity than is absolutely necessary." Olivia pushed the last word in, and Rowan let her. She needed the win.

In spite of Olivia's agreement, it took a while to actually organize their foray into the forest.

Now that Bron was completely out of commission, everyone from soldiers to villagers and mercenaries looked to her for instruction. Rowan thought he could understand why she was losing her patience more often.

He could understand the questions about defense repair and guard shift schedules. But most of what took up Olivia's time was stupid stuff like a mercenary arguing that a villager had stolen a monster carcass that he had marked. Rowan just wanted to stab everyone involved.

In fact, he reached for his spear to hopefully strike a more imposing figure and stop people from bothering Olivia with their trivial problems. That's when he realized what was happening.

Rowan scanned the pair and the other parties waiting for Olivia's arbitration, and he came to a simple conclusion. Those people were all just scared, and upset *because* of that emotion. They weren't there for her to solve their problems. They were looking to whine at a figure of authority. It didn't matter to them that the person in question had twenty better things to be doing.

And in his newfound wisdom, he decided to step in himself.

"Okay, that's it," Rowan said loudly. "Commander Olivia is leaving now because she has a previous appointment. You can disperse and solve these problems on your own."

Several voices immediately rose in protest, but Rowan was through with their nonsense. He lifted his spear by a fraction and slammed the butt down on the ground. The tip of the spear ignited in a haze of red mana. It was absolutely perfect for sending a message in a hurry.

"Do you think that your problems are so important that they need to get solved when we potentially have another monster wave on our hands? Olivia Sutton of House Sutton needs to join me on an important scouting mission. Or would you like to volunteer to scout instead?"

Rowan swept his gaze over the crowd, and they predictably backed away. He used the chance to tug Olivia out of her seat and quickly shuffle her toward the village gates. Surprisingly, when he turned to look at her reaction to the turn of events, she just looked amused.

"You know that I was dealing with relatively important duties for a commander, right?" Olivia said.

"Listening to people whine like children is considered an important duty?" Rowan countered.

"No, but relieving the rising tension in the settlement is. So we don't get a coup on our hands," Olivia said with a smile.

"Do you really think they'll do anything? They just want you to take their side in useless arguments. If something really important came up, we'd likely have heard about it, no?"

"Probably," Olivia admitted with a sigh, looking tired again. "But my father always taught me not to let these things fester."

"Did you see Bron spending all his time resolving petty disputes?" Rowan asked.

"Well, no, but he didn't need to deal with the aftermath of a demon attack," Olivia protested, though Rowan could tell that the farther they got from the village, the more tension left her body.

"All I'm saying is, let's just take some time to ourselves, get some scouting and hunting done, and see what greets us when we're back, okay?"

Olivia hesitated for a few moments, but by that point, she'd had stopped glancing behind them. "Fine."

Rowan's new build was working like a charm, and he couldn't resist taking another glance at his status screen. Especially the fact that his deck now held five cards instead of four, courtesy of his new Uncommon class.

**Rowan Clairfont**
**Level 20 Reckless Spear**
**EXP: 0/5,000**

**STR: 25***
**VIT: 12**

**DEX: 25***
**PER: 14**
**INT: 10**
**WIS: 11**


**Deck (5/5):**
**[Heart] Keen Spear (Epic, Passive)**
**[Class] Empowered Thrust (Common, Active)**
**[Class] Blood Siphon (Uncommon, Passive)**
**Persistent Regeneration (Rare, Active)**
**Lavish Feasting (Rare, Passive)**
**Blessings:**
**Blessing of the Stalwart Hero**

The screen was glorious. Rowan loved every single thing about it—his new stats, his new cards, the stars attached to his strength and dexterity thanks to the class. They were all great.

He'd felt a ridiculous surge in the quality of his strength and dexterity when he passed the twenty mark. And yet, that didn't even compare to what he felt when he picked his [Reckless Spear] and it improved the effectiveness of those stats even more.

Rowan knew it was ridiculous, but he could *feel* the higher weight of investing in those two categories compared to his other stats.

His body definitely reflected all the changes, at least. It wasn't like he had gone from a skinny kid to a ten-year bodybuilder. The muscles seemed more defined now, but that was mostly it. The real change was in the way he walked. There was a certain grace, an innate balance and strength that simply weren't there before.

Rowan certainly felt like a whole new person moving through the forest. The last time they'd visited, he'd still felt a little awkward and unsure. Now, he was positively thrilled at the idea of finding a monster to fight.

Thankfully, they didn't need to go too far for that.

When they were halfway through the cleared fields, a large black figure tore away from the trees and charged at them. A wolf. A quick glance at Olivia confirmed his suspicion that she was still running **Inspect** when she informed him the wolf was level 14.

Even just a few days ago, Rowan hadn't imagined a world in which he'd be so relaxed that he was almost negligent as a giant wolf sprinted at him. But he did feel that way. His spear lit up red, and when the wolf jumped at him, he almost rolled his eyes.

*The dang thing is so slow.*

Rowan dramatically twirled out of the way and stabbed at the wolf's side. The blade of his spear neatly parted flesh like it wasn't even there, and when he flicked it back, there was a giant burst of blood from the wound.

He had his new class card to thank for that.

**[Class] Blood Siphon (Uncommon, Passive)**
**Each wound your spear inflicts will provoke severe bleeding,**
**draining your foes of their life essence. The bleeding effects grow**
**in proportion to the damage dealt.**

**Blood Siphon** wasn't some fancy vampiric ability that healed him for damage dealt. It wasn't even particularly spectacular, as far as effects went. And it certainly couldn't apply to all enemies, either.

But as long as his enemies had something flowing through their veins, the card would be invaluable. It was a solid all-around card that made his attacks stronger and also gave him the chance to pick away at an enemy instead of trying for devastating attacks.

Not that Rowan was above using devastating attacks. His strike against the wolf had been strong enough to throw the beast back, and **Blood Siphon** had created a geyser of blood to add to things.

There was another side benefit. The card, or perhaps the [Reckless Spear] class, had the effect of dyeing mana bloodred. In Rowan's humble opinion, that made his **Empowered Thrust** glow effect much, much cooler. That was important, especially now that he had someone to impress.

The battle, if it could even be called that, ended shortly after. The wolf was dazed from losing so much blood so quickly that Rowan easily finished it.

Really, it struck him that the card might have been made for hunters. There was no need to drain blood from meat after **Blood Siphon** was through with them.

"This might actually be what I needed," Olivia admitted, sword shearing ruthlessly through a fox. She controlled her mana-edge card much better than before, using it only for the single strike rather than draining all her mana on just a couple of opponents.

"See? I told you it was a great idea for us to come out here," Rowan teased, strolling ahead of her.

They were taking turns dealing with whatever popped up, since it seemed highly unlikely that anything truly challenging was about to make a move against them.

In fact, they'd spent most of the day exploring, scouting, and fighting Common beasts that no longer gave them any experience. The one exception was a fox that had somehow made it to Uncommon.

Even then, that battle ended in record time, giving Rowan his first experience points at the Uncommon tier. He really hated thinking it or feeling that way, but he was worried he'd not get properly challenged any time soon. It was a conflicted feeling. No danger meant safety to everyone, but it meant stagnation for him.

"It seems like all the demonic creatures really did stick to the demon who led them here in the first place," Olivia confirmed his suspicions.

"Well, at least we don't need to worry about them sneaking up on the villagers and soldiers and just exploding, I guess," Rowan said.

"True. Honestly, it's a pretty well-known phenomenon."

"What, the sneaking?"

"No, the creatures-following-a-demon thing. For some reason, the higher-tier demons seem to have absolute control over the lower-tier ones and the demonic creatures."

"That's the reason he could more or less treat them as his personal army?" Rowan asked. One thing that had stood out to Rowan was the fact that the demon minions never broke rank. Even when the hounds were getting slaughtered, none of them ever backed away. The corrupted beasts, on the other hand, fought until their terror overwhelmed their bloodlust.

"Yeah. There are a lot of theories on why, but my money is on how they're raised, or that something imprints the demon's mana on them."

Rowan was silent for a few moments, his feet moving on autopilot, before something finally occurred to him. "Wait, does that mean that if we ever start seeing creatures like that again, we've got a demon inbound?"

Olivia grimaced, but she still nodded. "Exactly."

In spite of how much fun Rowan was having hunting monsters and chatting with Olivia, they eventually had to head back. She steered them toward Felton's Mill well before darkness started falling.

According to her, if the heroes of the village were still missing at sundown, it could cause a panic they didn't want to deal with. But as they stepped foot in the village again, Rowan hated it.

It felt like they were stepping foot in hostile territory. Everyone they passed stopped to glance at them, both discreetly and openly. Olivia took it in stride, but Rowan had to work on keeping his displeasure off his face.

The soldiers were skittish and nervous. They kept sneaking glances at the house Rowan knew Bron was located in. Mercenaries, funnily enough, seemed largely indifferent. Most of them would offer acknowledging nods or similar and then go back to their own tasks.

The villagers, on the other hand, alternated between being deathly afraid for their lives and acting like he and Olivia were the most awe-inspiring beings to ever walk the lands.

"You know," Olivia said, in a voice low enough that only Rowan could hear, "as much as I enjoyed that, I don't think I'll be able to join future scouting sessions."

"Why not? Do you really want to spend entire days just trying to solve petty disputes?" Rowan asked with a frown.

"No. The thing is, petty disputes or not, I have a lot of organizational stuff I need to do. There's food logistics, deciding on the best repairs, directing said repairs, organizing guard shifts, handling communications with the mercenaries, and more. It's a mess."

Rowan blinked. "And Bron was handling all this himself before? Doesn't he have assistants you can rely on or something?"

"No, I guess not. If he did have assistants of any kind, they're either hurt or dead," Olivia said.

"What about the village chief? Desimir was his name, I think?" Rowan offered.

Olivia paused in her step. "That's actually a good idea. I haven't seen him lately, but I'll go check with him."

"So I guess it's solo scouting trips for a while?" Rowan said. He hated the idea, not just for all the practical reasons but also because the trip today had been fun. It was a much-needed change of pace compared to the earlier fighting. And Rowan wouldn't have admitted it at the moment, but he was beginning to enjoy spending time with Olivia.

"Actually, I really don't think you should," Olivia said.

"So you'll find time in your schedule?" Rowan asked.

"No, you'll just have to sit around and look pretty," Olivia teased, sticking out her tongue. "How about partying up with Marcus and Milena?"

"Marcus? Milena?" Rowan asked. He had no clue who Olivia was referring to.

"The beast folk twins. They're pretty good. Plus, their party only has two members," Olivia said.

Rowan reeled from the information being thrown at him. For one, he had a hard time picturing the short and stout shield bearer being twin to the tall and slender mage. Rowan made the assumption that Marcus was the shield bearer while Milena was the mage. And second, perhaps more seriously, was the implication that Olivia was going to leave his party.

"You're telling me to leave you for a different party?" Rowan asked.

The baron's daughter sighed, briefly looking skyward. "Yes, Rowan, I'm telling you to go with a different adventuring party. They haven't actually accepted my suggestion yet. They might say no even if you agree to the plan."

"With my charming looks and personality?"

"More like because of your just-barely Uncommon level and tendency to do stupid stuff."

"You take that back!" Rowan faked outrage, placing his hand over his heart. "My stupid actions look genius in hindsight and you know it."

Olivia grinned. She turned toward the makeshift cooking tents near the central fire pit.

It didn't take long before Rowan heard the twins. Milena was laughing, or at least that's what Rowan assumed, based on the fact that the sound was an octave higher than normal laughter. It didn't particularly help that the sound was a blend of howling and laughing.

As he got closer, Rowan found quite the crowd of mercenaries gathered around them. The two seemed to be at the center of attention and were being plied with food and scavenged drinks.

Alcoholic drinks were quickly growing rare in the village. Though they had been plentiful when Rowan first arrived, the combination of the mercenaries and stressful sieges had wiped out most stores. Nowadays, most of the alcohol being consumed was an abomination that could have given Olivia's potions a run for their money.

But the shield bearer, Marcus, was earning every drink.

He hopped around the campfire as he gestured with a meat skewer like it was a sword.

"And then the hero threw that spear of his, and I swear he obliterated the huge mauler's head!" Marcus paused and spread his arms apart to show just how large the head was. Rowan didn't remember the mauler's head ever being that big. "Lady Sutton was incredible, too, and her potions burned so hot I thought she was summoning hellfire to burn its own spawn to cinder, and then two of us . . ."

Marcus's eyes widened and he suddenly trailed off when he saw Rowan and Olivia approaching. The mercenaries roared their displeasure and only quieted when they realized why he had stopped.

"I realize we're being rude, but I hope we can briefly borrow this bard of yours and his sister," Olivia said, amusement plain in her voice.

"Of course, Lady Sutton," one of the mercenaries was quick to agree. Before Olivia and Rowan could even bid them stay, most of the group had already retreated. Rowan would have found it funny if there wasn't a trace of fear and concern on their faces.

"My brother and me—That is, we didn't mean to insult you," Milena rushed to assure them, her eyes nervously on Rowan.

Rowan tried to make sense of things. This was a time where he really wished that it was socially acceptable to walk around with a spear in his hand. He had left his weapon near the wall after returning to the village.

Was there some kind of unwritten rule that people weren't supposed to talk about their exploits against demons? Or perhaps anything about the heroes was considered a forbidden topic? Or was it just getting caught gossiping about their employer that was the issue?

Regardless, Rowan didn't really find any reason to drag out the misunderstanding. "That's not why we're here, and we're not upset, I assure you. Do you two have a place we can speak in private?"

The twins tensed up at his question, but they eventually nodded, and Rowan followed them into the home they'd managed to rent from the village natives.

Olivia showed off her noble upbringing by claiming a seat first and motioning for the twins to do the same. If Rowan wasn't completely sure that the baron's daughter slept in the room next to his, he might have thought that this was Olivia's home with how confident she seemed.

Once everyone was settled, Olivia began the conversation. "You two are good fighters. There's no doubt about that. But you're also lacking. You have a tank and a mage. That's good if you find something that's slow. But the moment you're up against a fast opponent, they'll tear through you."

Rowan chose to be the good guy. "But you guys were invaluable in the fight against the demon. Saved all our lives several times. If it weren't for your magic, Milena, I don't know if we could have done as much damage without being hurt ourselves."

Neither of the two beast folk responded. They sat in their chairs and fidgeted under the combined gazes of Rowan and Olivia.

"That means a lot," Milena said. "Really, a lot. Our family . . ." She paused. "Thank you, Hero Rowan."

Rowan noted Milena's reluctance when talking about her family and filed that little tidbit of information away. "Well, I meant it. And it's with what you've done in mind that I'm asking this. Would you like to team up with me?"

Olivia jumped in to clarify things. "What Hero Rowan is asking is if you'd like to join his party as he goes out to scout and clear the surrounding monsters. It won't be completely safe and you'll receive no additional pay besides what you kill on these scouting trips. But now that the demon is gone, the danger should be minimal. We just need to keep the monster numbers low."

It was true, too. Rowan still wasn't entirely sure how corrupted beasts were made, but Olivia had explained that most of them were ordinary animals tainted with demonic mana. But they still held their original instincts, including a tendency for stronger beasts to drive their weaker counterparts to soften enemy defenses.

"With our scouts gone, we can't afford to stay idle," Rowan continued. "But since Olivia needs to lead the village, I have to face all the enemies on my own. I probably could, but it's not ideal." Rowan ignored the glare Olivia sent him for the bragging. "That's why I'd like for the two of you to join me."

The two beast folk stayed silent. Rowan waited just long enough for a shadow of doubt to cross his heart.

*Is the stock of a hero that low? Or do they think I'm that weak?*

Those doubts were quickly driven away when the twins released high-pitched squeals that reminded him of young puppies.

"Really? We'd get to be part of the hero party?" Marcus shouted.

"Temporarily," Olivia made sure to emphasize. "But yes. You get to be a part of the hero's party. That should be enough stories for the rest of your life."

"Yes. For as long as you'll have me," Marcus rushed to agree, then shot his sister a rueful look. "As long as I get to be with my sister."

"She's invited, too," Rowan added.

Milena smiled. "I would love to, of course. This is a tremendous honor. Thank you, Hero Rowan."

"Call me Rowan. Please. Thank you both, really. Here, I'll invite you in a second," Rowan said, navigating to his party menu. That's when he spotted Bron's name there and froze. The name was currently grayed out.

Olivia must have noticed something, because her gaze went blank as she looked at her own system screen. A moment later, she nudged Rowan. "Push Bron out. We'll talk about it later," Olivia whispered.

Rowan's heart thumped in his chest. He was the only one who could remove Bron from the party, but doing so felt like a betrayal to the man who had sacrificed everything for them.

In the end, he gritted his teeth and removed Bron from the party, then sent out the two new invitations. They accepted almost instantaneously.

**Marcus and Milena have joined your party. Full party assembled.**
**Conditions met:**
**Blessing of the Stalwart Hero has been fully activated.**

# CHAPTER NINETEEN

# Grace of the Divine

To say that Rowan wasn't amused would have been an understatement.

This whole time, while he was putting his life on the line and in danger of getting poisoned, corrupted, or otherwise tainted, he had been assured that the gods were favoring him. After all, Aristaeus had blessed him.

Now, he was being told that his blessing had only been half activated this whole time because it required him to assemble a full party?

"Rowan?" Olivia's concerned voice rang out.

*What if I never met Kayden? What if I had been forced to fight solo? Most of all, why in the name of all that was holy or unholy didn't the dang thing come with an instruction manual?*

Rowan's eye twitched, and he reread the notification. Then he did it again.

A soft hand landed on his shoulder, lightly shaking him. He still couldn't force his eyes away from the status screen. "Rowan, are you all right?"

"I'm going—" Rowan's rage session was cut short when icy-cold water slapped him in the face. "What in all that is good in the world was that for?"

"Sorry." Marcus set his mug down and raised his hands in surrender. "You were out of it. We do that back in my hometown. It was instinct."

"Thank you, Marcus. Please ignore Rowan's grouchiness. Now, what actually happened just now? They joined the party and you just shut down," Olivia asked, genuine concern in her voice.

Rowan opened his mouth to explain, then quickly changed his mind. He trusted Olivia, especially after everything that had happened recently. However, the twins were still very much an unknown quantity.

"Sorry, I got lost in thought." Rowan turned toward the twins. "Marcus and Milena, right? Thank you for trusting me. Do you mind if we call it a day, though? I'm still a little tired from everything that happened with the demon."

"Of course. Plenty of time to get to know each other tomorrow. Maybe we can go out and hunt a little. We've been cooped up in here for a bit too long," Marcus offered, earning a smile from Rowan.

"Thanks, and that sounds great. Olivia, how about we go visit Bron before retiring for today? I haven't seen him since the last fight, and I'd feel a lot better if we could do a quick check," Rowan said.

Olivia narrowed her eyes slightly, but nodded. "Sure. And thanks, Marcus and Milena. You two have been a great help. Know that you can count on House Sutton in the future. We honor our debts."

Before they reached Bron's house, Rowan pulled Olivia aside.

**Awakened Blessing of the Stalwart Hero**
**From Aristaeus, the God of Soldiers and Rural Craft**
**Grade: Unique**
**Description: You are the determined champion of the people.**
**Effects:**
**When fighting with allies nearby, the whole group receives full experience values of every slain enemy.**
**When fighting with allies nearby, your chance to receive Rare drop items is doubled, and your chance to get more than one drop item per downed enemy is three times higher.**
**When fighting with allies nearby, your damage resistance is two times more effective than what your stats suggest.**
**When fighting alone, you'll be more likely to encounter streaks of bad luck.**
**When fighting alone, your experience-gain rate and loot-drop rate will be halved.**
**Believers of God Aristaeus are more likely to provide aid and help in any way they can, provided it doesn't interfere with their personal goals.**

"What's wrong?" Olivia asked. "You were acting weird back there."

Rowan took a deep breath. It was time to take a leap of faith. "Here, take a look at this."

He sent over the blessing screen to Olivia. For a few seconds, the baron's daughter stood as still as a statue. Then, out came a barrage of curses. When she was done, she collapsed onto a nearby wall.

"Did this mess up your build?" Olivia asked.

Hearing that question, Rowan knew that he had made the right choice by trusting Olivia. *Anyone who first thinks of other people can't be that bad.*

"Why would it mess with my build? It's not like I'm going around fighting solo these days," Rowan said.

"You numbskull. The damage-resistance part. Did you always have that?" Olivia asked.

"No? That part's new. It used to be that I'd get bad luck fighting alone and that I got more experience and loot when fighting in a party," Rowan answered.

"But if you'd known about that before, you could have gone for a more defense-oriented build. Do you know what tanks would give to have a blessing like that? Every stat you spend on vitality pretty much doubles in effectiveness. Did you have a defensive class option?" Olivia asked in her Rowan's-definitely-done-something-stupid voice.

"No, not really. [Reckless Spear] was still the best option. There was one class called [Spear Wall] or something like that, which sounded pretty defensive. But I couldn't have taken that one anyway. I can't use a shield, so unless I'm counting on the spear to block everything, it was a dead end."

"Right. Your Heart Card," Olivia muttered. "I guess it's fine, then. If anything, I suppose this will patch over the class penalty you took on, at least a little. I just can't believe we missed something like that."

Rowan grimaced, crossing his arms. "And imagine if we never got around to picking up more team members. Then I'd have never unlocked the full blessing."

"I'm sorry." Oddly enough, Olivia really did sound remorseful, like it was all somehow her fault. "We didn't know. There's not a lot publicly discussed about hero blessings. We know most if not all of the blessings boost experience and loot gain, but that's about it."

"Hey, I'm not blaming you," Rowan said quickly, suddenly realizing that she might feel self-conscious. "Your family's only been good to me so far."

Olivia nodded tightly, but Rowan could see something was still bothering her.

"Have you seen Bron yet?" Rowan tried to change the subject.

"No." There was something about the way that Olivia said the word that told Rowan that he'd hit another wall.

"We should," Rowan said, forging on through the wall. "He'd appreciate it. I think it'd be good for us, too."

Olivia looked Rowan in the eye and evidently saw that he wasn't about to back down. Finally, she nodded and the two of them made their way to Bron's room.

It was a rather small room. Clean, but spartan. There was only a single bed and a small window. On the bed was Bron.

Thankfully, the officer looked like he was simply sleeping. He was lying on his back, and as far as Rowan could tell at a glance, hadn't moved an inch since the fight with the demon. His face and upper body also seemed to be in good condition, even if clothes got in the way of gauging that.

His arms, however, definitely weren't.

They were wrapped in thick bandages, and he could easily spot places where blood had seeped through, leaving ugly, dark-red patches. The bandages themselves were also soaked in some kind of green substance that shimmered under the light.

"How is he doing?" Rowan asked quietly, afraid to talk too loudly.

"He's fine. He'll make it. I think," Olivia said, facing Bron herself. "Problem is, we can't use potions on him. His body is *already* suffering from the effects of one, after all."

"Then what's up with the bandages?" Rowan pointed out, taking a closer look at those again. The closer he got, the more apparent the herbal scent became.

"Those are soaked in herbal juice. The plants have some healing properties, even when they're not processed. Under those bandages is a special medicinal paste, too. It will protect him from infections and enhance his healing," Olivia said. "That's why we haven't removed them to change the bandages yet."

"I guess fighting a demon isn't exactly the easiest thing to go through." Rowan pulled back. "Is it odd that I kind of miss him? He spent most of his time shouting at us, but I still feel that way."

Olivia's smile was small and hesitant, but it was still there. "I don't think it's odd. He was . . . is nice. I just want him to wake up already so he can take over command." She sighed, absentmindedly combing her fingers through her hair to untangle it.

"Things going that badly?" Rowan asked. "I know things weren't great when I stole you away, but I really thought they wouldn't give too much trouble to their baron's daughter."

"It's not that they want to make trouble. They're all just upset and worried," Olivia confided as she paced around the room. "And I don't have a single way to reassure them."

"Hey, we took down a demon together. Isn't that a lot of reassurance right there?"

"Exactly the problem, actually. What happens if there's worse beast waves? Is another demon going to show up? Can we stop it, especially without Bron? Everyone's panicking and asking questions like that." Olivia sighed. "Now that everyone knows what the worst case might be, they're all asking questions."

Rowan tapped his foot, looking at the floor. "And you really can't say anything to reassure them? Like reinforcements are coming?"

"Without scouts, I can't say anything for certain. If I promise reinforcements and they don't come, then we're in a world of trouble. We're blind right now. I don't know if . . ."

"Kayden will be fine," Rowan said, finally wising up for once. "If I know one thing about your father, it's that he's smart. He'll find a way to solve the situation and be here before we know it."

Olivia managed a small smile again, and Rowan cheered internally at how Olivia's mood was lifting. "It's not like there's anything else we can do right now."

"What about another Unique potion?" Rowan asked. "We don't need to use it, but just knowing that it's there would help everyone calm down."

"I wish," Olivia sighed. "Unique potions are called unique for a reason. I'm pretty sure we can no longer afford the base ingredients as a barony with this demon invasion. Let alone the special item to really make the potion Unique."

"Then I guess we pray that a demon doesn't show up. Or if it does, then we hope that it's weaker. And if it's not, then we trust that reinforcements come in time."

"Unless you've been holding out on me and are secretly a Legendary-tier [Spearman]?" Olivia teased.

"I wish. No such luck."


Venturing outside the walls without Olivia felt wrong.

The twins weren't bad company. For starters, they exuded an aura of strength. They were talkative and friendly, and their stories about places they'd visited were also vivid and fantastical.

But they weren't Olivia.

There was also the fact that the official mission they were on was scouting and culling nearby beasts, while Rowan's actual motivation for venturing outside the walls was to test out his blessing as surreptitiously as he could. He still didn't know how he would do that.

"You don't need to be so stiff, boss." Marcus grinned, offering Rowan a flash of his fangs and thumping a fist against his shield. "I know that I might not look all that reliable, but I guarantee that nothing's gonna break through my defenses today."

After getting to know Marcus better, all of Rowan's stereotypes about tanky defenders came crashing down. For starters, the man was built more like a dwarf than a beast folk. But he was also as goofy as they came. There was nothing that Marcus wouldn't laugh about, and especially after this morning, Rowan was surprised to see a smile still on the man's face.

"Sorry, I want to ask one more time. You're sure that you're fine with the loot-distribution rules?" Rowan asked.

"Yep. It would be kind of rude of us to push for more. I mean, we're technically being paid by the baron for defending the village. And he sent out a barony-wide recruitment notice for people to join your party as soon as you arrived," Marcus said. "We were actually on our way when we got stuck in Felton's Mill. In some ways, that was a stroke of good luck."

"Still, if you do end up changing your minds about that, do tell," Rowan said. The current loot distribution was heavily in favor of him and Olivia. The twins would only take cards that were useful to either of them. And even then, they'd only take the cards if neither Rowan nor Olivia needed them. "It's very generous, but I don't mind something more fair."

"We're happy with how things are," the sister, Milena, chimed in. Despite her smile, Rowan was still slightly afraid of her.

It was a lot of different things. Her black miasma made her seem like some kind of death mage, and there was something about a big wolflike lady that made him afraid of getting eaten.

Overall, the party was off to a good start. Whether that was because the twins were doing this because they were inherently kind or if they were being purposeful, there was a still a positive tone to the relationship. And Rowan didn't care much either way.

He only had one secret, which was his blessing.

Rowan hadn't said anything in front of Olivia before, but a part of him wondered how much of the blame for blessing information scarcity had to do with typical noble machinations and how much of it was down to the secrecy of heroes themselves.

Although he didn't regret sharing the details of his blessing with Olivia, Rowan had a pang of doubt creep into his mind soon afterward. Like he had done something wrong. Like he had exposed a crucial part of himself to an enemy's dagger.

The sensation felt more like a subconscious compulsion than any sort of logical reasoning. And the feelings could only have one source: the blessing itself.

*Is this some kind of default thing? Or does Aristaeus have a reason to keep things hidden? Maybe he just doesn't like the kingdom that threw him away in favor of a greater god?*

"Okay, I know this is going to sound weird," Rowan said, turning around and addressing the twins. "But I just got my new class and a new card to cover up a class penalty. I need to test it. So, I'm going to stand here and I need you to punch me while slowly upping the strength of your blows. You in?"

He was apparently a little too heavy-handed, because the twins froze like deer in headlights. Finally, though, Marcus smiled and nodded, while his sister started chuckling.

When Rowan arched a brow in her direction, Milena just laughed harder. "I'm sorry, I'm sorry. I just thought for a moment you were like one of those weird nobles we come across occasionally."

Rowan frowned. It was his turn to be confused. "I'm not following."

"Oh, come on." Milena grinned at him roguishly. "You left behind your special lady friend, led a pair of wolfkin twins into the woods, and then said you have a weird request."

When Rowan started sputtering and blushing furiously, the beast folk just laughed harder.

"Okay, well, when you put it like that." Rowan shook his head in exasperation. It was really looking like he would have to give up on ever getting normal party members, even temporary ones. First Olivia, now Marcus and Milena. *Perhaps no one in this world is truly normal.*

"You know, all that still applies," Marcus mused, stroking his chin slyly. "He *is* asking me to punch him. We don't know what humans like."

"I'd be plenty happy to punch you if you want to test your defense auras," Rowan offered, trying to emulate Olivia's sickly-sweet voice that she took up whenever he did something particularly stupid.

"No thanks, I'm really not into that," Marcus quipped. Even while grinning, he took up a proper punching stance. "How hard do you want me to start?"

"Light. I'm really entirely unsure of how effective this card is," Rowan admitted. The good news was that he could feel the blessing working. It was like some kind of thin film covered his entire body, observed only by his mind and nothing else. He couldn't touch it, and even Olivia had no way of proving that it was there.

As far as he could tell, the protective shield might or might not be real, but it only existed in his weird, intuition-like sense.

Marcus nodded, paused, then threw a punch. The strike was light and even a little slow, letting Rowan track everything fully.

About a quarter of an inch before the fist impacted Rowan's shoulder, the thin protective film stopped it, making the strike rebound slightly.

Marcus frowned, shaking out his hand. "That felt weird. It's the card effect, right?" Before Rowan could respond, the shield bearer got back into a punching stance. "Let's ramp things up, then. Let me know when to stop."

The results of their test were interesting. Rowan was almost entirely unaffected by anything under level 5. From there, things got a bit more complicated.

First, the film, even when "destroyed" by an attack, had a blunting influence. Second, from what Rowan could tell, it regenerated nearly instantly. And finally, it had about as much "defense" to it as Rowan's own body could withstand before sustaining damage.

It was better than nothing, but Rowan hadn't learned much about how it'd perform in a real combat scenario. In fact, most of Rowan's fights so far had been with monsters that probably would have ripped him in half if he didn't dodge their blows. That was true of the demon, the maulers, and even the hounds to some extent.

With the test done, the party got back to culling and scouting.

Culling was easy. It was basically just wandering around and taking down whatever unfortunate corrupted beast happened to think of them as prey. In fact, both Marcus and Milena took care of most of the small fries before Rowan even had to work.

Scouting was less easy. None of them could really contribute in a way that mattered. They could see that the forest had a lot of footprints, but none of them had any clue if those were from the previous monster horde or if there was a new horde brewing.

At least, those were his thoughts before Milena declared she was going to perform a ritual.

"What, exactly, do you mean by that?" Rowan asked. There was something more than a little ominous about hearing someone make that proclamation, especially when they carried around a skull staff.

"I'm a spell-casting class, but not like you might think. [Shamans] work best when given the time to prepare and set up. That's why you don't see me slinging around a ton of different spells in combat," Milena explained.

"Just watch," Marcus assured Rowan, smile again on his face. Honestly, Rowan wondered if he ever frowned at all. The man was eternally cheerful. "It's worth the wait."

In spite of her proclamation, Milena didn't start straight away. Instead, she paced around the small clearing she stopped them in, muttering something to herself before finally using her staff's pointy end to carve a large circle into the ground.

A smaller circle followed, just large enough for her to sit inside. Then she pulled various items and scrolls from her robe's many pockets, arraying them around the circle in some order that made no sense to Rowan.

Her initial preparations didn't keep her busy enough to stop her from talking.

"You see, [Shamans] are much closer to [Acolytes], [Diviners], and even [Warlocks] in the way we perform magic. We're pretty far from [Mages], [Wizards], and the like. We can use curses on the fly with the right staff, but if you want to do bigger stuff right, you have to do it slow."

"I mean no offense, but this feels like a lot of work." Rowan motioned at the circles she was busy fussing over. "Does this happen every time?"

Milena was adjusting one of the many crystals. As far as he could tell, she was just nudging it left and right.

"Not every time. But to do it right requires patience," Milena supplied, finally happy with that one piece and immediately moving on to the next. "When it works, we end up doing a lot more with a lot less mana. Most of the mana that our spells consume comes from the items we use or the natural mana of a place."

"Right, and I can see how that'd be useful for a noncombat situation. But wouldn't whatever you cast be easier to prevent or avoid in a fight, considering the time and exactness your spells demand?" Rowan countered.

"Yes and no. Once it gets started, the effects of rituals typically need to be dispelled or overpowered. There's simply no way to avoid them outright. Meaning, you need a strong curse breaker to do it. And they need to supply sufficient mana at once to succeed." Milena patted the animal skull she was handling. Rowan shivered.

"So if you do pull off a ritual, then it's pretty much game over? That sounds powerful, but what about the setup time?" It had been a couple of minutes since they stopped for the ritual.

"That's why we have [Defenders] and the like. To protect the ritual circle even on a battlefield and buy time. Anyway, I'm ready to get started." Milena took her seat, crossed her arms, and closed her eyes. A quiet chanting slowly took over all sound in the clearing.

Rowan felt goose bumps break out all over his body, especially when the various items started to react to her chanting. One of the scrolls she had put out unfurled on its own, bloodred ink glistening like it was still wet and ready to roll off the paper. The eye sockets of some kind of rodent skull lit up, and its jaws started clattering. Crystals of all kinds were now glowing, and some even seemed to *grow*, while others were suddenly flaking out of existence.

Most disturbingly of all, as Milena continued to chant, various forest critters slowly found their way into the clearing. A couple of squirrels and a singular fox, at first, but soon the branches above them were filled with all kinds of birds.

Rowan almost started swinging, but Marcus stopped him, motioning to wait. Rowan figured it out a couple of moments later when he took a proper look at the animals.

They weren't corrupted.

Somehow, that surprised him. He thought there would be extremely few, if any, regular animals left. But apparently, even though the corrupted beasts were plentiful, some smart animals still seemed to manage to stay out of trouble.

After what seemed like a small eternity but was really just a few minutes, Milena's voice fell for the last time. Her eyes snapped open, glowing a sickly purple, and the same light ignited in the eyes of every gathered animal, too.

Then the moment broke and all the animals took flight, some literally and some by speeding away through the bushes.

"That was intense," Rowan said quietly, and with a newfound respect for Milena's class.

"Why thank you!" Milena said in a sweet tone. Rowan got the feeling that she'd learned that particular voice from Olivia. "And now, we have all the scouts we need. Until the next sunrise, at least. I can recast that ritual if we want them to stick around."

"Uh, quick question. What does the ritual do? It looks cool and all, but what just happened?" Rowan asked.

"A temporary bond with the animals drawn to her ritual—" Marcus began.

"Shush. My ritual, my explanations," Milena said, cutting her brother off. "Anyways, I can feel the emotions of the animals. So I'll know if any of them feel distress or something similar. I'm a [Shaman], so I can also give them simple orders or directly possess their senses for a short time."

All Rowan could do was blink.

"Why were you not in charge of scouting before?"

"Because the spell is expensive and takes a lot of mana," Milena replied with a little sigh, though it was gone quickly. "Keeping the connection going and peering through their eyes is *costly*, you know?"

"How long can you keep it going?" Rowan asked. "Or what do you need?"

"The only reason I'm doing this now is because I know Miss Sutton is an alchemist," Milena said, proud of herself despite openly stating she was after Olivia's supplies. "As long as she shares one or two strong potions with me a day, I can more or less keep it up indefinitely. It won't be as good as a real scout, but it'll give us some early warning when we need it."

Rowan felt like the word *strong* was doing a lot of work there. But that was a different problem for a different time. He readied his spear again. It was time to blow off some steam.

The corrupted beasts in the forest had a very bad time that day.

# CHAPTER TWENTY

# Growing Pains

Rowan was pretty glad that Marcus and Milena were now part of his party. Outside of the fact that Milena was a single-person scouting platform with her [Shaman] class and Marcus could block pretty much any threat that came their way, the two were actually pleasant to be around once he was used to their shenanigans.

This was true, despite their almost opposite temperaments. Where Marcus was enthusiasm incarnate, Milena was quiet and lethal in conversation. She watched, she learned, she struck where it hurt. Her jokes quickly homed in on Rowan's non-existent romance with Olivia, and all of them hit true.

Rowan might have been bothered by those jokes, but he was too busy dealing with things to care.

"I don't like this," Olivia shared. She was huddled with Rowan and the rest of the party in front of the village. They were close enough to slip back in if there was real danger but far enough that they could see into the woods.

"It worked the last few times," Rowan said. He stared at the two birds flirting around the edge of a thicket that definitely hid a miniature horde. "Any time now, the beasts are going to take the bait."

"I don't know, I'm not getting a good feeling from this," Olivia said.

"It's our best shot. We can't risk going into the forest anymore, not with more monsters than ever," Rowan replied. "Milena came up with this. She baits a small number of beasts and they go into a rage."

As much as Rowan and the others had tried to cut the swarm around the village down to size, the monsters just kept coming. Marcus swore that they were facing at least a couple forests' worth of corrupted beasts at this point.

And now it was too dangerous for the party to venture into the forest by themselves. In fact, almost any activity outside the village ran the risk of getting swarmed by hundreds of different monsters.

"Olivia might be right," Milena whispered after she directed the birds to take a couple of low dives. "They're not biting anymore. It's like they *know* we're baiting them now."

"Is that even possible? Did one of the beasts get smart enough to take charge?" Rowan asked. He glanced back toward the village. They could get back to safety in under sixty seconds. Less if they had to run with their lives on the line.

"With this many different types of monsters? Unlikely," Milena said. "A corrupted beast needs to reach Epic to have that level of control. And if there's something that strong out there, it would have no reason to play games with us. We'd be dead already."

Rowan shuddered in spite of the relatively muggy midday air.

"Let's call it," Olivia said. "Not much that we can do if they aren't biting."

"What about the mana we spent on this?" Rowan asked.

Once it became too dangerous to go on scouting trips, Milena's temporary familiars were absolutely invaluable. The corrupted beasts didn't bother them most of the time. The bait plan had been put in place when Milena realized that her scouts were becoming meals for the increasingly hungry corrupted beasts.

"It was just a single potion. I've got dozens of them," Olivia said. She had been downright force-feeding mana potions to Milena, desperate to get any edge over their incoming foes.

"Look sharp, foes incoming!" Milena yelled.

The thicket belched out a mass of corrupted beasts. Milena directed the birds back toward them and Rowan prepared to fight. In the past few days, the average level of the corrupted beasts had risen from the low teens to upper teens, with a lot of the corrupted beasts at the max level 20.

All it took was for one thing to go wrong and an army of Uncommon monsters would start besieging the village.

The fight itself was rather simple. Rowan's **Empowered Thrust** was stronger than ever. Although his combination of cards was less flashy than before, it was undoubtedly much more powerful.

And that came in handy today, especially when a couple of Uncommon monsters appeared. Marcus would block, Milena would stun, and Rowan would deliver the strike that finished the fight. And in the cases where that didn't work, Olivia had a potion ready to seal the deal.

As soon as they took care of the small group of beasts, the party rushed back to the village. Luckily, no new hordes chased them, which meant that the retreat turned into a leisurely walk. Rowan used that chance to fall in with Olivia.

"That was fun, right?" Rowan asked.

"It was manageable." Olivia strained out a smile. "But it's time to go back to the hell we call home."

"At least the offending mercenaries were relatively quiet today so you could come with us," Rowan offered. "Hopefully, that trend keeps up."

"They know that what's happening is trouble. They won't put their own lives at risk at key moments," Olivia said. "No, now it's the villagers picking fights instead."

Rowan glanced over at the baron's daughter. She looked like she had aged since he first met her. She was no longer the carefree girl but instead a ragged battlefield commander.

"Seriously? We can't catch a break for even five minutes?" Rowan asked.

"Look at it from their point of view. We've been stuck here for this long, with no new messengers coming around and no reinforcements. Now they can't even go out to work," Olivia said with a sigh.

"So, they're making it everyone else's problem," Rowan said with a bit of bitterness in his voice.

"No, Rowan. They're scared, powerless, and have no clue what to do. Picking a fight with unpleasant mercenaries who have been bullying them probably seems like their best option," Olivia said. "Maybe I should have done the thing before."

The thing that Olivia was referring to was when she had been tempted to have some of the more troublesome mercenaries executed just to calm down the flaring tempers. She had run herself ragged trying to keep things civil between the mercenaries and the villagers, which was part of why Rowan had brought her along for the trip. There was nothing like hard fighting to get the blood going.

"No, I think you made the right choice," Rowan said. He meant it. "We need every hand that we can get right now. And there would have been morale problems in the village if we had gone through with it."

Part of the problem was also that the mercenaries and villagers outnumbered the soldiers so heavily. Out of the twenty soldiers that had set out from the baron's home, only eight were combat ready. Their unified spears were enough to take care of emergency beast attacks when Olivia or the hero party wasn't around. But they were entirely inadequate to deal with the rising issue of arguments around the village.

That was only exacerbated by the fact that there were Uncommon-tier classes among both the mercenaries and villagers who were stronger than the soldiers individually.

"Desimir's not helping?" Rowan asked.

"Not really," Olivia said. She sighed as she sped up and rejoined the twins. Her face turned hard as she crossed through the gate.

Rowan sighed, too. He wanted to help but had no idea how. The only thing he could do was to keep killing monsters. Each slain enemy was one they wouldn't have to deal with in the future.

As soon as they stepped back in the village, people crowded around Olivia like a tidal wave. But before she could start helping them, one soldier muscled his way to the front.

"Officer Bron," he sputtered, "woke up. A few minutes. Awake."

Rowan pieced the different sentences together, and while he didn't quite let himself believe that everything would finally be solved, his lips were already twitching up into a smile.

"We can't miss this, Rowan, come on." Olivia grabbed his hand and beamed up at him.

They made it into Bron's room and watched as the officer twitched and groaned as the motions tugged on his healing skin. Rowan was pretty sure he had seen the officer close his eyes when he saw them enter.

"Maybe I can do something to help him wake up," Olivia mused aloud, drawing as close to the bed as she could. "I have some oils and scents I can mix. I've never made anything like it, but I think it could work. Or maybe the potion'll explode."

"Or we could wait and let Bron have his break for a little longer," Rowan teased.

"Eh, I like my method better. Let me see here, I have some tickle root and . . ."

"Why," Bron croaked. His voice broke, cracking and faltering for a second, but gathered strength quickly again. "What is it going to take to get you kids to stop bothering me? Fighting a demon? I already did that." Bron's eyes fluttered open.

They were red.

Not bloodshot red. Not the "reflecting the flame of a candle" kind of poetic red. They were a solid, crimson red, no separation between the iris, sclera, and the pupil at all. According to everything Rowan knew about basic biology, that was impossible.

Yet Bron was looking at them like there was nothing wrong.

"You look like you just saw a ghost, so I take it I'm not looking good. How long was I out?" Bron's voice was still scratchy, and Olivia picked up a cup of water from the nightstand.

"Three years," Rowan replied without missing a beat. "The kingdom has fallen, and we might be all that's left. We have to rebuild from the village up. Every day is a struggle."

Rowan managed to keep a straight face right up until the man started squinting at him, then lost it and collapsed next to the bed in giggles.

"Ignore Rowan. It's just been a few days," Olivia scoffed, bringing the glass up to Bron's lips.

The officer went to grab it from her, but that only brought his bandaged hands into focus. He scowled like he could cow them into submission, but when that failed, he accepted his fate and sipped at his water.

A couple minutes of awkward maneuvering later, he was lying back again and breathing heavily.

"Well, never let it be said it's easy to kill a demon," Bron sighed as he closed his eyes.

When neither of the two responded, he opened his eyes, only to find Rowan looking solemn and Olivia on the verge of tears.

"I'm so sorry," Olivia whispered, clutching her hands together for lack of something better to do with them. "This is all my fault. If I hadn't given you that potion, you wouldn't be in this state right now."

The old lieutenant took her in then. Really took her in—all the signs of exhaustion, the way her robes always seemed at least slightly stained, the bags under her eyes.

"I'm guessing you're in charge right now?" Bron asked.

Olivia paused, as if she was afraid that she had done something wrong. "I was the highest-ranking official left."

"And the village hasn't burned to the ground? Everyone else wasn't eaten by monsters, either?" Bron waited for Olivia to shake her head in the negative. "Good, then you've been doing a good job while I took my sweet time recovering."

"You wouldn't need to be recovering if it wasn't for me," Olivia insisted, almost getting angry that he wasn't responding the way she wanted him to. She probably expected curses and castigation.

"Olivia Sutton, if it wasn't for you, I wouldn't be alive right now." Bron said her name slowly, and the way he did it left no room for doubt.

"But—"

"No buts, please. We won. I'll live. Neither of those two things would be true without you. I knew the risks. Besides, you got to me in time to give me that purging potion, no? So, you definitely contributed to keeping me alive." Bron smiled.

Olivia took that in for a few seconds. "But your eyes are all weird because of me."

"Really? What's wrong with them?"

"They're a solid red. Crimson. Looks kind of intimidating, really. You'll probably like it," Rowan said, because he could legitimately imagine Bron taking full advantage of his new eyes for added troop discipline.

Not that Bron needed it.

"All's well, then," Bron said. "Will I still be able to wield a sword, do you think?"

"I think so. Not today. Or tomorrow, or anywhere within the next two months," Olivia said.

"Hmm, so I'll be stuck with logistics duty for the foreseeable future. Not great, but I can work with that." Bron seemed about ready to try getting out of bed, too.

"I swear, if you try to get up I'll glue you to that mattress," Olivia hissed.

From how angry she looked, Rowan believed her. Evidently, Bron did, too. He sank back into the bed.

"Really, your father is such a nice, calm man." Bron looked at the ceiling. "Who did you inherit that temper from?"

"We both know that is a lie," Olivia laughed.

"What about my regeneration card?" Rowan asked. "Could that help Bron?"

Olivia paused as she considered it. "I don't think so. I've only ever used one set of phoenix materials. If anything, a Rare-tier regeneration card won't be able to negate the potion's damage."

"That was made with the materials from a phoenix?" Bron whispered reverently, his eyes huge.

"A single feather, but yes. Stolen from the family vault. At least my father was happy enough with the result not to punish me for it."

"And you gave the potion to me."

"I did."

The man stared at her for a few moments longer, then shook his head and gave up. "You are as impossible as your father was at your age. If you're not going to let me work, then let me rest. We'll talk more later."

Rowan traded a glance with Olivia before the two of them retreated, closing the door behind them softly. It was only once they were outside the house that Rowan spoke again.

"Bron, what kind of an officer is he? He can fight and lead. That doesn't seem like something an ordinary officer can do," Rowan said.

"He's a lieutenant," Olivia answered. She twisted her hair around her finger. "Usually, that's a rank for Uncommon classes, but he's a Rare class."

"Then why is he only a lieutenant?"

"Because he never wanted the promotion. And because back when we were a duchy, only an Epic class could become general of the territory's troops. He said he wasn't interested in anything above a lieutenant unless he became a general."

"And then your family got demoted?"

"And then my family got demoted. It turned out that his stubbornness was actually a good thing. If he was of higher military rank, there was a chance they wouldn't have let him follow my father here. This way, he slipped through. No one thought a lieutenant would have a Rare class."

Rowan smiled. He really should have known that the baron would not just send some random lieutenant to accompany his daughter.

"At least things should get better soon. He'll be able to help you out with all the logistics. I'm sorry I'm so useless at it," Rowan said.

"Don't worry. You just need to keep being the big bad hero." Olivia giggled a little, poking him in the side. "I'll take it slow with Bron. He does a good job of hiding it, but he's a lot more hurt than it seems. I'm just happy he's finally awake."

Rowan sighed and looked into the sky. The monster-baiting plan was mostly a no-go with how risky it now was. Maybe he could become a messenger to help take some of the load off Olivia.

Off in the distance, the sky was awfully cloudy, and he was willing to bet that before things were through, they'd be dealing with storms, too.

*Just one more piece of bad news.*

The clouds moved a lot more slowly than Rowan expected. It took two whole days before the sky opened up and released a deluge upon the world.

Most of the village had taken shelter in their houses, and guarding the walls was now a miserable job. One that Rowan was glad to do. The raindrops were like little swords that slashed against his skin, but he justified the suffering in that his patrols were like a beacon of light in the swamp of bad news.

Right when Rowan was feeling pretty good about himself, Milena rushed up to the wall to find him.

"We have a problem," she gasped.

"We have nothing *but* problems." The other reason why Rowan was on the walls was because he didn't want to deal with the problems on both sides of the wall. Cooped up, the villagers had started complaining about only getting meat for meals recently. Rowan wondered if they truly believed that there was a nice little farmers market down the street where they could shop for more supplies, and the hero party was just being stingy. "What's going on now?"

"Some kind of new monster," Milena supplied, looking worried. "Huge, snake or wormlike, large eyes and teeth. They're moving through the mud and shallow water a couple miles from here. I only spotted them because of the hawks under my control."

Rowan didn't groan or throw his head back dramatically. Spending more time with Bron had its benefits, including little things like how a leader should act in response to bad news. Subordinates were like a megaphone—they took cues from their leader on how they should act, and if Rowan was groaning, they'd only amplify that negative sentiment.

"I'm going to assume that since you're worried, those monsters are coming straight at us," Rowan said. "How long until they're here?"

"They're maybe an hour or two out. I really can't make any accurate predictions, though. Those things move all weird, and they move *quickly.*"

"Then I guess we should try to match their speed."

If there was one thing that near-constant attacks were good for, it was building up habits. At the start, it would take a couple of panicked minutes for people to take their positions and get ready for defense.

Now?

They were a well-oiled machine. Everyone, even the mercenaries, did their part. But none of that seemed particularly important when they all spotted the incoming monsters.

It was everything that Milena had mentioned and more. Their creator, some god or otherwise, had leaned all the way into prehistoric eel-monster designs. They had jagged teeth that were too large for their mouths, long and slimy bodies that were over three yards in length, and fish-like fins on the sides of their bodies. The fins weren't quite wings, but they would occasionally throw themselves into the air to better gauge their destination, gliding for a few meters before submerging back down again.

In essence, their new enemies were a nightmare fusion of flying fish, eel, and prehistoric vibes.

Lovely.

At least Rowan didn't have to rely solely on Olivia to gauge what the things were anymore. After some time experiments against weaker monsters, he had a consistent definition of what "entering combat" actually counted as.

Up high on the wall, he had more than enough time to swap out one of his cards for **Inspect** and get a better idea of what he was up against.

He couldn't say he much cared for the results.

**[Mudclad Lure]**
**Level 32**


**STR: 22**
**VIT: 26**
**DEX: 38**
**PER: 14**
**INT: 5**
**WIS: 5**


**Deck (5/5):**
**[Heart] Demonic Breeding (Rare)**
**Flawless Mimicry (Uncommon, Passive)**
**Vicious Lunge (Uncommon, Active)**
**Watery Grave (Uncommon, Active)**
**Hypnotizing Lure (Uncommon, Passive)**

Rowan shared the status screen around, earning himself a grin from Olivia. He returned the smile, replacing the **Inspect** card with something a bit more relevant for combat.

Right as Rowan was feeling good about himself, the eel that he'd scanned began to twist. It redoubled its efforts, slithered through the next bit of muck, and launched itself into the air. Where its previous hops were tiny glides, this was a full-on burst of violence that turned the eel into a living arrow. It aimed straight at Rowan's throat, and he tried to bring his spear forward to defend.

Thankfully, Milena was a bit more attentive than he was.

Miasma drowned the eel, stealing its momentum and slowing it down even though it was midlunge. From there, Rowan had it. His spear ignited crimson, and he thrust straight for the creature's gaping maw.

His strike didn't miss, spearing through the back of the eel's throat and out of its head.

The eel wasn't dead. In a truly horrifying display, its body thrashed for a moment before suddenly coiling around his arms and *squeezing*.

Even with bolstered defenses in his blessing and stats, Rowan still heard something crack inside his arm. His grip on his spear immediately weakened, and he almost lost the buff from **Keen Spear**.

Milena applied a double layer of miasma and Marcus rushed forward to strip the eel away from Rowan. In Marcus's hands, the eel finally died.

Before Olivia could take out a healing potion, Rowan activated **Persistent Regeneration** and all pain fled from his arm while a small part of the energy storage from **Lavish Feasting** vanished.

"Dammit, that was close," Rowan cursed. If he'd had his previous movement cards, there was a chance that he would have been able to dodge the attack in time. But the silver lining in everything was how well the combination of his two cards was working out. As long as he had enough energy, he could focus on damage output and berserk his way to victory.

"Ranged, fire!" Olivia shouted.

A volley of arrows flew out from the wall, only to land harmlessly in the mud. The eels were both too quick and too well protected by the terrain. Any attempts at area spells like fireballs were also quickly drowned out by the pouring rain.

"Hold!" Olivia yelled when she saw the eels mostly unscathed. "Melee fighters, forward. Ranged, keep your attacks ready. Use them if you see an opportunity, but don't waste them."

Rowan scanned the wall. The good news was that the eels were only coming from a single direction. The bad news was that almost all the defenders looked especially pale. He had to do something to turn the morale around.

Rowan thrust his now-healed arm in the air. "People of Felton's Mill. We've fought off monsters and demons. We've faced worse enemies. We'll overcome these eels. They're an opportunity for us. If anything, they'll be a stepping-stone in our path to leave our names in the history books."

The speech was a bit clunky, but it worked. Some of the defenders, especially the mercenaries, began grinning as they readied their weapons. Rowan's words were true: The past few sieges had thinned the village's population, but the ones who remained were mostly sporting levels in the high teens or even twenty. All they needed was a kill of an Uncommon-tier enemy and they could become Uncommon classes themselves.

Their enthusiasm also translated rather well into deadliness. The eels launched themselves into a blizzard of steel and mana, quickly falling without inflicting anything more than a few broken bones on the defenders.

Rowan himself did the very best he could to contribute. He went for smaller but quicker attacks without **Empowered Thrust**. Thanks to **Blood Siphon**, even these light attacks did appreciable damage.

But perhaps the most important factor was that the Mudclad Lures were not meant for siege attacks. They were individual fighters, focused on speed and stealth. Seeing them fly at the wall was scary, but once the initial shock was over, most people realized that the monsters were relatively easy to defeat.

*These eels are lurkers or assassins. A through-and-through ambush predator at home in swamps. Why are they here?* Rowan thought. Even though things were going well, he was beginning to feel a chill rising from the bottom of his heart.

It didn't help that some of the mercenaries were living proof of the adage that the only thing to rival human ingenuity is human stupidity. One loudmouthed mercenary somehow gave an eel the opportunity to wrap around his entire body. Marcus had to use his shield in a precise strike, and Rowan poked the eel to death thanks to **Blood Siphon**.

Outside of episodes like that, the defense of the wall went fairly well. When the eels finally stopped coming, a cheer from the village echoed even amid the heavy rainfall. There was plenty to be happy about. They were still alive and most of the defenders were now proud owners of Uncommon classes.

But the celebrations didn't extend to Rowan and Olivia. The two of them had grim looks on their faces as they made their way to Bron's room.

"Well, don't the lot of you look cheerful?" Bron said, giving them a sardonic smile. "The defense went that badly?"

"The defense went great," Olivia said with no real enthusiasm. "But . . . we've most probably got another demon inbound."

# CHAPTER TWENTY-ONE

# Risk of Rain

Rowan was beginning to learn that he really didn't like rain.

The downpour kept coming over the next day and complicated just about everything. Unpaved ground had been whipped into mud, squelching and trying its best to suck everyone down in a mire of immobility.

It also made combat anywhere other than the wall an absolute nightmare, which wouldn't have been as much of an issue if the enemies were using conventional siege tactics.

At some point over the night, the nightmarish eel monsters had decided that they didn't want to keep jumping up and losing their mobility. Instead, they dug down and made their way behind the walls. They'd either lie in wait and ambush those who were alone or make a beeline for the cottages containing civilians.

Given the rough and unrewarding nature of trying to fight the eels, Rowan had volunteered for eel-fighting duty with the rest of his party.

It wasn't all bad news, though. The constant infighting and grumbles that had plagued the village were mostly gone in the face of the monster threat. Along with the eels came small groups of corrupted beasts, and the teamwork of villagers and mercenaries was surprisingly good for how they had been at each other's throats just a week ago.

And the eels were now easier to fight than when they'd first encountered them. A single blast of cold air from the card that Olivia was rapidly growing to adore would catch the eels in place, freezing them into solid chunks.

Some died that way outright, while others had to be shattered into pieces, but it didn't much matter. Once they were popsicles, it was game over for them.

On the other hand, the rain was more than just a nightmare for their footing.

"Still having trouble?" Rowan directed the question at Milena, hoping the answer had changed since the last time he asked it.

The tired wolfkin just sighed and shook her head at him. "I'm sorry, but there's nothing I can do. This rain isn't normal."

And she was right. The water was starting to come down with ever-increasing ferocity. Some of the villagers were already complaining that just standing under it *hurt*, simply because of how hard the drops were landing.

"I can't believe we're blind again," Olivia grumbled. By the way she glared at the sky, it was obvious that she wasn't blaming their only [Shaman] for it.

"It's literally bringing my birds down." Milena looked, well, like a wet dog. "They can't even fly around in this downpour, let alone actually scout. We still have some of the other critters to rely on."

By some, Milena meant only a couple of animals positioned at faraway points. Without the means to recast the ritual, the familiars rapidly dwindled as the corrupted beasts exterminated their normal-variant counterparts from the forest.

"It doesn't matter much. Nothing is going to change from the scout reports. Corrupted beasts massing, demonic creatures attacking, things looking more dire by the day," Olivia said with a sigh.

Even with Bron waking up, he was months away from returning to duty. He was, other than occasional bits of advice on governance, entirely out of commission. Olivia was on her own, and there was very little Rowan could do to help her when it came to running the village.

"If we could get some food variety, I think it would help," Marcus volunteered, even though he was honestly just as enthusiastic about their meals as he used to be.

"And how do we do that? It's all the same old problems. We can't go out, and the stored vegetables are either going bad or eaten already. We're down to meat, like it or not," Olivia grunted.

Frankly, if it weren't for the fact that monster meat was edible, they would be *entirely* out of luck. A small village wasn't exactly the sort of place designed to house a bunch of soldiers and mercenaries through a long-term siege.

To make matters worse, even the monster meat they did have was starting to sour. The rain made it nearly impossible to smoke and cure properly. The warehouses were luckily still standing, but quite a few homes had collapsed under the weight of all the water being dumped on them.

"We might need to organize some kind of foray into the forest," Rowan admitted, turning the shaft of his spear to distract himself from what he was forced to say. "The villagers are running out of material to make repairs, to homes and the wall both."

"And risk our lives? Even if we do get the wood, how should we treat and prepare it for use under these conditions?" Olivia snapped. "But while we're on the topic, I'd like to get ingredients to replenish my mana potions. Assuming, of course, that the beasts haven't eaten them."

Olivia was right, of course. With the nonstop rain, it was impossible to make lumber without the use of magic.

It was just a bad situation all around.

"I really don't like how limited our options are," Rowan admitted, huddling a bit tighter into his frumpy, borrowed coat. He didn't even care how wet it was.

Marcus was about to say something, but the shield bearer froze, his eyes snapping up to the sky. He scanned it carefully, an unusually serious frown clouding his features. "Did you see that?"

"See what?" Rowan asked, raising his eyes skyward along with the rest of the group. He had to lean forward and up because the eaves of the house they were huddled up against were blocking most of his vision.

He failed to spot anything. The curtain of rain blinded him.

"I'm pretty sure I saw something up there," Marcus muttered, keeping his squinted eyes trained on the sky. "It was like some kind of shadow. No, wait, there it is!"

Olivia was faster to spot what Marcus had seen, though judging by the way she broke into quiet curses, it wasn't anything good.

"Look at this," she growled, pushing the status screen at them.

**[Skyfin Seeker]**
**Level 38**

**STR: 8**
**VIT: 10**
**DEX: 24**
**PER: 46**
**INT: 20**
**WIS: 15**

**Deck (5/5):**
**[Heart] Demonic Breeding (Rare)**
**Minor Aerokinesis (Uncommon, Passive)**
**Storm Lurker (Uncommon, Passive)**
**Grasping Cage (Uncommon, Active)**
**Amphibious Adaptation (Uncommon, Passive)**

"A new kind of bomber?" Rowan asked. His own experience with flying monsters so far had been with the type that picked a person up and dropped them from the sky.

"A scout. They have scouts now." To say that Olivia sounded bitter would have been an understatement.

"That's also the second water-based creature we've seen now," Milena muttered, narrowing her eyes in thought. Her tail, wet as it was, had poofed out a little, shooting straight up into the air. "It *could* be nothing, just a result of this recent weather change, but what if the cause and effect are reversed?"

"You're saying there's something out there *conjuring* this storm?" Rowan's voice was alarmed.

"A powerful demon could probably manage it. The problem is, if they're really capable of something like that, we have no hope of stopping them," Olivia said.

No one had an answer to that. The uncomfortable silence stretched between them, punctuated only by the rain and occasional eels that decided to take potshots at them.

"Forget about that," Rowan said finally. "What we need to worry about is how we're going to take those things out of the sky. We can't just leave them be."

"We need a ranged class. How we have a caster but no decent range is beyond me," Olivia said.

Milena's cheeks puffed up. "I'm sorry. All my strongest spells and curses are either midrange options or require like an hour of cast time."

"Guys, focus," Rowan interjected.

Finding their way to the top of the wall, the party found groups of close-range fighters clustered around ranged classes, ready to protect them if the eels made another appearance and lunged out of the rapidly rising water.

It wasn't a concern yet, but if the rain kept up, they'd eventually need to worry about flooding. Already, puddles were forming on the wall.

Olivia was in the lead of the group, walking confidently toward the nearest cluster of ranged attackers. Rowan and the twins were only a few steps behind.

So it was only by the barest of margins that he caught sight of a clawed hand rising out of a puddle and reaching for Olivia's ankle.

Instinct took over completely, and Rowan's spear blazed as he brought it down. He fueled the strike with as much mana as he could stuff into the relevant cards, and it *nailed* the wispy limb to the wood of the wall.

Immediately, a wail ripped through the air, and a creature shot out of the puddle.

The thing was *floating*, which unfortunately gave everyone a rather good view of its bare body. It was wrinkled, looking at once waterlogged and too thin. The overall shape of it was feminine, but it was more the long, flowing hair that gave that impression than any specific signs of gendered characteristics.

"Olivia, what the hell is this thing?" Rowan shouted. He felt a force tug on his spear as the spearhead ripped through the creature's arm, leaving the limb connected only by thin strips of muscle.

Yet it seemed to pay no mind to its injuries, and the wounds were healing before their eyes. The bone and muscle *slithered* back into place, reconnecting like snakes diving back into the burrow.

"Careful!" Marcus yelled as he positioned himself in front of Rowan.

The creature took a deep breath, parting its rotted lips and revealing rows of sharp, pointed teeth. It screamed, and its mouth cavity did a disturbing thing that made its teeth seem like they were spinning. Rowan was suddenly glad that he hadn't given the creature a chance to hurt Olivia.

The scream was mostly for intimidation. Just high-pitched and loud. Marcus relaxed slightly, and behind the shield, Rowan got a good look at the thing's face.

It looked like the rotting corpse of a person who'd died by drowning. Its eyes bulged and were on the verge of popping out of the eye sockets.

*Disgusting.*

Rowan circled around Marcus's shield and launched another attack. This time, the creature was on the lookout and drifted out of the way faster than Rowan thought it could move while floating.

His spear still sheared through a couple strands of its hair, proving he could indeed hurt it.

One of the mercenaries charged forward with a curved sword. The blade slashed effortlessly through the body of the creature, but it was like the man had tried to cut water. It was unharmed.

"Use mana! Regular attacks don't work!" Olivia shouted over the din of the rain and the rising chaos of battle. She sent over the results of an **Inspect** she had somehow found time to perform.

**[Waterlogged Wraith]**
**Level 41**

**STR: 12**
**VIT: 5**
**DEX: 41**
**PER: 60**
**INT: 50**
**WIS: 38**


**Deck (6/6):**
**[Heart] Demonic Origin (Epic)**
**Aquakinesis (Rare, Passive)**
**Water Veil (Rare, Passive)**
**Chill Touch (Rare, Active)**

### Waterlogged Gasp (Rare, Active)
### Mirror Image (Rare, Active)

From what Rowan could tell, the Waterlogged Wraith was either some kind of undead or outright a water demon. He didn't quite get the same feeling as he had when facing the Rotflower Cambion.

"Swarm it!" Rowan yelled. Behind the wraith, Olivia let loose a flood of mana that quickly crystallized into ice. Her attack frosted over parts of the monster's body, and it turned with a shriek.

The wraith's arms had wisps of cold air curled around them as it rushed straight for Olivia. Marcus got in its path before it could reach her, but when the wraith's claws struck the glowing shield barriers, ice erupted all over it, causing fractures to form. A second strike collapsed the barrier entirely, and the creature was soon reaching for the wolfkin directly.

Marcus tried to put his physical shield between them, but the thing's arms phased through it.

Milena's eyes erupted with black flames as miasma poured forward toward the wraith. The attack intensified when the skull on top of her staff also lit up in flames.

The creature ignored the threat but flagged when the miasma was sucked into its ethereal form.

Meanwhile, Rowan rushed forward again, all thought of defense abandoned as he aimed to deal a blow as crippling as he could manage. His spear, enhanced by **Empowered Thrust**, found purchase in the wraith's shoulder, and when he wrenched it up, it almost took the entire limb.

The wraith erupted into shrieks again, only made louder when several ranged sword slashes impacted its form and confirmed that mana was definitely effective.

Rowan wasn't sure that would be enough. Even as he watched, its arms started to reconnect to the rest of its body. Judging by the way the wound seemed to be absorbing water straight out of the air, he was guessing that its healing factor had something to do with moisture.

With the nonstop downpour, it was like the wraith had an infinite healing potion.

*There's got to be a limit somewhere.*

Rowan struck out again, this time aiming for the creature's face. Unfortunately, it had determined that he was a threat, and it did its oddly swift drifting maneuver, getting just out of reach of his spear.

The wraith's eyes were positively shimmering with mana as it glared at Rowan, and the arm he'd almost taken off snapped up to point straight at him. A wave of mana surged out of the wraith and slammed into him. For a moment, it seemed not to do anything.

Then Rowan choked, eyes widening in panic as he realized he couldn't breathe.

He stumbled forward, struggling to raise his spear. The panic and crushing realization that he was drowning crowded out any other thoughts from his mind. He collapsed to his knees, water spewing out of his mouth.

Attacks frantically slammed into the wraith. But it didn't care. Its arm was still pointed straight at Rowan, and its face was screwed up in malicious glee.

*It's going to die soon. Its vitality is a measly five*, Rowan thought, **Keen Spear** giving him just enough presence of mind to realize he was wrong. *Shit, the rain. It heals just as quickly as it gets damaged. They need to attack all at once.*

Rowan tried to speak, but only water came out of his mouth. As he tried to calm down, he heard shouting and screams in the distance, like a curtain call to his own demise. There was another battle raging on the wall, and he almost lost hope thinking that there was a whole host of wraiths devastating their defense lines.

Black spots began to dance in the corners of his vision, and he drew closer and closer to death. He was on the ground now, and all his struggles to take in oxygen had just resulted in a deep puddle growing around him.

And then Olivia was there, looking angrier than ever before and shimmering with mana.

She practically hugged the wraith before mana exploded out of her.

The full force of **Flash Freeze** erupted, and the wraith transformed from the figure of his nightmares into an ice sculpture. Under any other circumstances, Rowan would have likely found the thing's expression of shock amusing.

But as it was, he was a bit busy trying to cough the water out of his lungs. Olivia's attack interrupted the card's effects, and a moment later, she was on the ground helping him into a better position.

When the first breath of air blessedly hit his empty lungs, Rowan felt like he had been reborn. He managed to shudder out a thanks, his hand finding and briefly squeezing Olivia's own. Then he was scrambling back onto his feet, shaky as they were.

In the meantime, the twins and the nearby soldiers had taken to breaking and hacking the ice sculpture of the wraith apart. A brief check of his system window told Rowan that the thing was dead, but he certainly wasn't about to ask them to stop.

If anything, he stomped on one of its legs himself, getting a satisfyingly loud crack, before quickly scanning the wall to see what else had gone wrong.

Rowan found the defenders huddled behind the wall, thuds echoing out from their wooden cover.

"What?" Rowan was about to move forward and check, only for Olivia to drag him down.

"Do you seriously want to die today?" Olivia hissed, staying crouched as they approached the palisade of the wall.

It quickly became apparent that she was right to be angry, especially with the odd, thin projectiles hissing through the air above their heads.

They were technically out of combat, however, so Rowan switched out his **Persistent Regeneration** for **Inspect** and, when the salvo of whatever was attacking them paused, he risked a quick glance.

He didn't really have a name for what he saw. Groups of creatures that vaguely resembled snails completely covered in at least twenty-inch-long spikes were parked right outside their defenses, firing their spikes at them.

If there was one thing that cheered him up a little, it was the fact that the things looked nearly completely bald. But as Rowan looked, his joy faded at how quickly the spikes were regrowing.

**[Depthsworn Urchin]**
**Level 36**

**STR: 25**
**VIT: 16**
**DEX: 8**
**PER: 40**
**INT: 10**
**WIS: 20**

**Deck (5/5):**
**[Heart] Demonic Breeding (Rare)**
**Rapid Regrowth (Uncommon, Passive)**
**Quill Barrage (Uncommon, Active)**
**Pinpoint Accuracy (Uncommon, Passive)**
**Threat Detection (Uncommon, Active)**

That settled one thing: Each and every one of the enemies were aquatic in some way. That, more than anything, convinced Rowan the rain wasn't natural.

"How, exactly, are we going to take those things out?" Rowan asked, sharing his **Inspect** results with everyone around him and replacing the card with **Persistent Regeneration**. He realized that removing the regeneration card was a bit of a mistake. It was probably much better to take out **Empowered Thrust** the next time he wanted to inspect something.

"I can summon an omnidirectional shield around me for a little while," Marcus offered. "It wouldn't last as long as a shield wall, but I could cover us for long enough to make it down there and start stabbing things. That should also give our ranged attackers a chance to strike."

"That's an idea," Rowan said. He really didn't like the idea of jumping down into a field with urchins, eels, and probably even more water enemies. "Any other ideas?"

Of course, that's when something dropped out of the sky, engulfing the head of one of the soldiers hunkering down. It wrapped around their head completely, and muted cries erupted from the victim.

The people closest to the soldier were clearly stuck on what to do. Some had raised their swords, but they couldn't strike for fear of killing their own ally.

A moment later, the creature unfurled and lifted gently into the air, revealing itself to be a monster that looked nearly identical to a manta ray. And in a pattern that Rowan was coming to dislike very much, it had a massive mouth lined with teeth on the underside of its body.

The soldier's head was brutally savaged, flesh scraped away to a nearly pristine skull.

In revenge, the ranged classes let loose a barrage, bringing down the monster to avenge their comrade's death.

That was just the start of the swarm. All around Rowan, more and more of the airborne monsters were springing their own attacks.

In an ironic twist, the Skyfin Seekers had managed to sneak up on them in spite of the fact that they'd originally gone up the wall in search of someone who could snipe them down.

Fortunately, the things had pitiful amounts of strength and vitality, allowing the defenders to kill them quickly once they exposed themselves. Not as fortunately, this necessitated moving and fighting, which provided the urchins lurking below the chance to strike.

"We can't let this go on," Rowan cursed, biting down on his lip until he tasted blood. "It's going to have to be the two of us, Marcus. Let's go."

Rowan waited just long enough to receive a determined nod, and then he was vaulting over the wall, letting the gravity do the rest. A glowing shield expanded from Marcus, mercifully sparing them the fate of turning into pincushions.

And just like that, they were in the thick of it.

Rowan's spear blazed with mana, but he used only a carefully controlled amount. He had already reduced himself to a mere thirty-two points after the fight with the wraith, and he couldn't run out before he was done.

So, when Rowan rushed forward, he drove his spear into the nearest urchin and tore it out as a massive spray of blue blood shot into the air.

It was disgusting. It smelled fishy, and he danced away from it in case the urchins had some kind of corrosive blood. It was kind of glorious.

Rowan found that the spear countered the urchins perfectly. Their spikes were long, but his spear was even longer. Which meant that he could dig his spear deep into the monster's body and the spray of blood was directly proportional to the amount of damage he was able to deal.

Naturally, it was time for the hero to go on a slaughter.

A more innocent Rowan hadn't thought he would ever get used to fighting, but he was genuinely enjoying himself as he fought for his life by Marcus's side. There was nothing phasing through the walls. Nothing trying to poison him with its blood. No soldiers immediately around him whose deaths he was dreading because they'd rather die than let him get badly hurt.

It was just him, a member of his party, and enemies susceptible to bleed damage.

But like all good things, the time quickly came to an end. The two of them caught the attention of enough urchins for most to change their targets to them. And the barrage of quills was enough to force them right up against the wall while Marcus struggled to keep mana exhaustion at bay.

However, that allowed the defenders to finally do their job, too. They'd apparently cleared out the fliers, and with so few monsters shooting their way, slashes of mana came down on the urchins, intermittently at first and then in massive groupings.

The deaths of their fellows sent the urchins into a frenzy, but that ironically made it easier to deal with them. Rather than concentrating their attacks properly, they started panicking and shooting their quills in every direction, occasionally even hitting each other.

That's when Rowan decided to take a calculated risk. He rushed into combat again, leaving Marcus behind the safety of his shield. It was time for him to let the monsters get a taste of their own medicine.

Rowan couldn't dodge every quill sent his way but wasn't worried so long as he could protect his face. Using the combination of **Lavish Feasting** and **Persistent Regeneration**, any quill that sank into him was quickly pushed out by his regenerating flesh. Meanwhile, any strike that Rowan made on the urchins left their ranks eternally diminished.

And so, Rowan did his best impression of a berserker, ripping through every urchin in his way and dyeing the ground in their blue blood. The fullness of his **Lavish Feasting** energy plummeted, but there was more than enough of it to last the battle.

Finally, the last one fell, and a cheer erupted from the wall.

Rowan smiled wholeheartedly.

# CHAPTER TWENTY-TWO

# Unstable Footing

Rowan's smile lasted until he got back inside the village and saw the full impact of the siege on the village.

The urchins' quills and Skyfin bites had taken out more than a quarter of the combat-ready population of the village. The ones who remained mostly had Uncommon classes, but the constant battles were taking a toll on everyone, fighters and villagers alike.

The best reminder of that was how quiet the village was. There was no celebration. No large show of solidarity and camaraderie. Just the quiet shuffling of feet and grunts of the wounded as the designated healers tried to administer aid in the driest corner they could find.

*So why don't I feel the same way?*

Try as he might, Rowan couldn't find it in him to feel the same fear and concern that was apparent on everyone else's faces. It wasn't that he was entirely unbothered, but his feelings on the subject were muted. Controlled. It was just another setback to overcome.

*Is this the true me?*

Rowan tapped the butt of his spear against the wall he was leaning on and pondered. Then pondered some more, his eyes drifting toward Olivia, who was organizing watches and repairs with the healthy villagers.

*Maybe it is. Maybe this is really who I am.*

Rowan's gaze fell to his spear. It was hard to remember the last time he had been without a spear for any appreciable amount of time. He held it constantly whenever he was awake, and even when he was sleeping, it was on the ground next to him.

*The last time I went without it. Before the fight with the demon? The first corrupted beast wave? Before we left the baron's estate?*

Rowan stared at the weapon blankly, then fought down a shudder that threatened to tear through him. His hand tightened on the shaft, and the feelings halted and sputtered out, letting him breathe easily again.

So many things suddenly made sense to him.

He was never a coward. In fact, Rowan would argue that he was downright brave in comparison to most people his age. But even that had its limits. He was facing down murderous hordes without flinching. With a smile on his face. That wasn't normal. He didn't falter; he didn't collapse. It shouldn't have been possible for a normal adult to go through the changes he had and still stay sane. But he was fine. More than fine. Even when experienced soldiers and mercenaries faltered, he kept moving.

Rowan's breathing started to pick up once more, and again, focusing on his spear let him push the emotions away.

*That's good, right?* Rowan wondered. *It's a good thing to tune out the world. It lets me do my job. It lets me save more people.*

"Rowan? Are you okay?" It was Olivia's voice. Rowan's eyes snapped up to meet her green ones, and he almost flinched at the concern he saw there. "You look pale."

"I'm fine, really. I just need to—" Rowan paused as his mind desperately tried to come up with some excuse. He saw an exhausted soldier slumping against the wall of a house. "Just need to rest a little. Tough battle, you know?"

In some ways, Rowan wasn't lying. Even if he had no mark to show for it, he had gotten stuck by far too many quills for it to be healthy. A more sane person would be looking for some food to replenish energy stores.

"Okay then." Olivia didn't sound convinced, but she pulled back. "You did well out there today. Want to head on back and leave things out here to us?"

Rowan nodded, his grip on the spear redoubling as he made his way through the village. He absolutely hated seeing all the misery on everyone's faces, and it only made him walk faster and make his face even more resolute.

Back in his room and away from all the drama, Rowan simply piled his soggy clothes and armor in a corner. There would be time to deal with them later. He collapsed on the bed, one hand still lightly gripping his spear, hoping he would pass out on the spot.

He didn't.

*When did I become borderline disconnected from all my negative emotions? Do I want them back? And are they the only thing I'm missing out on?*

Time infuriatingly ticked by. Rowan tried to drop the spear. His fingers kept disobeying him. He tried to fall asleep. His mind kept finding new excuses. The storm raged on outside his window, making it hard to even tell the time of day.

At some point, Rowan snarled in disgust, pushed away from his bed, and paced around his room with his teeth gritted. Why was this bothering him now?

*You know why.* Rowan grumbled at himself, forcing his pacing to a stop and taking a deep breath.

It was the damned weather. The weather and constant attacks. With sunshine and good company, they could still pretend things were fine and the baron was just a few days away, ready to reinforce them even if everything went to the literal hells.

Now, the depressing clouds and the masses of beasts had stripped away the illusion, and everyone was on edge. Including him, apparently. It was just that the emotions had been buried much deeper and affected him in ways that were a lot more insidious.

The sum effect of everything manifested in the form of second-guessing how healthy it was to use his Heart Card as a crutch for emotional discipline. At least there was a really simple solution for that.

*Just stop doing it. Drop the thing.*

Rowan let the weapon clatter to the floor and felt the sense of purpose and focus fade like a tide receding. All the emotions came out. The voice in his mind was almost taunting him at how bad a choice it was to be without **Keen Spear.**

Before he could second-guess himself, Rowan threw on some simple clothes and was out in the hall, approaching Olivia's door. He had no idea what time it was. It could have been ridiculously late or just after dinner. All he knew was that she was there, the vague party-link sense telling him that much.

"Just come in already!" Olivia shouted from the beyond the door, making him jump. How long had he been hesitating?

Rowan pushed the door open to find Olivia watching him with an amused smile. He felt the urge to fiddle with his hands. It felt odd *not* holding on to his spear.

"You realize I could hear you thumping away with your foot in front of my door for the past ten-odd minutes, right?" Olivia's voice had that teasing lilt, but her eyes were worried and earnest.

He looked away, focusing on the floor instead.

"I'm sorry. Did I wake you up? I wanted us to go over the loot together, but if now's not a good time, we can just do that later." Rowan was fumbling, and he was fumbling badly.

He just really didn't want to be alone at the moment.

"Does this look like the room of someone taking the time to sleep?" Olivia scoffed and motioned around herself, and even with all his problems, Rowan had to admit she had a point. Every available surface was covered in papers, most with scrawls on them that were either circled or violently scratched out. Most of them were drafts of speeches.

"What's happening? Anything I can help with?" Rowan offered in earnest.

"That depends." Olivia sighed. "Do you know how to motivate an entire village? We lost Desimir, and the villagers have taken it hard. They're throwing a pout party."

"You mean a pity party?" Anger curled in Rowan's chest. It was only when Olivia placed a hand on his arm that he snapped out of it. Apparently, depression and bad thoughts were *not* the only thing his **Keen Spear** was keeping at bay.

"They've barricaded themselves inside their homes with whatever food they could hoard while we were fighting. Now, they're refusing to come out. The Skyfins went after the villagers, too. Now they're convinced that's going to be them if they venture out," Olivia said.

"Shit," Rowan cursed softly. "No repair crews?"

"Worse than that. They did most of the cooking, too, and equipment preparation and a whole host of other things," Olivia said. "We can't afford to lose them."

"So, what do we do?" Rowan asked.

"I don't know." Olivia looked a bit more pale as she exhaled those words. "I can't order the combat classes to bust down people's doors and drag them out to work. They're just scared, and I get that." She hunched in on herself. "Bron could have handled this. He could always—"

Rowan stepped forward and gave Olivia a hug. It was awkward, with him standing and her sitting, but she didn't seem to mind.

"You know that you're the only reason why we're alive right now, right?" Rowan said.

"I don't—"

Rowan stopped her right there. "You've been keeping this village together. If they don't appreciate that, it's on them. What you've done with a group of ragtag defenders is nothing short of incredible."

Olivia was quiet for a second before she returned the hug. "Maybe we should just fight our way out of here and go look for my dad, huh?"

"We'll be fine, you'll see," Rowan said. He knew that she was far too caught up in her duty to really go beyond just a joke. "We'll take the problems one at a time. And then when we finally get over this, we'll make sure to rename this place 'Olivia's Mill' so that they know who saved them."

That made Olivia giggle, and she pulled away. Swinging her legs down, Olivia grabbed a blanket from her bed and tugged Rowan toward the fireplace on the other end of the room.

"So you want to look over our loot?" Olivia asked. The two of them sat down on the floor and she threw the blanket over them both. Rowan was suddenly very aware of her squeezing right next to him.

"Yeah." Rowan fumbled the word out. "The twins. Passed." He took a small breath. "They decided to pass on everything, and I wanted to look with you to see if there's anything useful."

Olivia nodded, and they dived into the system interfaces together. Rowan ignored the battle experience notifications—there were more than he could count, most of them in the one to two hundred range.

"Is this normal? Two hundred and sixteen cards?" Rowan asked. He had been under the impression that cards were something extremely hard to come by. But his experience these past few days had been the exact opposite.

"For a hero? Probably," Olivia said. "But to be clear, there are more cards here than I would see in an entire month. Most people never make it past Common, even after a lifetime of trying. In peacetime, it takes an incredible amount of talent and hard work. But here? Most of the mercenaries are Uncommon and working toward Rare. Flirting with the line between life and death has its merits."

Rowan nodded. "Time for loot?"

"Time for loot," Olivia confirmed.

Rowan first went through his backlog of cards. He had been merging them together as much as possible, which had finally paid off when he combined ten **Relentless Advances** and found the Rare equivalent of the card.

**Obliterating Charge (Rare, Active)**
**Rush toward your enemy, building up extreme speed and damage**
**as you go. Your impact damage grows in proportion to the**
**ground covered during your advance, and your damage resis-**
**tance will be boosted by the same amount, making it incredibly**
**difficult to knock you out of your charge.**

The description was almost the same as before, but the image showed a creature knocking down an entire brick wall. It almost felt like a waste to keep such a card in his cardholder. But Rowan needed every card in his current deck.

There was another Common card, **Nimble Body**, that had grown to Rare tier.

**Feline Physique (Rare, Passive)**
**You can control your body with exacting precision,**
**allowing you to react to blows with extreme dexterity and speed.**
**Your ability to pass through obstacles and**
**tight gaps will also only be constrained by the**
**size of your skeleton.**

Rowan tried the card on and instantly felt a difference. After thinking about it for a few seconds, he swapped **Empowered Thrust** out for **Feline Physique**. The attack card could come back when he went into combat.

Then it was time for the new cards. Rowan worked through the wall of green and found most of the cards only suitable for scraping.

"This could be useful for a future scout?" Rowan said as he sent over a card to Olivia.

**Flawless Mimicry (Uncommon, Passive)**
**You can blend into your surroundings, causing your body to take**
**on their color and even texture. Only the most eagle-eyed scouts**
**will spot you.**

"Not bad," Olivia said. "Sucks that there's only one copy. But I guess we should be grateful for what we have." She began to giggle. "Oh, the things that I could do with that **Grasping Cage** or the **Watery Grave** card."

**Grasping Cage (Uncommon, Active) x 4**
**Summon a cage of air currents to toss around your enemy and**
**disorient them. The duration of the effect depends on the amount**
**of mana invested.**

**Watery Grave (Uncommon, Active)**
**Summon a sphere of water that will trap your enemy and suffo-**
**cate them. The duration of the effect is directly proportional to**
**mana invested.**

"From the Skyfins?" Rowan asked.

"Probably," Olivia answered, rolling for the cards. Rowan declined to partici-pate, and the five cards dropped into Olivia's lap. "Honestly, most of these cards aren't bad. They're just not right for us."

Olivia was referring to cards like **Vicious Lunge**, **Minor Aerokinesis**, **Hypnotizing Lure**, and many more. Most of them were decent cards, but they didn't fit in at all with Rowan's current build or card combinations.

"Scrap them?"

"Yeah, and then combine them," Olivia said. "No point keeping them. Fuse the Common ones together to make Uncommons and then the Uncommons into Rares. If you have enough, then let's go for some Epic cards."

Rowan found that not every card needed to be scrapped. The urchins had a card that caught his eye.

**Rapid Regrowth (Uncommon, Passive) x 21**
**Regrow a minor part of your body, like hair, fur, nails, claws, or**
**similar, very quickly at the expense of your mana.**

"Mind if I take the **Rapid Regrowths**?" Rowan asked. The card looked like a worse version of his own regeneration card. And when Olivia passed on them, Rowan immediately fused the two stacks of ten cards together, grinning like a loon at the result.

Two new copies of **Persistent Regeneration** stared back at Rowan. The sight of the blue Rare cards was enough to temporarily blow away his bad mood. Counting the one he already had in his deck, if Rowan could get seven more copies, he'd have an Epic-tier regeneration card.

Finally, the wraith had actually dropped not one, not two, but three cards, much to Rowan's delight.

**Mirror Image (Rare, Active)**
**Create convincing mirror images of your own body around you**
**using your mana, confusing your foes and confounding their**
**senses.**

The potential of the card was, frankly, huge. Especially for a squishy, weak backliner whose entire job was to lob curses or potions. That being said, Rowan knew how precious each slot of a person's deck was. He set it aside as he looked through the next two cards.

**Waterlogged Gasp (Rare, Active)**
**Point at a foe and conjure water directly within their lungs. At**
**the cost of continued mana consumption and keeping your focus**
**on your enemy, you can keep up the card effect indefinitely.**

Rowan could almost feel his lungs filling up again. The sensation of drowning wasn't one he wanted to reexperience. But on a combat level, this was yet another card that could appeal to both Milena and Olivia.

**Chill Touch (Rare, Active)**
**Channel the deadly grasp of winter into your hands, inflicting**
**severe frost damage to any enemy you touch. The damage of this**
**card can be scaled up through greater mana consumption.**

"This seems like an upgrade to **Flash Freeze**," Rowan said. If nothing else, it was a Rare-tier card instead of Uncommon.

"Only an upgrade on paper," Olivia replied. "I can't use it. Even if it does more damage, it requires me to touch my opponent. I'm not exactly the type to get personal with anything I want to fight. That's you."

Rowan took Olivia's teasing with a smile, which dropped a little as he got to the final entry on the list.

### [Heart] Demonic Breeding (Rare) x 21

"Should I just leave these for now?" Rowan asked.

Somehow, Olivia knew exactly what he was referring to. "Yeah, I don't want to deal with them right now."

"Sounds good." Rowan got to summoning the other cards and turning them into scraps. He happily worked away at that for a while.

"You know." Olivia's voice sounded next to Rowan. "You can talk to me about what's bothering you, right?"

Rowan hesitated. "Eh, it's not a big deal."

"Rowan." Olivia pulled away to look at him directly. "I'm your first party member. You've been there for me when I have my problems. I want to be there for you. I care about you. This isn't anything about duty or whatever, in case you somehow misunderstand. I consider you a *friend*."

"It's my Heart Card." The words tumbled out of Rowan's mouth.

"Explain, you doofus." Olivia groaned and actually punched him in the shoulder.

"It's called **Keen Spear**. It's the card that locked me into using just a spear." Rowan paused and saw Olivia nod as if she already knew that. "It helps me focus better when I have a spear. It's like everything's *clear*. I *know* what I need to do. I get better at wielding my weapon. There's this *awareness* I suddenly feel. It's just so much better than what I can normally manage, in every way."

Olivia put her hand on Rowan's but didn't speak. The silence settled on them until Rowan couldn't bear it anymore.

"It mutes my emotions. Fear, existential dread, embarrassment." Rowan tried to laugh it off, but Olivia was suddenly gripping his shirtsleeve. He ended with a quiet confession: "Now, I'm not really sure I can cope properly without it."

"You know, I thought you were a natural," Olivia muttered, bumping her head against his shoulder. "I had to train for years before I could really use my cards. There are cards that speed that process along. Nobles and wealthy fighters use them. The long-term effects are not pretty."

Rowan considered that. "It's my Heart Card. I can't remove it. And the effect activates every time I hold a spear, and I can't use another weapon to fight."

"You're not using it now," Olivia offered.

"Yeah, I'm not using it right now," Rowan said. He felt a bit better when Olivia pressed herself into his side again.

"I'll think of something, okay? Just promise me you'll actually talk to me about this stuff more in the future." Silence stretched, and Olivia grumbled. "Rowan, I need you to say the words."

"I promise." Rowan caved in. "I'll talk to you."

The two of them stayed in their spot, looking at the fire. All their worries and fears were outside the blanket. Inside, it was just them.

When Rowan woke up in front of the fireplace the next morning with the baron's daughter slightly drooling on his shoulder, he thought that his promise was worth it, at least a little.

# CHAPTER TWENTY-THREE

# Deer and Weasel

The rain never stopped.

And there was only so much water that the ground could take. At some point, it was like a switch had been flipped and the village became a swamp.

Water seeped into everything. Homes, food, and even the mood.

"I wish they'd cooperate at least a little." Rowan gritted his teeth, eyes scanning over the shuttered homes of the villagers. "Don't they realize we're the only thing between them and a pack of hungry monsters?"

"I would like to say that I don't blame them, but . . ." Olivia trailed off with a sigh.

"But this is getting ridiculous. I can understand feeling scared. What I can't understand is why they think hiding in their homes is going to solve anything. Even I can see that the mercenaries are on edge. They're going to do something drastic if this keeps up." Rowan disliked being pushy, but at this point, something had to give. Otherwise, the next wave of monsters would meet a village that was tearing itself apart.

"I know, I know," Olivia growled as she ran a hand over her face in frustration. "It's just that if I do something and things go wrong, it's going to be on *me*. Tell me some good news."

"The beasts, they seem distressed," Milena said. The beast folk was currently sitting cross-legged on the wooden wall in spite of the rain, eyes closed. Her face was scrunched up in concentration. "I can't get a good read. The best familiar I have left after that last attack is a fox. I'm trying to get closer, but I don't want to lose it. Give me a second."

"What are you seeing?" Olivia asked.

"I think . . . take this with a grain of salt. I'm really not sure if I'm seeing this right."

"Milena, please, you know I won't blame you for whatever you say. What's going on."

"I think the horde will rush us soon. I don't know why they haven't already. Some of the weaker ones have drowned. I think there's some kind of commander among them. Probably a wraith like the one we fought a couple of days ago," Milena replied in an unsure voice.

"You think that the corrupted beasts were holding back and massing in number?" Rowan furrowed his brows. That was tactics, something only the demon had employed.

"It makes sense." Olivia sighed, closing her eyes briefly. "They're too well organized. The Skyfins for scouting, the wraith assassin, the troop of urchins, the harassing lures. They *are* organized."

"So what's next is going to be a corrupted-beast wave. If they want to weaken us, now is the best time to just unleash all of them," Rowan concluded.

"Exactly. We need to organize our defenses before that happens. Spell casters for now. We'll need to save the archers for pinpoint attacks when the demons come." Surprisingly, it was Milena who said those words. Not Olivia. She looked down a moment later. "I'm not sure. Just a thought."

"A good thought." Olivia offered her a smile and bumped her shoulder. "We'll do just that. I'll go send the order."

It wasn't an easy thing to drag the right defenders up to the wall and force them to take station. Rowan couldn't help but show a bit of worry on his face as he watched the men and women slump against the palisades, miserable in the rain.

Five hours after they'd bolstered their defenses, Milena's fears proved true. A tidal wave of beasts gushed out of the trees, literally and metaphorically.

Funnily enough, the rain actually worked in the village's favor for once. They had the nice, tall wall they could attack and defend from. The forest critters, meanwhile, had to waddle and even *swim* to get at them.

Some of the small beasts were entirely submerged, and the smarter of the monsters clung to their larger comrades in arms. Interestingly, this didn't provoke a battle. Under normal circumstances, they would have started infighting over that kind of breach of personal space. But under demonic control, Rowan could see it all make sense.

"Should we go down there?" Marcus quipped.

"What? No. Why would you suggest that?" Rowan asked.

"Because most of those can't really hurt us." Marcus motioned vaguely at the slowly approaching horde. "And we could break them up into more manageable chunks for the troops by hunting down the stronger beasts."

Rowan blinked, then looked at the beasts again. The shield bearer was right. Despite their numbers, most of the attackers were at the Common rank. They might have all been at the max level 20, but they were still a walk in the park compared to the demonic creatures they had been fighting.

"Rowan Clairfont, if you so much as think about jumping into thigh-high water to fight a beast horde when we have a perfectly fine wall, I am going to strangle you myself," Olivia hissed.

Rowan hesitated. For all of about fifteen seconds.

"Catch you there." Rowan grinned at Marcus and *leaped* down the wall.

It was horribly annoying that he couldn't use any of his more interesting cards in his build, since his two free slots were taken up by **Lavish Feasting** and **Persistent Regeneration**. He couldn't remove the former without eliminating all the energy stores he'd accrued, and they didn't magically return when he reequipped the card. Meanwhile, the latter was just a no-brainer to keep when heading into combat.

"Keep them off my back, okay?" Rowan shouted over the rain at Marcus, and he didn't even wait for the nod to start wading into the slaughter.

It was oddly calming. Therapeutic, even. Rowan used his spear for what it was intended for. Combat and death.

Rowan buried the spear into the eye of a boar, then gracefully sidestepped the remaining momentum of the same beast while aiming at the throat of a wolf. The spear tip became dyed in red from the blood that gushed out. The beauty of **Blood Siphon** was that it was entirely passive. He didn't need to use a single drop of mana on the card for it to do its work.

About twenty or thirty beasts in, Rowan began to relax. He was absolutely bullying monsters that would have turned him into mincemeat just a few weeks ago. It was exhilarating. And it was good to feel **Keen Spear** go to work after being without the card for the past few days.

A deer with glowing horns jumped in his path. Rowan's eyes briefly widened. That was **Relentless Advance** if he'd ever seen it. The creature must have killed a boar and then added its card to its own deck. As it barreled toward him, Rowan carefully took a few steps back.

They were fighting in a flooded swamp. The mud sucked down on every step, which meant that although the deer was faster than Rowan, it wasn't a big advantage. And it wasn't quick enough to get to Rowan before Marcus did.

The deer collided straight on with the wolfkin's shield and came up short. It didn't even rock the defender back, and by the easy smirk on Marcus's face, he wasn't daunted, either.

Rowan took down two wolves and a fox trying to attack them from the flanks. Then, using the opening, he stabbed at the deer's neck.

It did the job. The spear bit deep into flesh, and when Rowan drew it back, deer blood swirled around their feet.

The animal released a cry of pain and somehow stumbled through the wound. Rowan advanced again, raising his spear for a final attack on the monster's head.

Rowan locked eyes with the deer. And everything felt wrong. The eyes he met belonged to a creature of perfect purity and innocence. Its tearful gaze struck straight through Rowan's heart, and he couldn't believe what he and Marcus had done. To raise his weapon against something like that was practically sacrilege.

When Rowan was ready to confess his sins, the deer reared up and stomped its front hooves on his chest. The air flew out of his lungs. He gasped, only to get a lungful of murky, disgusting water.

The only reason Rowan didn't panic and manage to drown in mere feet of water was **Keen Spear**.

He did a slow roll to the side and fought down his panic.

When Rowan came up, spitting water and gasping for air, Marcus was locked shield to horns with the deer and a wolf was preparing to pounce on his unprotected back. Rowan snarled in rage, his spear snaking out and catching the beast in the throat. He wrenched his weapon clear and rounded on the deer. He made sure to use **Empowered Thrust**, coating the spear in a red haze.

This time, there was no coming back for the deer. Not unless it could function without a head.

"You okay?" Marcus shouted.

"Fine," Rowan coughed. He leaned over and hacked up blood. Normally, that might have given him pause, but he could feel his regeneration kicking in and fixing him up. His chest was tight for a bit before he could breathe normally again. "The damn thing got me."

"That's for sure," Marcus laughed. He swung his shield in a giant arc, creating some space for the two of them. "I got scared there for a second."

"You and me both," Rowan grunted as he took a couple of deep breaths to make sure everything was functioning fine. The blow had been surprisingly devastating, perhaps the hardest he had been hit since rising to the Uncommon tier. "It's my class. Sacrifices defense in favor of attacks."

Rowan speared a couple of the beasts that crept closer. He used **Empowered Thrust** in its lowest form, just a single mana point per attack. That was enough to end pretty much anything in his way with a single shot each time.

"I'll say. If I could attack like you, I'd give up a couple points in defense as well," Marcus said as he came closer to Rowan.

"Yeah," Rowan grunted. He was beginning to learn a bit more about his class and the implications behind it. It was true that his blows were far more ferocious than before, but he couldn't underestimate any of his opponents.

*The "reckless" in the name means that I go all out, no matter what I'm fighting.*

Soon, the majority of the horde finally reached them. Even though the beasts were likely under the control of a demon, they seemed to have a bit of wiggle room in their orders. Instead of rushing toward the high wall, most of the monsters chose to wade their way toward the two stupid humans who were sitting out in the open.

Rowan gradually lost himself in the fighting. The bodies of the slain beasts piled up around his feet, gradually accumulating enough that he found himself fighting on dry ground, or at least something that was different from mud. And thanks to the baron's training, he could keep his footing even when the dead monsters rolled and shuffled under him.

Marcus was not quite so lucky.

The shield bearer, predictably, worked best on solid ground. His stat investments clearly favored vitality and strength instead of the dexterity that Rowan prized. As the bodies piled up, he began having more and more trouble moving around.

"I'll cover you," Rowan called out after dispatching another squirrel that flew off another beast to scratch at him. "Just make sure you don't let them get through to me."

Rowan danced around Marcus, protecting his flanks and back while using him as a semimobile wall. That, in turn, freed him up from having to worry about his own back and allowed him to unleash his full destructive might against the beast horde.

"Heavy hitter coming!" Marcus yelled.

Rowan spared a glance back and saw a bear, ten feet tall and built like a tank, rumbling toward them. It wasn't overly fast, but its slow momentum plowed through the other beasts like they didn't exist.

"Is that thing still Uncommon?" Rowan asked. He swung his spear out like a staff and poked at a few antsy beasts that tried to rush in.

"Is that really what's on your mind right now?" Marcus grunted as he braced himself. The bear's front paws started glowing well before it reached them, and it began to charge. Every time its claws came down, water shot up in the air, and any beast unfortunate enough to be in its way was trampled into the mud. "Brace."

The beast practically launched itself over the last few yards.

Its front paw landed heavily on Marcus's shield, creating a miniature light show as his cards struggled to absorb the blow. Somehow, the beast folk never backed up even a single inch.

Then the second blow landed and Marcus's defenses folded. The glow protecting him *shattered*, and he was suddenly thrown back with startling force.

The only thing that saved Rowan were his enhanced reflexes. He dropped down on the pile of bodies, letting the beast folk sail over his head and impact some of the Common beasts behind.

Almost by instinct, Rowan committed the strongest offense he could possibly bring to the bear.

Twisting his body in a way that made him sorely miss the **Feline Physique** card, Rowan channeled as much force and mana into his strike as he could. He pulled his shoulder back as the glowing mist surrounding his spear tip turned viscous and incandescent, and then shoved forward.

The bear never knew what hit it. The spear flashed through the air and found its way into the bear's chest. There was so much momentum that nearly half the length of the spear staff went into the bear, and the tip even poked out of its titanic back.

Rowan stared at the results of his attack, almost unsure that he was the one who did it. There was now a hole the size of his head running through the bear's body, and through it, he could see the dark cloud rumbling behind the monster.

*That's what . . . twenty points of mana does*, Rowan thought in mute shock as he quickly checked his status screen.

A gusher of blood exploded out of the bear's back. The beast paused, swayed, and collapsed forward. Rowan actually had to let go of his weapon to avoid getting crushed. Thankfully, even when temporarily separated from his **Keen Spear** effect, Rowan had more than enough speed and presence of mind to scramble on top of the bear's back and pull out his spear from the other side.

As soon as **Keen Spear**'s cool relief flooded through him, Rowan turned around to help Marcus.

The shield bearer was nowhere to be seen. And then Rowan found him. Or rather, he found a lump of Common beasts that made a tiny hill and assumed that Marcus was underneath. Wading his way forward, Rowan speared away the critters and unearthed an unharmed shield bearer. Even though his main defenses were down, the claws and fangs of the Common beasts weren't enough to even draw blood from the man.

*How much vitality does he even have?* Rowan was jealous of Marcus's defenses for a few seconds before realizing how much it would have sucked to been under a mass of wet, snarling beasts. *I'll take my current build, actually.*

"Thanks," Marcus said as he got back to his feet, almost entirely fine despite the scare earlier. "Same tactic?"

"Same tactic," Rowan replied as he left his back to the shield bearer.

Luckily, the strong Uncommon beasts seemed to be a bit of a rarity, and the two of them got a chance to catch their breath against weaker swarming Common beasts.

"I don't think I've ever been this disgusted while fighting for my life," Marcus quipped after dispatching a pair of boars.

"Or this wet," Rowan said. He was soaked with a combination of blood, water, and murky fluid that he didn't even want to find the provenance of.

"At least we're doing something." Marcus moved closer to the wall.

Hygiene-related trauma aside, things were actually going well. Their presence on the field made them a very obvious, very attractive target, which relieved much of the pressure on the defenders. Besides the numbers, the beast horde was surprisingly manageable.

As the wave eventually began to thin out, the beasts began to throw some curveballs at the two of them.

A flaming boar ran forward, somehow lighting itself on fire and probably hoping to score a lucky hit with its charge card. Marcus effortlessly stopped its charge, and Rowan quickly skewered it while using the bare minimum in mana.

Later, an owl divebombed down and attempted to sink its claws into them. That one was a bit harder to deal with due to a corona of wind surrounding it, but once Rowan figured out the trick, it was just a matter of stabbing upward at the right time.

And right when Rowan thought things were done, a massive trio of wolves came into the picture. The beasts all conjured clone illusions, quickly surrounding the two humans with real and fake wolves. It would have been tricky to deal with them if it weren't for the fact that it was still raining—the water splashed on the real bodies while passing through the illusion ones like nothing was there. Rowan made short work of them.

A small flash of movement danced at the edge of Rowan's vision as he finished putting down the last of the wolves. For the moment, he didn't think much of it. He had been dealing with squirrels for much of the day, and even when there were a dozen hanging off him, they hadn't been able to be more than just a nuisance.

So when lines of agony suddenly ripped their way up his legs, Rowan was a bit too shocked to scream.

Instinctively, he punched down to stop whatever was hurting him. The pain stopped for a second, only to begin again on his arm. When Rowan finally heard an angry screech and looked down, he realized that his worst enemy of the fight, funnily enough, was a weasel. And unlike nearly every other corrupted beast, it was utterly adorable.

The weasel had wine-red fur, with a perfect, snowy patch on its belly. Its eyes were large and glassy, and its whiskers twitched left and right in a way that would have had Rowan squealing in delight under any other circumstances.

As the pain caught up with him, Rowan was definitely squealing. Part of the weasel's wine-red fur was thanks to Rowan's blood, and each time it scratched down with its claws, three new wounds appeared on Rowan.

And it was using the arm as a death-delivery system to scramble toward Rowan's face.

"Shit," Rowan cursed. That was the only word he got out before the weasel hit his face and the world went dark on him.

Things seemed to suddenly slow down for Rowan, and he got confirmation of several of his suspicions and theories.

First, the reach of the spear was a double-edged sword. Its length was great when the opponent was something big and heavy, but in the case of a small and nimble enemy that could get past his guard? He was pretty much at its mercy.

Second, the weasel was definitely an Uncommon. The raw instinct it had to hide and then go straight for Rowan's face was something that hadn't been true of most other demonic beasts.

Third, **Persistent Regeneration** regrew organs, like a person's eyes. Or at least it felt that way. Rowan lost his sight when the weasel got to his face and a sharp pain blossomed from his eyes. But the healing process was surprisingly painless. Or at least it should have been.

Somewhere next to him, Marcus was screaming gibberish. The next thing that Rowan knew, he was getting bashed in the head. And the blows didn't stop when he fell to the ground. Finally, he heard a soft whimper by his ears and the attacks finally paused.

"Rowan? Are you okay? Rowan?" Marcus's yell was so loud that Rowan thought his head was going to split in two. Or maybe it had already been sawed in half with how bad everything hurt.

"I hope so," Rowan said, surprising himself at how calm he was. He could feel his eyes reforming, followed by flashes of colors and shapes that he didn't even have names for. "I really hope so."

"Holy shit. Thank Sarina," Marcus whispered. "I thought . . . I'm sorry."

Rowan blinked blearily into the rain as he got his bearings. Marcus was fighting desperately right above him to keep the Common beasts away.

For better or for worse, **Keen Spear** helped Rowan push through the horror of what had happened to him, and he was able to shakily rejoin the fight.

For the first few beasts, Rowan made sure to double-check that there were no critters hopping a ride and about to wreak havoc. He relied on Marcus to keep the monsters at an appropriate range and backed into the safety of his beast party member after each strike.

No small critter was ignored in favor of their bigger counterparts. If anything, the two of them fought those smaller demons first.

That might have actually saved them a repeat of the incident, because one of the smaller foxes that Rowan skewered managed to survive long enough to extend a paw farther than physics should have allowed and almost scratch Rowan.

Another Uncommon, by Rowan's reckoning, and another one that could have attempted to climb him like a cat determined to knock the ornament from the top of a Christmas tree.

Thankfully, the horde quickly dwindled, and soon the two of them were facing only a handful of beasts. Rowan dispatched them with ease, now completely healed thanks to **Persistent Regeneration**. And whether it was his imagination or post-healing hunger pangs, all the beasts looked delicious to him.

Every wolf, fox, boar, and whatever else the forest had disgorged was lying dead on the field next to them. It wasn't a pretty sight. The muddy swamp had turned into a bloody cesspool of fur, muscle, and beast parts.

"We're done?" Marcus asked when no new animals came to challenge them.

"I think so," Rowan sighed.

The wolfkin nearly collapsed on the spot. "I'm never going to suggest something dumb like that again. I thought you were . . ."

"Dead," Rowan finished for him.

"Yeah. I'm sorry, I didn't see the damn thing," Marcus said.

"No, not on you." Rowan looked at his companion. Despite a ridiculously high vitality score that left Marcus without so much as a single bleeding wound, the beast folk was exhausted. He had swung an incredibly heavy shield for, by Rowan's hazy estimate, the past three or four hours. "I think we both deserve a chewing out."

Rowan was feeling the effects of the fight, too, but mostly on a mental front. For one, he was pretty sure he would never look at a cute, fuzzy animal the same way again.

Quite literally, too, because he was in possession of a brand-new pair of eyes.

As Rowan surveyed around himself once more, he realized how low **Lavish Feasting**'s energy stores must have been. He wasn't just hungry. He was starving. He felt like his body was devouring itself. The beasts had never looked better.

Rowan shook the sensation off, then blinked when he realized it wasn't entirely his own. Whether it was because of the card's original owner or because of its inherent quirk, there was a tug in his chest that seemed to be urging him to feast right then and there.

And Rowan wasn't sure if he would have been spared from trying to gorge on the beasts if it weren't for **Keen Spear** backing him up. For the first time, he realized that literally shoving magical cards into the core of his being had some effects he couldn't entirely predict.

Now that he had a moment to reflect, even his use of **Persistent Regeneration** was not something done consciously. The card seemed to activate entirely on its own the second he was hurt in some way.

That wasn't troubling, but that did lead him down a disturbing train of thought.

*We bend the cards to our will. But the cards also shape us. The cards I decide to equip right now will influence me in ways I have no clue about.*

It was a sobering thought, one that Rowan didn't dwell on as he waded across the battlefield with Marcus and back to the gates.

Now, it was time for the real battle: enduring Olivia's scolding.

# CHAPTER TWENTY-FOUR

# Shoring Up Weaknesses

Rowan found a different Felton's Mill when he walked back through the gates. The soldiers and mercenaries, what remained of them, looked at him with awe and fear. They stood to attention when Rowan walked by, and he got the odd feeling that discipline for them would no longer be an issue for Olivia anymore. As he shuffled in front of them, cheers began to form.

"A hero's welcome," Marcus said happily.

"I mean, we just went out into a monster horde, almost lost our lives, but somehow pulled through. That deserves something," Rowan replied.

"I just hope Milena sees things the same way," Marcus whispered as he watched both Olivia and Milena approach them with very stormy expressions on their faces.

Rowan grinned as he saw the two of them. But his grin soon froze when Milena grabbed one of her brother's fluffy ears and violently manhandled him into a corner. Olivia, on the other hand, stopped a few feet short, crossed her arms, and just stared.

Even when the soldiers finally closed the gates, struggling against the push of the water, Olivia just stood there and stared.

"Umm." Rowan cleared his throat, unsure of what to say. He was pretty sure she would reach for her potion pouch if he tried to go around her. "I'm sorry?"

"Was it worth it?" Olivia's voice was tightly controlled, almost neutral, but he could *feel* the emotions hidden within.

Rowan took a moment to think. He had faced the strongest that the monster wave had to offer. It had been reckless, but there were definitely benefits. For one, even though it was only him and Marcus fighting, everyone in their party got the full experience for every kill thanks to his blessing. Second, the wall defense became easier thanks to them drawing away most of the heavy hitters. And last, he saw how the others now looked at him. Rowan wasn't just a person carrying the title of hero anymore—now he was a real hero to everyone in the village.

"I think so," Rowan admitted. "We're still alive."

For a second, Rowan thought Olivia might punch him. Or at least slap him. She surprised him by closing the distance and hugging him.

He hesitated for a fraction of a second, then reciprocated. His heart also broke when he felt the subtle tremors running through her, but he didn't regret the decision.

"I really thought you were going to die when you went down. Twice," Olivia whispered against his chest, and all he could really do was hold her a little tighter.

"We can't afford to just stand still and wait for things to happen anymore. If we want to get stronger, we're going to have to get into the thick of things," Rowan said softly.

When one of the soldiers awkwardly cleared his throat, the two of them suddenly realized that they were in the middle of the village and jerked apart.

"Ah, I was wondering if you want us to do something about all the bodies outside, Lady Sutton?" the man asked.

"No. The water's not great for the meat, and considering the way this one smells—" Olivia paused to jab a finger into Rowan's chest. "Keep the doors closed and make sure we have enough lookouts for when there's a new wave."

"Yes, ma'am." The soldier snapped off a salute, then started spreading the orders around.

"You know, we still have to deal with those bodies," Rowan said. "The rain will slow things down a bit, but when those dead beasts start rotting, we'll have a plague on our hands."

"That's a problem for later," Olivia huffed. "If the village falls, it won't matter if there's a plague or not."

"Olivia!" Milena called out as she sprinted toward them. "We need to talk."

Olivia glanced at the soldiers and mercenaries still around and led the way to one of the side houses. "Did your scouts spot something?"

"I'm not sure how to say this gently, so I'll just do it. There's an army headed our way. They're about two days away at their current speed, and the army *definitely* belongs to a demon," Milena said. "It's a big army. Hundreds. Maybe thousands? All of them at least Uncommon, from the looks of it."

Olivia paled, but didn't falter. "The same creatures as before?"

"Mostly. I caught a glimpse of some new types, but the eyes of a badger aren't really the best around in the middle of this rainstorm."

Everyone paused.

"Right, then." Rowan broke the silence. "So we have two days to prepare. That's plenty of time. Worst case, we die in a way fit for bards to recount in their tales. Best case? We live and tell the story ourselves."

Olivia laughed softly. "And who wants to join me while I break the news to the troops?"

Rowan really didn't want to, but when Olivia headed back toward the soldiers, he followed.

A couple of hours later, once the initial preparations had been set into motion and Rowan managed to find the time to change into something that hadn't been mauled by a rabid weasel, the hero party found themselves in Bron's temporary lodgings.

The officer was still barely able to move his limbs, but they needed all the brainpower they could get for what to do against the approaching army.

"Your father is probably fine. You do know that, right?" Bron rasped out.

Olivia's eyes snapped to the man, and for a moment, she gave off the impression of a deer in the headlights, frozen yet ready to bolt. Then the fight went out of her, replaced by a defeated look. It was as if she took the approach of the army as her personal failing.

"You say that, but look at what's happening. There is a literal demon army marching right for us. If he's fine, and that's a big if, then why? How did this happen?" Olivia asked.

"I don't say this lightly, nor do I mean it as an insult, but Olivia, your father is not perfect," Bron said slowly. "If he were, he would still be a duke."

Olivia flinched like he'd struck her and hunched in on herself, prompting Rowan to draw closer to her. Bron glanced at the two of them before he continued.

"There's no use thinking about this if it's only going to distract you. What level are you all?"

"I'm still only level 38. Incredibly close to 39, but I'm not going to make Rare before the army gets here." Olivia drew a shuddering breath. "The problem is, I really don't see how we fight another demon. That last one took everything we had, and . . ."

"And here I am," Bron joked. "Still alive, although barely. Hero Rowan?"

"28," Rowan replied. He was beginning to see how difficult it was to level up.

**Rowan Clairfont**
**Level 28 Reckless Spear**
**EXP: 1,645/60,000**

**STR: 30***
**VIT: 12**
**DEX: 30***
**PER: 20**
**INT: 10**
**WIS: 11**

**Deck (5/5):**
**[Heart] Keen Spear (Epic, Passive)**
**[Class] Empowered Thrust (Common, Active)**
**[Class] Blood Siphon (Uncommon, Passive)**
**Persistent Regeneration (Rare, Active)**
**Lavish Feasting (Rare, Passive)**
**Blessings:**
**Awakened Blessing of the Stalwart Hero**

"That's not bad, considering that you were still a Common class when we set out," Bron said, lightening the mood.

Rowan promptly poured a bucket of cold water on the officer's efforts. "But it's slowing down. The experience requirements kept ramping up by five thousand for each level until level 25. Now, they're increasing in increments of ten thousand at a time. Honestly, I can't imagine how much experience it'll take to go from level 39 to 40."

"And we don't have another Unique potion to rely on. We don't even have a Rare class to lead us into battle this time. And that's before we consider the fact that this approaching demon is clearly leagues beyond the last one we fought," Olivia finished miserably.

"Well, about that. Maybe I can help," Marcus cut in sheepishly. "Me and Milena both, actually. We were on the cusp of getting to level 40 before the battle. That's sort of why I was so eager to go out and fight. And surprise? We both have Rare classes now."

Olivia and Rowan could do nothing but stare for a long moment, before the hero broke into a smile and dragged the wolfkin into a hug, slapping his back as he did.

"You oaf! You could have said something sooner," Rowan exclaimed.

"Honestly, it's mostly thanks to the wave," Milena said in her gravelly voice, her face stretched into a grin.

"It really is great, you know?" Marcus continued, pulling out of the hug and completely missing the fact that Rowan had tried his best to bruise his friend's back with those gentle pats. "It might have taken us months or even years to get the experience for that last level."

The hero's hand was numb, and Marcus looked like he was none the worse for wear. Rowan wasn't bitter about it. At all.

"The two of you," Olivia cut in. "You have Rare Heart Cards?"

Marcus traded a glance with his sister. "We do. It's part of why we decided to become mercenaries. There was no other way to use our gifts back home."

"I see. I hate to just ask this, but what can you do now?" Olivia asked.

Marcus didn't even hesitate. "I'm an [Aura Guardian]! The class card I got now lets me extend my defensive stats to nearby party members and allies, nullifying a certain amount of damage dealt to them and taking on the rest myself. Unless I choose to pass on absorbing damage, no one is dying before me."

Rowan was beyond impressed. Olivia was less excited. "And the penalties?"

Marcus paused, and Rowan had to resist the urge to chuckle at the way his ears and tail drooped.

"You can pretty much count me out for any kind of damage dealing," Marcus said. "My mobility is also a *bit* worse. And, obviously, if I take on too much damage, I can still get hurt."

"I'm an [Elder Shaman] now," Milena volunteered. Her voice was slightly less raspy than before. "I got a pretty useful ritual that I can perform for this upcoming battle. There's just one slight problem."

The wolfkin hesitated, crossing her arms in front of her chest protectively.

"Go on," Olivia said, and Rowan was surprised at how gentle she sounded. He wasn't sure when it had happened, but it seemed like the two had grown quite close.

"It's a summoning ritual. I can call forth the spirits of past warriors to fight for me. They'll be at the same tier as me. However, it's expensive. Mana-wise. On my own, I can maybe keep them around for five, ten minutes. I'm going to need a lot of potions to use them in fights."

"What about the summoning time itself? How long does the ritual take?" Olivia asked.

"It's not long, comparatively speaking. I can complete the final steps of the ritual in five minutes or so."

"In other words, you can hold back on the ritual and then spring it if we're losing or need an edge for the boss fight?" Olivia asked, her eyes taking on a far-away quality. She was making plans already, and Rowan wasn't sure whether to be excited or worried.

"Yes, but if the warriors perish, I won't be able to resummon them. They're fixed summons and take time to regenerate before I call on them again."

"That's fine. That alone gives us a ton more options than we used to have just ten minutes ago. I'm thinking about a basic defensive formation, with you in the reserves," Olivia reassured Milena with a smile. "I'll fight on the front. It's not ideal, but with the size of the incoming army, I'll probably hit the level cap at some point during combat, too."

"When that happens, come to me," Bron interrupted. For most of the conversation, he had been content to let Olivia and Rowan lead the way. But he now shimmied up in his bed to sit straighter.

Olivia nodded. "I'll need to be out of combat for a bit before I can apply stats or upgrade my class anyway. When that happens, Milena, you might need to use your ritual if the line starts to waver. But once I come back with [Combat Alchemist], I'll be much more useful."

The next item on the agenda was about the villagers. Thanks to Rowan's recent heroics, they seemed a lot more willing to listen than before. And Bron urged the group to take advantage of that.

"If the rain keeps up, some of the weaker houses are going to collapse," Bron warned. "You have to move them into the better houses, whether they want to or not. If Skyfins are part of the next invasion force, then a few odd villagers are going to panic, and that'll spread to the rest of the defenders if we don't plan ahead."

"I'll make sure of it," Olivia promised.

The last item was something from Rowan's list.

"We have a lot of Uncommon cards from the past few days. Should we distribute them? Maybe some of the villagers or mercenaries can use them," Rowan asked.

"Don't," both Olivia and Bron said. The baron's daughter paused while Bron continued on. "It's never a good idea to be equipping new cards before a battle unless the card's the same tier as your Heart Card. And even then, it's best if they use the cards that they're familiar with."

"Right, no distributing cards, then," Rowan said. He looked at Marcus and Milena. "But what about you guys? We got a couple of cards that you might find useful."

Rowan brought out **Titanic Physique**, **Waterlogged Gasp**, **Chill Touch**, **Mirror Image**, and even **Rot Shield**.

Marcus sorted through the cards and picked out **Rot Shield**. "With my new class, **Rot Shield** might come in handy. I'll have to test it out, but if the rot mana covers everyone inside my aura, it'll be a big deal."

**Rot Shield (Rare, Active)**
**Summon a film of rot mana that will cover your body and protect**
**you from blows, damaging your enemies and their weapons in**
**the process.**

"It's yours, then," Rowan said. "What about you two? Would the other cards be useful for you?"

He already sort of knew the answer. Olivia had seen every card with him and already picked out the ones that she liked.

"This one if no one else wants it," Milena said, pointing at **Mirror Image**. Olivia shook her head. "Both my casting and my rituals force me to hold still. If I had that, I could at least distract any enemies from going directly for me."

**Mirror Image (Rare, Active)**
**Create convincing mirror images of your own body around you using**
**your mana, confusing your foes and confounding their senses.**

"You don't want the **Chill Touch**?" Rowan figured she had the same problem with the card as Olivia.

"Thank you, but no." Milena winced a little. "I'm not made for front-line fighting, in spite of the way I look."

Rowan nodded and pulled the rejected cards back. They'd either go into his pack to wait for sale when and if they survived their current circumstances, or he'd eventually scrap them. Either way, that was that.

With the agenda complete, the twins stayed around for a few more minutes making small talk before they left to prepare for the upcoming fight. Rowan lingered behind when he noticed that Olivia wasn't leaving.

"Olivia? There are only two ways to get [Elder Shaman]," Bron said slowly as he slumped back down in his bed. "Incredible talent or as a stepping-stone to the Epic [Ancestral Shaman] class, which is only available to what passes for royalty among the beast folk."

"And?" Olivia answered. Rowan could swear he saw a smile briefly play across her features.

"I'm just saying be careful, you brat," Bron rasped as he closed his eyes.

"I will. We just have bigger problems right now," Olivia said teasingly.

Rowan couldn't really blame her. They were stuck in a remote village with defenses barely passable against beasts. Political intrigue of the beast folk was the least of their concerns.

Rowan didn't sleep well that night.

Every time he closed his eyes, he saw the rabid look in the weasel's eyes as it went right for his face.

He knew the decision to stop **Keen Spear** at night was stupid, especially in the middle of what was essentially wartime.

He also knew that if he didn't stop right then and there, he probably never would.

As Rowan tossed and turned, he realized that he missed home. A life where the biggest worry he'd have was about the next exam or trying to find a job. Now, he was fighting monsters and living minute by minute. There were good parts to his new life, but the experience just slowly sanded away at his emotional defenses.

After a zombielike next day of preparing for the incoming siege, Rowan knocked on Olivia's door the following night.

She answered and they had tea. It was nice. They fell asleep in front of the fireplace again, and Rowan didn't have a single dream or nightmare.

# CHAPTER TWENTY-FIVE

# Downpour

It was once again raining on the day of the battle.

And for once, Rowan was glad to be on the wall. The flooding in the village had reached his thighs, making almost everything impossible. Their defenses were now concentrated on two points: the walls and the cluster of safe residences.

"Everyone's been taken care of?" Olivia's amused voice greeted him as soon as his head peeked over the palisade.

"Not easily or quickly, but yes."

"I'm honestly surprised that as many of them cooperated as they did," Olivia confessed, looking out over the field of the upcoming battle.

The demon army was still not visible, but they could see the shaking of the trees in the distance. Milena had reported that the assault was being led by the urchins, and apparently the massive slugs were simply bringing down every tree in their path.

The watery field was also still covered by the piles of beast corpses, which had been roughly pushed away from the walls. The manpower and effort required to clean everything up hadn't been worth it.

In fact, they were even hoping the corpses could hold back some of the demons. At the very least, they'd break up any charge a little as a sort of sick, floating barge.

"Well, it turns out that 'you are going to be murdered by ghostly water demons' is motivation enough to do as they're told. For *most* people."

"It's done now. Besides, look." Olivia gestured as the shaking and cracking was finally drawing close.

With a loud crash and water spraying into the air, the final trees were cleared, revealing a long column of urchins.

If anything, they were bigger than the ones Rowan had faced previously, their spikes more numerous and longer. Partially covered by the water, they looked like miniature islands floating toward them. But the bad news didn't end there.

Right behind them was a stretch of churning water. It was like the water was boiling, multiple geysers incessantly spraying into the air. When the head of a Mudclad Lure broke the surface for a moment, Rowan realized that it was an old enemy. Just hundreds, if not thousands, at once.

And if that wasn't enough, there was a whole army of colorful aquatic human-oid monsters marching forward. Each and every one of them wore equipment. Some were dressed in only armor, tattered and mottled in places. Others bore spears, clubs, or even a sword.

Above the marching army, a whole host of Skyfins swarmed. And at the tail end of the procession were wraiths. Only four revealed themselves at the start. Then, emerging from a patch of forest, a fifth drifted up.

*That one's different. Maybe a commander?* Rowan marked out the last wraith in his head.

The army was imposing.

The army was terrifying.

However, what really worried him and every other defender were the three shadows far up in the sky, beyond even the highest soaring Skyfin.

Two were smaller, and they twisted and snaked through the sky without rhyme or reason. The outline of their bodies was snakelike. The moment they were vis-ible, the rain intensified.

The final outline absolutely dwarfed every other creature Rowan had ever seen.

"There's our demon," Rowan muttered, and he didn't even bother to hide his bitterness. After all, everything seemed meaningless compared to that demon.

From what he could see, the demon could flatten a good quarter of the village just by landing on it. And that was just its size. It had Rare-tier lackeys when the last demon they fought off was a Rare-tier itself. And its very presence was enough to send the atmosphere into a conniption.

"That's an Epic." Olivia's voice was quiet and without her usual fight. He risked a glance, and she was watching the sky as blankly as the rest of them.

"Imagine all that sweet, sweet experience," Rowan said, forcing his voice to stay cheerful. "Wonder if I could just skip the Uncommon tier entirely if we hunt that thing down."

Olivia laughed. A smile sneaked onto her features. "Well, I guess I'm defi-nitely getting into the Rare tier today."

Rowan nodded, delighted by the spark of light that was once again dancing in her green eyes.

"Okay. Okay, we can do this," Olivia said, pumping herself back up. "It's odd that they chose to lead with the urchins, but we can punish that. The urchins are ranged dealers. Marcus, get ready to apply your aura as soon as you can. Everyone else, buckle down. They're going to try to drive us out with their barrage, and we need to outlast it."

Rowan wasn't too worried about the quills. Getting his head blown off or his brain mushed would probably kill him, but with his **Lavish Feasting** replenished, nothing short of that would put him down permanently.

Still, he did as he was ordered, getting closer to the palisade and taking cover.

"Do you want me to start working on the ritual?" Milena posed the question, eyes roving over the many demonic creatures arrayed before them.

"Not yet. I want you to wait until the urchins are gone. Maybe more. Speaking of—" Olivia took a deep breath to steady herself and took a look at Rowan. "Everyone, let them get as close to us as possible. With all this water they've provided, I have a gift for them."

Rowan reinforced her authority.

"Friends. If I may call you all friends," Rowan said, his voice ringing out. They were lucky that the demons were once again only attacking from a single side, which meant most of the defenders were within shouting distance. "Today, we fight an army from hell. They'll be mean and tough. And it'll be a hard fight. But the measure of a man is determined by his greatest challenge. This is a damn big challenge. We can ask for nothing better to prove our mettle."

As Rowan's speech fell, shouts emerged from the defenders huddled against the wall. Rowan flashed Olivia a grin, who returned the smile.

On the other side, the demonic party didn't pause or deliver grand speeches. They began their assault as soon as they were in range. The quills *thunked* into the wood of the wall, and quite a few defenders flinched when some of the arrow-like quills managed to pierce through the palisade and poke their tips out.

In spite of that, the soldiers and mercenaries held still and waited.

Even if they weren't a hundred percent convinced they were going to survive until sundown, they were still willing to gamble their lives on the hero and his party.

The demonic creatures got closer.

With the shrinking distance, the quills gained strength. Enough that the barrage of attacks cracked and splintered the top of the palisades.

Still, they waited.

At some point, Olivia's hand had found its way into Rowan's. He wasn't sure which of them was shivering. It might have been both. He gave her fingers a reassuring squeeze anyway.

Closer and closer the demon's army drew, until it was time.

"Stay down!" Olivia screamed, squeezing her eyes shut as she took out a potion bottle in her other hand, gave it a light shake, and threw it as far in the direction of the advancing army as she could.

The burst of power that followed was deafening. It reminded Rowan of a mix between a lightning storm and the sounds given off by a Tesla coil he used to have as a kid. And the potion was definitely a close cousin to them, judging by the zaps of electricity lashing wildly through the air, making his hair stand on end all the way up on the wall.

Rowan didn't think that the urchins, whatever they actually were, were capable of screaming. Obviously, he was wrong, since their voices rose in a haunting tune of suffering. The Mudclad eels were screeching underwater, too.

When the screeches died down, Rowan risked a glance to find the entire field of urchins and at least half of the eels floating lifelessly in the water.

*This is what Olivia is good at,* Rowan thought. He could count on a single hand the different healing or enhancing potions that Olivia used. *But attack potions? They never seem to run out.*

"Do you have any more of those?" Rowan whispered.

Olivia giggled. "Impressive, huh? I used all but one of my lightning potions to distill them and supercharge that one. Do you know *how much* mana I used up keeping that thing stable until now?"

Rowan's smile cramped. "And if you failed to do that?"

"Well, I mean, we had a demon army headed our way anyway, so . . ." Olivia trailed off, giving him a cheeky grin and looking not at all apologetic.

*Perhaps Kayden was right—Olivia should not be allowed to continue down this path.*

"Did that give you enough experience to level up? All the way to Rare?" Rowan asked, taking another glance beyond the wall.

It wasn't only the defenders that were still reeling from the effectiveness of Olivia's assault. The humanoid part of the demon army had paused, and if his eyes weren't deceiving him, some of their ranks were actually brawling with each other.

"Yes. Holy Aristaeus, that was a lot of demons," Olivia said with a hint of disbelief in her voice.

"Then give out your last orders and go. I'll hold the line until you get back."

Olivia took courage from that, and her voice rang out clear and loud. "Milena, wait for them to start advancing again, then start your summoning. Marcus, keep everyone alive. Rowan, you're in charge while I'm gone. The rest of you, stay alive—that's an order! I'm going to get out of combat for fifteen minutes to rank up. And once I'm back, we'll make them pay!"

A cheer rose up at her proclamation. As Rowan thought, the fact that Olivia was this powerful as an Uncommon-tier crafting class was already a major accomplishment. Having her come back as a Rare tier? It was a massive morale booster.

Olivia straightened up, quills no longer being a concern, and made a beeline for the closest house. Seeing no reason to continue hiding, Rowan followed her example.

"Everyone, back to your positions. Get ready to deny them approach to the walls," Rowan commanded, his voice steadier than he actually felt.

To the demons' credit, and to Rowan's frustration, the minor scuffle in the enemy army was quickly resolved. One of the wraiths drifted forward, and moments later there were a few ice sculptures and obedience in enemy ranks once again.

Milena stepped up to the ritual circle that was shielded from the rain and took her place in the smaller of the two circles, just like she had back in that clearing when summoning familiars.

That, however, was where the similarities decisively stopped.

When Milena started up her quiet chant, the sound of her voice thundered and echoed like she was shouting at the top of her lungs. The sheer force caused ripples on the water that grew with every passing moment. More impressive was the way her voice shifted and changed, suddenly sounding like countless others had joined in.

Rowan tried but failed to distinguish between them. He'd almost manage to separate one voice from the rest before they merged again in perfect harmony, the one he'd been following disappearing and turning into something new.

Milena had set up an odd, old flag right next to her in the inner circle, and now it flapped, raging, as a wind formed an invisible barrier against the rain.

The flag itself had started off unremarkable, with a simple, faded design in some brown-black shade. Yet, as Rowan watched, the color of it shifted and grew richer. It shone with an inner crimson light now, light refracting across it in a glossy way that convinced Rowan that what he was seeing was blood.

Then, between one moment and the next, a crack formed in front of the village gates.

The blackness of the crack was absolute, yet Rowan found it oddly reassuring instead of terrifying. Rather than the gaping maw of a beast, this was the color of repose, of gentle rest and forgotten woes.

A leg appeared, leached of color and almost see-through. Its owner, a woman warrior, stepped out in a perfectly casual, disinterested manner. She carried a massive shield in her left hand, easily larger than Rowan, yet barely big enough to cover her torso. In her right, she bore a wicked, jagged blade. It, too, was perfectly proportioned to its wielder.

The warrior surveyed the field, took in the dead and approaching demons, and *laughed*.

As if that was the signal, more and more figures streamed past her. Absolute behemoths, smaller and more agile figures, a female wolfkin who wielded a bow, oversized even for her massive stature. More and more warriors joined the fray, until Rowan could count sixty-four ghostly figures.

At the very front was the first warrior to cross the threshold between realms, and she screamed out in a bestial voice as she charged.

Whether by wraith-induced discipline or the fact that they outnumbered the strange warriors thirty to one, the odd humanoid monsters didn't falter. That quickly changed as the first line of monsters fell almost as soon as the warriors breathed on them. Milena had downplayed the power of this ritual. It was about to be an absolute slaughter.

Or it was. Until one of the outlines in the sky decided enough was enough.

It plummeted out of the clouds, and Rowan saw a creature that was neither dragon nor serpent. The demon had a superficial resemblance to dragons from Chinese myths, but only in the sense that both were snakelike and flew without wings.

It had jaws that stretched for nearly half the length of its body, and two rows of eyes that stretched the full length. Its tail ended in a finlike appendage, and long spines lined its back, quivering and dancing with an electric charge that fluttered between them.

Rowan thought about using **Inspect** before deciding to keep the card in his cardholder. For one, he didn't need a headache before battle. And second, it didn't matter what the demon was. He needed to kill it, otherwise it would kill him. That was all.

The creature swooped down at the charging warriors, only to rock sideways when a glowing arrow dug deep into its side. The projectile remained inert for a moment, then exploded, sending a shower of blood and fleshy chunks into the air.

That only made the creature angrier.

It screamed an unearthly sound, then dived toward the archer with an outsize bow. The archer nocked another arrow with an unconcerned expression on her bestial face. Her next attack threw the creature off course, and it crashed into the ground. Before Rowan could blink, the other warriors fell upon it, laughter and screams of bloodlust rising into the air as they hacked their way through.

Rowan almost thought that would be it. One of their greatest foes would disappear from the battlefield.

But that was wishful thinking. A burst of electricity, even greater than what Olivia had produced, erupted from the serpent-dragon. Behind him, Milena coughed out a strangled gasp and dropped the potion bottle she was holding.

"Sister." Marcus rushed over, trying to shield her from whatever was hurting her.

Milena put out a hand to stop him. "I'm fine. Just my mana." She fumbled for her mana potion and downed it in one gulp.

Rowan glanced outward and saw that several of the glowing figures were gone completely, and more than a few were flickering precariously. The creature had paid a price for its attack, too. Its originally vibrant spines were now dull, a mere few sparks left where once electricity raged.

But the demonic creature was already regenerating. Wisps of flesh unspooled from its insides, weaving themselves into new rough scales and healing its wounds in mere moments.

"Oh great heroes, heed my call," Milena whispered. Her voice slowly grew louder with each word. "You fight, not for victory or life."

The monster's jaw unfurled, revealing tongues and tentacles that fought with the remaining warriors. With both sides wounded or missing strength, the fight was nearly even.

"You need not fear the oblivion," Milena continued. "You were already consigned to it. The only thing to brighten the darkness is a flame of glory. Your flame of glory."

The warriors pulsed. Rowan could almost see what they would have looked like had they been alive. And they began hacking into the serpent creature, ignoring any attacks that the monster made in defense. Ten, maybe twenty warriors perished, but their sacrifices bore fruit.

The serpent tried to fly and escape. But every attempt was beaten back by the archers' arrows or the warriors' axes. It struggled, thrashing its tail and tongues.

"Kill and spread your name, even to oblivion," Milena screamed. The warriors pulsed once more, and the first woman warrior began a sprint at the creature's head. At the peak of her momentum, she leaped high in the sky and slammed her shield on the monster's head. Raising her blade so far back that her arm almost looked like it had dislodged from her shoulder, the warrior smashed down and plunged the weapon deep.

The monster shuddered and opened its mouth wide. Only a weak whimper came out. The warrior answered with her own scream. She raised the shield again and pounded the blade deeper into the monster. One more shudder and the creature went still.

Rowan almost celebrated. Except the second creature chose that moment to emerge from the skies.

It didn't bother to defend its twin, or even avenge the murder. Instead, its many malicious eyes focused on the wall and the defenders arrayed on it. It opened its mouth, and its many spines started to glow with even more intensity.

And then the wall was gone.

# CHAPTER TWENTY-SIX

# Damming the Tide

A few moments earlier, the serpent-dragon had unleashed a torrent of laser-like energy from its mouth. The energy blasted into the wall and the creature craned its head to the side, reducing a whole stretch of the wall to crackling rubble.

The only reason people hadn't died yet was because of Marcus. The shield bearer made full use of his new class as a faint glow washed over every soldier and mercenary and left sparkles on their skin.

When the attack finally sputtered out, the defenders quickly picked themselves up from the fall. Marcus, on the other hand, swayed before almost toppling over. Rowan saved his friend from meeting the ground in such a way.

"Mana," Marcus rasped. He coughed up a wad of blood and his face went bone-white. Rowan fumbled through his bag to procure a mana potion that Olivia had left behind and only stopped when Marcus began giggling. "I just bit down on my cheek. I'm not hurt."

"Holy gods, you scared me," Rowan said.

"Have more faith in me. I'm of pretty tough stock," Marcus laughed as he drank a mana potion procured from somewhere on him. The color returned to the wolfkin's cheeks as he got to his feet. "But that bastard isn't a pushover, either."

Rowan looked back to the serpent monster. It was sagging in the air, but its eyes still glowed just as bright as before. Almost immediately, Rowan felt a burning hatred for the creature. It had just taken away the village's best defense, and yet it simply floated. Its eyes looked calculating, patient. Almost like it was taunting them.

Rowan and Marcus were at the edge of the destroyed wall. Below them, the defenders were starting to reorganize and try to plug the massive hole in the wall.

But no matter how hard they tried, it was impossible. Thirty men, side by side, could march on top of the rubble and into the village. There was no way that the defenders would be able to stop the monsters now that they had lost the wall.

As Rowan watched, the giant monster finally turned its head and trained its gaze on the warrior who had just taken down its sibling. The female warrior looked up and returned the stare.

And then it dived toward the warriors.

"Rowan! Rowan, are you all right?" Olivia's panicked voice rang out from below, and he leaned over the palisade to spot her rushing their way.

"We're fine!" Rowan bellowed back over the rain. He glanced over the wall and found that the demonic army was moving forward again. Now that the urchins and eels were gone, they were facing the humanoid soldiers of the army. And the bulk of the army was marching.

"My warriors, they're almost gone," Milena cried out, rising from her ritual circle and swaying dangerously.

"Stay down," Rowan yelled.

He swiveled in the direction of the second flying serpent. The female warrior was still in the battle, her shield and sword raised high. But she was alone. The serpent wasn't in much better shape. Its bottom half had been sawed away, and green-blue blood stained the surrounding water.

As if encouraged by the attention on it, the serpent sent one of its tongues forward as quick as lightning and caught the warrior's waist. With a triumphant hiss, it squeezed and the summon was split in half.

"Enemies incoming!" Marcus roared. A couple of the Mudclad Lures had apparently survived the battle and were now ambushing the still-recovering defenders on the ground. Without the wall to add height, the mercenaries quickly began taking lethal hits from the monsters.

Rowan ignored the chaos as he sought out Olivia's eye. She noticed his glance and dipped her head. An unspoken conversation passed through the two of them.

*Olivia's Rare now. That should help*, Rowan thought. He nodded back at her and glanced over the wall one more time. There were at least two thousand in the demonic army, not including the wraiths that hovered at the back. It was going to be a tough fight.

"We can't hold the wall," Rowan hollered, shouting at the top of his lungs to be heard over all the mess. "And I won't let innocents get slaughtered. Everyone, in front of the wall. We march out to meet them. Your hero will be with you. You'll march alongside three Rare classes. Together, we will bring victory back to Felton's Mill!"

A cheer, as desperate as it was, went up from their troops. The ones still on the walls scrambled down the wooden steps, rushing to meet their enemies.

Rowan took the quicker way, jumping straight down into the water and finding Olivia waiting for him.

"Nice speech," Olivia quipped.

"Tried my best," Rowan responded. "So, Rare now, huh? How's your stock?"

"Enough to last me through this fight, at least," Olivia grumbled, narrowing her eyes at the incoming frog men. "I suppose if we make it through this and more monsters show up, we might as well just serve ourselves up on a platter anyway."

"That's not very positive thinking," Rowan teased. For some reason, he felt more alive than ever in the moment. Perhaps it was because the two giant flying serpents were now either dead or wounded. Or it was the fact that he was finally going into battle after watching others do the fighting for him.

"Save it," Olivia laughed. When the demonic army was close enough for the ranged classes, she turned to address the men assembled behind her. "Fire at will! Doesn't matter where you shoot. There are so many out there, you'll be hitting something."

Rowan flashed his spear forward, striking out at the water. When he pulled it back a moment later, there was a wiggling eel on it. He used **Empowered Thrust** and the mana tore the monster into two.

Above him, the first arrows and glowing sword slashes flew forward.

Still smiling, Rowan rushed into the battle. The first enemies he slammed into were weak, even weaker than the eels or the urchins or even the Skyfins. The massed army was full of Uncommons, but they were at the very start of the tier.

Right behind him were the soldiers. They had outsprinted even Marcus, which spoke either to their own improvements or the weaknesses in the wolfkin's new class. But as they tore into the demonic ranks, Rowan was glad to have them at his back. The soldiers fell into lockstep with each other, the product of countless hours of training, and speared anything that even dared to look their way. Their movements were slowed by the water, but they somehow kept up with Rowan's slaughter.

"Rowan!" Olivia yelled from somewhere behind him.

Rowan risked a glance back.

"Snake!" Olivia pointed a finger forward at the flying monster that was now trying to wobble its way back into the sky. The thing was barely crawling upward, and its many wounds were still weeping green-blue blood, its regeneration lagging as ropes of flesh unfurled sluggishly.

Rowan nodded. He waited a couple moments for Marcus and Olivia to reach him, and together, the three of them began sprinting forward. The soldiers helped part the way, charging forward to attract the attention of the demonic army and drawing them away from the hero party.

When the soldiers were gone, Olivia dipped her hand into her potion bag and retrieved a light-yellow potion. Rowan expected Olivia to lob the potion at the army and force them out of her way. Instead, she kept it in her left hand and grasped at the air with her right. Instantly, yellow light bloomed and coalesced in midair, and she was soon holding a ghostly replica of the potion. It was almost like what Blake, Rowan's classmate, had done when he summoned the solid arc of light back when they first came to this world.

But Olivia was no Blake. With a smile verging on manic, she lobbed her new potion forward and it exploded, sending a surge of electricity through the water. The ropes of lightning struck down the nearest demonic soldiers before traveling back to Rowan and lightly nipping him on the legs.

"There! Make me run out of potions now, why don't you?" Olivia cackled, conjuring another lightning potion and repeating her assault.

The enemies faltered for the second time. Though they were corrupted beasts or demonic creatures, the attackers were made up of flesh and blood that could be cowed. And Olivia was leaning into that advantage, conjuring the potions two at a time and flinging them in every direction.

The path toward the wounded serpent opened up, and Rowan locked eyes with the beast. There was a surprising depth of emotions there, and he saw the serpent realize that it was about to die.

Before Rowan could make that understanding come true, the sky darkened with a flock of Skyfins.

The flying nuisances dived toward the hero party, set on stopping them from taking the serpent out of commission. Rowan did his best to attack faster than he ever had in his life, but there was just no denying the absolute blanket of enemies trying to cling to their bodies. In fact, if it weren't for Marcus's aura, they likely would have been covered in minor wounds already.

"Marcus, protect us," Olivia screamed, and Rowan could barely see her through the mass of leathery wings even though she stood right next to him.

Marcus got the message. The aura he was sharing with them flared, growing in power and intensity.

And then Olivia began unleashing her potions.

It didn't really matter where she threw them. All she had to do was chuck them into the sky and they were guaranteed to hit a monster.

Once, twice, thrice . . . the lashes of lightning and the peal of thunder were dizzying and entirely too close. The residual energy snaked down, striking at the hero party, the water, and the surrounding monsters.

The party had the benefit of a Rare-tier class's defense.

The monsters did not.

But Marcus's protection wasn't without cost. Rowan saw the shield bearer's knuckles around his weapon go white as his face paled. The beast folk fumbled at his waist pouch with trembling fingers and barely managed to pull out a mana potion. Rowan bridged the gap and helped uncork the potion before unapologetically shoving it into his mouth.

*I'm sure there's a joke somewhere in there*, Rowan thought a bit absentmindedly as another flash of lightning erupted above them.

Olivia didn't even notice. She continued her assault, so taken by her newfound ability that she began to target clumps of monsters who were trying to march past them for the village. Rowan was willing to bet a good number of cards that her class came with a sizable mana pool increase.

Rowan made sure that Marcus was okay. Then, forcing his body to move as quickly as it could through mild paralysis and continued attempted lightning damage, Rowan shot forward. Blessedly, he was out of the lightning pretty quickly. For all that Olivia's potions were destructive, they were also fairly short-ranged.

The snake creature was still trying to take off higher. It was starting to make progress and was now almost two yards off the ground.

Marcus's aura disappeared from Rowan, and a shred of doubt crept into Rowan's mind. Maybe it was better to wait for the others before trying to fight a mythical serpent.

A wave of calm washed away that doubt, and a plan began to form in Rowan's mind. Steeling himself, he sprinted to the nearest demonic soldier. Instead of cutting it down, he leaped and landed straight on its shoulders. The creature flailed, starting to topple back, and its wild swings brushed across Rowan's thigh. But the temporary stable, dry foothold allowed Rowan to propel himself into the air once more.

Rowan's jump pushed the poor demonic soldier firmly into the water, and the combination of strength and dexterity let him cover the final distance between himself and the flying serpent. Rowan landed heavily on the lower portion of the serpent and jammed the tip of the spear as deep into the creature's flesh as he could.

The serpent thrashed and Rowan was almost bucked off. It even lit up in a weak corona of light. However, Rowan's weight and its injuries were pulling it down to the ground again, and Rowan started *climbing*.

In movies and video games, heroes would often climb giants to bring them down. And for the first few seconds, Rowan thought that he was going to be one of those heroes. His grip strength was more than enough and he could create new handholds with his spear.

And then the serpent twisted around and he came face-to-face with it.

Not even **Keen Spear** could hold back the fear Rowan felt when looking at the tongues and teeth. Its mouth began to glow, the same as when it collapsed the wall. And Rowan was definitely less sturdy than the wall.

Rowan did the only thing he could think of. He found a handhold on one of the monster's wounds, pulled his spear out, and jammed it into the roof of the monster's mouth.

Typically, the length of steel and wood would mean that his weapon would be very firmly jammed inside the brain of the thing. However, seeing that he wasn't sure it had one, he ripped the blade to the side, tearing apart its soft insides.

A torrent of green-blue blood drenched Rowan as the two of them tumbled out of the sky.

For a moment, Rowan experienced a very real moment of panic as he somehow ended up underneath the bulk of the monster. But then he landed in the water, and even though the monster had collapsed on top of him, he barely felt the impact thanks to how deep the water was.

When Rowan emerged from the water, it was to the final peals of lightning behind him. After what felt like hours of the bombardment, the silence was deafening.

Even the demonic army seemed unbalanced for a moment. And then they surged toward Rowan and his companions. At least the Skyfins were gone. Olivia's rampage had reduced them to numbers that were now negligible.

As Rowan readied for another round of fighting, a sudden spike of cold made him whirl around and swipe out with his spear.

The body of the spear went right through the hand rising to point at him, and the glowing spearhead tore a hole right through the rising wraith's chest. The unearthly scream of its rage shook the water field, and even several of its own troops hunched away from it.

Rowan didn't let up on the assault.

He leaned inward for a second body strike. Pulling the spear back, he aimed for the wraith's head next. There was no chance that he was going to let the wraith use its card to fill his lungs with water from the inside again.

The wraith seemed to sense his determination, and its entire body shimmered before nearly becoming one with the water that surrounded it. Having no better idea of what to do, Rowan raised his spear above his head.

Mana swirled around its tip, building to uncomfortable levels that he almost couldn't control. Then he brought it down, detonating the blow against the fading body of the wraith.

The effect was as extreme as it was immediate.

The collection of mana *shredded* through the frail body of the undead water spirit, interfering with its attempt to flee. Instead, it caused globs and strings of ghost flesh to shoot in every direction, absolutely covering Rowan in the stuff.

*Oh god, it's in my mouth. It's in my mouth!*

Rowan fought the urge to retch or wash out the taste with the water around him. The only thing that stopped the latter impulse was the knowledge that whatever was in *that* water was just as bad.

Still, that was one wraith down, and just four more to go.

Behind him, a shriek broke out, and he spun around to see another of the wraiths lit up by the thrashing lightning bolts.

A second potion silenced it, permanently.

*Three to go.*

Olivia's [Combat Alchemist] class was living up to all its promises and then some. Where the wraiths had taken the entire hero party before, they were now barely a threat.

Rowan tried his best to carve his way back to his companions. The demonic soldiers weren't all that much of a threat individually. There were just too many of them.

They were ready to throw body after body just to slow him down. And their ability to cooperate with each other made them some of the most skilled demonic creatures Rowan had seen. Their relatively uniform skills allowed them to attack in unison, creating a far more devastating blow than should have otherwise been possible.

As Rowan fought them and carved a path forward, he realized the power of the humanoid creatures.

*These things aren't individual fighters. They're like feints in a boxing match— they encircle their opponent, tire them, and then step aside for another to deliver the finishing blow.*

Rowan slowed down and swung his spear around, eyeing every shadow to see if there was a wraith. The demonic soldiers used this chance to tighten their lines.

The fighting was hard and Rowan could feel his energy reserves plummeting. Only when he identified their cards did the fight get easier.

First, they had some kind of card that made their bodies extremely sticky to everything and everyone other than their fellows. When some of the soldiers pulled at his spear, he had to use mana to unstick the weapon.

The second card was some sort of poison attack. Most of the time, the demonic soldiers used their weapons normally. But every so often, the attack would leave behind a sickly purple trail. It was some kind of poison, and when one of the demonic soldiers accidentally hit their comrade, the unfortunate creature's veins turned black in seconds.

*Don't touch that, even if I have to get hit by something else. Got it. Better a pin- cushion than a puddle of melted organs.*

The final detail that Rowan found was surprisingly similar to the Rotflower demon he had fought before. When he sheared through the neck of one of the creatures, he spotted a thin, green root rapidly pulling back.

The creatures were somehow *nurturing a plant* inside them, likely a poisonous one. Or perhaps the plant was controlling them.

Rowan couldn't be bothered to find out. By that point, he was close enough to Olivia and Marcus that he could bully his way forward and take the hits, count- ing on **Persistent Regeneration** to heal him back up. It took more energy than he would have liked, but grouping up with his team was worth adding a few wounds.

"Rowan, you okay?" Olivia said once Rowan was back in Marcus's aura shield.

Before Rowan could respond, a trio of wraiths materialized around the three of them, choosing that moment to strike. They plunged their hands into the water and webs of ice shot forward.

Rowan tried to spear one of them, but they were too far and one of the soldiers stepped in front of the blow anyway. And then it was too late; the ice was close enough that he had to back up.

"Shit," Rowan cursed. "Olivia?"

Olivia answered by lobbing her lightning potions. The electricity arced against the ice, but because of the distance, it wasn't enough to stop the wraiths. The ice gradually squeezed inward, forcing the hero party to bunch up.

Rowan slammed his spear down on the ice, and the weapon bounced back up. Trying again, he used **Empowered Thrust** against the ice layer and successfully pushed ice back in one direction. But the ice from the other two wraiths kept coming forward.

"We need to do something," Rowan said as he retreated to the others.

"That's quite the observation," Olivia quipped. "Marcus? You got any ideas?"

The wolfkin didn't respond. Rowan swung back and found Marcus with a giant grin on his face.

"Marcus?" Rowan asked.

In response, the glow around the heroes changed colors to a strange yellow-brown. Marcus pointed at the wraiths. The ice they had been producing had touched the aura generated by the shield bearer. As he stepped forward, the ice began to retreat. It was like he had something to counter the cold. Rowan looked closer and saw that the ice closest to Marcus took on a yellow tint before disappearing.

"How is he . . ." Olivia asked.

"Rot Shield," Rowan said as he sprinted forward, using Marcus's momentum as a launching pad into one of the wraiths. The spear tip impacted right on the wraith's head. And then Rowan was once again in water. He ran to the next two wraiths that were still locked in an invisible battle with Marcus and lopped off their heads as well.

And then the world went quiet.

The demonic army, or at least what was left after the wraiths' ice attack, retreated. Only desperate gulps for breath and the thumping of rain were left on the battlefield. Rowan wasn't one hundred percent sure, but if the previous demon's behavior was anything to go by, then this new one could likely detect him, too. And with the army now gone, that meant it was time for the demon itself to fight.

Right on cue, the massive shadow overhead slowly started to lower, heading directly in the direction of the hero party.

"Potions, now," Olivia ordered in a hurry, drawing out only three mana potions. "I'm out after this."

Behind them, Milena rejoined the group. Rowan had lost track of her after the wall had fallen, and she still looked a bit more pale than before. But she was there. Rowan took one of the potions from Olivia and downed it.

"Take these, too." Olivia handed out potions that looked oddly familiar to Rowan. They were a stat booster, Common level, just like the one he'd drunk for the initial demon fight.

"No other variants? You could have at least done something about the taste," Rowan joked as he watched the demon's descent and slugged his potion back. The taste was about as foul as he remembered it to be.

"Really? We've been in a party together for *how* long and you're already complaining about my cooking?" Olivia's voice was as strained as Rowan's, but at least the twins chuckled at their banter.

"You sure you don't have some final super-special potion squirreled away?"

"Yes, I'm sure, Rowan." Olivia sighed, eyes flashing with regret. "I didn't exactly know I'd be coming here to fight not one but *two* demons. I turned almost everything I had over to my father. I thought he'd need it more."

That was actually a bit of a scary thought. If this was Olivia at her poorest and least prepared, what in the world would she have been like if she was still the daughter of a duke and with full access to every potion she wanted?

"Well, we'll manage, I guess," Rowan muttered, just as they got their first proper look at the demon.

Surprisingly enough, the creature that revealed itself was not hideous, at all.

Its body was a pale, luminescent blue, and a sightless head with two horns jutted out of the front of its body. It had two pairs of wings, though they could just as well be called fins, with long bones connected by faintly glowing membranes.

Its tail was long and sinuous, and all up its spine, blue, coral-like plants swayed and released a soothing glow.

Rowan quickly realized exactly what the demon reminded him of. *A blue sea-dragon slug. That, crossed with a crystalline coral reef.*

Were he entirely honest, Rowan was entirely content to simply gaze at the creature. It swayed in the air like it was buoyed by invisible waves, and it was so beautiful and serene that he had difficulty imagining it as a demon.

Then lightning, hail, and torrential winds started to pick up around it, and Rowan was rudely reminded of exactly what they were dealing with.

"It's Epic," Olivia whispered. That shouldn't have come as a surprise, given everything that had happened so far, but the confirmation still slapped Rowan like a brick. An Epic-tier demonic ruler of storm and sea there to drown them.

The time had finally come for the final confrontation.

Rowan was not at all sure they were ready.

# CHAPTER TWENTY-SEVEN

# To Fell a Giant

The demon was enormous, and Rowan, for the first time in his life, realized how small a human being was. He struggled to move. Not because of some tangible or fear effect, but rather because he saw how insignificant he was in comparison to the demon.

The demon was like a floating castle. There was no way Rowan, hero or not, could even hope to bring it down.

Rowan had expected the demon to look closer to a humanoid, like the first demon he'd faced off against. This was not that. The only thing they had in common was their power. Air around the demon shimmered blue, and the rain kept falling like it was celebrating the return of its favored son.

It was impossible to defeat the demon.

Still, he had to try. He was the hero.

Rowan took a quick glance at his companions. Seeing him move must have jogged them into action, since they also broke out of their stupor and downed their own potions.

"Marcus, can you throw me?" Rowan asked. Although his voice was firm and emotionless, his mind was turning to humor to justify the suicide mission. *Perhaps I'm getting used to taking magic drugs and fighting magic enemies. I'm going native.*

"Maybe," Marcus muttered, letting the empty potion bottle plop right down next to him. Rowan was almost upset at the casual littering. "It's a long shot."

"We need to bring it down lower somehow. If we leave it up there, we're as good as dead," Rowan grumbled, glaring at the demon. "I don't like our chances if it stays up in the sky and blasts us with ranged attacks. And don't say that it doesn't have them. It's bending the weather to its whims."

"Even if you can get up there, what are you going to do?" Milena asked before volunteering a bit more information of her own. "I have a ritual, but I don't know if it's going to be enough. And the costs . . . they're staggering."

"Hold on." Olivia chose that moment to speak up, her free hand dipping into her potion pouch and producing a dozen different ingredients. She half crouched in the water and combined them. Gradually, a potion began to take shape under her hands. It looked fairly innocent until Olivia produced a card and shoved it into the potion. Almost immediately, the potion bubbled a vibrant yellow-green and looked entirely *vile.*

Rowan forced down his unease as he watched it take shape. He wanted to stop things, to knock the potion out of Olivia's hands, to pick her up and get as far away from it as possible. The only reason he didn't try was because his urge to not touch it was much greater.

"Olivia? What's that?" Milena, thankfully, made the query for him. "It feels cursed, far too cursed, and that's coming from a shaman."

"Let's just say I can use a lot of things as material if properly motivated. If we can get this potion into that thing above us somehow, I guarantee we'll at least have a fighting chance. Just don't get into contact with it yourself," Olivia said.

That went without saying, in Rowan's opinion. Still, he eyed the flying demon once more. It was just floating there. It had announced itself and was now waiting. Just like the first demon, it was giving the hero party time to think and plan before they fought it. Was it a matter of some kind of honor? Complete assurance that weak humans could never do a thing against it?

Rowan turned his gaze back in the direction of their troops. They were bloodied, bruised, tired, but definitely not broken. The soldiers and mercenaries had mostly survived the assault, despite the overwhelming numbers of the demonic army, and most of the ranged attackers now readied their attacks against the demon.

If Rowan had more time, he would have waded over to them and asked where they got that courage. But he thankfully had his own pool to pull from.

"Okay. So the plan right now. I fly up there, maybe hurt it so that it's lower, hopefully feed it Olivia's potion. And then we win. Question is, can you throw me up there, Marcus?" Rowan phrased that last sentence as a challenge, hoping the levity would be infectious.

It wasn't. Marcus looked like he'd bitten into a lemon, but eventually he nodded. "Oh, I just need to launch the hero hundreds of feet into the air? Easy. No problem. At least you're not in heavy armor."

"Well, then, I go up, and you go to rally the troops. I think I can take out one of its wings, but that still leaves three. We need to damage at least one more," Rowan said. He wasn't sure at all if he could damage anything of that beast. But his courage was starting to spread among the party.

"Let's aim for the front. That way, if it does start destabilizing, at least partly, its mouth will be closer to me," Olivia suggested, and Rowan nodded. He had no objections to that.

"I'll slow it down," Milena offered. "It won't be much; I've never fought against anything like this before."

"It's better than nothing," Rowan said, offering his companion a smile. Then he turned to Marcus. "It's go time."

"Jump on the front of my shield, in three, two, one." Marcus counted down, positioning his shield somewhat parallel to the ground.

Rowan didn't bother with a running start. With how much water was bogging them down, it would have been a waste of time. The stats he'd earned allowed him to leap straight onto the shield. Right as his toes touched down on the metal surface, Marcus *heaved*.

The upward movement of his bulging muscles was only part of the equation.

It was the sudden corona of blinding light that actually gave Rowan most of his propulsion.

Marcus had chosen to expand his shield aura as far and as explosively as he could, and Rowan could do little other than brace himself and struggle to blink spots out of his eyes as he was repelled by the bright barrier and launched up into the sky.

Thankfully, his perception stat was high enough to shake off the blinding effects in mere seconds, letting Rowan see where he was headed.

Marcus's all-out attempt was impressive. Rowan rose and kept flying higher. For a second, he was lost in the feeling of being weightless. When he remembered his mission, Rowan lit up his spear with mana. The potion he had swallowed earlier had replenished most of his mana, and he poured it all into his spear without reserve.

And then Rowan thudded against the monster. His spear, supercharged with all his mana and all their hopes, pierced past the creature's hide and deep into the flesh of one of its wings.

The demon screamed, and Rowan screamed with it.

It was the blood. The moment he'd dealt his blow, a deluge of blue blood had erupted out of the wound, drenching him. Unlike the Rotflower, this blood wasn't directly corrosive. There was no smoking where it touched his armor, and it didn't eat through anything. But there was an energy in the blood, and it sought to pierce into Rowan's body, burning and altering it. His own mana rose up in response instinctively, and the sensation eased.

*What the hell is wrong with demons? Can't they just have normal blood?*

Rowan kept his grip on the spear, dangling in the sky. The demon listed the tiniest bit in his direction, and Rowan dreaded the idea of it doing a barrel roll, but it quickly rebalanced itself.

The retaliation began. Wind and rain whipped up, slamming against Rowan with almost enough force to dislodge him. But it seemed unable or unwilling to strike too hard so close to its own bulk, sparing Rowan from anything worse than just water and air.

Rowan gritted his teeth, steeling himself before pulling himself higher and sticking his fingers right into the edge of the wound. The demon's hide was tough and strong enough to fully support his weight without tearing, even if it was a struggle for his fingers to find purchase in the oddly spongy flesh.

The moment he was secure in his hold, Rowan ripped out his weapon, sending another burst of blood free, then stabbed up again.

This time, the spearhead actually bounced. It glanced against the creature's hide, leaving a shallow gorge and almost destabilizing him.

Upset he'd basically wasted mana on an unsuccessful strike, Rowan tried again. This time, when he doubled the amount of mana used, the attack went through.

It also left him at around twenty points of mana, in spite of the fact that the battle had started mere moments ago. There'd only be enough for one more strike.

Blood once again erupted from the beast, and Rowan prepared for more pain. Shockingly, it never came. Instead, a sickly film snapped around his body, and the liquid started to bubble and steam against it.

Rowan recognized it as Marcus's aura combined with the **Rot Shield** card protecting him.

But Rowan soon wore a small grimace when he realized the new effect was making the wound he was using as a handhold slowly sizzle and liquefy. He had to scramble for a better hold.

Before Rowan could stab his spear into the demon again, it started moving erratically through the air. When the wing went up, Rowan got a dizzying view of the thing's back. In the center of it, right above its spine, was a pile of metal.

Then, the world turned upside down, and Rowan almost lost his lunch.

As the creature began its maneuvers, Rowan clung desperately to his spear and what little hold he had. For the first few seconds, it was all he could do to pray for strength in his arms. But when Rowan found himself still up in the air after a particularly lunch-losing dive and twist, he began to get used to the motions. And he began to think.

Piercing the hide? Difficult. Preventing a wound from closing and hopefully bleeding it to death? Doable.

Rowan gave his spear a jerk, feeding it minimal mana just to do some damage and worsen the wound. It worked. Blue blood started pouring consistently from the wound instead of petering out relatively quickly like it did before.

Things got more difficult when salvo after salvo of colorful slashes and arrows erupted from the defenders, even as they were forced to scatter due to the thunderbolts cracking out of the sky and aiming directly for them. Most of the attacks did nothing against the creature's hide, but some shredded through the thin webbing that presumably helped it fly.

It was working. The demon listed to the front and lost height.

Soon, lightning wasn't the only thing that struck down from the sky.

It flapped its wings against the ground, summoning massive slashes of condensed air that sent water bursting away from points of impact. The rain itself condensed into spikes, stabbing and striking the soldiers and mercenaries.

Some of the water strikes were turned away by the aura defenses, accompanied by the grunts of Marcus's pain. However, the wind strikes that found their targets always reaped a life. They left behind disemboweled or mutilated bodies floating on the water, making the defenders even more desperate to dodge.

Milena was, amusingly enough, on Olivia's back. The baron's daughter struggled under the weight, yet she still doggedly avoided the blows coming from above, desperate to keep ahead of the strikes.

Above Milena's head, a massive storm cloud of miasma was building up. Screaming and weeping faces flashed through it, responding to the quietly muttered incantation the shaman was wholeheartedly focused on.

Rowan wasn't sure what did it. It might have been the constant barrage of attacks on the creature's left fin, or perhaps the relentless prodding of his own spear. But the demon's descent got faster and faster.

Twenty yards from the ground. Ten. Five.

Rowan's instincts kicked in just in time to stop him from being driven deep into the water and potentially squished to death. He ripped his spear out of the demon's side and kicked off against its hide, putting much needed distance between himself and the falling hazard.

When the demon crashed into the water, Rowan was already back on his feet and charging at the creature's head. Or at least what should have been a head. The neck simply opened up to rows of concentric teeth that moved like a blender, sending an odd, resounding sound into the air.

"Guys?" Rowan whispered as he realized that there was no vital spot to attack.

Olivia answered with her actions. She pitched the revolting potion forward like she was a baseball player. The small glass vial sailed through the air, landed well inside the creature's mouth, and was swallowed without a sound.

At the same moment, the ritual Milena was performing also surged forward. The horde of ghosts rushed into the demon, seeping into every single opening it could find, like a legion intent on devouring it from the inside.

At that, finally, the behemoth briefly paused.

From the stunned silence of all combatants, it was obvious they expected something to happen.

And something did.

The demon surged forward, its bizarre neck-mouth extending and snapping out to close around a soldier who hadn't retreated far enough. The man's screams mercifully lasted only for a moment, but the wet crunching that echoed out was far worse.

Rowan managed to get out of the way and found himself directly behind the demon. Its tail was whipping back and forth surprisingly quickly, and an unlucky mercenary who stood too tall was immediately beheaded.

Still, that gave Rowan a unique opportunity.

The demon's tail was huge, like the rest of its body, but it still came down to a tip, and there was little to stop him from dealing a crippling blow to the area where the tail was only as thick as his wrist. Instead of trying to make his way back to the group assaulting the demon from the front, Rowan eyed the whipping tail.

The moment of respite also let his mana regenerate thanks to his higher stats. Rowan waited. And waited. When he spotted his chance, the hero struck.

He aimed straight for the middle of the tail, where the demon's spine lay, emptying out nearly all his mana. As the tip of his spear sank into demonic flesh and scraped against cartilage and bone, he even managed to give his mana a *twist*.

In a shower of blood and pieces of flesh, a large chunk of the demon's tail detached from its body.

**Blood Siphon** did the rest. A literal geyser of blue blood sprayed out, staining the nearby water. The tail, or what was left of it, thrashed wildly.

The demon attacked blindly and with no real target, simply trying to punish whatever creature had dared hurt it. In practical terms, that meant that the area around it lit up with electricity, and a gust of wind sent Rowan streaking away from the demon.

He landed on the water with a painful splat before it parted and swallowed him. Even that didn't give him a reprieve, however, since the demon had now created a mini pool of tidal waves that spread out in all directions. It was hard to even orient himself in the water.

If it weren't for a hand suddenly gripping the back of Rowan's armor and roughly pulling him out of the water, he might have actually drowned then and there.

Rowan came face-to-face with one of the soldiers. The man just offered him a nod of respect and motioned back toward the colossus.

Even hurt, bleeding deeply from its mangled tail and front wing, the demon was still not flagging. If anything, it had finally overcome its rage and was now eyeing up its arrayed enemies. It roared again, extending its odd mouth fully, and made to lunge.

Then it faltered, swayed, and almost collapsed.

"Attack! Attack immediately!" Rowan heard Olivia bellow, and he didn't hesitate to follow the order.

He rushed forward as quickly as he could, his spear lighting up weakly with the six points of mana, the dregs of his mana pool.

If he had to pass out to wrap up the battle, so be it.

All around him, it seemed like the soldiers and mercenaries were following the same logic. Their attacks struck the demon's sides, now actually doing damage and creating new wounds.

Rowan couldn't believe his eyes. Where he needed to pour large amounts of mana to even pierce the demon's skin, his measly six-point **Empowered Thrust** now penetrated so deep that he almost lost his spear.

The reason why became apparent quickly.

Where the demon's blood once ran blue, it now came out as a sickly greenish-black. Its near-impenetrable hide was breaking out in what resembled sores, and its crystalline look made it easy to spot the blackened, pulsing veins.

Rowan had no idea how she'd done it, but Olivia had poisoned the demon somehow, weakening the beast enough to make it possible for them to damage it.

The alchemist herself was out there, slinging potions in a continuous stream of explosions against the demon's side.

Now, entire sections of the demon were starting to resemble a pincushion.

Even Milena was attacking directly. Instead of her usual curses, she had her arms up, and bolts of black energy erupted from her hands, striking the demon. Wherever they touched, they worsened the effects of the poison. Under concentrated fire, an entire section of the demon's hide was starting to rise up and slough off, revealing wiggling and necrotic muscle.

Some of the soldiers were completely covered in the demon's blood and kept fighting even though the blood was starting to eat into the soldiers themselves. In fact, one of the mercenaries was actually *inside* the beast. The red-haired woman was wielding two short swords like a dance, and she was outright burrowing through the demon's flesh with her chain of attacks. It was like watching a drill at work, and their enemy's cries had long since turned unceasing.

But the demon *would not die*.

Even with how savaged and punished it was, it still continued to attack. Not even the constant downpour of rain had weakened, only lagging once or twice when a particularly large attack landed on the demon.

Recognizing the fact that the creature was not going to go down until it was thoroughly ripped apart, Rowan led the charge against its limbs.

"Cripple it! Try to stop it from attacking and moving!" Rowan screamed out for whoever was around him to hear, then dived headfirst into trying to outright sever the colossus's wing.

Rowan was forced to wield his spear with both hands near the very tip of it, tearing and mangling the limb with short stabs.

The demon's efforts redoubled, and it tried to spin and lurch in place, catching the occasional unlucky human with its lunges. Some were caught by its maws and swallowed, and some were mushed into paste by its bulk.

No one dared retreat or try to run.

Each and every one of them knew that if the demon was allowed to catch its breath, it would eventually find its way back to them. And that would mean death. Every soldier and mercenary threw themselves into the assault with wild abandon, joining swords, maces, and even some daggers to Rowan's efforts.

Their work resembled that of butchers more than soldiers.

The water around the demon had long since been churned into a muddy mess by the battle, but now it had taken on the sickly tint of the colossus's blood.

It was almost tempting to stop, Rowan found. He wasn't striking so much as he was allowing his arms to fall and deliver blows at that point. Even the burning ember of the potion churning in his gut wasn't enough to entirely overwhelm the sheer exhaustion he was feeling.

Yet, it wasn't for nothing.

The demon was slowing, weakening, and even its unceasing bombardment was losing some of its intensity.

Then, finally, with an even louder wail, one of the thing's wings gave out and collapsed into the water, completely detached from the rest of its body.

That freed up the soldiers to join other groups, and their grisly work doubled in intensity.

By the time all four of its limbs were severed, the demon was on the verge of death. No one was brave enough to climb up to where the spikes on its back still twitched and sparked with electricity. Nor were people foolish enough to go near its thrashing legs.

However, the attackers had carved deep into the creature's sides, going nearly as deep as some of its vital organs.

As soon as that much progress was made, ranged attackers showed their worth again.

Without having to literally dig into the demon, they bombarded its insides, weakening its cries and causing ever-increasing amounts of blood to seep out of its body.

Rowan had no clue what finally did it. What he did know was the immense relief when his system pinged away at him and he risked opening it for long enough to look at the very top of his combat log.

**[Draconic Sea Slug Cambion] +624,080**

*That's a very big number*, Rowan noted absently, trying to stop his swimming mind from suddenly collapsing under the weight of relief.

All around him, the soldiers and mercenaries slowly stopped attacking, catching onto the fact that the battle was won. It was a subdued cheer that erupted at first. Then, it rapidly gained in volume, until it seemed to be louder than the lightning and thunder conjured up by the demon.

Rowan, too, allowed himself to scream until his voice went hoarse. The adrenaline, the knowledge that he'd get to *live*, the relief of knowing that none of the hero party members were dead—it all coursed through his body.

No one could trump the twins. Their loud, earsplitting howls rang out, and Rowan was convinced that even the baron, wherever he might be, was able to hear them.

"Everyone, back away from the demon! Get out of its fluids, people!" Olivia was the only one still with reason, trying to push everyone away from the corpse of their enemy.

"Olivia? What was that potion you fed the demon?" Rowan asked, brushing his hair out of his face with some frustration. It was getting way too long, and the persistent rain was driving it right into his eyes in thick, vision-obstructing clumps.

"I used a card," Olivia said. When she saw that Rowan didn't understand, she tried again. "People think that the only things you can use in potions are herbs and minerals. They're not."

In that moment, Rowan thought that Olivia's confidence looked beautiful. Then, of course, what she was saying caught up to his brain.

"Wait, what card did you use?" Rowan eyed the demon's blood with a newfound sense of horror.

"**Plague Incubator.** We're not using it, so when I thought of ways to take down the demon, I just . . ."

"Are you telling me we're standing in the middle of a potential plague outbreak?" Rowan asked as calmly as he could manage, the dread over just how far all the water could take the plague pooling in his stomach.

Olivia, looking contritely away from him, murmured something in response that he couldn't hear properly over the rain.

"You're going to have to repeat that, because all this rain is making me nearly deaf," Rowan grumbled, glaring at her a little and brushing his hair away again.

Then he froze and his head whipped up to stare into the sky. The same rainy sky, which hadn't let up even with the demon slain.

"I'm sorry, okay. I'll tell you next time," Olivia apologized. "But this was the only way I could think of to weaken an *Epic-ranked demon* enough for us to kill it. We'll find some priests who can purify the land and make the plague go away. Rowan? Rowan, are you that mad at me?"

Rowan ignored her, terror and worry and disbelief all warring inside of him. *There's no way, right?*

The sound of footsteps rang out loud and forceful, overwhelming even the splatter of rain. Tremors boomed in the land.

Every single eye fell to the beast, hands gripping weapons and faces going pale.

No one could really see the top of the dead beast properly. It was too tall. But whatever was happening came from above the monster. The footsteps made their way up the demon, following its spine, and finally became visible just short of the creature's head.

It was a knight. Completely covered in heavy armor, with water sloshing out of its many openings and joints. Underneath its feet, the beast sagged.

The knight finally stopped, hand coming to rest on the massive, sheathed sword on its side, and it surveyed its surroundings like a noble standing on a lavish balcony and looking over their domain.

"Impressive, mortals." Its voice rang out like the deepest current of an ancient sea, or the most violent storm. "You have slain my mount. A pity. Yet it seems you've proven yourselves worthy of serving me."

As Rowan took in his new opponent, he wondered if sinking into the water where he stood was an option.

# CHAPTER TWENTY-EIGHT

# Electrifying Endings

Rowan wondered if this was where he was going to die. Or if his line in the history books would be "Hero Rowan perished at Felton's Mill, a nothing village in a tiny barony."

His mana pool had been burned down to dregs and was now just a minor spark in his chest. His body felt drained and wrung out, and even the power of the potion that had burned inside of him was fizzling.

But he was going to fight to his last breath. Literally.

"Shouldn't you be more upset than that?" Rowan shouted, trying to hide how tired he was with sheer volume. "We massacred your army and killed your mount."

The demon scoffed; the sound came out like someone throwing a rock into a well. "You have simply passed my test, mortal. Nothing more, nothing less. I did not expect you to succeed. Yet, the result pleases me."

Rowan knew that the demon was waiting for him to ask about the test. But every second he kept the thing talking was a bit more mana and for the others to recover a bit more energy. "So you sacrificed everything for a test? What a waste. Besides, why in the world would that *please* you?"

"Everything?" The demon laughed and water splashed out of the armor even faster. It was like it had an ocean hidden within the confines of the armor. "What makes you believe that was everything?"

A loud, keening wail tore through the air. Hundreds of wraiths appeared. Rowan lost count of how many there were, especially with the way they swayed and seemed to overlap with each other. That wasn't all. Behind the wraiths were hulking figures. On paper, they seemed to be the same species as the humanoid soldiers that Rowan had just fought. In practice? Rowan was pretty sure he'd be dinner if they charged forward.

"How?" Rowan asked weakly, even as his hand tightened on his spear. "How did you slip your entire army this far into the barony?"

"Humans think that all demons are the same kind of idiots that assault the same defensive point," the demon scoffed.

"The baron's defense still holds, then?" Olivia asked. She seemed to take courage from Rowan's words and joined in the conversation.

The demon knight turned his helm in her direction. For a second, Rowan thought all was lost and he was about to lose patience. "You will be a particularly valuable addition to my troops. Such skill with potions. Yes, the baron holds fast still. He will fall, of course. All will, before our king's might."

"And the demon we fought before?" Rowan asked before Olivia could say anything. "The Rotflower? It also went around the baron's army."

"Demon? That thing was barely a cambion. A wretched halfling of a descendant," the knight scoffed, sounding something between amused and affronted. "To think a fool I sent ahead to scout would try to steal an amusing find such as you lot from me. Losing to his appetites! You seem to have done well, however, inheriting his power."

Rowan shuddered, fighting the urge to step back. He didn't feel an **Inspect** hit him, or any other attempt to breach his privacy. Had the knight demon simply seen him fight, or did it have a way to tell?

"What test did we pass? What do you want from us?" Rowan asked.

"Want? I do not want or ask. I claim. You have survived. Proven yourself capable and useful. So you will be claimed and added to my troops. Making proper demons out of your companions will take time, but you'll find yourself serving under my king soon."

"I'm afraid I'm not open to coming under new management," Rowan snarled, taking a fighting stance in spite of his weary limbs. Ever since the demon had shown up, the rain had been pulling him down. It almost demanded he stay still and obey.

"Or I could just eat you," the demon offered. "Would you prefer that?"

"I'd prefer it if you just died," Rowan responded in his most sarcastic voice.

Rowan's spear tip ignited with red flames, and every ounce of energy and strength he had left was dedicated to the strike he was making. Next to him, Olivia's hand brought up another deadly potion. The twins, too, leaped into action. Milena's miasma overtook Rowan, and he felt **Rot Shield**'s power intensify around his body. He charged.

It didn't matter.

An explosion of pressure and mana swept out of the demon knight and knocked everyone back. Rowan was almost forced to kneel on the spot when he was slammed back down to the ground.

"How amusing. It would be a waste to eat you here. Perhaps our king will demand your soul regardless, and if he does, I shall turn it over, yet to lose such ardor and potential would be the utmost waste indeed," the demon said slowly. "Hero, will you watch your companions get eaten because of your stubbornness?"

Water exploded away from the demon as it suddenly appeared in front of Rowan, hand clasped around the hero's neck.

"Brave yet also foolish. The classic hero. You would think me the same as a near-unthinking beast, recently elevated to the status of cambion?"

A tidal wave rose around Rowan and the demon. All around them was water and more water.

"No, I think you're worse, you—"

Rowan didn't get to finish his insult. The demon's fingers squeezed, cutting off any expletives or retorts Rowan might have had.

He tried to strike again regardless, his spear aiming for a chink in the knight's armor even from his awkward position of having his head fixed in place by immovable fingers. The spear clanged against the knight's armor, sputtered, and died. Rowan couldn't summon a single more spark of mana, even when his life literally depended on it.

"Again, a dazzling show of will. I will see it turned to mine own goals." And with that proclamation, an explosion of black mana ignited on the demon's hand, burst into a wriggling mass of black tendrils, and then engulfed the hero.

Rowan found himself in utter darkness. A tidal wave of sickly emotions aimed for his very core and tried to *burrow in*. He couldn't help it, he screamed. Even without knowing what was happening, every instinct told him he couldn't just surrender to what was happening.

Rowan roared at the sticky blackness, trying to swat it away with his hands or kick it with his feet. Neither worked. It just inched closer and closer to his heart. Just as Rowan thought he was fully lost, a light ignited within him. It was weak. Still, it made the relentless advance of shadows halt and twitch.

Rowan recognized the glow. It was the subtle glimmer and shine of the card he'd seen the very first day he arrived in his new world: **Keen Spear.**

Most of the light that came off the card was purple and struggled against the pure black wave. A few rays of the light were different, however. They were golden, warm, and divine. Those rays actually drove back the darkness.

"Exceeding expectations. Hero," the demon whispered. "Why did they send such a promising hero out to the frontier? Did you lose favor with the human king? The demon king cares about merit above all else. No more politics. Just power. Pure, raw power."

The waves of darkness redoubled. For the first time, Rowan felt pain and his heart wavered.

*Perhaps it'd be easier to just give up. The kingdom has done nothing but shun me since I arrived. They don't even want me.*

The glow protecting him weakened by the moment, and the tendrils of darkness didn't hesitate to tear new paths through Rowan's body in pursuit of his card's brilliance.

*No, there's Kayden, who trusted me. There's Bron, who almost sacrificed himself for me. There's Marcus and Milena, who joined my party. And there's Olivia.*

Rowan steeled his heart. He felt the strength flow out of him as the darkness took more and more of him. But he circled his defenses around his Heart Card. He would not just fold and let the demon win.

"Really? You want to fight to the bitter end? Wouldn't it be easier to give up, to be granted limitless power?" The demon's voice slithered into Rowan's ear. "Or do you want me to destroy you instead? I must tell you, it's painful."

Rowan didn't even dignify that with a response. He bent the golden rays and wove them around the purple glow.

Then the pain came. Rowan screamed, as it felt as if his own heart was being consumed, one nibble at a time. But, oddly, the demon was screaming right alongside the hero.

"Is there some law where a hero takes the stage only when all is lost?" A new voice joined their conversation. Rowan almost lost his defenses as he realized who it was.

"You think your attack hurt me?" the demon snarled.

Rowan's awareness of reality was abruptly restored as he saw the knight tilting its head up against the sky.

"No, but this attack will." A thick, purple bolt of lightning connected the heavens with the earth in an unceasing stream of electricity that had chosen the demon as its lightning rod. For several eternal, painful seconds, this meant Rowan was the target, too. Then the demon's fingers unclenched and Rowan was practically launched away from it by the surge of electricity.

Even before he impacted the water, Rowan found his balance and landed feet first. Around him, the lightning was snaking through the thigh-level lake and burning up the demonic creatures.

Even the demon was clearly caught in the effect of whatever was happening. Eventually, the knight screamed in sheer frustration instead of pain, and his mana shot into the sky, cleaving the lightning apart from within.

"You survived that? That's odd. Everything I used that spell on before died." Kayla's voice rang out again. Hovering in the middle of the sky on a glowing platform was a whole group of figures, foremost among them Kayla and the tower master Rowan had seen once before.

"You'll need more than that," the demon said, his voice oddly calm. "So, another hero. This is turning out to be quite the fruitful trip."

Kayla laughed. She began to chant, and a second voice echoed her words. The hero almost seemed to glitch. An ethereal version of Kayla twisted in the air around her.

A spark ignited far above the battlefield. It wavered and trembled, but with every passing moment it turned into something greater, something that made the surrounding air quiver and the surface of the water dance.

"Stop them!" the demonic knight screamed. For once, its noble visage cracked as its visor snapped open, revealing a skull of pure, snapping darkness wreathed in abyssal waters. The skull unhinged its jaws far too wide for something living, and a zap of pure power erupted from its mouth.

It was aimed straight for the chanting heroine. The tower master waved her hand and a ghostly outline of some ancient and mighty fortress sprang up between the demon's beam and Kayla. The attack slammed into the fortress, yet the ramparts didn't even shake.

For several long, drawn-out seconds, the knight kept up its assault before it petered out.

Behind the demon, its army surged forward. Serpents rose into the air while the ground troops found their enemies in Rowan and the remaining defenders.

"To arms! Defend yourselves!" Rowan roared. He swung around to find Olivia and the twins already around him.

Frankly, every inch of Rowan's body was in agony. He felt like someone had shoved barbed wire into his veins and then poured bleach on top of the wounds, just to be sure he suffered enough. Even attempting to draw a single point of mana caused unspeakable agony to surge through him, for a moment wrecking him so badly he nearly nosedived into the water.

*No mana, then.* Rowan gnashed his teeth together to stay upright. *I'll die on my feet.*

But no dying was happening today unless it was a demonic creature. The tower master waved her hand again. A giant tidal wave erupted in front of the defenders and barreled toward their enemies. Rowan thought that it was just a strength spell, but when the wave touched the monsters, they simply disintegrated. It was like the water had been turned into acid.

The lead demonic soldiers barely had the time to scream as they met their ends. And those that tried to run found themselves outpaced by the wave. From Rowan's perspective, the massive demon army was literally feeding itself into the grinder that was destroying it.

Meanwhile, the demon was being driven mad by its attempts to attack being rendered useless. It finally drew its sword, a blade of pure obsidian. A strange screech reverberated in the air like the abused strings of a harp.

The spell was also done.

A giant orb hung in the air, sparking with plasma and shedding intense light. The demon seemed to grin as it jumped upward and slashed.

It was like the sun had been summoned. Rowan heard a terrible sound before his ears decided that enough was enough and shut down. For the next few seconds, his world was awash in white light.

Rowan could make out the barest of shapes in his vision. The demon slashed again and again at the sun but was battered back each time by invisible pulses of energy. Some parts of the sun's flames rushed up into the sky and blew away the demon's clouds. Water and fire fought in the air until one of them fell back to the ground.

The battlefield was silent as everyone waited to see who had won. Only Kayla disregarded the chance of her enemy surviving, directing her attention toward Rowan. Her mouth opened with a smirk, but before she could say anything, a screeching scream resounded.

From the water erupted the figure of the demon, which had definitely seen better days.

Most of its armor was melted away, or bunched up in grotesque splotches of dripping metal. Even standing there, nearly beaten, the demon was still an impressive sight.

"How? I pulled mana from the others for that attack. And I used everything I had," Kayla snapped, her angry eyes narrowed on the struggling demon. "This can't be right."

"Stupid apprentice, didn't I tell you? Demons are different from the monsters we've had you hunt thus far. You need to finish the job with grace," the tower master said as she made a grasping gesture at the demon. The former knight, now little more than a water wraith, gasped as it was snatched up by the neck. It struggled to do or say something, but it was useless in front of the tower master's might. "Now, I'm literally holding it still for you. Kill it so we can finally move on from this place. I hate the rain."

Kayla raised an arm, and a ball of flame ignited atop her cupped palm. The flame was a cheery orange-red at the start before turning blue and then a blinding shade of white. The spell, whatever it was, shot forth and engulfed the demon. The knight managed a single cry before it was reduced to nothing.

For the first time in what felt like months but was realistically at most a week and a bit, light broke out over the village. For as far as the eye could see, not a single cloud marred the horizon.

Rowan felt numb. An enemy whose mount had tormented an entire village, whose army could have overrun the village, whose own strength seemed limitless, was gone. Reduced to nothing. In moments.

He couldn't help but stare blankly at the spot where the demon had struggled so recently, just letting his thoughts wander. Was he really so useless compared to other heroes? Were his struggles so trivial that a couple of Kayla's spells could defeat them?

Olivia grabbed Rowan's arm, clinging to it almost protectively. He went to ask what was wrong but got his answer a moment later.

"Long time no see, stranger," Kayla said with a smirk, a brow rising inquisitively at the way the baron's daughter was clinging to him, but she didn't comment on the situation.

"Hey, Kayla. How have you been?" Rowan watched as Kayla descended with pure glory.

"Good, good, though I can't say the same thing about you." Kayla's eyes flicked around, and the horribly invasive feeling of an **Inspect** washed over Rowan, making him grimace. "Really, my guy, you need to do better. What are you doing at Uncommon still? You do realize you need to at least get to Epic, right?"

Rowan struggled to keep his face straight. His friend had always been cocky. But the newfound feeling of authority, of what seemed an unquenchable belief in her innate superiority? That was new. It felt like he wasn't talking to his friend, not anymore.

"Little hard to do when I'm trying to stay alive," Rowan said, an edge seeping into his voice.

"It's not his fault." Olivia spoke up. "We've been defending this town, keeping everyone here safe. He didn't have the time to dive into some dungeon all day." Olivia seemed convinced that was what Kayla was doing. True or not, the heroine didn't seem to care to correct or even acknowledge her.

"I really missed you guys, you know? Well, you in particular. I can still go visit Blake, even if he's stuck doing paladin stuff all the time nowadays. Why'd you have to go and join some frontier baron?" Kayla sighed, shaking her head.

"We do not have time for this, apprentice," the tower master said from her platform. "You insisted we stand around in the rain for days. Now we need to rush the final leg of our journey."

"One second!" Kayla yelled back.

Rowan frowned. "Kayla? When did you get here?"

"Oh come on, Rowan, you were handling it." Kayla smiled. "And you obviously needed the experience. Where would you be if I stole it all? Really, I was doing you a favor! Have to go now, though, bye-bye! Make sure to visit more often, okay?"

Without another look back, Kayla shot back toward her platform. She had been hovering just above the water the entire time, while Rowan was mired in the thigh-deep swamp.

As Rowan watched her go, he got a sinking feeling in his gut. This wasn't the Kayla he knew. The gratitude he had felt for her saving him and the rest of the village was countered by the dread that one of his few friends in this world wasn't the same person anymore.

*I hope Blake is still the same.*

# CHAPTER TWENTY-NINE

# Cloudbreak

Kayla had changed.

It was true that she had been friends with Blake for far longer than she was friends with Rowan. But Rowan thought he knew her well enough. A brash, rough, but likable friend he could trust.

All that was now in question. Kayla had shown up, saved the day, and promptly left. If that was all, he could still keep the illusion that she was the same person he'd once known. But the fact that she'd outright confirmed that she had somehow hung around for *days*, just watching while the soldiers and mercenaries died, left a cold, bitter feeling in Rowan's chest. Things would never be quite the same between the two of them again.

But then, had Rowan changed, too?

He was almost eager to dismiss the thought. A part of him wanted to cling to the person he'd been when he was summoned. It was a reassuring bit of familiarity and certainty in a world that had only grown progressively more unfamiliar.

It would also be a lie.

Rowan had changed, too.

The Rowan from even a couple of weeks prior would not have charged a giant flying monster for a chance at victory. He would also not have been brave enough to look at that same demon and ask others to charge with him.

Yet, he had. What did that say about him? Was this something that had always been inside him, or was the world molding him into a fabled hero?

Rowan didn't have an answer to that. What he did know was that if he hadn't done anything, even more people would have died. He also knew that Kayla had saved him from succumbing to the darkness. Her spell had not only taken down the demon but also cleansed the artificial lake formed on top of the village.

"Rowan!"

The scream of his name made Rowan flinch. He spotted Olivia almost immediately and tilted his head in confusion. "Olivia?"

"Are you okay? I've been calling your name forever!" Olivia hissed when she finally reached him, dragging him down and checking him for wounds.

"Yes? I'm all right?" Rowan mumbled, still confused.

"You don't look like it. You look like someone stabbed you and then killed your puppy," Olivia said as she rested her hand on his chest.

Rowan took a moment.

*Is this shock? Am I in shock?* His eyes scanned the scenery around him. He lingered on the soldiers and mercenaries, and even his own party members. No one looked like they'd just won. They looked, well, defeated. They were all looking at him, expecting something that only Rowan could give.

*I'm supposed to be a hero*, Rowan thought as he took a deep breath, shot a smile to Olivia, and stepped toward the troops who had followed him into what was near-guaranteed death.

"We have won." Rowan's voice echoed out, spreading a bit oddly because of all the water. "The demons brought an army and unleashed the wrath of nature against us, but we *won*."

He saw the realization ripple through soldiers, mercenaries, and villagers. They seemed to be in shock that they were still alive. Only Marcus and Milena broke into smiles.

"Yes, we've defeated the demon," Olivia said, picking up where Rowan had left off. She had the hint of a smile on her face. "And our king has finally sent reinforcements. The full might of our kingdom is now turned on this breach. Baron Sutton, my father, will soon be free to return and assist everyone so we can recover from this trial fully. There will be no more threats to fight, and no more comrades lost."

Cheers slowly went up. Every defender tried to add their own voice to it. Hidden underneath all the suffering and exhaustion, there was a bedrock of strength. They'd been tested, pushed to the brink, but they'd survived. And Rowan was proud of each and every one of them.

"We were challenged and we have proved our mettle, but now it's time for us to recover and sort things out after our victory," Rowan shouted, pitching his voice a bit higher to get over the din of conversation and celebration. "I need everyone who's hurt to step forward." Rowan paused, taking a deep breath. "The water's mostly clear now, so those that are healthy will become a search party. We need to find anyone who's underneath."

Rowan motioned at the expanse of water, and the mood sobered up right quick. Although he was loath to cut short the celebrations, he felt even worse about leaving the corpses of people who had fought and died for the village to rot under the waves.

Under Olivia's leadership, everyone broke up into their designated parties and worked through the slog of immediate issues before they could begin resting.

Rowan helped, too. Even after being put through the wringer, Rowan found the strength to push through and contribute to the cleanup effort. He searched the water, counted and recounted the survivors, and helped with the wounded.

As he dragged his tired body back to the rest of the party, he found them already in deep conversation.

"You were chucking firebombs and electric burst potions left and right," Marcus said. "Your class card allows you to copy them? Why didn't you just summon copies of healing potions?"

"What's my class called?" Olivia grumbled, almost going into her full angry-with-arms-crossed mode.

"[Combat Alchemist], right?" Rowan offered.

"Exactly. Combat. [Combat Alchemist]. Not [Healing Alchemist]. Or [Versatile Alchemist]," Olivia said with an edge in her voice. "Now, would you say a [Combat Alchemist] could replicate the effects of healing or support potions?"

"Sorry, didn't mean to pry!" Marcus quickly begged off, and Rowan remembered that asking questions about someone's class could be considered rude.

"No, it's not that." Olivia deflated like a popped balloon. "It's just that now the problems start for me."

That caught Rowan's attention. "Problems?"

"It's . . ." Olivia paused.

Marcus picked up on the cue. "We won't tell anyone. It's not like we *know* enough people to gossip with. But if you want some privacy . . ."

While Marcus acted friendly with everyone, he and his sister typically kept a distance from just about everyone. It wasn't that they were purposefully difficult. There was something there holding them back, though, and somehow Rowan and Olivia had at least broken through that a little. But trust was a two-way street, which Olivia knew as well as anyone else.

"No, it's all right," Olivia said. "It's just that I've wanted this for so long. And now that it's come, I'm not sure what to think. My father wasn't super thrilled when I told him my plans for my class. He doesn't like how I could be called on as a member of nobility."

"Called on?" Rowan asked.

"If there's a war, or any sort of armed conflict, nobles with a combat class are expected to respond to the summons from the crown. My family isn't exactly in good graces at the moment, so I might be shunted off to the most dangerous areas and battlefields," Olivia sighed.

"Isn't that, I don't know, kind of a moot point at this time anyway?" Rowan asked, a little amused. It wasn't like anyone could avoid combat at a time when there was a demon invasion happening. "We all need to fight demons."

"Maybe." Olivia glanced at the dead monsters around them. "If I were a normal alchemist, I'd be asked to stay home and produce certain potions once the conflict with the demons really kicks off. Even as a healing-focused alchemist, I'd at most get stuck in the back lines, healing and taking care of the wounded."

"Wouldn't they want as many healers on the front lines as they can manage?" Rowan asked. His confusion seemed to confuse the rest of his party in turn.

"Rowan, healers are rare and valuable," Milena said. "The protection of healers of any kind is prioritized beyond any other class, to the point where Common healers, if they're actually competent, get preferential treatment."

"But, then, what happens to the front lines?" Rowan asked. If everyone was left fighting mostly without healing support, they'd run out of steam much faster. Olivia was figuratively if not literally a godsend with all she'd done with her healing and mana potions.

"They just rely on potions. Of course, some healers want to fight on the front lines. They either have their own parties or want the faster experience gain that kind of combat provides. That's allowed, since no one's going to chase off a healer," Milena supplied.

"That's why my father wanted me to be a regular alchemist or at least a healing-focused one. And why I reacted so badly. Sorry, Marcus," Olivia apologized.

"No worries, really." Marcus waved her off.

They fell silent again, and Rowan was too busy with his thoughts to try and remedy the lack of conversation.

It wasn't only Rowan and Kayla who had changed. Olivia might have led a peaceful life, taking her place among the nobility when her time came. Instead, Rowan had jumped into her life and she now had a different future than the one Kayden had planned.

"Rowan?" Marcus called.

Rowan looked up. He had been shuffling forward mindlessly for the past few minutes as he thought about the changes in his life since coming to this new world. In some ways, he had become a person unrecognizable to his past self.

"Yeah," Rowan replied and saw why Marcus had called out to him. The shield bearer had found a mercenary partially buried under two monsters. Together, the two of them pulled the man out of the water.

"Drowned, poor soul." Marcus mumbled a prayer for the body as Rowan brought it back to the center of the battlefield. Olivia and Milena split off to help the others find the bodies and count the survivors.

Rowan refused to think in terms of numbers. He really didn't want to, but even a cursory inspection revealed that the number of dead approached almost half of what they'd gone into battle with.

So almost everyone was carrying a body of some kind as they returned to the village. Although they had won, the army marching back to Felton's Mill looked more like a ragtag group of survivors than one returning in triumph.

Only, it was even worse than that.

"Look sharp," Olivia called out. "We have a welcoming committee."

A sizable group of villagers had ventured out from where they'd hidden. Most of them had some sort of implement that could double up as a weapon. For a few drawn-out, awkward moments, the two sides eyed each other up.

There was no forgetting the way that most of the villagers had acted, refusing to participate in the final battle against the demon and its army. Still, Rowan hoped that they weren't about to try and run them out of the village.

"Is this how you welcome an army who fought and bled and died for you?" Rowan asked. No one answered his question. After a few moments, Rowan tried a harder tack. "We went against an entire demon army and lived to tell the tale. Are you sure that you want to offend us? Offend me? A hero?"

At that, the villagers finally put down their weapons. No one met his eyes or tried to strike up a conversation, but they helped see to the dead and assist the more wounded soldiers to somewhere where they could rest.

*Sometimes, you need fear just as much as kindness*, Rowan thought. And with that, a long-forgotten chime sounded within him.

### You've gained an insight about the world.
### +1 Wisdom

Perhaps because of his new wisdom, Rowan noticed the expression on Olivia's face and almost immediately understood what was causing it. He grabbed one of the nearby villagers.

"Where's Bron? The officer. Is he all right?" Rowan asked.

The villager squirmed under the attention but still answered. "Hero . . . Hero Rowan. None of the monsters tried to get past you to strike at us. He's fine."

"Great," Olivia said as she took Rowan's hand. "Now stop torturing this poor guy and let's go find Bron."

Rowan smiled as they ran, hand in hand, through the village. For once, it felt like something had changed for the better.

Rowan found Bron in the room he'd left him in.

"Finally," Bron grumbled the second they opened the door. His eyes trailed over the two of them, searching for any sign of injury. "Can't you let an old man know you're fine earlier so he can rest properly?"

Olivia laughed as she plopped down on the foot of the bed a bit more force-fully than necessary.

"How did it go?" Bron asked. "The villagers don't seem to know much, understandably."

Both Olivia and Rowan went silent, unsure of what exactly to say. That they had won even though the battle had almost become a slaughter that would have ended in a bunch of newly corrupted humans running around if they hadn't been saved?

"Well, we're alive. The demons aren't," Olivia said, earning a tired chuckle from the man. "Really, you look worse than we do."

"Next time someone needs to drink a potion that invokes phoenix fire in an attempt to make the drinker go through a doomed attempted at rebirth and completely stonewalls all attempts to heal or regenerate, I'll let you handle it," Bron said back. He winced a moment later, realizing the effects his words had on Olivia.

"We just finished fighting a demon army. Don't tell me we're going to fight each other next," Rowan said, drawing out a truce between the two of them. Sometimes, their friendly quips went a bit too far, and Olivia definitely could not take as well as she could dish. "I'm glad to see you're doing better, though, Bron."

"No thanks to these villagers," Bron grumbled. "What's the damage?"

"Half of the mercenaries, most of the soldiers. We almost lost," Olivia said as she began ticking things off her list. "But Rowan's friend Hero Kayla appeared at the end of the fight and finished the demon. She left in Father's direction."

Bron nodded. "That's good. The job of defending the invasion doesn't just fall to House Sutton. The kingdom will likely soon send an army to bolster the ranks of the frontier."

"An army that we will need to feed and clothe and shelter," Olivia said bitterly.

"The price of safety," Bron joked. "I'm glad the two of you are okay. But you're soaked and getting my bed wet. Get some rest. I'm sure it's been a long day."

It had been a long day. Olivia jumped off the bed and quickly excused herself with an apology thrown in for good measure. As they walked back, Rowan could tell she was still bothered, so he slipped his hand into hers voluntarily for the very first time.

The baron's daughter gave him a wide-eyed look. When they finally walked up to the pair of doors that led to their respective rooms and he made to disengage, she didn't let him.

Rowan didn't fight it when she tugged him in the direction of her room.

It was a little funny, watching her blunder around her room trying to get the fire started with only one hand. She had the logs in quickly enough and did a neat trick where her mana shifted into small sparks. But even then, it took a bit of finagling to work everything out.

"You should really put that by the door, you know. Then you could have helped me," Olivia groused.

Rowan's death grip on his spear was more than a little awkward, especially since he could have at least contributed a little in the fire making. As it was, both of his hands were full.

"I know," Rowan answered but stayed in his spot, eyes trained on the fire slowly gaining in intensity.

Olivia didn't push him. She simply stood there, in front of the hearth, watching him. After a few moments, Rowan relaxed enough that he could walk over and lean his spear against the wall. But even then, his hand was still clenched over the spear. He was afraid the emotions churning away inside his chest were more than he could deal with on his own.

It was only when Olivia laid her free hand over his white-knuckled one that Rowan unclenched and stepped back.

The rush of emotions that **Keen Spear** had been holding back came to the front. It was like the world's worst cocktail of feelings. There was grief at the lives he had seen disappear, fear at what could have happened had the demon won, and anger at Kayla for just waiting while she could have stopped everything. He shut down.

Olivia guided Rowan into a sitting position by the fire, the two of them side by side as they enjoyed the first hints of warmth that seeped into them.

After what felt like hours, Rowan whispered, "Thank you."

"You're here for me, too, you know?" Olivia said, trying to sound teasing and coming off as miserable. Seeing Bron always left her in a foul mood.

"I am. I will be." Rowan bumped her shoulder a little, or tried to, but with how close together they were, they just listed to the side for a moment.

"So we have no secrets between us?" Olivia said. Rowan noticed that her tone was slightly different than before and glanced at her with a confused look. She returned an unimpressed look. "You knew the other hero well, didn't you?"

Olivia didn't really need to clarify which hero she was referring to. But Rowan stayed his execution for a moment. "Is that typically how it goes when summoning heroes? They know each other?"

"Not really. They can be just two strangers, all caught up in the summoning together. Now, stop dodging the question."

"Yes, I knew her. Know her." Rowan paused. "She's a good friend. I think— It's complicated," he tacked on weakly, entirely unsure if that was still the case or not.

"Just a friend?" Olivia challenged, arching her brow.

"Just a friend, maybe less," Rowan assured her. "If anything, her and Blake were a thing, for a little while at least. Or maybe they still are? I don't know, their relationship was sort of complicated." Rowan was rambling and Olivia let him. "It's kind of hard to explain. Do you have casual dating in this world? Even if you don't, think of it like a flame that flickers in and out. It never extinguishes but also never burns too bright for too long."

When Rowan finally stopped, Olivia was there with her next question. "And you never had an unsaid love for the beautiful, otherworldly heroine?"

"No, Kayla is . . ." Rowan stopped, taking a moment to think again and really process what he thought about her. Even when he would have sworn up and down that she was one of his very best friends, there was really only one way to describe her. "She's complicated."

Olivia giggled and placed her head on his shoulder. Rowan could feel her wet hair press against his skin.

"You seem to use that word a lot when describing her," Olivia said. "Complicated."

"Well, it's true, and that was before we all got pulled into this world." Rowan was grumbling and it only made her giggle more. He liked the sound. So of course, he had to say something dumb to ruin the moment. "You know, we find ourselves here an awful lot after every fight."

"I guess we do. Are you complaining about it?" Olivia's voice had a hint of challenge to it and Rowan pressed his lips tightly shut before he could say something even dumber and actually ruin things.

"I wouldn't trade this for anything," Rowan said and felt his cheeks light on fire.

"Good." Olivia snuggled into his side more.

# CHAPTER THIRTY

# Startling Discoveries

For the next few days, everything was peaceful. And Rowan made the most of it. Ever since his summoning, he had been thrust into battles of political intrigue or raw strength. The time to relax and rest was very much welcomed. And Rowan spent it doing stuff he'd always wanted.

"Can you tell me what you're doing here?" Rowan asked.

"It's all about what we can do now to better our fields in the future," the farmer admitted nervously. "It'd be a waste for all this water to just evaporate. It's enough to rejuvenate the fields for a long time. We can super-saturate the ground and keep it fertile and watered for much, much longer than it normally should be."

"And you're doing all this with your cards?"

The farmer looked around and leaned forward. "I'm only telling you this because you're the hero, Hero Rowan. But I'm the only Uncommon farmer around, and my family's been saving up cards for generations. We've got a couple of good cards that would make any farmer jealous."

And he wasn't lying. His thirty fields had turned into giant sponges, sucking up all the water in only two days.

"So how long will the water keep?" Rowan asked. In his head, he was comparing the effect to **Lavish Feasting**.

"Years. If I manage this well, I can pass it on to my children and their children as well," the farmer said excitedly.

"This means that you'll be safe from droughts in the future?" Rowan asked, genuinely curious. Here, farming was still a relatively manual affair with hand tools and oxen. Even so, there were things that made it magical.

"Yes and no." The farmer dropped his head. "There's a limit on how much water can be stored this way. Long droughts hurt still. And not everyone can put in the extra watering work. So it's more likely that when the drought comes, we'll have to share this water."

"It's still really impressive," Rowan said, and he meant it.

The farmer smiled at that. "Not as impressive as you, Hero Rowan. And I wanted to say sorry about the way we acted during the siege. We all knew that you were helping us. It's just that . . . our whole lives, we were told that we were safe. And now there are monsters and corrupted creatures? It's not the life that I signed up for."

"It's okay," Rowan said. He had already forgiven the villagers. Olivia kept a longer grudge, but even she was softening to them. The people of Felton's Mill might have been real bastards when everything was on the line, but they were decent people in peacetime. Especially since they were cleaning up the battlefields and repairing the walls without any prompting.

*In fact—* Rowan glanced back at the wall where a woman was performing literal miracles.

"She's quite something, isn't she," the farmer said, standing up to look at the sight as well. "Besides the late Desimir, she's the only other Rare class in the village."

"Rare?"

"Of course. She's the whole reason the world even has a place called Felton's Mill."

The woman strolled toward them. She was pushing the latter half of her fifties, which meant that she was firmly among the oldest in the village. But it was a young fifty. The system's stats added a spring in her step and gave her the vigor of someone half her age. It also helped that everywhere she stepped, damage and grime retreated.

"Hero Rowan," the old woman said. "Glad to see you out here."

"Yeah, I wanted to ask. How do you do that?" Rowan asked, gesturing at her feet.

"Walk with me, young man," the woman replied. Rowan waved goodbye to the farmer and walked back toward the village with the woman. "It's one of my family's most cherished cards. **Stellar Upkeep** is its name. A long time ago, someone in my family must have served the nobles."

"And you chose it as your Heart Card?"

"Oh, young man," the woman laughed. "It's not like there was much competition. The other options were mostly Common with a few Uncommons sprinkled in. Do you know how much money it'd take to get a good Uncommon Heart Card without being blessed with it?"

Rowan nodded. He stuck his spear in the ground and breathed deeply. None of the villagers commented on the fact that he went everywhere with his spear, but he caught them glancing at it, as if wondering why the hero was always armed.

The simple answer was that he needed **Keen Spear** to feel at peace. The horrors of men dying, monsters trying to eat him, and the demon corrupting him was enough for a whole lifetime of bad memories.

Inspired by the conversation, the hero took a quick glance at his status screen, much changed by all the fighting and the terror of what they'd been forced to face.

**Rowan Clairfont**
**Level 37 Reckless Spear**
**EXP: 185,430/240,000**

**STR: 39***
**VIT: 12**
**DEX: 39***
**PER: 20**
**INT: 10**
**WIS: 12**

**Deck (5/5):**
**[Heart] Keen Spear (Epic, Passive)**
**[Class] Blood Siphon (Uncommon, Passive)**
**Ravaging Lightning Lance (Rare, Active)**
**Persistent Regeneration (Rare, Active)**
**Lavish Feasting (Rare, Passive)**
**Blessings:**
**Awakened Blessing of the Stalwart Hero**

Rowan was proud of his progress, even though a part of him had expected to finally step into the Rare tier after all the fighting.

The amount of experience he needed to advance to another level was almost astronomical at this point. Which made the fact that people got to Rare or Epic in peacetime all the more impressive. But he hadn't exactly walked away from the battle a pauper.

The experience was obvious, but beyond that, and much to the hero's excitement, he'd finally gotten the chance to replace his very first class card. Now, he had something much better.

**Ravaging Lightning Lance (Rare, Active)**
**Unleash the wrath of the heavens upon your foes and ravage their**
**bodies with lightning. You can either summon blasts of lightning**
**lances out of thin air at a much greater mana cost, or channel**
**that attack through a spear-type weapon for reduced cost and**
**increased effectiveness.**

It wasn't the same as **Empowered Thrust**, and Rowan genuinely hoped to eventually get his hands on an improved version of that card since it felt easier and more natural to use. But there was no denying that **Ravaging Lightning Lance**, courtesy of the demon knight and its mount, was definitely an upgrade.

That wasn't to say the Rare card was easy to use. The first time he equipped the card, Rowan had almost fried himself when the lance arced back and hit him. It was only one time, but that didn't stop Olivia from using that as a laugh about a dozen times already.

"Well, thanks," Rowan said, snapping out of introspection as he caught sight of his menace of a companion. He ran forward to greet her and then stopped dead in his tracks.

In the distance were two familiar figures riding toward the village. A man and a woman. The two riders were at the head of an army. Knights rode behind them while a massive group of ordinary soldiers marched in orderly rows. They had obviously been through a battle, with splotches of red and brown among their ranks.

"I can't believe they're only just getting here! The mages left over a week ago," Olivia grumbled.

"You think they're reinforcing us because they expect more demonic trouble?" Rowan asked. Olivia turned around and stared into Rowan's face. "Did I say something wrong?"

"No, I thought that maybe . . . Did Father ever teach you about the emblems of the noble houses and their colors?" Olivia's fingers were twitching toward his own, but she restrained herself.

"He did," Rowan said. "Oh—Oh."

Understanding dawned on Rowan as he realized what he was looking at. The army was sporting the colors of House Sutton. And unless there was a second hidden army somewhere in the barony, the two riders at the front were . . .

All of a sudden, Rowan's heart tightened. He stole a glance at Olivia and saw that she was fidgeting on her own. In theory, the two of them had just saved a village from getting destroyed and fought off demons far above their weight class. They hadn't done anything wrong; he *hadn't* done anything wrong.

And yet, Rowan couldn't help but be nervous meeting Kayden again. Especially with the knowledge that he had been spending the nights after the last demon battle staring into a fireplace with Olivia and falling asleep together.

Olivia took a few hurried steps forward before catching herself and falling back again. She even schooled her expression into a dignified look. And then she did what seemed to have turned into instinct for the two of them when they were stressed over the last few days—she grabbed Rowan's hand and gave it a squeeze.

Almost immediately, a cold shiver raced down Rowan's spine, and he wondered if it was worth trying to get her to let go. But before he could decide one way or another, he felt the full weight of a gaze land on his shoulders.

Rowan stiffened. *I guess come hell or high water, we're doing this.*

Kayden Sutton came into view first. And when Rowan could make out his face, he saw a snarl forming on the baron's lips. His wife, Camilla, looked oddly smug.

*You know, it might not be too late to change my name and move to a different kingdom.*

Kayden gave the briefest of nods toward Rowan and Olivia before he waved his knights off and went to visit Bron. After a lot of ceremony and logistics, Rowan found himself alone in a room with the Sutton family.

Luckily, Olivia drew the first shot. "You could have come to visit a bit faster, you know?"

"There was a lot to do in the aftermath of the invasion, dear," Camilla said, pulling Olivia closer and adjusting her clothes in spite of the younger woman's protests. "There's a lot of work to be done to recover from all this."

"How bad was it?" Rowan attempted to steer the conversation into safe grounds and was immediately met with Kayden's full attention. The baron had been throwing glares Rowan's way whenever he could without his wife catching on. Now, Rowan had just handed him the perfect opportunity.

"It's not as bad as it could have been," Camilla answered. "Kayden, stop doing that and come sit."

The baron grunted and settled down on one of the seats with a kind of wince that Rowan recognized. He, and the rest of the hero party, had been showing the same expression for the past few days, a by-product of pushing too far in combat and taking too many potions. Although Rowan's stats showed that he was stronger than ever before, his body was tattered. He needed time to let his wounds heal and replenish the stock he'd drawn on.

"Losses?" Olivia asked quietly, her eyes fixed on her father. After all, if Rowan could recognize potion overuse, so could the alchemist.

"Four more settlements were attacked, aside from Felton's Mill. A city and three villages. The city's fine. I had experienced troops stationed there, since it's closer to the frontier than I'd like. Two of the villages were wiped out, and one is mostly still standing. None of them were actually attacked by powerful demons, though." Kayden sounded tired as he spoke, and his wife went over to stand by him, her hand firmly on his shoulder.

"Powerful as in . . . Epic?" Rowan ventured.

"Epic," Kayden sighed.

"How could something like this happen? What was the frontier doing?" Olivia hissed.

"It's not entirely their fault," Kayden said, though reluctantly. "Such a surge in demon activity shouldn't have been possible for several more months. The defenses simply weren't set up to handle them yet."

"And I'm sure that failure has nothing to do with the fact that our family's territory is first in line of any invasion force," Olivia snapped out.

Almost instinctively, Rowan reached out to take Olivia's hand. The brief smile that earned him was worth the glare he got from the baron and the wry look on the baroness's face. Rowan toughed it out. For all of Olivia's impulsiveness and short temper, she was true to herself. She wasn't one of those calculating people who measured every word or hid themselves behind elaborate rituals. She was just herself.

"Perhaps, Olivia, I think . . ." Kayden winced and tilted his head the tiniest fraction up toward his wife. "Ah, what I mean to say is this. Olivia, I would suggest not sharing any such accusations in public. It wouldn't do much at this point. And most nobles have interests tied up in the frontier. They don't want this as much as I do. One of the towns fell in the wave, and its commander was lost. An Epic-tier combat class."

"Interests?" Rowan asked. "What does that mean? Isn't it practically a death sentence for anyone not strong enough to be sent there?" Rowan was picturing the frontier to be an inhospitable hellscape staffed by the unlucky souls in the kingdom's army.

"The nobles all have their own towns along the frontier. It's a business to them. What they want is the constant stream of cards coming out of the frontier," Camilla said.

"But the system assigns the cards to the combatants. So they all signed contracts like me?" Rowan asked.

"No," Kayden said as his eyes sparkled. "Rowan, you see my army. I train them, give them equipment, and lead them into battle. But for any monsters they kill, they get to keep the cards. That's the iron law of the kingdom. You fight? You keep your reward. So tell me, how do the nobles get their cards?"

Rowan could see that this was a test, and the realization made it that much harder to think. He tried to stall for time. "Are these soldiers that are stationed on the frontier?"

"Soldiers and mercenaries."

"And you said that there were towns, right?" Rowan said slowly. Camilla nodded encouragingly. "The soldiers and mercenaries, they need a place to rest, food to eat, and even entertainment. And the noble houses control that. Cards would be the currency of frontier towns."

"Well done," Camilla said. "The towns are built by the nobles. They own every single shop or service. So they get to set their own prices."

"And I'm guessing the prices aren't pretty." Rowan didn't even bother keeping the disgust out of his voice. "They're sucking the blood of people who are dying to keep the kingdom safe."

Kayden shrugged, and Rowan noticed Olivia looked particularly uncomfortable. When he arched a brow in question, she blushed.

"We used to own one of these frontier towns," Kayden said.

"But it was managed fairly," Olivia rushed to say. "It was one of the biggest because of our practices, but then House Sutton was demoted to . . ." She trailed off, and Rowan didn't need to ask for clarification.

"Be that as it may, it is in the best interest of nobility to keep things running smoothly in those towns," Kayden said, picking up the conversation again. "For one of them to be reduced to near rubble? It goes to show that this wasn't just some plot to hurt us. This was a genuine demonic invasion."

"Dad, was it dangerous? Are you all right?" Olivia's voice softened, and Rowan watched the baron's weariness and bad mood melt away.

"I'm fine, I assure you. The rewards we got from the invasion also more than compensated any losses we took." A small smile rose on Kayden's lips as he looked in Rowan's direction. "Speaking of, considering how you protected Felton's Mill and helped save Olivia from danger, I won't ask for my share of the loot . . . this time."

"Dad!" Olivia blushed.

"A contract is a contract," Camilla chimed in, too, her eyes dancing with the same mischief Rowan saw in Olivia's green irises. "Of course, such things could be waived for *family*."

Kayden choked. Olivia's face turned scarlet. And Rowan thought that if a hole opened in the ground, he might just jump in it.

"Dear, ahem, you can't say things like that," Kayden whispered as he tried to keep his voice in control.

"I take it that you haven't heard, then?" Camilla laughed. She looked so self-satisfied it bordered on smugness.

"Heard what?"

"Oh my! I can't possibly share such sordid details. What if someone overhears?"

Kayden whipped his head around, leaned forward, and stared daggers into Rowan. "What is she talking about?"

"Oh dear, don't do that," Camilla said as she kept her arm on the baron. Kayden flinched as he half-willingly leaned back in his chair. "A little bird told me that they were sharing private time in the hero's very own bedroom. They were *on the bed*."

Rowan almost jumped out of his chair, but Olivia beat him to it. "We were discussing loot! And we were just tired! We couldn't have done anything even if we wanted. Which we didn't!"

"People also said that our daughter likes to stroll through the village hand in hand with the hero—why, we even saw them do it," Camilla continued.

"I was just keeping hold of him so he doesn't wander off and so we get where we need to go faster!" Olivia protested.

"They often spend time together, all alone."

"I needed to plan and deal with all the logistics after Bron was hurt. Rowan was the only one who could help."

"You know, they even say that the hero hasn't slept in his own room for the last week."

As Olivia faltered in her response, Rowan ventured his own attempt. "We just have the blankets set up in front of the fireplace and kind of doze off together?"

Kayden's face turned the same shade of red as Olivia's. His next words were spat out like he was chewing on gravel. "We should talk, Hero Rowan."

Olivia stood up. "You can't kill him. I didn't even kiss him yet or anything."

Her father's attention briefly switched over to her. "Yet?"

Olivia grabbed Rowan's hand and ran for the door. Somehow, they made it through, and when Rowan risked a glance back, he saw Camilla with both hands on Kayden's shoulder. She gave him a wink as the door slammed shut behind them.

Thankfully, Rowan found a way to stay out of trouble for the next few days. Kayden was more than a father; he was the baron whose barony had just been ravaged. Between training his army and coordinating the relief and rebuilding efforts of his entire barony, the baron was too busy to execute whatever scheme he had thought up.

And so Rowan found a way to torture himself: practicing and training with his new card and finding new combinations for his deck. With three passive cards, there wasn't much that he could do, but **Ravaging Lightning Lance** was like a cave—there was always more to attempt and explore.

When things began settling down and a messenger came to fetch Rowan, he thought that Kayden was finally settling debts. But he walked into a room to find the baron dressed in noble clothes while a pompous-looking stranger stood in the center.

"Hero Rowan?"

Rowan caught Kayden's eye and the baron gave an imperceptible nod. "Yeah, that's me," Rowan answered.

"Good." The stranger pulled out a scroll from his pouch and slowly unfurled it. "In the name of the king, I hereby inform you that one Rowan Clairfont, his party, and any support you deem fit to outfit him with are to present themselves at the town of Rest's Remorse in no more than three weeks. You will find the details of his deployment here. You are dismissed."

The stranger rolled the scroll back up before tossing it into Kayden's lap. "Baron Sutton, the order has been delivered. If the hero doesn't show up, you'll be held responsible."

Kayden nodded gravely. Without another word, the man turned around and left the room. As the footsteps faded away, a silence settled between Rowan and Kayden.

For a few seconds, Rowan wondered how he should break the ice. "Where's Rest's Remorse?"

"The frontier."

# CHAPTER THIRTY-ONE

# Side Story: Light

Blake was worried and doubting himself. The former wasn't an odd or unusual thing, especially since his friends always seemed to get into trouble. But it *was* rare for him to doubt his own decisions. He was the kind of guy to fully commit once he made up his mind.

He had convinced himself that there was enough work at the capital that he couldn't put off everything and go visit Rowan. But every moment of crouching in the shadows of an alleyway was putting that decision more and more in doubt.

"Hey there, I'll help with that," Blake said as he stepped out. It only took him two steps to cross the street and arrive in front of a grandmother struggling with a crate of apples. "Where do you need this to go?"

"Over there." She pointed at a shop in the distance.

"Sure thing." Blake slowed down to walk at the same pace as the grandmother. As he strolled at what felt like turtle speed, he tried to convince himself that staying in the capital was better. He had, after all, written a letter and slipped it into the official scroll of royal notice. He hoped it would not be needed, but sometimes, it was better to be safe than sorry.

"Right here is okay," the old lady said. When Blake gently placed the crate down, she took one of the apples and offered it to Blake. "You're a real gentleman, you know that?"

Blake smiled. "As long as I keep getting treats like these, I'll keep being a gentleman."

He bit into the apple as he strolled away from the shop. The fruit was bland, almost bitter. It was a horrible taste. But he kept chewing and swallowed before taking another bite. He wasn't about to discard her appreciation by throwing it away, no matter how much he wanted to.

*This would be the kind of thing that Rowan notices. Everyone else sees me as an ever-on-the-move guy, happy to just rush into things without much thought. Only Rowan knew that I care about one thing: helping people.*

Blake was *not* the kind of guy to worry too much about whether people liked him. He just liked helping people. Or, in Rowan's words, Blake was the type of person who had a hero complex.

*But look at where we are now. In an entirely different world and heroes of a kingdom. Look at how things played out for good ol' Blake.*

"What *are* you doing?" A hiss rang out to his left from one of the alleys, and the hero gave a friendly little wave. "You do realize that we are waiting for the signal to kick off an extremely important *secret* mission?"

"I know," Blake muttered when he managed to swallow the bitter fruit. "But that's no reason to be rude or not to help someone in need."

"Really?" the voice hissed back.

"It's better than . . ." Blake gestured at himself. He looked more like a rogue or some disgusting assassin than a hero blessed by the light goddess Sarina herself. Blake sighed, rubbing the front of his armor that was covered in a thick cloak. His disguise covered all emblems of Sarina, and he even dimmed their glow by cutting off the flow of divine energies to his armor, something that made him extremely uncomfortable.

The radiance had started when he got his Rare class and only intensified when he advanced to Epic-tier [Holy Paladin]. He already missed its reassuring warmth and the presence of his goddess bolstering his will in the back of his mind. He genuinely felt partly crippled without that connection.

"How much longer do we have to wait?" Blake asked, eyes already roaming the streets again.

The old lady had been an excellent find, but an unfortunately small number of people needed help so late at night. He perked up for a moment when he saw a group of men stumbling along with a woman between them but then overheard her scolding them for drinking too much.

Just a group of friends making their way home, not an attempted kidnapping or worse.

Blake sighed.

"We're all in position. Well, *most of us*," an inquisitor of Sarina whispered, glaring at Blake meaningfully. "We're just waiting for . . . confirmation for when the illegal gathering starts."

Blake nodded, pleased. Confirmation was indeed important. He had stepped in just the other day when a group of inquisitors had been a bit too eager to perform their duties.

Protecting the sanctity of the light was all well and good. Terrorizing citizens was not.

He could forgive them for their errors, however. He had the reassurance of a god's will burning inside his chest. Even though he wasn't a [High Priest], his class and blessing afforded him a genuine connection to his goddess. In fact, he was better than a priest. The church had said that he was the closest person to Sarina they had seen in generations. And he would bring down the justice of his goddess's wrath on anyone who deserved it.

Blake felt his energies reach out for his armor and quashed them. He wouldn't be the one to jeopardize the mission.

"How many of the participants have we managed to identify?" Blake asked, looking for the next best distraction.

The man hesitated, much to Blake's ire. "Unfortunately, none so far, other than the host of this meeting. They've been exceedingly careful, and we can't risk alerting them before the time to strike comes."

*Cruel, brash, and incompetent.* Blake's estimation of the man's character had been plummeting for some time, but that was the one final nail in the coffin. *I'll have a chat with the [High Priest] after this. This must not be the quality of Lady Sarina's servants.*

Even without their connection at full power, he felt a trickle of amusement and approval from his goddess. Immediately, the night seemed just a tiny bit brighter and the wait more bearable.

By the time the light in one of the windows of a building across the street turned on, Blake had a small smile on his face.

And just like that, Blake had a purpose in life again.

He threw off his cloak and charged *through* the gates of the small yet opulent building they had been keeping an eye on. By all accounts, the building was a "gentlemen's club" meant for the gathering of the capital's elite. In other words, a place to drink, gamble away money, and make secret dealings.

Blake hated it.

He relished the chance to break down the front doors, sending the nearby guards literally flying with the explosion of his radiant aura. Already, a glowing shield adorned his left arm, and a long sword hewn out of pure light was clasped in his right. He was a true vision of divine might and fury, and the way his goddess sang to him through the warmth in his chest only reinforced that notion.

Unfortunately, he was instructed to spare every evildoer he came across, so they could be properly detained and questioned. Blake blunted his sword so that it wouldn't send any limbs flying and began swatting away at the men and women dressed in finery and wearing thick masks. He took great care in disabling each and every one of them so they couldn't run.

As he ventured deeper into the building, the infidels managed to mount some minor resistance. They were actually halfway competent combatants, and one of the women resistors might have managed to draw blood had his glowing aura not stopped her blade. It halted just a fraction of an inch from his jugular and Blake might have been a bit rough when he backhanded her across the room.

"Our main target is deeper inside the building. We have reliable information that they're having a much more clandestine meeting there. Main supporters only," a voice whispered in Blake's ear. He was much too focused on *not* murdering the fool trying to stab him through the eye with a rapier to respond.

For all his power and toughness, healing from that kind of an injury would still be difficult. Not impossible, but difficult.

The man suddenly sped up and his blade ignited in black energy. Every strike began shearing through Blake's aura. There was a good chance that the man had synergetic cards that weakened or nullified healing. So Blake tried his best to dodge.

Unfortunately, dexterity really wasn't Blake's main stat. He needed far too much wisdom and strength for that to be possible. After one particularly close call, Blake decided enough was enough. He burned through an immense portion of his mana pool to charge at the man in a corona of golden mana.

Blake slammed into the man, and the ridiculous expenditure worked. His opponent's blade almost bit through and cut his skin, but before it could go farther, its owner was launched into the ceiling with a loud squelch.

Blake winced a little, hoping they could find him a healer in time to prevent death.

Finally, though, he was through and staring at a heavily warded door.

"We'll need a couple of minutes to take down the wards," the inquisitor said, but Blake was far too upset to listen properly. There was no guarantee that the people on the other side of that door weren't fleeing already.

Blake fell to his knees, his weapons unraveling into light as he clasped his hands in prayer. "My goddess, please open the path for your servants, so that your will be done and your enemies cleansed."

The prayer wasn't something the clergy was likely to approve of, especially since it was short, sincere, and to the point.

However, if his goddess was displeased, she didn't show it.

A halo of light erupted around Blake, and he immediately stepped forward, pushing on the warded doors. The wards sparked and tried to devour him, but he was more than just mortal. In that moment, he wasn't mere flesh.

He was the partial avatar of his goddess, and such trickery was beneath him.

The ward imploded inward, blasting the doors open and even damaging the walls of the room. The shudder of the building might have worried Blake if he didn't know his goddess was there with him every step of the way.

Blake strolled into the room confidently, only to freeze at the sight within. At the very back of the room, a massive portrait of some ancient noble was pushed to the side, revealing the gaping hole of a tunnel heading into darkness.

Most of the people in the room were already in the tunnel, with only two men left behind to guard the passageway. One of them was almost purposefully unremarkable. His features seemed average on every count. The other, however, was much more distinct. The man's golden hair glittered under the light of the chandelier, and his forest-green eyes glared at Blake with a kind of barely tampered anger typically reserved for one's worst enemies.

The man's fingers were tightly clasped around a sword, and Blake had a moment to note how odd they looked before he stumbled.

It was like someone had hit him over the back of his head with a baseball bat. Everything was spinning around him and he almost bent over to puke. Even the support of his goddess was thrown into disarray, and that was the very first time such a thing had ever happened.

Blake lost track of the two men as he tried to get his headache under control.

"Hero Blake, are you okay?"

"Why are you asking after me? Go chase . . ." Blake paused as he saw the wards enveloping the passageway the two men had escaped into. He pushed aside the inquisitor and tried to bull through those wards. But without the goddess's support, he could only take several steps into the tunnels before his mana was burned out and he was launched back, painfully. Someone had taken the time to layer ward after ward on every single inch of that tunnel.

"We're working on it, but the complexity of the ward network . . ." The inquisitor cringed when Blake turned his eyes on him.

*I'm definitely purging this entire group of inquisitors from the order.*

"Record this," Blake said. "One of the leaders had some kind of identity-concealing artifact, or just a deck based around subterfuge. Can't offer much about him past the fact that he was male. The other, platinum hair, ice-blue eyes. Built as thick as a house. Should have seen his hands—like bricks, really."

"We'll track down someone with that particular description," the inquisitor offered.

Blake just sighed, desperately wishing his party members were with him. They could have caught the back-room participants. But the unfortunate side effect of having a princess and two daughters of high nobility as your party members was that they were weak-willed. And rather fond of their beauty sleep.

Well, that and it was "politically insensitive" to take them along.

*Especially when the infidels are nobles. There's no other explanation. A commoner organization couldn't have wards this intricate or manpower this strong.*

Oh well, he'd just have to do better next time.

# CHAPTER THIRTY-TWO

# Side Story: Gossip

Kayla was having the time of her life. Not even her master's grumblings about wasting a week's time watching "incompetent buffoons" struggle against demons could get in the way of that.

In fact, she was pretty sure that hidden under all that grumbling was a happy spirit. Out here, the tower master didn't have to split her attention between paperwork, overeager students, or kingdom politicking.

That was a shame, since Kayla rather liked standing in for her master when it came to those things.

"It was a valuable learning experience, was it not?" Kayla ventured, keeping her voice carefully composed. It wouldn't do to let her master hear the taunting notes. "I got to see the difference in the way regular classes approach combat as opposed to mages."

"Girl, you will learn *nothing* from barbarians who are content to swing their sticks around," the tower master snapped as if the history books were not littered with barbarians breaking mages in two thanks to the unique strand of magical arrogance.

But Kayla wasn't like those foolish mages. She was a good mage.

"You can't tell me that the shaman wasn't at least a little interesting," Kayla countered. Truth be told, she was a little jealous of the party assembled around Rowan. Both the shaman and the alchemist showed incredible promise. Potential that would be wasted under Rowan's direction.

"Her people can be promising, yes, but the fact that we're talking about a her instead of a he means that she won't go far," the tower master answered.

Kayla furrowed her brows as she tried to glean the tiny bit of information her master had let slip. The tower master was anything but sexist, especially considering the fact that the system more than evened the playing field. So it was either something about the class evolution or the shaman's race.

Sometimes, her master's teaching style was a bit infuriating. She had very rigid ideas about how Kayla's education ought to be structured and tolerated very little deviation. And so, Kayla had to go behind the woman's back and treaty with the various factions inside the towers for her unanswered questions. In a way, that was fun.

But out here on the road, there was little that Kayla could do. She settled back into her chair and plopped open her favorite book. The book wasn't some grizzled ancient tome like one would have expected of a mage. Rather, it was quite modern and printed on clean, floppy paper. And as she began yet another read-through of the book, she started with the introduction.

*Reader,*

*You might be shocked to find the definitive compendium of spells to be so modern. After all, is it not better to plumb the ancient past of our craft for god-killer spells and rituals that can raze entire cities? To this, I tell you: no.*

*As startling as it is to learn this, mage is not an ancient class. Before us came ritualists, cultists, witches, warlocks, thaumaturgists, and so many more classes. Some of these paths were mighty. Some of these paths were lacking. Some exist still, and some have been lost to the ravages of time.*

*They all opened up the path to what we have today: magecraft, and the prestigious beginner class of [Mage]. In fact, the time since the appearance of mages is measured in centuries rather than the uncountable eons that some of the other classes can lay claim to.*

*To understand this, you need to accept that the perceived immutability of the system is an error. Even the very term "system" is something that only took root in recent history, when the cycle of demon kings and hero summonses started.*

*It is a term brought to our world by the otherworldly visitors, along with their strange scientific and magical knowledge.*

*So, here I inform you of this: Classes can be forged, changed, and even lost to us.*

*This is why the storied and ancient classes, such as the humble [Farmer], have so many options and permutations in their deck builds. Farming has long since been turned into a subtle science, one improved by every system user to ever wield the class. The cards for it, too, are frighteningly effective and simple, to a degree of stark beauty.*

*In contrast, less popular classes have fewer choices, fewer paths, and much less effective decks.*

*Some classes have even entirely faded from system memory, such as the once fabled [Mind Reaver] knights of the ancient divine empires. If someone wanted to claim such a class themselves today, they would have to reinvent it from scratch.*

*This means that the very system we use is growing, changing, and improving alongside us. Take heed of this, reader, and work to emulate it!*

*—Magus Zorian the Sky Breaker*

Kayla loved the introduction and could prattle on for days about it. But the rest of the book was equally interesting. On every read-through, she always learned something new about the spells and cards. Even the basic ones often led to some sliver of knowledge that she could squirrel away for future use. And the higher-tier spells were like riddles, to be teased apart line by line. Some were out of her reach still, even with her Epic advancement, but she could see the path to gaining mastery over them. And she was getting closer.

All good things come to an end, however, and so did her master's patience.

Mere hours after they'd started their blisteringly fast journey by flying over the terrain, the tower master called for a break and dismissed them all to set up camp for the night. The old mage herself waved her hand, and an opulent tent that was much bigger on the inside materialized in the clearing she had chosen.

"You will handle my camp setup. I will be practicing some of my spells," Kayla informed one of the other apprentices offhandedly and then strolled toward the depths of the forest.

The apprentice dipped her head low, as was proper.

As Kayla walked, she ran through a whole host of spells. Spells meant to hide and conceal. Spells meant to protect and hinder. Spells meant to check that a particular, frustrating old cow wasn't under an invisibility effect and trying to follow her.

Again.

Seeing all the diagnostic spells come back clear, however, Kayla finally relaxed. Once she was a decent enough distance away from camp, she spoke.

"How did the meeting go?"

A figure materialized out of the darkness of the night, blurry and with indistinct features. The only thing really recognizable was its female gender.

"Well, Mistress, the meeting was interrupted, of course, but that will only feed into their discontent. The important actors fled with our aid. The captured will not spill any secrets they shouldn't. Those who know too much will choose to commit suicide instead of talk," the figure said.

"I'm sure they will. So very self-sacrificial of them. What about our plans for the frontier?" Kayla asked.

"The kingdom has been sufficiently weakened by the early demonic activity. The fact that they couldn't even predict the wave speaks volumes. It does give us the opportunity to offer aid," the figure replied.

"Don't push them too far yet. My own position is not quite as secure as I'd like. We need as many nobles as possible backing me if we want to pull this off right," Kayla warned.

"Of course, Mistress."

Kayla didn't like the sound of the response. There was just a hint of insubordination behind the words. Which meant that Kayla needed to be a bit more clear about her intentions. Her hand shot forward, lightning quick for a mage meant to be casting spells, and wrapped around the fool's jaw. "You do realize what we're doing here. If we are discovered, we will be wiped out to the last. Do. Not. Mess. This. Up. For. Me."

She wrenched the figure's head to the side.

"Yes, Mistress." The reply had the proper amount of respect now.

Everyone always acted tough until they got physically pushed around by the fragile Cunning Hero. Where Blake was blessed with the title of Radiant Hero, Kayla got the short end of the stick with "cunning" as her hero modifier. It was better than Rowan's, but that really wasn't much to gloat about.

Kayla spun around on her heels and started stalking back toward the camp. She didn't need to say anything else. If they somehow managed to mess up, she'd deal with them herself.

Her mind was instead preoccupied by the memories of Rowan in combat. She hadn't expected him to turn out even remotely as promising as he had. In fact, she had expected him to become another failure like Blake. But there was hope yet.

Having an extra hero on her side would make everything so much easier, and she really did hate knowing that, at some point, she'd have to kill that heroism-obsessed moron herself.

He was cute, but not cute enough to let him jeopardize everything she was working toward.

# Author's Note

Hello! Valentine here!

Thanks for reading *Legend of the Spear Saint*.

I've always loved fantasy books, with plenty of childhood favorites like *Eragon*, the Black Magician trilogy (though I'm willing to admit that one wasn't really the best book series to hand off to a kid), and more.

*Legend of the Spear Saint* is not quite like those. Namely, I wanted to try writing my own spin on the hero-summoned-to-a-new-world-but-something-goes-wrong genre. There's something inherently appealing about the genre to me, even though execution can sometimes be tricky.

In *LSS*, cards are at the heart of everything. The starting point for the idea was a thought that anyone could grow stronger by a combination of talent, hard work, and a bit of strategy. A person can become a better fighter or crafter through them. But they're not the end-all, be-all. They won't do all the fighting for a person or make someone immortal until all their health points run out. In fact, in this series, those aren't a thing at all!

Anyways, that's all for now. Enjoy the story and I hope to see you again in Book 2!

A. T. Valentine

# About the Author

A. T. Valentine is the author of the Legend of the Spear Saint series, originally released on Royal Road. He strives to write the best possible books across a variety of genres. Valentine resides in Potomac, Maryland.

# RESPAWN YOUR CURIOSITY
## *follow us on our socials*

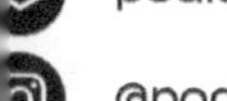
podiumentertainment.com

@podiumentertainment

/podiumentertainment

@podium_ent

@podiumentertainment

9 798889 539393 2